FOLLIES

Rosie Thomas is the author of a number of celebrated novels, including *Bad Girls, Good Women*, *A Simple Life* and the Top Ten bestsellers *Every Woman Knows a Secret*, *Moon Island* and *White*. She lives in north London, and when not writing fiction spends her time travelling and mountaineering. Her most recent novel *The Potter's House* is now available in Arrow.

Acclaim for Rosie Thomas:

'Rosie Thomas writes with beautiful effortless prose, and shows a rare compassion and a real understanding of the nature of love' *The Times*

'Compelling ... a master storyteller' *Cosmopolitan*

'A story full of passion ... will keep you reading long after bedtime' *New Woman*

'Honest and absorbing, Rosie Thomas mixes the bitter and the hopeful with the knowledge that the human heart is far more complicated than any rule suggests' *Mail on Sunday*

'Outstanding' *The Good Book Guide*

Follies

Rosie Thomas

ARROW

Published by Arrow Books in 2002

1 3 5 7 9 0 8 6 4 2

First published in the United Kingdom in 1983 by Fontana

Arrow Books
The Random House Group Limited
20 Vauxhall Bridge Road, London, SW1V 2SA

Random House Australia (Pty) Limited
20 Alfred Street, Milsons Point, Sydney,
New South Wales 2061, Australia

Random House New Zealand Limited
18 Poland Road, Glenfield
Auckland 10, New Zealand

Random House (Pty) Limited
Endulini, 5a Jubilee Road, Parktown 2193, South Africa

The Random House Group Limited Reg. No. 954009

www.randomhouse.co.uk

A CIP catalogue record for this book
is available from the British Library

Papers used by Random House are natural, recyclable products made from
wood grown in sustainable forests. The manufacturing processes conform to
the environmental regulations of the country of origin

ISBN 0 09 940643 8

Printed and bound in Great Britain by
Bookmarque Ltd, Croydon, Surrey

MICHAELMAS TERM

CHAPTER ONE

In a moment, she would see it.

The train swayed around a long curve, and then rattled over the iron arches of a little viaduct. Helen pressed her face against the smeared window, waiting.

Then, suddenly, it was ahead of her. The oblique sun of the autumn afternoon turned the spires and pinnacles to gold, and glowed on the rounded domes. The light made the stone look as soft and warm as honey, exactly as it had done for almost four hundred years.

The brief glimpse lasted only a few seconds, then the train shuddered and clattered into an avenue of grimy buildings and advertisement hoardings. But when Helen closed her eyes she saw it again, a sharp memory that was painful as well as seductive. She loved the place as she had always done, but she was a different person now. She shouldn't have come back. Home was where she was needed now, not here under these honey-gold spires. Yet her mother had insisted, her face still grey with strain. And Graham, with all the sudden maturity that had been forced upon his thirteen years, had told her that it would break their mother's heart to see Helen give up now. So she had repacked her cheap suitcases with her few clothes, the paperbacked texts and the bulging folders of notes, and she had come back.

Helen opened her eyes again as if she couldn't bear to think any more.

The train hissed grudgingly into the station and she stood up as the doors began to slam open. Two foreign tourists, encumbered with nothing more than expensive cameras, reached to help her with her luggage. A deafening crackle overhead heralded the station announcement.

'Oxford. Oxford. This is Oxford.'

The tourists smiled at each other, pleased to have their destination confirmed. They bowed to Helen before they left her.

Where else? she thought. Even the air was unmistakable, moist with the smell of rivers and the low mists that the autumn sun never shone strongly enough to dispel. The yellow and gold leaves in the roadway beyond the station entrance were wet, and furrowed by bicycle wheels.

Helen picked up as much of her baggage as she could manage and went in search of a taxi. It was an unaccustomed luxury and uncertainty sounded in her voice as she told the driver, 'Follies House, please.'

The oak door was heavy, and studded with iron bolt heads. A drift of crisp, yellow-brown leaves had blown up across the threshold, giving the house an abandoned air.

Helen stopped pulling at the iron ring that hung unyieldingly in place of a doorknob and stepped back to peer at the narrow windows set in the high wall. There was nothing to be seen, not even a curtain in the blackness behind the glass. The traffic, roaring close at hand over Folly Bridge, seemed miles away. It was the gush of running water that filled the air, the river racing between the mossed arches of the old bridge.

Helen glanced down at her luggage, piled haphazardly in the pathway where the taxi driver had left it. Her mouth set in a firm line and she turned back to bang on the door with her clenched fist.

'Anyone ... at ... home?' she shouted over the hammering.

From startlingly close at hand Helen heard footsteps, and then a rattle before the door swung smoothly open.

'Always someone at home. Usually me,' the fat woman answered. Helen remembered the facts of the loose grey hair, the billowing, shapeless body and the alert little eyes in the dough-pale face. What she had forgotten was the beautiful smile, irradiating the face until the plainness was obliterated. 'I'm sorry to disturb you, Miss Pole,' Helen murmured. 'The door wouldn't open. Helen Brown?' she added, interrogatively, afraid that the woman might have forgotten, after all.

'You call me Rose, pet. I told you that last term, when you came for the room. Don't forget again, will you? Now then, for the door you need a key.' The ordinary-looking Yale swung at the end of a strand of dirty orange wool. Rose fitted it into the lock and showed Helen how the door moved easily on the latch. 'Simple, you see.' Rose waved towards the stairs. 'No-one to help with your stuff, I'm afraid. Gerry's never here when you want him, and I'm far too infirm.' The smile broadened for an

8

instant, then the fat woman turned and disappeared into the dark as quickly as she had materialised.

Helen scuffled through the leaves and stepped into Follies House.

The hall was dingy and smelt of cooking, but the grandeur was undimmed. It was high, four-square and wood-panelled to the vaulted plasterwork of the Jacobean ceiling. The bare wood stairway mounted, behind its fat balusters, to the galleried landing above. In the light of an autumn afternoon the atmosphere was mysterious, even unwelcoming. Yet Helen felt the house drawing her to it, just as she had done the first time. It had been a brilliant June morning when she had applied to Rose for a room. 'Not my usual sort,' Rose had told her bluntly. 'Mostly I know them, or know of them. Reputation or family, one or the other. But you've got a nice little face, and Frances Page won't be needing her room next term, not after all this bother.'

'I know,' Helen had said humbly. 'Frances is in my College. She told me there might be space here.'

'Oh well', Rose had said, looking at Helen more closely. 'Why didn't you tell me you were a friend of Frances?'

And so it had been arranged.

Now, after the long, sad summer, she was here. Usually her family had come with her, driving up to her College in the little car. Helen shook her head painfully. This time she was alone, standing in the muffling quiet of a strange house. Again, through the stillness, she heard the pouring gush of the river as it tumbled past the house and on under the bridge, and the sound soothed her. Determinedly, one by one, she hoisted her cases and boxes over the doorstep and into the hall. With the last one she kicked the door shut on the fading yellow light outside and began the climb towards her room with the first load.

Follies House was square, and the first-floor gallery ran round the four sides. Doors led off to each side, but Helen made for the staircase which led on up to the third floor. Servants' quarters, she thought with a faint smile, as she panted up into a smaller corridor, even dustier, with uneven, wide oak floorboards. There was no name-card on the low oak door in front of her, but the room was hers just the same. Helen pushed open the door and dropped her burden gratefully on the worn carpet.

The room was the smallest of Rose's undergraduate quarters, Helen knew that, but the size was unimportant. What mattered was the view. It was a corner room, no doubt freezing cold in the coming damp of the Oxford winter that already seemed to hover in the air. But there were windows in two of the walls, square windows with stone facings set in the red Jacobean brickwork, with cushioned window seats in the recesses beneath them.

Helen knelt on one of the seats and, through the fog of her breath on the cold glass, stared out over Oxford. Due north, ahead of her, was Carfax with its ancient tower, the crossroads that was the nominal centre of the city. Beyond that lay Cornmarket with its chain-stores and shoe-shops, and beyond that the dignified spread of North Oxford.

Helen turned away to the second window. There, to the east, was the heart of Oxford. The towers and pinnacles and domes were familiar to her now, but the sight of them spread out before her never failed to thrill her.

A little bit of this is mine, thought Helen, as her eyes travelled from the distant perfection of Magdalen Tower, along the invisible but well-remembered curve of the High past All Souls' and St Mary's, to the magnificence of Christ Church's Tom Tower in the foreground. *I do belong here*, she whispered to herself, and knew that she was glad to be back. Glad, in spite of and also because of the deadening sorrow that she had left behind in the cramped rooms of her parents' house.

As Helen knelt on her window seat and watched the teeming life passing to and fro over Folly Bridge, up and down St Aldate's and past Christ Church, a figure appeared in the ribbed archway beneath Tom tower, over the main entry. It was a young man in a soft tweed jacket, breeches and tall polished boots. He stood for a moment with his hands in his pockets, watching the shoppers and cyclists and homebound office workers with an air of faint surprise. Then he shrugged, adopting an expression of mild resignation in place of the surprise, and began to stroll towards the bridge. Several of the faces in the crowd streaming past him turned to watch him pass, but the young man was oblivious. He merely lengthened his stride, lifted his head to taste the damp smells of leaves and woodsmoke that mingled with the exhaust fumes, and smiled in absent satisfaction. With the wind blowing the fair hair back from his narrow, tanned face and the brilliance of his smile, he attracted even more attention.

Helen, high up in her window, stayed at her vantage point long enough to register the fact of Oliver Mortimore turning out of Christ Church and down St Aldate's. He was the kind of Oxford figure whom she had spotted and categorised for herself early on in her life there. She had expected him, and would have been disappointed not to have discovered his kind. She knew that he was 'a lord, or an earl, or something' because a breathlessly impressed friend had told her so. And she knew that he drove a fast car, and had beautiful friends and expensive tastes, because she had observed as much for herself. Oliver Mortimore was a famous figure in Oxford, well-known even to Helen, even though he moved through its world at a level that couldn't have been further from her quiet round of library, lecture room and College.

Helen smiled tranquilly and sat for a moment more, immersed in her own thoughts as she stared unseeingly out at the view. Then, reminding herself that there were things to be done, she swung her legs briskly off the window seat and set off for the next armful of possessions.

Her foot was on the last step of the broad lower staircase when the front door banged open. It brought with it a gust of damp, river-redolent air, a small eddy of dead leaves, and Oliver Mortimore. In the dimness he stumbled against Helen's shabby pile of belongings, lost his balance and fell awkwardly. Oliver swore softly. 'Jesus, what is all this? Looks like a fucking jumble sale.'

Helen sprang forward, contrite. 'I'm sorry. It's all my luggage. Stupid place to leave it.'

Oliver looked up at her, and the frown disappeared from between his eyes.

'I didn't see you there,' he said. 'Sorry for the language. Good job I didn't break my leg on your impedimenta, that's all. It's the first Meet tomorrow.'

Helen nodded politely, evidently not understanding, and Oliver grinned at her as he scrambled up. She saw that there was a long scrape in the high polish of his boots, and had to resist the impulse to kneel down and rub the blemish off such a vision of perfection. At close quarters Oliver Mortimore was not only the most beautiful but also the most physical man she had ever encountered. He radiated such confidence, such highly-charged

11

animal pleasure in his own existence, that he set her skin tingling in response. He made Helen feel hot, and shapeless inside her clothes. Oliver held out his hand. He was six inches taller than Helen, but it felt like twice that.

'I'm Oliver Mortimore,' he said lightly. 'Who are you, and why don't I know you?'

'I know who you are,' Helen countered. 'You don't know me because there's no particular reason why you should. My name's Helen Brown.'

'And what are you doing at Follies, Miss Brown?'

Helen moved forward under his gaze to pick up one of the scattered boxes.

'What I'm doing is moving in. I'm going to live here for a year.'

Oliver was staring at her now with undisguised interest.

'Oh really? You're not in the usual run of socialites and harpies that Rose collects around her, are you?'

He was so clearly stating no more than the obvious that Helen found herself laughing with him.

'I imagine not. Frances Page let me inherit her room. We're friends,' Helen told him crisply, 'in a way.'

Oliver raised his eyebrows, but politely made no other comment on such an unlikely-sounding friendship. 'Ah, unlucky Fran,' he said. 'Perfectly okay for one's own use, of course; but not very clever to start dealing in the stuff. Still, if you're a girl with expensive tastes and no cash, like Fran, the books do have to be balanced somehow.'

Helen looked away. She didn't care to hear muddled, aristocratic, silly Frances spoken of so lightly. For the time that they had lived in adjacent College rooms, she had been a good friend to Helen. She hadn't been sent to prison for what Helen thought of as her witless dabbling on the fringe of the cocaine-peddlers' world, though she could have been. But she had been sent down from Oxford, and Helen missed her.

Oliver was counting up the remaining items of Helen's luggage.

'Cases, three; cardboard boxes, miscellaneous, secured with string, four. You can't possibly manage all this yourself. Where's bloody Gerry?'

He picked up the nearest box. 'Oof, what's in here? Rocks or something?'

Helen put out her hand. The material of his sleeve felt very soft. 'Books, mostly. Don't bother, really. Rose told me I'd have to cope myself, and I'm quite ready to.'

'Lazy old trout.' Oliver had already started for the stairs. 'Where's your room?'

'Top floor.' Helen had no alternative but to pick up the remaining case and follow him.

Oliver chuckled. 'Good old Rose. Trust her to have stuck you right up there. Who're the lucky occupiers of the smarter quarters this year?'

'No idea. Isn't this Gerry one of them?'

'God, no. Gerry is Rose's half-brother. He calls himself a writer, but he's actually a drunk and a lecher. He also claims to be a distant relative of mine, because Rose is, but I find that hard to swallow. You'll be seeing lots of him, which is hard luck.'

They reached the door of Helen's room and Oliver shouldered it open. He dropped his armload and strolled over to the window. 'Nice view, anyway. Hey, you can almost see my windows over at the House.' Oliver flexed his shoulders inside their second skin of tweed, easing them after the long pull up the stairs, then turned back to Helen.

'Come and have tea with me, won't you? Tomorrow. No – wait – Friday. Yes?'

Helen looked straight back into his tanned, smiling face for a long moment before she answered. But there was no possibility that she could refuse.

'Yes. On Friday, then.'

To her amazement, Oliver leaned forward and kissed her, quite casually, on the corner of her mouth. 'Cheer up,' he said softly. 'You should smile a bit oftener. You've no idea how much it suits you.'

From the doorway he waved, without looking at her again, and Helen heard him clatter away down the stairs.

For a moment she stood stock-still in the middle of the room, absently touching the corner of her mouth with her fingertips. Then she sank down at one end of the narrow bed. Follies had cachet, Helen knew that. The idea of Helen Brown, who had none at all, living there had given her some rare moments of private amusement over the summer. And now here she was, in the house for barely an hour and already she had been invited to tea and kissed by Oliver, practically a being from another planet. Helen rocked back on the bed and laughed out loud, a

13

transforming giggle that Oliver would have approved of. It was absurd to think anything of their encounter, let alone to take it as an augury for the new year, but she would do it anyway. It was a good one, Helen was sure of that.

Chloe Campbell registered the road sign as it flicked past her on the motorway. Oxford 15 miles. Shit, almost there. A little shiver of nervousness snaked along her spine before she realised it. Well, there was nothing to be apprehensive about. Nothing at all. Chloe jammed her foot down on the accelerator and swung her slick, little black Renault Gordini out into the overtaking lane. A glance in the mirror showed the family saloons dropping satisfactorily away behind her, and she relaxed her too-tight grip on the wheel. Nice little car, she thought. Thank you, Colin. Thank you, but goodbye in the end, just the same. Goodbye to a lot of things, come to think of it.

Chloe, darling, are you serious about all this?

The question was addressed to her own reflection briefly glimpsed in the mirror. The huge green eyes with their sooty black lashes were perfectly made up as usual. The dark coppery-red hair gleamed over the diamond ear-studs, just as always. But where were all the other things she used to identify herself by?

Chloe began her reckoning once more, already repeated once too often since she had left London.

No job, to start with. She had resigned from that, her ridiculously well-paid job as a top copywriter in a smart little ad agency. Well, except for the money, that was no great loss. Trying to create the perfect lines for the perfect housewife in her dream kitchen with the superlative packet soup bored Chloe nowadays, like so many other things.

No lover, either. All the available ones bored her too, and it irked her to think of the unavailable one. Leo Dawnay, damn him. All of this was really because of him. Leo was in the business, the perfect Englishman who had made it his particular business to trade on that on Madison Avenue. A big joint campaign had brought him briefly back to London, and into Chloe's bed. It was Leo who had said it as they lay wound together after one of their long evenings of love-making.

'You don't have to be so competitive in everything. You've got an intellectual chip on your shoulder, that's your problem.'

'What? That's crap.' Chloe sat up and the sheets fell away from her silky shoulders. 'I've got twice the wits of any of the little graduate mice that they send along to type my letters and answer my phone nowadays. When I was eighteen I just wanted to get on with life, not moulder in some dusty library.'

'Well', Leo had said coolly, 'you mentioned graduates, not me. But you're twenty-eight now, and perhaps you've done enough getting on. Take some time off. Test yourself a bit. You'd enjoy it.'

Leo, of course, had been at Balliol. And had taken a First.

'I don't need it,' Chloe had whispered into his thick, black hair. 'What I need is you. Again.' And his hands had moved across her belly and between her legs once more with unquestioning assurance. In the fierce pleasure of the moment Chloe had forgotten his words, but later they kept coming back to her. She thought about them when she recognised the uncomfortable feeling that permeated her life as boredom, and she remembered them again when she realised one day that she wasn't interested in the challenge of pitching for a major new account. She felt that she was running along in comfortable, well-oiled grooves, and that she wasn't thinking about anything, any more. She began to be afraid that even falling in love with Leo had been no more than a way of filling the vacuum that yawned in the centre of her life.

Another day she had pushed aside the story boards for a new bra commercial and typed a letter to the Principal of an Oxford College, making the choice just because she had seen the College featured in a magazine.

'That's that,' she thought. 'The answer will be no, of course.'

But with surprising speed, the letter had led to an interview with the austere Principal in her book-lined drawing room. Then, after some hasty reading, there had been papers to write on Victorian novelists and Romantic poets. She had been interviewed again, making her joke to her friends that she felt that she was being looked over for the chairmanship of Saatchi and Saatchi, not a commoner's place at an obscure women's College. At last the Principal had told her: 'We have a policy here, Miss Campbell, of accepting mature students and other unusual folk. You're more mature than most, of course, and you'll have a lot of catching up to do. But we think you'll make a useful contribution to College life, even if you turn out not to have a first-class mind. Would you like to come up this October?'

At first, going to Oxford had been no more than a teasing idea for Chloe. She had wanted to prove to Leo that she could win a place, and she had wanted to show him that it impressed her so little that she could turn it down without a second thought. Then she had found herself enjoying the preparation for the entrance papers, hurrying home to dig poetry books out of the inner pocket of her briefcase instead of going out to cocktails and dinners with friends from the agency. She had started to use the cool, remote thought of Oxford as an antidote to her grating London world.

Yet, even so, when the moment finally came she was shocked to hear herself saying, 'Thank you, Dr Hale. I'll do my very best. And I'd like to start in October.'

Now, Leo was back in Manhattan, or with his top-drawer wife up in East Hampton or wherever it was. Chloe Campbell was slowing down before the Oxford bypass, her car loaded with her expensive but not-too-new-looking leather suitcases, piles of crisp empty notebooks and brand new standard texts, and feeling as apprehensive as any sensitive adolescent on the way to a new school. It was too late now. Chloe negotiated the tangled city traffic, and parked the Renault defiantly half on and half off the pavement on Folly Bridge. Only a single window in the old house showed a light.

Chloe hitched her shaggy wolf-pelt jacket closer around her and began to pick her way down the slippery stone steps. Her hair looked as bright as a beacon in the wintry dusk. Before she reached the front door which had barred Helen's entry, it swung open and Gerry Pole lounged out. His grey sweater was filthy and his lined face was unshaven, but the tattered remnants of a more wholesome romantic youth clung about him. Chloe responded with a brief flicker of interest as Gerry grinned at her.

'One of Rose's new tenants, I take it? And very lovely, too. I'm Gerry Pole, by the way, token male on the premises . . .'

'Oh good,' Chloe said quickly, waving up towards her car perched on the bridge. 'Perhaps, then, you could possibly give me a hand with my things? So inaccessible, down here.'

'Delighted.' Gerry smiled again, showing off the attractive crinkles around his pale blue eyes and revealing uncared-for teeth.

So Chloe made her entrance into Follies House burdened with nothing more than her handbag and her portable typewriter. Gerry obligingly toiled to and fro with the leather cases and set them carefully down in Chloe's first-floor room. The long windows looked out on almost total blackness now, but the little lamps inside glowed invitingly on panelled walls and solid furniture. Chloe looked around her with approval. The panelling was painted soft bluey-green, like a bird's egg, and the curtains and faded Persian rugs stood out against it in warm reds and garnets. She laid her typewriter down on the bare desk and switched on the green-shaded library lamp to make a little, welcoming circle of light.

Here, Chloe thought with a sigh of satisfaction, she could work. Books. Peace, calm and no hassles. Perhaps this crazy idea was going to work out after all. A little sound from behind her reminded her that Gerry was still hovering by the door. She shot him a brilliant, dismissive smile.

'Thanks very much. I expect we'll be meeting again soon, if you live here too?'

'Oh yes, certain to.' Gerry rubbed his dry hands expectantly. 'I could more than do with a drink now, in fact, after all that lifting. Won't you join me? I've got a little something...'

The flip-flop shuffle of down-at-heel slippers came up the stairs and along the gallery towards them. A second later the mass of Rose's bulk filled the doorway. She jerked her head at her half-brother and, with surprising speed, he was on his way.

'Another time, then,' he winked at Chloe and vanished.

Rose eased herself down on the foot of the bed and rested her podgy hands on her spread knees. The two women smiled.

'Still not quite sure about it, eh?' Rose asked. Chloe took off her jacket and stood stroking the fur absently.

'Not a hundred per cent,' she admitted. 'Or even fifty. Sometimes it feels like a crazy decision to have made, three years up here reading George Eliot and trying to make ends meet on a grant. Not that it isn't perfect to be at Follies House,' she added warmly.

Rose chuckled fatly and her little eyes flickered over the diamonds in Chloe's ears, the discreet but heavy gold chain around her neck and the supple, rust suede of her tunic dress. 'Don't tell me that girls like you ever have to manage on a grant,' she murmured. 'And you'll enjoy it here, mark my words. All

17

kinds of people to meet, for a start. Different from your London ad men.'

'I hope so,' countered Chloe fervently.

'Look at me,' Rose went on. 'I just have this house, nothing else. But enough goes on here to keep me looking forward to tomorrow.' As she winked at Chloe she looked, for an instant, very like her half-brother. 'So long as I choose the right people to live with me here at Follies, I have everything I need in these four walls. Which is just as well, because where could I go outside with a face and figure like mine?' The white hands fluttered vaguely over the forbidding fleshy mass. Chloe could do no more than turn the talk with a question.

'Who else lives here now? Since Colin Page's sister left?'

Rose's face brightened in anticipation. 'Ah. All new this term. You, dear, of course. A little mite called Helen, who you shall meet in one second, unless my predatory young cousin has swept her out of the house already. And by the end of the week there'll be a pretty love called Pansy. Such a beautiful name, isn't it? There's just the three of you. I think you'll make such an interesting combination.' Rose's fingers knitted across the mound of her stomach as she nodded happily at Chloe. Just for the moment she looked like a complacent puppet-mistress with her pretty dolls on sticks, waiting for the show to start. The idea amused Chloe rather than alarmed her. Why shouldn't Rose live a little through her lodgers, after all?

The landlady heaved herself to her feet and padded to the door.

'Helen!' she shouted up into the darkness. 'Helen darling, come down and meet a new friend.'

Chloe wasn't sure who she had been expecting as another member of Rose's 'family,' but the figure who appeared obediently a moment later came as a surprise.

'Helen Brown, Chloe Campbell,' Rose said easily. 'And now I'm off. Tell me if you need anything simple. Anything strenuous, ask Gerry.'

'Hello,' Chloe said to the girl in the doorway. Helen was small and fine-boned, too thin, with collarbones that showed at the stretched neckline of her royal blue sweater. In her grey corduroy skirt she might have been a fifteen-year-old schoolgirl, but something in the poised tilt of her head told Chloe that she was older, twenty or perhaps even a little more. Her skin was very pale and creamy under a mass of short black curls, and the huge grey eyes in the heart-shaped face were smudged underneath with violet shadows.

'Hello,' Helen responded warily. There was an exotic atmosphere in the room that wasn't just compounded of expensive scent and suede, nor of the rich colours and fine proportions that were missing from her own room upstairs. The atmosphere came from the girl herself, prowling like a taut red-brown tiger on the Persian rug. Yet as soon as Chloe smiled at her it was different again. She looked ordinary, friendly and inquisitive now. Chloe seized Helen by the wrist and propelled her to an armchair.

'For God's sake, sit here and talk to me while I get my bearings. It's my first day at Oxford, and you're the first real person I've met. Are you new, too?'

Helen shook her curls vigorously. 'No. My last year. But it's my first time living out of College. Follies isn't exactly my natural habitat either. It's been a strange day.'

Chloe was rummaging in one of her bags. At length she lifted out a green and gold bottle and brandished it triumphantly. 'Share this with me? It won't be very cold, but it'll do.'

Helen watched the champagne sparkle into a pair of glasses and then lifted hers to Chloe. The strangeness of the day evidently wasn't over yet, and something inside her didn't want it to be.

'Welcome to Oxford,' she toasted the newcomer.

'And to Follies House.' Chloe's bright green eyes glittered at her over the glass and they drank together.

They finished the bottle as Chloe unpacked. Helen sat curled up in the armchair with her cold feet underneath her and listened as the other girl talked. The champagne sent unfamiliar waves of warmth and lassitude through her veins, and she found herself sinking into the cushions and smiling at the warm colours and scents around her. Chloe's cases seemed to contain unbelievable piles of silk and cashmere and butter-soft leather, marching ranks of shoes and boots, and handbags in soft, protective wrappings.

There were other pretty, more eccentric things too. A huge, fragile butterfly gaudily painted on rice paper swung airily on one wall. A silver-framed mirror bore the raised motto 'Look, but linger not.' Chloe made a mock-grimace into it as she swung it into place on the mantelpiece. A collection of heart-shaped tortoiseshell frames all seemed to enclose pictures of different men. All these Chloe laid out among the vanity cases, silver hairbrushes and tiny crystal bottles.

All the time, as she moved to and fro, Chloe went on talking. Had Helen but known it, she needed to talk more than anything else. She needed to put London firmly behind her; Leo and the agency and San Lorenzo and everything else. Almost by accident, the possibility of Oxford had today become reality. Chloe was so used to feeling confident that it was doubly disconcerting to be nervous and apprehensive. Talking to this quiet girl seemed to help. She told Helen everything, but it was as much for Chloe's own benefit. The explanation helped to put this mad, life-changing decision into perspective. She had no need of an Oxford degree and it was exactly the abstract, stringent challenge set by gaining one that Chloe knew she needed.

With the last drop of champagne she smoothed a remaining square of tissue paper and tucked it into the last empty suitcase. Helen, who had drunk the lion's share of the champagne as she listened, smiled vaguely up at her.

'So here I am.' Chloe gestured theatrically. 'Unfettered, and as yet unlettered . . .' they giggled happily, '. . . although Dr Hale is about to put that right. And feeling much, much better.'

She stopped in front of Helen and put her hand over the younger girl's. 'Thank you for listening to all that. You're a good listener, aren't you?' On impulse she knelt down and took both of Helen's thin hands between her own warm ones.

'Helen, I've done all the talking, like a self-centred old witch. Now you tell me some things. You're sad, aren't you? Why's that?'

Helen looked into Chloe's concerned eyes and in an instant the champagne, her loneliness and this unexpected warmth from a woman she barely knew blurred inside her. Boiling tears swept down her face. In an instant Chloe's arms came round her and Helen's face was buried in soft suede and the thick mass of dark red hair.

'What? Helen, what is it?'

There was a second's quiet before she answered. 'My father. My father killed himself.'

At once Chloe's arms tightened around the younger girl's thin shoulders, but she said nothing.

'Yes,' said Helen after a moment, speaking as softly as if to herself. 'It was in the summer. The middle of August, when the world was hottest and brightest outside. Daddy must have found that very hard, looking inwards at the darkness gathering for him in our house. I suppose it had been dark for weeks before that, months even. At the end, it was as if everything positive and hopeful had wilted, through lack of light. Even our love for him seemed to have no life in it any more, because he couldn't lean on it. Right at the end, in the last hopeless days, I was still sure that it would brighten the gloom for him. But it didn't, because he killed himself.'

'Why did he do it?' Chloe whispered, as gently as she could, and felt an answering movement that might have been a shrug.

'It's a banal story, I suppose,' Helen told her with a new bitterness in her voice. 'He lost his job. Not a particularly high-powered job, or anything, just as a middle manager in a middle-sized manufacturing company. My father was always a quiet man – grey, they call it here – quietly doing what he was supposed to do. He came home in the evenings on the train, mowed the lawn, listened to the radio, did what was involved in being a husband and father, but mostly he just did his unassuming job. He must have enjoyed it ... no, perhaps needed it is nearer the truth. Because when they took it away, he collapsed inside. They did it all particularly brutally, just pushed him out with a tiny amount of compensation. But that's not unusual. In my father's case, I think he knew from the first moment that there was no chance of finding another job. And he wasn't the kind of man who could turn round and just create another life for himself. He was too mild, and puzzled, and overwhelmed by the circumstances of the life he already had. He just let himself feel shamed and rejected. There was no money, you see. He had no prospects at all, and there was nothing he could do for us or anyone else. So he retreated further into the dark and silence, leaving us behind. Until the day came when he went into the garage, locked the doors and turned the car engine on. He lay down on a tartan knee rug that we used to keep on the back seat. Do you know, he was still wearing a tie?'

'What about your mother?' Chloe asked.

'She loved him. It was the worst kind of shock for her. She's not very good at being alone.' Helen rubbed her face with the flat of her hand and, as if noticing that Chloe's arms were still

21

around her, stiffened and drew back a little. Chloe let her go, noticing the tired pallor and the shadows under her eyes.

'And you?' she asked. Helen shrugged again.

'There are money problems, of course. My mother does some part-time supply teaching, and there's a tiny pension. But my brother is still a child, really, and needs everything. And there's a big mortgage, the three of us to clothe and feed, all the household bills. So much money to find, from nowhere...' Helen's voice trailed away hopelessly. When she spoke again the reawakening of anxiety had drained away all the colour that the champagne had put into her cheeks. 'I shouldn't be here. I should never have come back. The right thing would have been to get a job, doing anything, anywhere. Whatever brings in the most money. I can help a tiny bit out of my grant, but...' The shrug, when it came again, was defeated, '... it isn't enough.'

'But they insisted, your mother and brother, that you did come back? Said you'd be letting them down, and your father, if you didn't?'

Helen smiled wryly. 'Exactly. How did you know that?'

Chloe laughed at her. 'Because it's what any right-thinking people would have said. It matters, doesn't it? You're probably very bright.'

Helen was too natural to attempt a modest contradiction.

'I'm bright enough. I could get a First, if I'm lucky. Before Dad died I'd wanted to stay on and do research. Now, of course, I'll have to look for something that's more of a paying proposition. But not to have got a degree at all, that would have been very hard.'

As she watched the anxiety in Helen's face, Chloe felt the weight of her own privilege. Her own background was not wealthy, but never at any time since her early and rapid success at her job had she had to deny herself anything. Travel, new books, designer clothes, a luxurious flat were as much an unquestioned part of her life as they were remote from Helen's. Chloe reflected that even her place at Oxford had begun as a move in her sexual game with Leo. Set beside Helen's difficulties and her family's sacrifices, that suddenly seemed frivolous and wasteful. She shook herself in irritation and turned to listen to Helen again. The other girl's face was brighter and more animated now.

'It's strange to be back here, after so much. And in this weird house...'

'Isn't it?' Chloe grinned at her.

'...I'd only been in the house an hour before Oliver Mortimore appeared, kissed me, and asked me to tea on Friday.'

'Who's that?'

Helen's smile transformed her face and the grey eyes shone with amusement in the absence of the shadows. She had no idea why she was talking like this to Chloe, but it felt perfectly natural.

'Oh, a bright star in the local firmament. Rich, titled, amusing, and the most beautiful young man you ever saw.'

'Love the sound of it,' said Chloe, 'but does such a sum of perfection do anything as ordinary as have tea?'

The sound of their laughter reached Rose as she slid across the dark hallway below, and it brought the flicker of a satisfied smile to her broad face.

'Now I'm sitting here drinking champagne and talking to you as if I've always known you,' Helen went on. 'Odd, isn't it? It feels a long way from home, too, and that isn't fair.' The sadness flooded back into her face.

'Listen to me, Helen,' Chloe said firmly. 'It would be wrong to destroy the value of being back here by immersing yourself in guilt and grief. That would make your family's sacrifice useless, wouldn't it? You can't forget your father's death – how could you? – and you shouldn't try. But you can find your own strength to carry on positively, where he couldn't.' Chloe broke off and bit her lip. Her face reddened as she met Helen's serious, straight gaze. 'I don't know why I'm preaching at you,' Chloe said uncomfortably, 'particularly when I've got the feeling that there are several things for me to learn myself before too long.'

The silence stretched on for a second or two before Helen broke it. 'You're right, though. Thank you, Chloe. Tea on Friday with Oliver,' she added lightly. 'I'll have to be profoundly positive to cope with that. Will you ... do you think you could lend me something beautiful to wear?'

There was relief in Chloe's face as she responded warmly, 'With pleasure. To seal the deal, let's go out and eat now – I'm ravenous. You tell me where's good, and I'll treat you. Okay?'

'Sounds wonderful.'

The two girls left Follies House together and climbed the cold, slippery steps up to the bridge. Inside her Renault, Chloe revved the engine decisively and glanced at Helen's profile beside her. 'Well then, Oxford, here we come,' she murmured into the icy air.

On Friday afternoon Helen slipped through the great wooden gates of Christ Church and crossed to the porter's glassed-in box, incongruously snug under the splendour of Wren's tower.

'Oliver Mortimore's rooms, please?' she asked, remembering that Oliver had made no mention of where he was to be found. Perhaps he just assumed that everybody knew.

'Canterbury Quad, Miss,' said the porter, pointing, and gave her a staircase and room number. Following his directions Helen came out into the sunlight in Tom Quad. For a moment, nervous but unwilling to admit to herself that a mere tea-party could intimidate her, she stood to admire the view. Cardinal Wolsey's great unfinished quadrangle seemed to capture and intensify the Oxford light. The gold of late autumn afternoon sunshine was reflected from the deeper gold stone, the rows of leaded windows, and the flat face of the water in the fountain basin. The space seemed immense and airy, yet the proportions made it intimate, too. The only sounds, magnified in the stillness, were the faint splash of water spouting from the statue of Mercury, and the whirr of cameras belonging to a distant group of Japanese tourists. Ahead of her the smooth green lawns rolled away to encircle the fountain and its fringe of lily pads. An undergraduate in a fluttering black scholar's gown brushed past Helen and it occurred to her that, tourists apart, this scene must be almost unchanged since the sixteenth century.

Then in a babble of noise a crowd of jostling people emerged from one of the archways and simultaneously a blare of music burst from an upstairs window. Helen jerked herself back into the present and walked on towards whatever awaited her in Oliver's rooms.

She found Canterbury Quad without difficulty. Built more than two hundred years after Tom Quad, it still looked to Helen profoundly ancient and magnificent as she stared up at its classical proportions. She was used to her own College, of which the oldest parts were late nineteenth-century, and to its comfortable air of being a random collection of reasonably well-preserved outbuildings to something much more important.

Oliver's rooms were on the first floor of the central building. Helen read the white-painted names on the board in his staircase doorway: Mr G.R.S. Sykes, Lord Oliver Mortimore, Mr A.H. Pennington. At the top of the stone staircase she came to Oliver's outer door, open, and then tapped lightly on the inner one.

'Cm'in,' someone shouted. Helen squared her shoulders inside the vivid scarlet of Chloe's brief sweater dress, glanced down briefly at what felt like far too much leg which it left on show, and went inside.

The room seemed at first sight to be uncomfortably full of people, all of them women. The atmosphere was charged with smoke and the sound of laughter and clamouring, insistent talk.

'...all through the Vac, darling. Not just in London, but in Italy as well...'

'...so I told him to stuff it. No, honestly, he was such a swine...'

'...Mummy bought it in the end, it was so funny...'

Everyone seemed to know everyone else very well indeed. Helen's first impulse was to turn and run, but then she saw Oliver refilling someone's glass. There was no sign anywhere, Helen realised, of a teacup or a piece of buttered toast. The carpet was cluttered with glasses and ashtrays.

'Hello,' Oliver said beside her, surprising her again by his height. His kiss, quickly brushing her mouth, surprised her less this time but had no less of an effect. Oliver took her hand and helped her to pick her way through the sprawled legs and gossiping bodies. 'You look very pretty,' he told her casually. 'Red suits you almost as much as smiling.' A blonde girl with a sulky face jerked her head up to look at Helen as she passed. There was a sofa in the corner, occupied by yet another pair of girls. Oliver eased her down between them, and they made room for her reluctantly.

'You must know Fiona? No? And Flora? Well then, now's your chance. This is Helen, and this ... is ... Helen's drink.' Oliver handed her a glass, winked, and went away.

Two surprised faces stared at Helen. Politely, but insistently, with their questions, they tried to find out who Helen was and where she fitted in. It gave Helen a kind of half-satisfaction to

25

demonstrate that she didn't fit in anywhere, but once that was done the girls went back to their conversation, leaning across her in their animated talk. Helen wriggled back against the cushions to look at the rest of the room.

It wasn't all girls, she saw now. Three or four young men, in jeans and sweaters like Oliver, lounged among the more carefully-turned-out girls. The striking exception was a dark, confident-looking man with a high-bridged nose and long hands that he used to make incisive gestures as he talked. He seemed older than the others and was dressed differently in a loose, pale jacket and beautifully-cut trousers with front pleats. He evidently felt Helen's stare from across the room because he stopped talking, and his eyes held hers for a second. Then he raised his eyebrows in surprising, friendly complicity. Helen guessed at once that he didn't belong here either, but he was making himself ten times more at home than Helen herself. After a moment he came over to her and helped her up from her captivity between Flora and Fiona.

'More room on the window seat,' he grinned at her. 'I'm Tom Hart.'

Expertly he ensconced them on the cushioned seat where they were half hidden from the rest of the room by loops of curtains.

'Well?' he went on, lighting himself a cigarette. Helen shook her head at the held-out pack. He sounded American, she thought. What was he doing here?

'Helen Brown,' she told him, and to forestall a repeat of her interview with Fiona and Flora she added 'I don't know Oliver from London, or from Gloucestershire either. I'm not a friend of Annabel, whoever she is, nor of any of these people.' Helen's small, firm chin jerked towards the chattering roomful and Tom grinned at her again. 'I met Oliver once, at Follies House, which is where I live, and he asked me to tea. God knows why, now I come to be here.'

She lifted her glass to Tom and took a gulp of the cold white wine.

'Quite,' said Tom equably. 'But I think that one might as well make the best of Oliver's excellent Alsace, now that one is here. Noll!' he shouted, and Oliver drifted over to refill their glasses.

'Take very good care of her,' he told Tom smoothly when he

saw Helen behind her half of curtain. 'I shall be needing her as soon as all the rabble has gone.'

Tom ignored him. 'Follies?' he asked her. 'Where Frances was going to live?'

Helen nodded, and Tom's face set harder for a moment. 'I miss her,' he said. 'She's very unlucky, and very helpless.'

Helen knew from that moment that she and Tom would be friends.

'Mmmmm.' Tom was looking harder at Helen now. 'D'you act at all?' He turned her face to the light and stared a little too deeply into the grey eyes.

'Act?' Helen blinked and caught herself blushing. 'No, not at all. I couldn't. Far too inhibited.'

'Pity. I'm directing the OUDS major next term. *As You Like It*, you know. I thought you might like to audition for me.'

'No, thanks.' Helen shuddered at the idea. 'But I'll come along and see it. Will that do?'

Her turn had come, she thought, to ask questions. 'You're American, aren't you? Are you studying here?'

Tom Hart laughed at the idea. 'Hell, no. Well, not in the conventional way. I'm a theatre director, and I'm spending a year or so at the Playhouse here. Purely in an assistant capacity, you understand, as they keep reminding me. My old man's in the theatre in New York. Management.' Something flickered in Tom's face, as if a disagreeable memory had bothered him for a moment, before he went on. 'I needed some time away from home, before deciding what to do for real, so here I am. One of my projects now is this students' Shakespeare. As a matter of fact, in a brilliant piece of innovative casting, Oliver is to be my Orlando.' Tom confidently waved away Helen's start of surprise. 'You'd be amazed. He moves beautifully, and he has a real unaffected feel for the verse. You may think he's a mere aristocratic thicko, with a flair for nothing more taxing than horses and dogs, but you'd be wrong.'

Helen's gaze travelled from Oliver, tall and tousled in the middle of his friends, and back to Tom. There was something in the way that the American looked at Oliver, with both fascination and a kind of unwilling admiration, that puzzled her.

'Anyway,' Tom went on quickly, aware that Helen was watching him, 'Orlando himself isn't a character endowed with a great deal of brain. No, Rosalind's the important one, and I

27

can't find the right girl anywhere. I was hoping I might spot someone here amongst Noll's grand friends, but they're all far too old already. Look at them.' He waved his hand expressively across the room. 'Twenty years old and experienced enough for forty. I need someone fresh, and full of innocence, yet with that sexy edge of natural cleverness and the beginnings of maturity. A bit like you. But not really like you,' he added, with beguiling frankness.

'Thank goodness.' Helen smiled back at him.

Oliver was seeing people to the door. There was a flurry of kissing and hand-waving, then when Oliver turned back into the room Helen saw the sulky blonde girl jump up and push her arm through his. There was a possessive glow in her face and Helen thought, at once, *Of course he would have someone*. The little, frivolous flame of excitement that she had been shielding went out immediately. The blonde girl tugged Oliver's head down to hers and kissed his ear, then let him go with a tiny push.

Tom stood up and pushed his hands deep into his pockets. 'Time I was off,' he told Helen. 'Sure you won't audition for me?'

Helen shook her head. 'No. I'd be no good. I'm too busy, anyway. I have to work.'

Tom stared at her for a moment. 'Jesus, you can't work all the time. That'd be very dull.'

Helen was aware of a prickle of annoyance. She felt that this dark, forceful man was pushing her in some way and she recoiled from the idea.

'I am dull,' she told him dismissively.

Tom's face remained serious but there was an underlying humorousness in it that threatened to break out at any minute. 'Somehow I doubt that,' he said, very softly. 'But it was only an idea. See you around.' With a casual wave that took in Oliver as well as Helen, he was gone.

Helen realised that she was almost the last remaining guest. The blonde girl was at Oliver's side again, turning her pretty, petulant face up to his. 'Oliver,' she said in a high, clear voice, 'so lovely to see everyone again. But,' and there was no attempt to lower the upper-class tones, 'the mousey girl in red, who on earth was she?'

Oliver's good-humoured expression didn't change, but he shook his hand free. 'Don't be such a cow, Vick. I don't know any mice. Where's your coat?'

28

'Don't bother, darling,' Vick said sweetly. She blew him a kiss, danced to the door and slammed it behind her.

At last, Helen saw that she was alone with Oliver. He came, picking his way through the debris of bottles and glasses on the floor, and held out his hands to her.

'You've such a sad face,' he said. 'Didn't you like my party?' His hands, as they closed over hers, felt enormous and very warm.

'I liked Tom Hart,' Helen told him carefully. 'I'm sorry about looking sad. It must be just the way I am.' There was no question of confiding anything to Oliver. Helen was still surprised that she had let out so much to Chloe. Yet Helen was shrewd enough to know that the very remoteness of Oliver's world from her own was part of the unexpected, exotic fascination that she felt for him. She was clever enough too to guess that whatever it was that Oliver saw in her, he wouldn't be attracted by the poverty and awkwardness of her background.

She felt, for an instant, guilty of disloyalty, but she turned the thought away deliberately. What was it that Chloe had said? 'Find your own strength to carry on. Positively.' Well, she would do just that.

'I shall have to try and cheer you up,' Oliver was saying lightly. 'Here. Have another drink. Always helps.' He filled her glass up with the heady, flowery wine and came to sit beside her on the window seat. His long legs sprawled in the faded blue jeans, and his forehead rested against the window pane as he stared out. After a moment's silence, in which Helen's eyes travelled from the clear-cut planes of his face to the tiny pulse that jumped at the corner of his eye, Oliver said, 'So quiet. Just the light and the dark out there. No talk. No noise or confusion. Do you ever wish that you could keep moments? Freeze them or something, just the odd minutes when everything is right. There are so bloody few of them.'

Even in your life? Helen wanted to ask. Perhaps after all he wasn't such a bizarre choice for Orlando. He had the face of a romantic hero, and there was enough of uncertainty in it now for her to imagine him as a boy in love with an illusion.

'Times when I want to stop everything, and say yes. Like this. This is how I want it to be?' Helen answered him. 'Not very many. Some, perhaps.' Like now, she could have added. Being here with you, of all strange people, talking like this.

Oliver stopped staring out into Canterbury Quad as if after all he was rejecting this moment as one to be kept.

'Well, what shall we do? More drink?' He waved the bottle and when Helen shook her head he refilled his own glass and drained it. 'Mmm,' he murmured, and lifted Helen's hand from where it lay in her lap. He traced the shape of her fingers and the outline of her nails with his own forefinger and then, with his face turned away from her into the room, said, 'Would you like to go to bed?'

The words seemed to hang, echoing, in the air between them.

Helen was not a virgin, but never in the course of the single, bashful relationship she had known had there been an instant like this. Half of her, astoundingly, wanted to say – just as casually – yes, let's do that. But it was a hidden half that she was far from ready to reveal, even to herself. The practical, careful Helen of old, the one who took stock and who watched intently from the sidelines, was the one who answered.

'No,' she said, as if considering it. 'Not yet.'

'Yet?' Irritation flickered in Oliver's blue eyes as he stared at her. He seemed to see her, very close at hand, yet not to notice her at all. 'What can you mean, yet?'

'People,' Helen told him mildly, 'usually leave a decent interval between meeting and going to bed.'

Oliver's quick, sardonic smile surprised her. 'A decent interval, then. How many days? How many dinners? God, I hate waiting. And I hate decency even more. It's a proletarian idea, hasn't anyone told you that?'

Helen was stung. She jumped up from the cushions, and as she moved she saw Oliver's eyes on the length of thigh showing beneath her scarlet hemline. Her blush deepened and she lost the sharp retort which had been ready. Oliver stood up too, grinning, and then swung her round by the shoulders. His mouth found the nape of her neck under the black curls and he kissed her.

'Ah, a warm place at last,' he teased. 'You're dressed to look like a flame, but your skin feels as cold as marble. Funny girl.' Then he turned her round to face him and kissed her mouth, deliberately, still smiling against her closed lips. 'Don't worry. If you prefer decency, we'll let it lie for now, like a fat bolster between us.' The good humour in his voice changed everything

30

for Helen. He did understand, then. The sensitivity she had guessed at was there in him, waiting. Helen stood in the circle of his arms for a second and wished that it was all different. If she had said yes ... If she had been a different person.

Flora or Fiona would have said yes, and they would have been able to keep him for a while. And now he was moving away from her, disentangling himself as he had done from the blonde Vick. *Oliver.*

'Come on,' he said kindly. 'I'll walk you back to Follies. I'd like to drop in and see old Rose for half an hour before Hall.'

Helen nodded dumbly. As they walked together across the Quad the ancient bell, Great Tom, struck six. The long, tolling notes lapped sonorously inside her head, uncomfortably like a knell. Yet Oliver drew her arm snugly through his as they turned down St Aldate's. He was whistling softly, a single phrase over and over again, as if he was trying to tease the rest of a forgotten theme out of his subconscious. Helen fell into step with him, half carried along by the support of his arm. He was wearing a shabby, brown leather aviator's coat with a lining of tightly curled sheepskin, and in the warmth of a deep pocket his hand still held Helen's. Remembering the first of his questions, she knew that this was a moment she would like to freeze for herself. If only it was possible to keep him here, beside her, just like this.

When they reached Follies Oliver handed her elegantly down the steep stone steps to the island, walked her up through the silent house and stopped outside her door. His eyes glowed very bright and amused in the darkness.

'I'll be back,' he told her, 'to check out the bolster before too long. Such uncomfortable, old-fashioned things.'

'That's good,' Helen responded equally brightly. 'I shall look forward to that.'

Oliver raised his arm in a half wave and turned away again. Helen stood listening until the sound of his footsteps had been swallowed up in the recesses of the house. She heard a burst of radio music followed by a door closing, then silence. The thought of her own cold, empty room was uninviting. Helen slipped down the stairs to the grander spaces of the gallery below.

'Come in,' Chloe's low, musical voice answered her knock at once.

31

Chloe was sitting curled up in her armchair in a pool of lamplight. There was a red-embered fire burning in the grate and her hair was glowing even brighter in the double warmth of the two lights. She closed her book with an exaggerated gesture of relief and grinned up at Helen.

'Well, and how did it go?'

It was easy to tell Chloe things. Helen clasped dramatically at her heart and stumbled forward into the light. 'Wonderful. And awful. He asked me to go to bed with him and I said no. Oh God, Chloe, what shall I do?' It was half a joke, but only half. Something intriguing had come in to fill a cold, empty space inside Helen, and now she didn't want to let it go.

Chloe's eyebrows lifted a fraction. 'Horny little bugger,' she said, amused. 'You were quite right to tell him to get lost. He'll be back, love, don't you worry.'

'I hope you're right,' said Helen softly. 'I want him to be back, very much.' She didn't, in her preoccupation, see the quick anxious glance that Chloe shot at her.

After an hour of sitting with Rose in the impenetrable untidiness of her kitchen, Oliver stood up restlessly. He drank the remains of the dark brown sherry in his glass and made a face. Rose went on impassively with her sewing, not looking at him. 'Before you go,' she said, 'what are you doing to that nice little thing upstairs?'

Oliver shrugged himself into his coat without answering, turned to go, and then as an afterthought sketched a kiss in the air between himself and Rose. 'Doing nothing at all, darling Rose. All the treasures are kept securely locked away, as you must have guessed. Bloody boring. And now, *au revoir* or I shall be late for Hall.'

Rose, left alone in the kitchen, smiled a little and went on sewing.

Oliver took the steps into the misty dampness shrouding the city two at a time. He noticed the outline of a big car parked on the bridge as he came level with it, then as he swung out on to the pavement he saw that it was a white Rolls. Beside it, a man in a peaked cap was lifting a heavy trunk. Three other people were standing close together in the orange glare of the street lights, moisture from the mist beading brilliantly on their hair and clothes. The tallest was a thickset man in an expensive overcoat; one of the two women was clinging affectedly to his arm.

But it was the other woman who drew Oliver's startled attention.

She looked very young. Over a cloud of pure white fur, the face was as innocent as an angel's, and as expressionlessly beautiful as if carved in marble. Oliver stopped dead. At once, the face burned itself into his memory. He knew that he had never seen it before, yet it was familiar, even down to the faintly startled reflection in the depths of the immense eyes. And the girl went on looking back at him, her lips slightly parted and the street lights darting jewels of dampness among her snow-white furs.

The thickset man made an irritable sound and Oliver wrenched his attention from the girl.

'Can I help?' he asked politely.

The man stabbed a finger towards the square black bulk of Follies House.

'Is this Follies House?'

'That's right.'

'Jesus, will you look at those steps!' The accent was mid-Atlantic, but beneath it were the unmistakable echoes of London's East End. 'Hobbs, can you get all this down there?'

The chauffeur leant over the parapet. 'Yes, Mr Warren, I think so.'

The other woman clung more tightly to the cashmere sleeve. 'Oh, Masefield, it's so wet out here. My hair.' Without a word her escort opened the passenger door and handed her back into the Rolls. Hobbs bent to lift the trunk again. The girl stared back at Oliver, motionless. The shroud of mist seemed to swallow all the sounds around them, so that they moved in eerie, silent isolation.

'Can I help?' he asked again, but the thickset man glanced at him only briefly. 'Thanks. No.'

The girl in white ducked her head and followed her father down the steps. Hobbs bent to the trunk again and bumped awkwardly after them. The woman sat in the car, staring ahead of her and rhythmically stroking her hair.

Oliver walked away, back up St Aldate's to Christ Church. He whistled to himself as he went, the same few, unfinished notes. Now he knew. The man was Masefield Warren. More, the white girl was his daughter, Pansy. Her face, wide-eyed and startled, was familiar from the flashbulb shots of a hundred gossip columns. Pansy Warren was not only beautiful, she was the heiress to her father's by now uncounted millions.

As Oliver walked back under Tom Tower the rest of the little whistled tune came spilling out, unchecked.

CHAPTER TWO

Oliver came looking for Helen again on Sunday morning.

On Sunday mornings Oxford was always full of the peals and counterpeals of church bells, and today they sounded louder and even sweeter than usual. The skies were clear after the days of rain of the term's beginning, and the trees without their muffling shrouds of leaves let the echoes through with extra clarity.

Helen was planning to do some reading in a library with a view over lawns and towers. It is Sunday, she told herself, as she gathered up her books. You must work as hard as you can, for Mum's sake and Graham's, but it can't be flat out all the time.

When she came out of the front door of Follies House she saw Oliver at once. He was leaning on the parapet of the bridge, watching her. He made no move as she climbed the steps towards him, feeling clumsy in her thick overcoat and encumbered by her books. But as soon as she came level with him, he smiled. Helen was struck at once by the way his face, the same features that must have belonged to the parade of illustrious ancestors stretching behind him, was repossessed by the smile to become Oliver himself, unique. He stepped forward, blocking her path.

'No work today,' he said firmly. 'Don't you know it's Sunday?' One by one he took the books from under her arm. 'Come with me instead.'

He wasn't being persuasive; he was simply telling her what she must do.

'We can go anywhere you like. The whole world's waiting.'

Helen let him unburden her, unable to protest or insist that indeed she must work.

'Books, books,' Oliver was saying breezily. 'I was sent out for tutoring last term to a man called Stephen Spurring. He kept trying to make me go to gloomy seminars with anxious girls from Colleges I've never heard of...'

'Like me?' Helen was laughing in spite of herself.

35

'No. Not a bit like you. You don't go to seminars and adopt a Marxist interpretation of *Wuthering Heights*, do you?'

'Oh, all the time. Stephen Spurring's very highly thought of, you know.'

'Then you must stop it at once.' Oliver stood squarely in front of her and cupped her chin so that she looked up into his face. He was mock-serious, grinning at her as he dropped his hand again so that she wanted to say, *Come back.* 'It can't be good for you. And highly thought of by whom? Hart has discovered that Spurring has got some kind of senior-member responsibility for *As You Like It.* Of all the tedious little men.'

So Oliver dismissed the bright star of the English faculty. How confident he is, Helen thought, as she followed him.

Oliver dropped the pile of books haphazardly into the well behind the seats of his open car. It was waiting for them at the kerbside, looking to Helen absurdly low-slung, sleek and highly polished. She had often seen Oliver driving around town in it. Now she said, 'It's such a pretty car. What kind is it?'

He opened the passenger door with a flourish, handed Helen into the leather bucket seat and swung his legs over the door on his own side.

'A Jaguar,' he said, with deep satisfaction, patting the walnut fascia. 'XK150. Rather old now, and quite rare.' The engine roared throatily into life and Oliver beamed. 'Looked after for me by a little man in the Botley Road. He just loves the innards of old cars, isn't that lucky? Me, I don't have any taste for sprockets and oil. I just want to drive her, the faster the better. So, really, the three of us have a perfect relationship.'

Helen watched him, fascinated. She had never met anyone so vibrantly pleased with life, and so certain of himself. The introspective moment of the other evening when he had sat staring out into the darkness of Canterbury Quad, and Helen had thought that after all he might make the perfect romantic hero, was forgotten.

They were bowling through the wide, tree-lined streets of North Oxford now, where the pavements were drifted over with golden leaves. The few people who were about were strolling with newspapers under their arms, or walking dogs who scuffled in the piles of leaves.

'Where are we going?' Helen asked.

'Where would you like to go?' Oliver countered. 'Anywhere in particular?'

'No.'

'Well then, you might as well leave it to me. We're going to have lunch, as it happens. And to see a man about a dog.'

Helen asked no more questions. Instead she sat back in her seat and let the wind blow away everything but the immediacy of this extraordinary morning. When she closed her eyes, the sunlight and the shade from the trees flashing past dappled patterns through her eyelids. When she opened them again there was the long, black car bonnet in front of her, the outskirts of the city dropping away, and Oliver beside her. He drove negligently, one hand on the wheel and the other resting on the polished wooden knob of the gear lever. They sliced in and out of the traffic on the busy road and then, suddenly, they were in the open country. Helen felt the acceleration pressing her back into her seat as the car surged forward. The shadows swept over her face, faster and faster, and the wind whipped her hair back.

Oliver glanced at her, sidelong. If Helen had known him better she might have recognised the small, secret smile with which he always congratulated himself on getting his own way. When she looked round at him again the smile had vanished and he asked, casually, 'Warm enough? My coat's in the back if you need something to put over your knees.' It was the brown leather aviator's coat which he had been wearing the other evening. Helen instinctively pulled her own well-worn duffle coat more tightly around her.

'I'm fine. Thanks.'

The car swept on. They were in the Cotswolds now, driving through villages built of honey-coloured stone and past winter-ready fields showing countless shades of brown and ochre.

'It's a beautiful day,' Oliver said, stretching back in his seat and bracing his arms straight against the wheel. 'Better than mouldering with all that lot in some library?' He jerked his head backwards at the pile of books behind them.

Much better, Helen told herself, shutting her mind resolutely to the niggling voice of conscience and another, much fainter, murmur of apprehension. She didn't feel safe with Oliver Mortimore. But then, what was so appealing about safety? Helen wriggled a little deeper into her seat and stared along the low line of the Jaguar's bonnet at the open road hurtling towards them. She thought, fleetingly, of Chloe; feeling safe wouldn't be high on Chloe's list of priorities, she was certain. Perhaps, after all, it didn't come so high on her own either. Helen couldn't explain to herself why she had been swept up by Lord Oliver Mortimore. But it gave her an unfamiliar glow of flattery and excitement. And now she was here she would enjoy it, whatever was to come. The recognition of that whatever, too, gave Helen a thrill of recklessness. She so rarely did anything without thinking very hard about it first. But there just wasn't any leeway for thinking, where Oliver was concerned. He had just happened to her, and she was ready to accept that.

Just as he would have to accept her.

Helen was clear-sighted enough to know that there was nothing to be gained by pretending to be something she wasn't, in the hope that would make her more interesting to him. Whatever it was that he had seen in her in the first place would have to go on being enough, and Helen lifted her chin determinedly at that. But she definitely wanted him to go on seeing something in her. Her eyes were drawn to him again as he sat negligently at the wheel. He was unusually good-looking, yes, but his attraction was more magnetic than that. It was the ease, the casualness and the assurance that drew Helen, who possessed none of those things. She felt as if she wanted to warm herself by him. And there was something else, too. She thought she detected a sensitivity in him, under all that urbane gloss, that made him doubly attractive. A little mysterious, too.

Be careful, Helen's sane little inner voice warned her. Another, louder voice responded. I'm always careful. This time I just want to see what happens. I don't care if it isn't real. If it doesn't last any longer even than today.

The Jaguar was slowing down. They had left the main road and, at the end of a much narrower road, they came to a compact little village. A cluster of stone cottages around an uneven triangle of green, a church with a squat stone tower masked by a belt of yew trees, and at the apex of the triangle, there was a pub. A mulberry tree was painted on the sign over the low door.

Oliver switched off the ignition and his smile flashed at her again.

'This is where we'll have lunch.' Again, there was no possibility of disagreeing with him, even if Helen had wanted to. Instead, she let him escort her across the green to the door under the mulberry tree. Oliver's arm sat lightly across her shoulders as they walked. Inside, there were log fires and high-backed oak seats.

'You're always so cold,' Oliver grinned down at her. 'We'd better sit close to the fire.' His hand touched the nape of her neck again, just briefly, under the tangle of black curls.

'Morning, Lord Oliver,' the man behind the bar greeted him. 'And Miss.' This was Oliver's home ground in some way, Helen realised.

'Hello, Bill. Drink, Helen?' A quick glance round the bar confirmed Helen's instinctive choice.

'Sherry, please. Dry, with ice.'

'Quite safe, but a little dull.' Oliver's voice was teasing. 'I'm going to have champagne, and I think you should too.'

The drinks arrived at once, Oliver's in a silver tankard and Helen's foaming in a tall, narrow glass. Twice in one week, Helen thought, amused. And I've hardly ever even tasted real champagne before. How odd things are. She raised her glass to Oliver in a quick, half-ironic toast and there was a flicker in his eyes as he responded.

'You are pretty,' he told her. 'Why do you try to hide it?'

'I don't,' she said, quickly defensive. 'Anyway, being pretty isn't everything.'

'You'd be surprised.' He was laughing at her: 'What else is there? Tell me with special reference to Helen Brown, please. I didn't have a chance to talk to you at my tea-party. And we did get off on rather the wrong footing afterwards.' Oliver took a long pull of champagne and looked at her expectantly.

'Mmm, your tea-party.' Helen picked the least dangerous avenue out of his questions. 'Are those people all friends of yours?'

Oliver shrugged, not interested. 'Acquaintances, mostly, not many friends. Except Tom Hart. He's very different, and rather formidable.'

Helen remembered the dark, intense face among the pink-and-whiteness of the English upper classes, and smiled a little. She remembered him, too, as much less formidable to her than the closed ranks of Oliver's social peers.

'Don't change the subject, anyway,' Oliver reprimanded her. 'Don't you like talking about yourself? Every other woman I know adores it.' He leaned back in his seat and clasped his hands behind his head, waiting for her to speak.

Helen was silent. How could she talk to this suave, privileged

39

young man about any of the things that mattered to her? She knew, instinctively, that Oliver would just be puzzled, and probably embarrassed, if she told him about the problems that beset her now. She had no desire to talk to him about her father, or even her mother and brother at home in their underheated little house. And then, the things that didn't really matter were so dull. She couldn't hope to amuse Lord Oliver Mortimore by giving him the details of her quiet, work-filled life and the few small diversions that she allowed herself. She felt herself colouring under his stare before her resolution to stay true to herself came back to her.

'No,' she said coolly. 'I'd prefer not to talk about me.' The amiability in Oliver's face didn't fade, but Helen was aware that he was staring at her with a shade more curiosity in his eyes. Unexpectedly, she grinned at him. 'Doesn't that make me fascinatingly different from all the other women you know?'

Oliver shrugged briefly. 'Different, anyway.' He raised his hand in a gesture to the barman to show that he wanted more champagne.

Aware that she had dampened the conversation, Helen cast about for a neutral topic to fill the silence between them.

'Where do you live? When you're not in Oxford, I mean.'

Oliver frowned over his tankard. 'Quite near here. At least, my family does. Thankfully, as a younger son, I'm not expected to involve myself too closely in all that.' Helen could only guess at what 'all that' might be. She had a dim vision of a feudal hierarchy presided over in baronial magnificence by Oliver's father. What would he be? A duke? A viscount?

'What about you?'

Helen told him the name of her home town and Oliver looked blankly back at her. 'Ah. Is it nice?'

'Not especially. But then we can't all have Gloucestershire estates.' I shouldn't have said that, she thought, as soon as it was out, but Oliver only smiled his brilliant smile.

'No,' he agreed as if she had made a telling point. 'It's a pity.'

Helen was realising as she sat in her corner, caressed by the glow of the champagne and the warmth of the log fire, that she and Oliver were even further apart than she had first thought. They might as well have come from different planets. Yet, surprisingly, the knowledge excited rather than depressed her. Covertly, Helen watched him lounging opposite her. He was playing absently with his silver tankard, turning it to catch the reflection of the fireglow. His fine blond hair was reddened by the warm light and his cheeks were faintly flushed by it. The aquiline features that reminded Helen of a marble knight on a marble tombstone were softened, so that he looked – as he did when he smiled – more like Oliver himself than Oliver the scion of a noble house.

I want him. The words sprang into Helen's head unvoiced, and for an instant they shocked her. *What* do you want, she made herself ask. A share, came back the answer from the other, hidden Helen. To share a little bit of him, because he's exotic and glowing and – perhaps – more than a bit dangerous. And to share through him all those things that I admire and have never had, like certainty and assurance. Not the money, or privilege necessarily, except that those things make it easier to have the others. I do want him, she thought, but I'm not making a very good job of getting what I want. If I was Flora or Fiona, I could giggle and gossip; maybe he'd think I was stupid but at least I wouldn't be sitting here in silence.

As if to help her out, a waiter in a sleek, black jacket came over to their corner.

'Your table is ready, Lord Oliver.'

'Great. Are you ready, Helen?'

Under his casual demeanour, Oliver sometimes displayed beautiful, rather old-fashioned manners. His hand was under her elbow to help her negotiate the single step up into the dining room. He waved aside another hovering waiter and pulled out Helen's chair himself, settling her into it and shaking out her thick, white linen napkin before laying it across her lap.

'What d'you think?' From across the starched white cloth Oliver waved around the little dining room. Helen peered about her. The light outside was brilliant, but in here it was all absorbed by dark walls and heavy oak furniture. Small, shaded lamps on each table cast pools of light, but the rest of the room was dim. There were only a dozen tables. The other diners were mostly much older than Oliver and Helen; men with port-wine complexions and silvery moustaches, women with high voices and well-cut tweeds.

'I've never been to one,' Helen told him, 'but it looks like I imagine the dining room of a gentleman's club.'

Oliver laughed, surprised. 'You're quite close. Except that

the food's a million times better. And, considering it's really only a country pub, it has the most amazing cellar.'

He means wine, Helen reminded herself, dispelling the image of a mysterious cobwebby recess beneath her feet.

Oliver nodded to the still-hovering waiter. At once a bottle was reverently brought, wrapped in a white napkin. Oliver tasted the half-inch of red wine which was poured into his glass, frowning, intent. Then another sharp nod to the waiter gave him the signal to fill Helen's glass. She watched, intrigued, then picked up her glass and sniffed at it as Oliver had done. The wine smelt rich, fat and beguiling, quite unlike the smell of any wine she had tried before. And a single sip told her that it was indeed something very different.

'This,' said Oliver, 'is burgundy. Gevrey-Chambertin, Clos St Jacques. Not quite the very greatest, but as good as one can find almost anywhere.' He turned his glass to the light and looked at it intently, then drank. 'Yes,' he said at last, and Helen knew that she was forgotten.

After a moment Oliver looked up again and recollected himself. 'One comes here for the game,' he told her. 'We're having grouse, okay?' She nodded, not caring if they were going to eat penguin.

In fact the food when it came, didn't appeal to her. The meat tasted strong and not very fresh. Helen ate what she could and gave all her attention to Oliver. In response, he set out to amuse her. She realised that when he chose, he could be excellent company. He made her laugh with stories of his own casual irresponsibility, and he swept the conversation along without making any more awkward demands on Helen's self-protective quiet. He seemed to live in a world of parties, weekends in Town, as he called London, dining clubs – and, even less intelligibly to Helen – dogs and horses.

'Do you do any work?' she asked.

'Not a jot.' His beguiling smile drew her own in response. 'I shall get a Third, of course. Just like my father. And his father, for that matter. My brother didn't bother with a degree at all. What difference does it make?' He shrugged amiably. 'More wine?'

Half-way through the meal Oliver drained his glass, tipped the empty bottle sideways, then signalled to the waiter to bring another.

'Another?' Helen said it out loud, in spite of herself.

'Of course another.' Oliver looked faintly surprised. 'The days of the one-bottle lunch are, as far as I am concerned, ancient history.'

He drank most of the burgundy, but he took care, too, to refill Helen's glass whenever she drank a little.

After the grouse came thick, rich syllabub in little china cups, and then brandy which made even Helen's fingers warm as she wrapped them round the glass.

When they had finished, one of the self-effacing waiters brought the bill. Helen tried to look away, but curiosity dragged her eyes back to Oliver's negligently scribbled cheque. It was for an amount almost exactly equal to the money she would have to live on for the rest of the term.

When they came out into the late afternoon sunshine, Oliver's eyes were hooded and he was talking just a little more deliberately than usual, but there was no other sign of how much he had drunk.

Once again he flung open the Jaguar's passenger door with a flourish and waved her towards it.

'Can you drive all right?' she asked, knowing that it was a pointless question.

'Perfectly.' His arm came round her shoulders again and with one finger he raised her chin so that he could look down into her eyes. 'Don't worry so much', he told her. 'Don't be so frightened of everything.' His hand moved to tangle itself in the mass of black curls and Helen felt the tiny, caressing movements of his thumb against her neck. He smelt of leather and wool and very faintly of dark red burgundy. For a moment they stood in silence. Helen was waiting, half apprehensive and half eager. Then Oliver laughed softly, deep in his throat. 'You seem so timid. But you aren't, really, are you? What door do I have to open to let the other Helen out?'

The other Helen. She caught her breath, thrown off balance by his sudden astuteness. Ever since he had kissed her, up in her bare room at Follies House, two Helens had been sparring inside her. She had no idea which one was her real self. How could she begin to find an answer for Oliver?

He didn't wait for one. Instead, he took her hand firmly and guided her into the car. 'Come on. We've got things to do.' Oliver hoisted his leather coat out from behind the seats and tucked it around her. Helen buried her nose luxuriously in the sheepskin lining.

'Where?'

'I told you. To see a man about a dog.'

The car shot forward. Oliver was driving even faster than before, but it seemed to Helen just as competently. He was very sure of where he was going.

The sun was low behind the trees now, and the shadows were thickening between the hedges in the narrow lanes. For a mile or so they skirted a long wall that looked as if it might enclose a park, then suddenly Oliver swung the wheel and the car skidded in through a gateway flanked by tall stone posts. They passed a low building that might have been a gatekeeper's lodge, its windows warmly lit behind drawn curtains. Beyond the lodge was a driveway, arched over with massive oak trees. As they sped towards it, Helen became aware of the dark, crenellated bulk of a big house sitting squarely on a little rise ahead.

Beside her, Oliver's face was expressionless.

To one side of the house was an outcrop of lower buildings, and Oliver turned the car decisively towards them. A moment later they were in a cobbled yard, the roar of the Jaguar's exhaust thrown back at them by the enclosing walls. Oliver vaulted out of the car and simultaneously one of the stable doors swung open. A shaft of yellow light struck across the cobbles.

'Evening, my lord', said the little man who had come out to meet them. He was toothless, brown-skinned and dressed in moleskin trousers and a coat so ancient that all the colour had been drained out of it.

'Hello, Jasper', said Oliver, grinning at him. 'Where are they?'

'End barn, my lord.'

'Come and see them too, Helen. This is Jasper Thripp, by the way. Miss Brown, Jasper.'

'Evening, miss,' said the little man, and hobbled towards the door of the end barn.

Uncomprehending, Helen followed them.

Inside the barn were the mingled smells of bran, paraffin from a heater, and warm milk. In a large box near the heater was a beagle bitch, surrounded by a warm, wriggling mass of brown, black and white-patched puppies. Oliver stooped over them, murmuring endearments to the mother as he lifted each pup in turn. His face was soft in the harsh light cast by the bare, cobwebbed lightbulb overhead. As he turned the puppies to and

44

fro, running a practised finger over their legs and backs, Helen saw that his hands were long and sensitive like the hands in an eighteenth-century portrait. At length he nodded and smiled at Jasper. 'Three first-rate, and a couple more pretty good. Yes?'

Jasper sucked at his toothless gums. 'Yup. I'd say so. She's done well this time, the old gel.' They were talking as equals now.

When the last of the pups had been gently returned to the security of its box, Oliver moved aside briskly. The softness was gone from his face, replaced by the more familiar authoritative mask.

'We'll give them a couple more weeks, then pick the ones we need for the pack.'

'Right you are, my lord.'

Master and servant again, Helen thought.

'And now, let's have a drink before I take Miss Brown off. There's a bottle in the tack-room safe.'

They retraced their steps to the door from which Jasper had emerged. The tack-room was stuffy and crammed with ranks of saddles and bridles, folded horse-blankets, combs and brushes and mysterious bottles and jars. Oliver was rummaging in an ancient green metal safe. Triumphantly he produced a whisky bottle and three thick tumblers. Helen shook her head at his invitation, but Oliver and Jasper both took liberal measures.

The old man drained his at a gulp, murmuring first, 'Here's to 'em, then.' Oliver tossed his drink back too, then stood up to go.

Jasper eyed him. 'Will you be taking Cavalier or The Pirate to the Thursday meet?'

Oliver was zipping himself into the aviator's coat. He took Helen's hand and squeezed it.

'Neither. Got to work this week.' Seeing Jasper's face, he laughed delightedly. 'Well, rehearse anyway. I'm in a play, did you know?'

'I'm sure you'll be the star of the show, my lord,' said Jasper drily and picked up a saddle from one of the pegs. It was clear that he had a low opinion of anything that took the place of hunting in his lordship's life. Oliver was still laughing as they climbed back into the car together. Helen could swallow her curiosity no longer.

'What is this place? The house? Who's Jasper?'

It was almost completely dark now and she could barely see

45

Oliver's face. But she did see that he hesitated a moment before answering, poised with his fingers on the keys in the ignition. And she was certain, too, that after a moment's hesitation he looked backwards over his shoulder in the direction of the big house. Then the car's engine roared into life again.

'Jasper is an old ally of mine,' he told her. 'He's part groom, part gamekeeper and a fund of useful knowledge. He taught me to ride when I was about three. Nell – the dog you saw – is as much his as mine, and he's in charge of the pups. I'm the Master of the House beagles this year, and I want to present the best of the litter to the pack.' There was pride in his voice as he spoke.

He does belong to another world, Helen thought. I don't know what he's talking about half the time.

As an afterthought, Oliver said quietly, 'And the house . . . it's where my parents live.'

The car surged forwards so fast that Helen was jerked backwards in her seat. She settled back, ready for the return drive to Oxford, but Oliver merely drove down the little rise away from the house, took another road across twilit parkland from which a damp mist was already rising and drew up in front of a cottage that might have belonged to a groundsman. It was screened on three sides by tall trees and all the windows were dark.

Helen followed Oliver through the drifts of leaves to the front door and stepped inside after him. When the lights came on they blinked at each other.

'Home,' he said.

The door had opened straight into a low, square room. It was shabby, filled with a mixture of what looked like outworn drawing room furniture and outgrown nursery pieces. The atmosphere was unmistakably welcoming. Helen looked round at the worn chintz covers, overlapping and unmatching rugs and the plain cream walls with an air of relief. She suddenly felt more comfortable with Oliver than she had done all day.

'Make yourself at home while I do the fire.' He knelt down at the open stone hearth. 'Or, better still, be an angel and make some tea.'

The kitchen was at the back. Helen hummed softly as she rummaged in cupboards to discover thick red pottery mugs and a homely brown teapot. When she carried the tray in, Oliver was lying on a rug in front of the fire, his head propped against the sofa cushions. He watched her as she put the tray down on the floor and then rocked back on her heels to meet his eyes. Oliver patted the cushions beside him, but Helen ignored him for a moment. Instead she poured tea into the red mugs and then handed him one. Then she wrapped her thin fingers round her own. Emboldened by the cosy domesticity of the little room, she asked him, 'Why do you call this home? If your parents live over there?'

'I've used this little house to escape to for years. When I was younger, to escape from the family. Nowadays, when I'm here, which isn't often, it's to avoid the tourists.'

'Tourists?'

'Mmm. The house is open to the public. Hordes of it. We've retreated to one of the wings, like survivors in a sinking ship.'

'What is this place?' Helen asked again.

'It's called Montcalm.'

Of course. Oliver's father, then, was the Earl of Montcalm. And this blond boy who was laughing at her in the firelight came of a family whose history stretched back to the Plantagenets.

'Didn't you know?' he asked her.

'No,' Helen said humbly. 'Or, if I did know who you were, I'd forgotten.'

'How lovely.' Oliver was laughing delightedly, and her own laughter echoed his. 'Come and sit here.'

Helen went. Her head found a comfortable hollow in the crook of his shoulder, and his chin rested in her hair. In front of them the fire crackled and spat. Helen let her eyes close, thinking of nothing but the sound of their breathing and the immediate sensations that lapped around her. Oliver's sweater was rough against one cheek and the heat of the fire was reddening the other. She felt his mouth moving in her hair.

'Comfortable?'

'Mmm.'

Gently, Oliver began to stroke her cheek. Instinctively, Helen turned her face closer to his. Her body felt soft, warm after the day's bright cold and relaxed with the ebbing of tension.

Very slowly, Oliver bent his head and kissed her mouth. Even as she felt herself respond to him, answering his kiss with a kind of hunger that surprised her, Helen heard a cold little voice inside her head.

You know that there will be no going back, after this?

You could still stop him.

47

You could still play safe.

No. I don't want to be safe. I don't want to lose him. I don't care what happens. This is all that matters now. This room, the firelight, the roughness of the rugs beneath us. Oliver.

His hand was on her breast now and his mouth was more urgent over hers. Like a suicide pushing away the lifebelt that drifted just within reach, Helen shut her ears and eyes and let herself be submerged in him.

'You look so fragile,' he whispered, 'but your strength is all inside, isn't it?'

He lifted her from the cushions and peeled her sweater off. Her eyes focused on his hands, portrait hands, insistent as they took off the rest of her clothes. Helen's skin was creamy-pale, but the light and warmth made it rosy now. Intently Oliver's fingers traced the line of her collarbone and the tilt of her small breasts, ran over the smooth flesh that stretched tight over her ribcage and then grasped her waist. She felt herself pulled towards him and her hands reached, in turn, at his clothes, wanting to touch him too.

At last, they faced each other, kneeling naked in the red glow.

'Now,' he said, and she echoed him on a long breath. Helen's fingers slid over him as he waited for her.

The dreamy languor which had bathed them both was gone in that instant. A flash of longing for him swept through her, making her gasp aloud. Her fingers knotted in his hair as they came together and her head arched back, and further back, as his mouth slid from hers to her throat, and then to the hardness of her nipples. His hands explored her, relentless now, and she felt herself open to him like a flower.

'Oliver,' she murmured, 'Oliver.' It was the first time she had called him by his name, but she felt as though it had been in her head for her whole life. His eyes were closed and his breath was coming in quick gasps.

Still kneeling, Oliver lifted her effortlessly and then drew her down on top of him. He pierced her with a single thrust and at once she felt a wave of pleasure so intoxicating that she cried out loud. Her legs wound around him, jealously imprisoning him inside her. Poised, they moved together, at first slowly and then fiercely, unstoppably.

Helen felt the deep buried stirrings of her own climax with the first low moan in Oliver's throat. Her back arched, taut, as he ground deeper into her. Then her fingers clenched, once, and fell open as the liquid currents shot through her veins, pulsed, extinguished everything except the man within her and then, slowly, exquisitely, receded.

By infinitesimal degrees, time started up again. Helen lifted her head from where it had sunk against Oliver's shoulder. Looking down at him she saw that his face was soft, just as it had been when he bent over the tiny pups. Sweat had damped his fine blond hair so that it lay close against his head and his eyelashes were dark and spiky. For an instant, Oliver looked almost vulnerable. Helen stroked the hair back from his face and laid her cheek against his.

Beside them the fire sank deeper into its own red heart.

After a moment Oliver stirred and smiled lazily at her. 'So that was the door.'

'Door?' Helen was bewildered.

'The door to let the other Helen out.' He chuckled. 'You surprised me. So much heat under that cold skin.'

Helen felt herself blushing, and uncertainty took the place of the peaceful satisfaction of the moment before. Had she done something wrong? Her knowledge of sexual manners was so slight that she might well have. She had simply trusted in the force of her own instincts to guide her and she had believed that Oliver was doing the same. Now, she saw, that could have been a mistake. It was all so confusing, not least her disconcerting longing to please him.

What was the right thing? She felt that he had been surprised by her refusal of him the other evening, and now after her passionate surrender of herself, he was no less surprised.

'Did I do something wrong?' she asked simply.

'Wrong?' His blue eyes were very bright. 'No, of course not. You were charming. Just not very like other girls. Or like what I expected.'

I'm not like Flora and Fiona, Helen thought. Or like Vick. I know that. But what did he expect? She wanted to ask him, wanted to make him talk, but the words eluded her. Instead, she became uncomfortably conscious of her nakedness, and she reached out for the tangle of clothes beside them. Quickly, acutely aware of the clumsy awkwardness of putting on clothes, she pulled on her crumpled shirt. Then she saw that Oliver was looking away from her, into the depths of the fire. He seemed utterly unconscious of his body, and at once Helen regretted her prudish scramble to get dressed.

Uncomfortable, unexplained hot tears pricked behind her eyes. What's the matter with me, she asked herself bitterly.

Oliver lay calm and unmoving. His body was evenly and deeply tanned, every inch of it. Helen knew that meant remote, exotic beaches, or very fashionable ones where everyone was free of stupid inhibitions. He looked fit, too, with the flat belly and developed muscles of the all-round athlete. Alongside him Helen felt herself bony and uncoordinated, as well as pallid from lack of sunlight. There had been too many weeks of not caring what she ate, too many nights with very little sleep.

With his eyes fixed on the fire, Oliver put out a hand and caught her wrist.

'Stop jumping about,' he ordered her. 'Lie still, here.' He made space on the rug beside him and obediently Helen lay back with her head against the cushions. His fingers encircled her wrist, and, as if to underline her own image of her body, he murmured, 'So thin and brittle. One false move and it might snap. Poor Helen. You need feeding up.' And he laughed again, pleased with the idea.

In the quiet that followed, Helen collected herself. What else did you expect? Or want? You shared those moments of love-making with him, and in those moments he was yours. Nothing can take that away. And now, what point is there in wishing it had happened some other way? Or hadn't happened at all? You wanted to give yourself to him, because what else could you have offered? And he's still here beside you. With his fingers around your wrist. Take what you've got, and believe in your own convictions.

The threatened tears were gone now, and the determination was back in Helen's face again.

Oliver sat up and reached for a log from the basket. When he threw it on the fire, the embers glowed hotly and sent out a last fierce blush of heat before settling again.

He let go of her wrist and leaned away from her to fumble in one of his pockets. When he settled himself, Helen saw that he was holding a key ring, with a small, silver propelling pencil dangling among the keys. Quickly, Oliver unscrewed it and Helen saw that it was not a pencil at all, but a hollow tube. Oliver patted his pockets again and then produced a tiny silver-backed mirror. Finally from his wallet he extracted a single, crisp pound-note.

'I can't stand the ostentation of people who use fifties,' he told her. Helen watched, bewildered.

Frowning with concentration now, Oliver shook a tiny drift of white powder from the tube on to the mirror. Then he held it out to her.

'Snort?' he asked, casually.

'What is it?'

'Cocaine,' he answered, enunciating the word very carefully. 'What did you think?'

'No', Helen cried out before she could bite back the word behind her teeth. Suddenly, and with startling vividness, she remembered Frances Page being driven away in an unmarked car by a young and pretty policewoman and a creased middle-aged man who bore no resemblance to the drug-squad officers of television serials.

Oliver shook his head. 'It's harmless, you know, unless you're very stupid. And it is instant sunshine.' He offered the mirror again, as if it were chocolates.

'No. Thank you.'

Oliver shook his head again, as if to say please yourself, then rolled the crackling note up into a narrow tube. With a sharp sniff at each nostril the white powder vanished from the mirror.

This time the tempo of their love-making was languid and dreamy. To Helen each movement seemed slowed, as if replayed before her eyes by an unseen camera, but yet more piercingly sweet than she could have believed possible. The world beyond the little circle of firelight, beyond this coupling of tanned skin with her own pale translucent flesh, meant nothing.

This was Helen's first experience of living for the moment, of being absorbed in the sensations of the instant, and she was transfixed by it. At last Oliver drifted into sleep with his head heavy against her breast. For a while Helen stared over the crest of blond hair into the greyness of the dead fire. Then she, too, closed her eyes, as if surrendering herself once again, and then slept with him.

It was very late when the black Jaguar slid alongside the steps leading down to Follies House.

Oliver switched off the engine and glanced sideways at Helen. Her chin was sunk against the collar of his coat which he had wrapped around her, and she seemed to be lost within her own thoughts.

'Follies,' he said, to nudge her back into awareness. 'I told you I'd deliver you back, safe and sound.'

Helen stared at him, her face drained of colour by the orange street lights. Something in her expression made Oliver uneasy.

'You're not sorry are you? About today?' He had meant it lightly, half referring to her missed day's work, but Helen interpreted it differently.

'No, not sorry. Stunned, perhaps. And bewildered. But happy too.' She smiled at him, and her small, cold hand reached out for his as it rested on the gearstick. 'Are you sorry?'

Her question disconcerted Oliver but he kept the lightness in his voice as he answered. 'No, why should I be? One only feels sorry if things turn out badly. And this evening wasn't bad. Not bad at all.'

There was a small silence before Helen spoke again.

'Will you come back again? Soon?'

'Of course. I'm always in and out of Follies. Rose likes to see me about the place.'

Helen nodded, accepting that.

Oliver leant back to gather up her books from where they lay scattered behind the seats. He glanced at them before handing them over.

'God, serious stuff.' His voice was teasing. 'Do you work all the time?'

'No,' said Helen in a small voice. 'I didn't work today, did I?'

Once again, a little silence hung between them before she took the books from his hands. 'It's late,' she said, as if reminding herself rather than Oliver.

'Mmm. And Hart has decreed that tomorrow work starts on the play in earnest. Something tells me that he's likely to be a slavedriver.'

Cheerfully Oliver climbed out of the car and opened Helen's door. He helped her out and they faced each other in the livid light. As he looked down at Helen's pale, heart-shaped face framed by black curls, Oliver saw that there was something unfamiliar in the huge eyes that met his. It was something that he didn't want to confront too closely. Instead he kissed her lightly on the cheek and swung her round to face the steps.

'Safe home,' he told her.

'Goodnight.' Her fingers touched the cuff of his jacket for a second before she walked away.

Oliver leaned on the parapet to watch her go and noticed again how slight she looked. He remembered how light she had felt in his arms, like a small bird, and how the strength of her passion had seemed at odds with that fragile body.

He frowned and turned abruptly back to his car.

Before he drove away he glanced up at the square dark shape of Follies House. Lights showed at three long windows on the first floor, and Oliver knew that they were the windows of Pansy Warren's room. The frown disappeared and Oliver was whistling as he eased the Jaguar away towards Christ Church.

Slowly Helen climbed through the dark house to her room. She had wanted, as she said goodnight, to seize hold of Oliver and never let him go. Even as she heard his car purr away she felt cold with the loss of him. But she squared her shoulders and, inside her head, tried to laugh away her feelings. Anyway, she reminded herself, he'll be back soon. He told you so himself. Perhaps tomorrow. Or if not tomorrow, the next day.

CHAPTER THREE

Stephen Spurring folded *The Times* into three, vertically, as he always did, and propped it against the coffee pot. The dining room was quiet, with thin autumn sunshine reflecting on the amusing pieces of high Victorian furniture collected by Beatrice and himself years ago, but from the kitchen came the confused babble of bickering children's voices. Beatrice herself could be heard from time to time, refereeing in the state of constant war that seemed to exist among their children.

Stephen stirred his coffee very slowly. This moment of privacy, 'Daddy must have some peace over breakfast, darling, because he needs to think,' was a legacy from the early days of their marriage, and he still clung tenaciously to it. It was little enough, Stephen thought. In a very few minutes Beatrice and the children would get into one car to do the round of bus stops and school gates, and he would take the other into Oxford. The day would officially have begun.

In the meantime, there was his oasis of quiet and the newspaper. When he glanced back at it the print blurred obstinately in front of his eyes. Damn. His reading glasses were upstairs, and the thought irked him. Needing glasses at all made him feel old and creaky. Irritably, Stephen abandoned the paper, picked up his cup and went over to look out of the French windows. The gardens around the old stone rectory looked very bright, gaudy with autumn colours. As he stood watching a grey squirrel bounced jerkily across the grass.

Thirty-nine wasn't so old, Stephen told himself.

It was October again now. This was the time of year when everything came to life for him after the long silence of the summer, just as it had done for the last twenty years. Twenty? Had he really been in Oxford for that long? Stephen smiled wryly, reflecting that this was the last year before middle age. Well, there was still time. For what? he might have asked himself, but he chose not to.

He was surprised to find himself humming as he picked up his briefcase in the black-and-white tiled hallway. A glance in the ornate gilt hall mirror cheered him further. Stephen had never belonged to the dusty corduroys and down-at-heel shoes school of University teachers. Today he was wearing a soft grey tweed suit, and a bright blue shirt without a tie. He looked sleek, and younger than his age even with the threads of grey in his silky hair. Satisfied, Stephen went on into the kitchen to say goodbye to his wife.

Beatrice looked round at him, tucking the loose strands of dark hair behind her ears as she did so. It was a gesture that she had used ever since he had known her, and it still made her look like a schoolgirl.

'Goodbye, darling,' Stephen murmured. 'Have a good day. I might be a bit late – faculty get-together.' They kissed, automatically, not meeting each other's eyes. Stephen reached out to touch his younger son's shoulder as he passed, but Joe jerked his head away. Sulking about something, Stephen remembered, but couldn't recall what. Five minutes later he was in his car, ready to drive the numbingly familiar ten miles into Oxford.

Beatrice watched him go, half regretfully. Fifteen years felt like a long, long marriage, but her husband still had the power occasionally to make her catch her breath and wish that he would stay. Even though she knew him much better than he knew himself, and that knowledge left no room for illusions, she still half loved him, half craved for him. Well, she reminded herself, the days of ducking guiltily out of whatever they were supposed to be doing and staying at home alone together were far behind them now. Beatrice reached for the tendrils of hair again, then remembered the marmalade on her fingers from Sebastian's plate. She wiped them slowly on her apron, staring out of the gateway where Stephen had disappeared. She was still tasting, as she did every day, the odd mixture of frustration at her dependence on him and the satisfaction that, in spite of everything, they were still together.

'Mum? My gym shirt?' Eloise's voice came demanding from the doorway. Gratefully, Beatrice stopped thinking and began to rehearse the daily list: *clean football kit, riding lesson after school, three things beginning with J for Sebastian to take with him.* Another day.

Stephen was still humming under his breath as he strolled into the packed lecture room. The sight was familiar, but it still touched him. There were the dozens of fresh faces, the clean notebooks and brand new copies of his own *Commentaries*. The size of the audience was gratifying. Stephen had given not a thought to his lecture, but that didn't matter. He had delivered this introduction to his pet subject so many times that it was as familiar to him as his own name. He put his unnecessary sheaf of notes down on the desk and smiled around the room.

'Okay,' he said softly, as if speaking to just one of the faces turned up to him, 'I'm going to talk to you today about love. Romantic love, sexual love, real love, as we find it in the greatest of Shakespeare's great comedies.'

There was a ripple around the room as pens were unscrewed and eager hands began to scribble down Stephen's words.

Chloe Campbell was the only person who didn't move.

Instead she cupped her chin in her hands and looked intently back at Stephen. Fortyish, she thought, and not a bit like the stooped academic she had expected from reading the lecture list. This Doctor Spurring was slim, not tall, but undeniably sexy. His hair was just a little too long but it was well shaped. He wasn't conventionally good looking but his eyes were a startling clear blue. And his mouth, almost too full and curved, looked as soft as a girl's. There was something in his voice that attracted her too. Under the conventional, cultivated tones there was something – someone – else. Was Stephen Spurring a Yorkshireman, Chloe wondered, or a Geordie perhaps?

After his fifty-five fluent minutes, Stephen began smoothly to wind up his introductory lecture. All around her Chloe saw that there were sheets of notes with underlined headings and numbered points, now being clipped with satisfaction into new folders. Dr Spurring was an excellent teacher, she realised, but she hadn't written down a single word of his instruction. Stephen Spurring the man interested her far too much.

When Stephen came out of the lecture, hitching his black gown familiarly over his shoulder and thinking cheerfully of coffee and the rest of *The Times* he found three people waiting for him. Two of them, he saw, were Oliver Mortimore who was lounging characteristically against the wall to watch the girls streaming past, and an intent-looking Tom Hart from the Playhouse. The third was a girl. Stephen had glimpsed her mass of dark red hair in his lecture audience, and now he took in green eyes, an aura of self-possession and a direct, challenging smile. He had no idea who she was, and wished that he did.

He turned reluctantly to Oliver and Tom.

'Still no Rosalind?' he asked, without much interest. Stephen was the senior faculty member responsible for student drama productions, and usually he enjoyed the involvement. He liked the passionate enthusiasms of his undergraduates, and even more he liked the steady trickle of pretty would-be actresses that it brought him into contact with. Yet this particular production, Tom Hart's *As You Like It*, threatened to be less agreeable. To begin with, casting Oliver Mortimore as Orlando was an absurdity. The boy knew nothing about Shakespeare and seemed to care less. Stephen guessed that he had agreed to act the role simply out of amusement and curiosity. And Oliver was devoted to amusing himself, the older man thought with dislike. He stood for so many of the things that Stephen had despised Oxford for twenty years ago, and mistrusted even now – inherited privilege, too much money, the unquestioning belief that life owed to its brightest and most beautiful the leisure to eat, drink, ride horses and indulge themselves in and out of bed. Stephen, with no such privilege behind him, had little time for Oliver's kind. Then there was Hart. He irked Stephen too, although the reasons were less clear-cut. His very presence, the suggestion of foreign, Broadway glitter which he brought with him, was a mystery. He was difficult to place, and so just a little threatening. Stephen waited without enthusiasm to hear what the two of them had to say.

Tom didn't hesitate. He started talking quickly in the confident manner that annoyed Stephen. 'We've got a couple of girls coming to audition for Rosalind at twelve. Can you be there?'

It was a mere courtesy that the senior member was invited to approve of the casting, at least in Tom's view. Stephen hadn't wanted Oliver, but that was just too bad.

Stephen frowned and glanced at his watch. The way that Tom Hart always addressed him as an absolute equal didn't help, either. But he wasn't going to give up and take a back seat, because that was probably exactly what Hart wanted.

'If I must,' he answered. 'Just don't keep me hanging about for too long.'

'Of course not.' But there was more irony than courtesy in the response. Cocky bastard, Stephen thought, and turned away deliberately to the red-haired girl who was still waiting at his elbow.

'Dr Spurring', she held out her hand, 'I'm Chloe Campbell.

I just wanted to say how much I enjoyed the lecture. And to ask you a couple of questions.'

Stephen saw that she had the clear, creamy skin of the true redhead, coupled strikingly with dark brows and eyelashes. She also had a wide, curving mouth which seemed made for laughter as well as for other, more intimate things.

'Ask away,' Stephen smiled at her. He looked round and saw with pleasure that Tom and Oliver had gone. 'Or better still, let me buy you a cup of coffee, and then you can ask me.'

With a touch of his hand at her elbow, Stephen turned Chloe round in the direction of the senior common room.

'In here,' he murmured.

Chloe found herself sitting in a deep, leather-covered armchair in a sombre, quiet room. There was a log fire at one end, and at the other a long white table covered with a white cloth and trays of china and silver. There was a promising smell of fresh coffee.

This is more like it, she thought.

Chloe had already admitted to herself that her first days in Oxford had been very short on glamour of any kind. She hadn't come up expecting immediately to dine off gold plate in ancient halls while the greatest minds in the world sparred wittily around her, but neither had she anticipated quite so many anoraks and queues, and so much junk food served and eaten cheerlessly in plastic cafeterias. And Follies House had been lonely, echoingly quiet. She had heard the third lodger, Pansy whoever-it-was, arriving with huge quantities of luggage, but she had left again immediately, apparently for a long weekend. Helen had been there and Chloe would have liked to see her, but she vanished disconcertingly early every morning with a forbidding pile of books. Chloe's only chance of companionship had been with fat, chuckling Rose in her witches' kitchen. Pride was the only thing that had kept Chloe from turning tail and running back to London.

But this was different. This peaceful room with its scattered figures in black gowns was more what she had expected. And here was Stephen himself, leaning over to pour coffee, his eyes even bluer at close quarters than they had looked across the lecture room.

'Cream? Sugar?' he asked, then handed over a deep cup with, she saw in amused satisfaction, the University crest emblazoned on the side.

'Well?' he asked, smiling a lopsided smile that made Chloe shift a little in her chair and forget, for a moment, the bright opening that she had planned.

'Ummm ...' Now they were both laughing. He's nice, Chloe thought. Nicer than anyone I've met for, oh, a long, long time.

'Dr Spurring', she began, but Stephen leaned across at once and rested his fingertips lightly, just for an instant, on her wrist.

'Stephen,' he told her. 'Even my students call me that.'

'I *am* a student,' she told him, half regretfully. 'A mature one, as they say. That's one of the things I wanted to ask you about, as it happens. I'm very new to all this, you see. I haven't read nearly enough. And I've been out of the way of – oh, just thinking properly, for years and years. Will you give me some advice about where to start? Tell me what to read, to begin with. Not just reading lists, but what's really important. I feel at a disadvantage. And I'm not used to that', she finished, candidly. She had intended to make herself sound interesting for Stephen Spurring's benefit, but she seemed to have blurted out something that was closer to the real truth. I've only made myself sound naive, Chloe thought, with irritation.

'You? Feel at a disadvantage?' Stephen leaned further back in his chair and grinned at her. 'Come on ... Chloe ... look at yourself, and then look at those kids out there.' He waved in the direction of the window and its view down a flight of steps crowded with people hurrying between classes. 'Okay, apart from your obvious advantages, and you don't need me to list those, you're a little bit older. It can't be by very much ...' he smiled again, into her eyes this time, 'but you've had the chance to live some real life. Adult life. Which means you know yourself a whole lot better, and you understand people and their funny little motives more clearly. Isn't that true?'

Chloe nodded slowly. 'Yes, but...'

'Listen. What could be more important, particularly in our field, in literature?'

Our field, Chloe thought, suddenly proud. I really am here, talking to this clever man, who's still got the sexiest mouth I've ever seen. Even better, he's not going to start the bitchy business gossip in five seconds' time, nor is he going to try to get me to put some work his way. I'm glad I'm here. This is where I want to be.

'... what matters is what comes from you', Stephen was saying. 'Your own ideas, drawn on your own experience. That's better than having read and being able to regurgitate every work of criticism on every set text there is. And that's why you're lucky. Literature is about people, after all,' he said softly. 'Men. Women. Their loves and their tragedies. Yes?'

Yes, Chloe thought. 'In your lecture you said...' but Stephen interrupted her.

'In my lecture, in my lecture. I'm a teacher. I have to put things across in a certain way because that's what I'm paid to do. But as a human being, as a man, I might think differently. I'm not just a don, although students tend to forget that.'

I won't tend to, Chloe told herself, I can promise you that.

'You know,' Stephen's eyes travelled over her face, from her eyes to her mouth, 'I envy you. Having put whatever, whoever it is behind you, to come here, you're starting afresh. Make sure you enjoy it, won't you?'

Was he challenging her? They were looking intently at each other as Chloe whispered, 'Yes, I will,' and it was a long moment before either of them spoke again. In the end it was Chloe who broke the silence. She reached forward to the silver pots. 'More coffee?'

Stephen shook himself slightly. For both of them, it was the signal to slow down just a little. Chloe always thought that the anticipation was half the fun, and she didn't want whatever was going to happen with Stephen Spurring to unfold too quickly. She was delighted to find that Stephen's understanding matched hers perfectly.

'Thank you. Well,' he said, in quite a different, polite voice, 'what does bring you here? Thirst for learning, or something more necessary?'

He was an easy audience, Chloe found. She made the edited version of why she had decided to come to Oxford sound as amusing as she could, and she gave him a quick, vivid sketch of her London advertising life. Stephen laughed with her, admiring her animated face as she talked. The morning's good humour consolidated itself inside him. At length, he made himself look at his watch.

'Oh God, I'm due to watch some auditions at twelve. I must go.'

'With the young Apollo and his business manager?'

Stephen laughed. 'Exactly. I'd forgotten you were there.'

60

'Who are they?'

'The tall, fair one is Lord Oliver Mortimore.'

Chloe saw again the aquiline good looks and the unmistakable hauteur in Oliver's bearing as he stood back to watch the world go by. Just as if it was there for his benefit alone, she thought, and her heart sank for Helen's sake. Helen's eyes had been just too bright when she talked about him, and her bewildered eagerness had been just too obvious. Chloe sighed. A mismatch, she thought, if ever there was one, and the only person likely to be damaged by that was Helen herself. Well, perhaps it would come to nothing anyway.

'Do you know him, then?' Stephen was asking.

'No. It's just that a friend of mine does. And who was the other, the business manager?'

'You're quite close to the truth, as it happens. Tom Hart, son of Greg Hart and heir to just about the entire New York theatre business.'

'What can he be doing here?' Chloe asked, interested. Hart was a famous name.

'God knows. Nothing to do with the University. He's got an assistant directorship at the Playhouse, so I suppose he's dabbling in front of the scenery instead of behind it. He seems to have a dramatically clear idea of who he wants to know over here, anyway. He attached himself to young Mortimore within days of arriving in Oxford, and now he's cast him as Orlando. Not that they make a bad pair – they're both as self-satisfied as each other. I'm responsible for seeing that they don't make a travesty of the production...' Stephen made a quick, boyish face, '... and so I try to sit in on things from time to time.'

'Look, why don't you come along too, if you're not doing anything else? It might interest you; they're looking for Hart's idea of the perfect Rosalind.'

'Yes, why not?' Chloe wanted to see if her first impression of Oliver had been the right one, and she was more than happy to spend another hour in Stephen Spurring's company.

Once more she felt the light touch of Stephen's guiding hand at her elbow, and they walked down the steps together and out into the wintry sunshine. As they turned in the direction of the theatre, Stephen peeled off his gown and bundled it under his arm. Chloe tucked her hands deep into her pockets and let herself enjoy the cold air in her face and the play of the light on the stonework around them. They were crossing the inner

quadrangle of the great library, the Bodleian, and unconsciously Chloe's step slowed as she looked up at the ancient
façades.

'Mmm, yes', Stephen said beside her. 'I must have walked
through here a million times, and it can still stop me dead in
my tracks. On the right day, and in the right company, of
course.'

They paused for an instant in silence, and as Chloe's gaze
travelled downwards she caught sight of a familiar, slight figure.
Helen was standing under the great arch that led through into
Broad Street, silhouetted against the intricate tracery of the
wrought-iron gates. She was carrying a stack of books that
looked too heavy for her thin arms, and was struggling to hoist
a heavy bag over her shoulder.

Chloe waved at once, and called out 'Helen! Over here!'

Helen stopped at once and they caught up with her a moment
later. It was Chloe, she saw, with Stephen Spurring. She
couldn't prevent a smile from escaping. It was so perfectly in
character that Chloe should already have secured for herself a
tête-à-tête with the heart-throb of the faculty. Helen herself
suspected that Stephen was more two-dimensional than the
image he projected, but she was well aware that he cut a wide
and successful swathe through the hordes of women surrounding him.

'I was just going to lunch,' she told them quickly, not wanting
to interrupt whatever it was they were doing together. 'If you
go early it doesn't take so long, and I want to get back to
work...'

'Hello, Helen,' said Stephen easily. 'I haven't seen you since
last term, have I? Good Vac?'

Helen bit her lip, but it wasn't a question that needed to be
answered. Stephen had cocked his head to one side to read the
titles of the books under her arm.

'Mmm, mmm, good. Oh, don't bother with that one,' he
pointed. He was effortlessly back in the role of teacher again.

Impulsively, Chloe took Helen's arm. 'Look, we're going to
the Playhouse to hear some girls audition for your friend
Oliver's play. Come with us. That'll be all right, Stephen, won't
it?'

'I should think so,' Stephen said without enthusiasm. He
would have preferred to keep this effervescent, glowing girl to

himself rather than have half the students in town accompanying them.

'Really?' Helen's face lit with a wash of colour that spread over her pale cheeks. 'I'd love to come along and watch. You know, Tom Hart even asked me to have a go, so I'd be intrigued to see what people have to do.'

It was something else that had brought the blush to her cheeks. Oliver had asked her, too, one morning during the breathless week that had just passed.

He had come strolling into the library where she was working and she heard the rustle of people turning to stare before she looked up herself. Oliver leant over and took the pen out of her fingers before kissing the knuckles. The girl next to Helen gasped audibly.

'Come and be my Rosalind,' he said. He made no attempt to whisper and she heard his voice carrying to the far corners of the room. But no-one tried to say hush to Oliver.

'I can't act,' she murmured.

Oliver's eyebrows shot up. 'A good thing too. Don't ever try to act with me, because I'll know.' He kissed her, a gentle experimental kiss as if they were alone in the world. Even here, Helen felt herself tremble in response. 'No,' he said meditatively. 'You don't pretend anything.'

Helen left her papers in a drift on the desk and stumbled out of the library.

Oliver followed her, bestowing his dazzling smile on the rows of readers.

'Oliver,' she gasped, shaking with laughter, 'don't do this. What must all those people think, in there?'

There was a narrow stone window beside them, with a dizzy view down to an oval of lawn set like a green jewel in an ancient ring. He drew her into the window embrasure and held her there against the smooth stone.

'It doesn't matter to us,' he told her, 'what anyone thinks. Does it?'

Helen looked up into his tanned face and saw his tongue against his even teeth. 'No,' she said, almost believing him. 'Not one bit.'

Oliver reached out to her and undid one button at her throat.

'Cold, and then hotter than fire,' he murmured. 'You know, I came to ask if you would sit in at a rehearsal for us. Read

Rosalind's lines and help me to concentrate. But now I don't feel like rehearsing at all. Come back to the House with me. *Now.*'

'I can't . . .'

'Oh yes, Helen, you can.'

They laughed at each other and she repeated, delighted at how easy it was, 'Oh yes, I can.'

He took her hand and they ran down the spiral stairs, along a cobbled lane and across a little square, and out into the brightness of Canterbury Quad. Oliver banged his oak behind them and locked the inner door.

'You see?' he asked. 'It's easy.'

'Yes,' Helen said. His closeness chased everything else out of her head. She was shaken by her own urgency, and she looked down unbelievingly at her own hands between them.

'Never say you can't', he said, with his mouth at her throat and then moving so that his tongue traced a slow circle around her breast. 'There isn't much time.'

Helen felt a beat of cold anxiety. She looked down sharply but his face was hidden from her.

'Why?' she asked, feeling that she was stupidly not understanding something. 'Surely there's all the time we need?'

She wanted to look into his eyes, but his head was still bent. She thought that there was something stiff about his shoulders.

'There's only ever *now*, this moment,' he said. 'Try to understand that. I don't want to hurt you.'

'You won't,' she reassured him.

But even as he reached to unleash the floodwater dammed up inside her, she was sure that he would hurt her. At that moment she knew too that she didn't care.

'I love you,' she said afterwards, so softly that she was sure it was inaudible. But Oliver stirred and opened his eyes. He stared at her before his quick smile came back.

'That's very reckless of you,' he told her, and she couldn't gauge his seriousness from his voice. 'Shall we go out to lunch? We definitely need to be fortified after expending all that energy. I think oysters and Guinness, don't you?'

The moment was past and she let Oliver take her hands and draw her to her feet. He watched her dressing so appreciatively that she forgot her embarrassment, and she felt herself growing more comfortable with him.

Outside, the black Jaguar was parked in a space marked 'Reserved for the Dean.' When Helen was settled in the low seat, Oliver bent so that their eyes were level.

'I like you. And I enjoy your company,' he said. Then, as if the admission surprised him, he vaulted into his seat and the car shot forward into the cold air.

If this is all, Helen thought, it will just have to be enough. It's more, much more, than I've ever had before.

Helen stared unseeingly at Chloe and Stephen, deep in conversation just ahead of her. In just a few minutes she would see Oliver again. A blurry kind of happiness mixed with apprehension gripped her, and for a panicky moment she thought that her knees might give way beneath her. Then as they reached the door of the Playhouse, she saw Chloe and Stephen pause for her to catch up, and she hurried blindly forward.

The unflattering house lights were on inside the theatre, revealing the worn red plush seats and the threadbare patches in the crimson carpet between them. Three or four people were sprawling in the front stalls, with Tom Hart's dark head prominent among them. Helen took all this in in a second, and then she saw Oliver. He was sitting centre stage with his legs dangling over the edge, intent on a paperback copy of the play.

Stephen strode down the centre aisle towards them.

'Right,' he said crisply. 'Let's not waste time.' He settled himself in the third row, and Chloe and then Helen slid in beside him.

Oliver looked up. There was a flicker of surprise when he saw Helen, then a cheerful wave of greeting. He held up his play text with a grimace, then went back to studying it.

Helen was oblivious of everything else. She missed Tom Hart's brief nod of greeting, and the frisson of irritation which vibrated between Tom and Stephen.

'You won't mind my bringing a little audience to keep you on your toes,' Stephen said easily.

'Not particularly', Tom answered. 'Okay everybody. We're reading Act Three, Scene Two, Rosalind and Orlando. Ready?'

Chloe watched the director with interest. With his quick, economical movements and his authoritative manner, he looked a natural leader. His dark, sardonic, good looks interested her without attracting her. An arrogant young man, she thought, as she watched him positioning Oliver and the plump girl who was to read Rosalind. But clever, too.

Tom had settled himself at the back of the stalls.

'When you're ready,' he called, and the scene began.

'I will speak to him like a saucy lackey, and under that habit play the knave with him...'

'Speak up, Anne. We hope that the audience will fill more than just the front row.' Tom's voice was cool, businesslike. The scene started up again.

Helen watched, spellbound. It was Rosalind's scene, but this Orlando was more than equal to it. Tom Hart's right, she thought. Oliver does have a feel for it. All the self-confident grace of Oliver's natural movements stayed with him on the stage. And the loose, half-ironical lightness of his manner spoke subtly for Orlando. The girl opposite him had a sweet, melodious voice but her body looked wooden beside his.

Chloe leaned across to Helen. 'If they're going to play it in doublet and hose,' she whispered, 'that girl's legs are too fat.'

'Thank you,' Tom called. 'Can we try it again with Belinda now?'

Another hopeful Rosalind climbed on to the stage. This girl was taller and slimmer and she moved well. But as the to and fro of the elegant, sparring speeches began again, it was still Oliver who drew all the attention. He looked gilded on the stage, as if he were already spotlit instead of quenched by the dull house lights like everyone else.

Stephen fidgeted in his seat and peered impatiently at his watch. 'So much for the perfect Rosalind,' he murmured.

There was a shade less confidence in Tom Hart's manner as he retraced his steps to the stage.

'Thanks,' he said briefly. 'Stephen, could we talk about...'

From the back of the auditorium a clear voice cut across the ripple of talk.

'Is this the right place for the audition?'

They turned to stare at the newcomer.

Helen heard the soft hiss of indrawn breath before she turned round too.

A girl was standing against the red velvet curtaining that hung over the exit doors. In the second before she spoke again, she looked almost too pretty to be real, like an exquisite statue without the warmth of flesh and blood. But as soon as she moved, smiled her question again, animation came flooding back and lit her face up.

'The *As You Like It* audition?'

Still no-one answered. The girl came down the aisle towards the stage. She had silver-blond hair, cut fashionably short and feathery to show the oval perfection of her face. Her wide-set dark blue eyes flicked from one to another of them and she smiled again, teasingly, and with a little challenge now. Although she was young, no more than nineteen, the newcomer was evidently used to the effect of her appearance.

'Who is this vision?' Chloe breathed to Stephen.

'No idea. But I'm not going without finding out.' He winked at her, and Chloe had the pleasurable sensation that there was already an understanding between them.

Tom collected himself first. 'Yes, we're auditioning now. You'd like to read for us?'

The girl turned her dazzling face to him.

'May I? I don't want to butt in. Let me explain first – my name's Pansy Warren, and I've just come to live at Follies House. The landlady, Rose Pole, told me that you were looking for a Rosalind. I'd love just to have a try. I've acted a little bit, at school and in Switzerland, but...' Pansy shrugged, self-deprecating.

'Okay.' Tom's voice was crisp again. He handed his copy of the text to Pansy and helped her up on to the stage. Oliver bent to take her hand, and between them they led Pansy into her scene as if she were a piece of priceless china.

Helen sank lower in her inconspicuous seat. I could never, she thought, ever have walked in here as she did, unknown and unexpected, and asked to be auditioned. But then I don't look like that.

There was a faint shadow on her face as she watched the players begin on the familiar lines again.

Pansy was wearing a loose roll-collared sweater that masked her slim, small-breasted figure, jeans, and soft suede ankle boots. With her cap of tousled hair she looked completely the girl-dressed-as-a-boy which the scene demanded.

'Love is merely a madness,' read Pansy, 'and I tell you, deserves as well a dark house, and a whip, as madmen do.'

Her voice was soft, but surprisingly resonant.

There was no need for Tom to tell her to speak up.

67

She's good too, Helen told herself. Good in the same way that Oliver is. She doesn't care who is looking at her, or what they think. She can just be herself because she's sure of being right. Like Oliver, she doesn't have to try.

Helen was too intent on Pansy herself to notice something else, but Chloe saw it. There was a crackle between this Orlando and Rosalind that had been completely missing from the earlier attempts. There was a new edge of seriousness in Oliver's performance as the youth in love with love, which made his posturing credible. Before, it had only been amusing.

And Pansy's Rosalind, although she was mocking her lovesick youth, showed the girl's attraction to the young man too.

That was right, as well.

'With all my heart, good youth,' said Oliver softly.

'Nay, you must call me Rosalind.' The balance of humour and longing in Pansy's exit line was perfect.

They want each other already, Chloe thought. And people like those two always get what they want. She shot a quick glance at Helen's rapt profile and sighed for her.

The spatter of involuntary applause brought Oliver and Pansy to the front of the stage, flushed and pleased.

'Weren't they good? Wasn't Oliver good?' Helen was beaming at Chloe.

'Very good,' she answered shortly. 'Unless the director is as blind as a bat, Follies House has provided the world with a Rosalind. What do you think of our house-mate?'

They looked at the slim, silvery figure between Tom and Oliver on the stage.

'How exotic to be living in the same house as someone like that. But she looks nice, don't you think?' Helen kept her voice deliberately neutral.

'Mmmm.' Chloe thought that indeed she looked nice, but it wasn't the kind of niceness that Helen would benefit from.

Clearly the auditions were over. The two disappointed Rosalinds had slipped away and now Tom was flicking off the lights. Helen stood up uncertainly, longing to go to Oliver but too shy to make the first move. Behind her, she heard Stephen Spurring murmuring to Chloe, 'There's still time for some lunch. Would you like to?'

Tactfully, Helen hurried to pick up her things. She didn't want to make Chloe feel that she should be invited too. 'See you later,' she said firmly. Oliver and Pansy were still standing at the edge of the stage.

When they spoke, neither of them mentioned their first meeting in the mist on Folly Bridge. Instead they let the memory of it hang between them like a shared secret.

'You read well,' said Oliver. 'It was a good scene.'

Pansy's clear eyes looked straight back at him.

'Thank you. You weren't too bad either. Quite good, in fact.' When she laughed, Pansy's prettiness took second place to her overflowing vitality. It was an irresistible combination. 'We should do quite well together. If your friend the director gives me the part, of course.'

'Oh, I think he will. Unless he casts you as my Rosalind, he'll find himself with no Orlando either.'

Oliver vaulted down from the stage and, reaching up for Pansy's hands, swung her down beside him. At once Tom went to join them.

Helen saw that they were absorbed and oblivious of her.

Don't get in the way, she told herself. They're busy. He's busy.

She walked away to the exit briskly enough, but then she found herself lingering bleakly in the deserted foyer. She wanted to see Oliver. The prospect of going back to her books without even a word from him seemed impossible. But how could she go back and interrupt him?

She was still hovering indecisively when the three of them came out. They saw her at once.

'Hello again,' Oliver said lightly, as if they had last met at a bus stop or in a cinema queue. 'What did you think of it?'

'It was good,' Helen said weakly. 'Both of you ... very good.'

Is that all? Then, more sternly, she reminded herself, what else could he say? In front of ... other people?

'Are you part of the cast?' Pansy asked warmly. At close quarters her eyes showed a dozen different shades of blue. She was wearing a scent which reminded Helen of summer gardens.

'No. But we will be seeing each other again. I live at Follies House too.'

'Really? That's wonderful. Isn't it weird? And the woman who runs it all, Rose, what d'you make of her?'

'Be careful', Helen warned her, 'she's a relative of Oliver.'

Oliver shrugged, not interested in the turn the conversation had taken. 'A very distant one, for whom I accept no responsibility.'

Tom was impatient too. 'Let's go and eat, for God's sake. Come with us, Helen. Are you sure you can't do something for my production? Backstage, perhaps. ASM...'

'I'll think about it', Helen told him absently. Her eyes were on Oliver, wanting him to echo Tom's invitation, but he had said nothing. Please, she wanted to beg him, it's me. Don't you remember our days together? Didn't they happen? Then the other Helen, coolly reasonable, reminded her. Don't grovel. He'll hate that.

But as they turned to leave, it was Pansy who took her arm. 'Please come. Let's get to know each other if we're to live in the same house.'

Helen went, incapable of walking away from Oliver just yet.

The pizza parlour next door was crowded and steamy. Oliver hung back with an expression of distaste but Tom strode past the queue and secured a table.

'No, I'm afraid it's mine,' he told the protesting party who had been just about to take possession of it.

'Neat,' said Oliver, with grudging approval as they sat down.

When the pizzas came, Oliver scowled at his. 'Why are we eating this garbage?'

Helen remembered the splendours of the meals they had shared and smiled to herself. She stopped herself from murmuring how the other half live. Tom, completely uninterested in food except as the means of supplying himself with more energy, said briskly, 'This isn't a gourmet outing. We're here to do business.'

The conversation centred on the production.

They were drinking red plonk, over which Oliver had also made a wry face, and Tom raised his glass to Pansy. 'Here's to you,' he said. 'You're not quite the perfect Rosalind, but you'll do.'

'What d'you mean, not perfect? I shall be a theatrical sensation, just wait and see.'

Helen sat quietly, watching and listening. Plainly Oliver and Tom had eyes for no-one but their new Rosalind. And Pansy bubbled between the two of them, laughing delightedly and turning her perfect face from one to the other. It must always be like this for her, Helen thought. She must always be the centre of attention. No wonder she can just stroll into auditions and expect to be heard. Not only to be heard, but to walk off with the part.

Helen's gaze took in Pansy's expensively casual haircut, her light all-year-round tan, and her tiny, jewelled wristwatch. I don't suppose anyone ever denies her anything, she thought. Jealousy was an unusual emotion for Helen but she felt jealous of Pansy now.

Oliver was leaning negligently back in his chair, but his eyes were fixed on Pansy's face. He had forgotten Helen, but she was no less electrically aware of him than ever. The four of them were packed close around the little table, and her skin prickled with the nearness of his long sprawled legs. The sight of his fingers curled round the wineglass brought a flush to her cheeks and the sound of his voice, not even what he was saying, obliterated the clatter of the noisy restaurant. Yesterday, just to have been close to him like this would have been enough to make her happy. But the intrusion of this beautiful, assured newcomer had changed all that. Helen looked from Pansy to Oliver, whose *dégagé* air had completely disappeared, and felt a twist of apprehension.

She turned back to her unwanted food, oblivious of everything but the threat that suddenly loomed in front of her. She didn't see a pair of her College friends gazing round-eyed across the room at the sight of quiet bookish Helen Brown in such glossy company. It would have come as a surprise to Helen to know that she was part of a striking picture, with the two bright blonde heads and two intensely dark ones bent close together.

At last Pansy looked at her tiny gold watch. 'God, look at the time. I was supposed to be at a tutorial five minutes ago.' She made the word sound archaic and faintly ridiculous. And she made no move to get up. Instead, she poured herself another glass of wine and beamed round at them. 'Still, I expect he'll wait for me. I'm not a real student anyway, I'm just doing a one-year art history course. To please Daddy, really. He wanted me to come to Oxford to meet the right people. Future kings of Broadway. And lords, that sort of thing. And brilliant women dons.' Generously, she included Helen too, and Helen felt herself warming in response to Pansy's friendliness. 'I have to do something while I'm here and I don't know anything about art or history, so it seems as good a choice as any. Daddy said doing a typing or cookery course wasn't "suitable", and Kim backed him up. Kim's my stepmother. My third stepmother, actually. She's all of twenty-seven, and acts like seven. You must all meet her, it's a real eye-opener.'

'Why?' asked Tom, interestedly. 'Does she beat you and dress you in rags, like a proper stepmother does? Even though she's a bit young for the job?'

Pansy laughed merrily.

'Just the opposite. I don't care much about clothes, but Kim endlessly drags me round to shops and fittings and designer shows. And she's too languid to mix a cocktail, let alone beat me. But if you think I'm not very bright, you should meet Kim...'

'I suspect you're quite bright enough,' Tom said quietly.

'You are a darling. And don't worry, I've got enough native wit to handle Rosalind. Inherited from Daddy, no doubt. Oh Lord, he'll be furious if I don't even get to my first lesson. I don't even know where the place is.'

Pansy fumbled in the soft Italian leather pouch bag that was slung over the back of her chair and brought out a list. 'Ashmolean Museum?'

Oliver, who had been watching her with fascination, suddenly stood up. 'I'm going over there. I'll take you.'

Solicitously, just as he had done yesterday for Helen, he drew back her chair and helped her to her feet. Pansy put her hand on his arm, thoughtlessly accepting it as her right to be escorted and protected.

"Bye, then.'

'Oliver...' Helen had no idea what she wanted to ask him, but he half-turned in response and she thought his face softened.

'I'll see you soon,' he said. 'At Follies.'

He was gone so quickly with Pansy that Helen found herself staring at the empty space where they had been.

I'll see you soon. She would have to be content with that.

Opposite her Tom was staring blankly too. It was a moment before they faced each other and realised that they were alone.

'Well.' Tom was smiling crookedly. 'Shall we finish the wine?'

Helen pushed her glass across to him. Instinctively, she liked

Tom Hart and – more than that – he was Oliver's friend. She could at least talk about him.

'I've never met anyone like him before,' she said softly.

'Oliver? Neither have I. He's got a lot of style, and I admire that. He doesn't give a damn about anything either, and I don't think that's just because of who he is. Although that helps. Think of living in a place like Montcalm. Of coming from a family like that ... holders of the highest offices in the realm for hundreds and hundreds of years.'

You're impressed by that, Helen thought. Am I? Am I? Perhaps.

Tom was still talking. His dark eyebrows were drawn together over his high, beaked nose and his mouth, usually compressed in a sardonic line, curved wider as he looked into the distance.

'That's quite something, you know, to a Jewish boy like me. My family tree goes back no further than my great-grandfather. He was called Hartstein, and he arrived in New York with no more than the clothes he stood in. He scraped a kind of living for his wife and kids by doing piecework in the garment trade. The business he slaved for happened to have a sideline in theatrical costuming. My grandfather had a flair for that, took it over at the age of twenty, and ended up a celebrated costumier. And my father – well, my old man has a flair for everything. Greg Hart owns five Broadway theatres now, and a string more across the country.'

'I think that's more impressive than just being born a Mortimore,' Helen told him gently.

Tom smiled at her in response, and she saw that although his face was stern and his mouth ungiving, there was real kindness behind his dark, hooded eyes.

'Perhaps.'

'What about you?' she asked. 'What are you really doing in Oxford, if you've got all that waiting for you in America?'

Tom picked up a fragment of bread from the tablecloth and rolled it between his fingers into a grey, doughy ball.

'I'm in disgrace, as it happens. Serving out a year's exile in the guise of doing my apprenticeship in the British theatre. By the time I get back, my old man reckons all the fuss will be forgotten.'

Helen stared at him, intrigued. She had forgotten herself enough not to worry about being tactful. 'What fuss?'

73

'D'you really want to know?'

'Of course. What could be bad enough to deserve being banished from home for a whole year?'

Tom laughed shortly. 'It's not so bad. I miss New York, that's all. Do you remember that production of *The Tempest* that was so successful in the West End last year? With Sir Edward Groves and Maria Vaughn?'

Helen nodded, dimly recollecting having read about it.

'My father brought the production over for his summer season. With the original cast, starring the theatrical knight and his new wife Miss Vaughn.'

Helen remembered that, too.

'Well. Whatever Maria had married her knight for, it had nothing to do with bed. In spite of the fact that she's very interested in that side of things herself. Most of us are, after all. When I was offered the choice, before the run had even started, I was hardly likely to turn her down. She's very beautiful, and disturbingly sexy. Before long we were screwing each other at every possible opportunity. At my apartment, in her hotel room, in her dressing room. And that's where Sir Edward caught us at it. Careless of me, really. The scene that followed was high drama – threats, screams, hysterical weeping, the whole works. It culminated with Sir Edward stamping down to my father's office and announcing that the Hart family was not to be trusted, so he and Maria were off back to London and fuck the opening night. Greg flung himself into the scene like the old trouper he is. There were more accusations of filial disloyalty, immorality, perfidy and general filthiness. Of course, Edward really had no intention of missing out on the chance to bestow his Prospero on Manhattan. They compromised by despatching me to England instead. This job was fixed up for me in about forty seconds, and here I am.'

Helen thought for a moment. 'Isn't it rather hard on you? Surely your father must have seen your side, just a little?'

Tom laughed again.

'Oh, it's much more complicated than that. You see, Greg certainly had Maria carved out for himself. He does quite a good line in leading ladies – he's always been very successful with women. And he's used to thinking of himself as the young phenomenon. Suddenly, there he was, seeing that his own son had cut him out. What would it be next, he must have asked himself. His theatres. His whole empire, perhaps. So, get rid of the little bastard for a convenient space of time by packing him off to Oxford, England, to produce piddling student productions of the classics.'

'Did you have to come?'

The answer came without a trace of hesitation. 'Oh yes. If I want to get the business in the end, I do. And I want it very much. I love the theatre.'

'Except for piddling little productions in Oxford.'

Tom shot her a quick glance, his eyebrows raised. 'Yes. I asked for that. I didn't mean it, except as a comparison with what I could be doing if I was back home. Of course this show is just as important in its way as the biggest musical spectacular on Broadway. That's why I've taken so much care to get the casting right. And it's why I'm so pleased with Oliver and Pansy. Particularly Pansy. I knew as soon as she walked into the theatre that she was the one I was looking for. She's amazing, isn't she?'

Tom's habitual cynical expression had melted, replaced by an enthusiasm that was almost boyish.

'Yes.' Helen didn't want to talk about Pansy Warren. She switched the subject again. 'And you? Will you make a wild success of being here? It's what happens in all the books.'

'Not wild. There's hardly scope. But I'll do well enough.'

Helen knew that he would, from the determined lines etched in his dark face. Tom Hart was bound to succeed in whatever he did. It was in his blood. You're probably quite ruthless, Helen thought. You can be kind too, but you wouldn't let that impede you where it matters. Probably you just feel genuinely sorry as you plunge the hatchet in. I know I wouldn't like to cross you.

Tom was looking at her now, his gaze level. 'Why am I treating you to this self-centred recital? It must be something to do with your having such a calm, attentive face.'

I don't want to be just a calm attentive face. A sudden spurt of resentment took possession of Helen. I want to be beautiful, like Pansy and Chloe, the kind of woman that people look at, not talk at. I want to be rich, and confident, and amusing. It's not fair. And then at once she felt ashamed again. You're so lucky in so many things, she reminded herself. Think of Mum, and Graham. And Dad.

Tom turned from signalling to the waitress and saw a

brightness in Helen's eyes that might have been the start of tears. His hand touched hers.

'What is it? Did I say something?'

She shook her head fiercely. 'No. I just ... remembered something. Look – it's late.'

'I know. I must go too.' When the bill came, Helen remembered that Oliver and Pansy, unthinking, had left without paying their share.

'Can I go halves with you?' she ventured.

'No. Of course not.' Without even looking, Tom dumped a fistful of notes on the plate and stood up.

It's just different for them, Helen told herself. It's wrong of you to feel resentful.

Tom left her with a brief goodbye at Carfax. Helen turned to watch him for a moment as he walked off down the long, golden curve of the High. His clothes were stylish, almost flamboyant, and with his alert face and purposeful walk, he stood out in high relief from the anonymous blue denim crowds that drifted around him.

As soon as he was gone, Helen was surprised to feel the loss of his bracing company. The lunch had been uncomfortable, but for some reason her sharpest impression now was of this brisk American. He was as different from the ordinary run of University people as Oliver himself. Helen thought he was more than a little frightening, because his cleverness made him intolerant, but she remembered the kindness she had sensed in him as well as the flash of vulnerability when he had looked at Pansy Warren. She liked him, too, for the straightforward way he had told her the story of his exile to Oxford. Tom Hart would not be easy to know well, she reflected, but once he had committed himself, she guessed that he would be a valuable friend. Helen wondered if Pansy, in her glancing appraisal, had seen that too. No, she wouldn't have. Beside Oliver's glitter, Tom seemed saturnine and acerbic. And it was Oliver, inevitably, who had scooped Pansy up and spirited her away.

Helen sighed, stuck her hands in her duffle coat pockets and began to walk down St Aldate's towards the river and Follies House.

As she stepped into the hallway and let the massive oak door swing to behind her, Helen knew immediately that there was something different about the old house. The dim, spidery spaces of the hall were deserted and looked just as they always did, but there was light filtering through from somewhere. And then the noise began – unbelievably loud rock music that bounced off the panelling and echoed along the stone floors. When she looked up, Helen saw that the door at the head of the stairs was open. A shaft of bright sunlight shone through it.

Pansy was at home.

Helen knocked on the door jamb and, knowing that she wouldn't be heard above the music, peered inside. Pansy was dancing alone and with her eyes shut. She was smiling a small, happy, secretive smile.

'Hello.' Helen had to shout. Pansy opened startled eyes.

'Hel-lo. Sorry. D'you ever feel so happy that you just have to dance? Wait while I turn it down.'

'That was a short tutorial,' Helen said into the new quiet.

'He didn't wait, can you believe it? I wasn't that late.' Pansy was wide-eyed, genuinely surprised. 'Anyway, it means I've got a lovely free afternoon now. Don't go. Stay here and talk while I sort some of this junk out.'

Unlike Chloe, Pansy had made no effort to settle into her room. Suitcases and a huge trunk were all open, the tumbled contents showing that their owner had rummaged through in search of the things she needed without bothering to unpack anything. Pansy was standing in the middle of the jumble now, staring round in exasperation.

'God, what a mess. I hate all this stuff. Wouldn't life be easy if we were all allowed to own only ten things each.'

Pansy, like Chloe, seemed to possess an unbelievable number of clothes.

'No,' said Helen a little sadly. 'It's nice to have things. I love clothes.'

Pansy glanced across at her and then scrabbled in another suitcase.

'Do you? Would you like these? Kim bought these for me because she thought they were Oxford-y. I'll never wear them, and they'd suit you.'

There were two Shetland jerseys, one in soft, sugared almond pinks and one in stronger blues. They had little round collars with picot edgings. She was holding out a skirt too, folds of pale grey fine wool challis.

There was a small, surprised silence.

'I couldn't possibly', Helen said stiffly. She would have loved

77

to own such pretty things, but it was impossible. She was not so hard-up that she needed to accept Pansy's casual largesse.

'What a pity, because I won't wear them.' Pansy shrugged dismissively and tossed the clothes back into the suitcase.

The silence was uncomfortable now.

Helen knew that she should go away, but it was unthinkable to leave without having mentioned Oliver. She had the impression that his name hovered in the air between them, waiting to be uttered.

'Are you pleased about the part?' she asked at last.

'Oh, yes. So long as it doesn't mean too much hard work. Still', Pansy was holding an evening frock up against herself, her head on one side to consider it. It was a frothy mass of Zandra Rhodes squiggles and ruffles, '... with two lovely men like that about, even rehearsing shouldn't be too much of a bore.'

Now that the opening was here, Helen shied away from it.

'Tom Hart's rather exotic for Oxford,' she said.

'Mmmm. I wouldn't choose him, though. Bit too saturnine and Jewish, if you call that exotic, for my taste.'

Of course, Helen thought, you do only have to choose. *Not Oliver, please.*

'But Oliver, that's different. Bit unfair of him to be so beautiful and a Mortimore, don't you think? What can a girl do, confronted with that?' And Pansy laughed, pleased with herself and with the pleasant prospect ahead of her.

Helen felt a slow, dull crimson flush creeping over her face. Her chest and throat felt tight, and her fingers itched with a sudden urge to slap Pansy's bright face. The violence inside her astonished and frightened her. But this girl would take Oliver away, she knew that now, and in that instant she hated her. She must say something. Not let him go without a struggle.

Helen struggled to make her voice sound cool and light, but when at last it came out it shook and cracked.

'Yes, Oliver and I . . .' she faltered, not knowing how to put it.

Pansy swung round in genuine surprise.

'*You?*'

Helen flinched. As she stared back at Pansy, she felt the ugly flush deepening over her face and neck. It was so humiliating, that surprise, the more so because it was completely natural. What could Oliver, it said, with his looks and his charm and his position, see in a little mouse like you?

'Yes,' Helen said, finding defiance in the anger that threatened to choke her. 'Me. Why not?'

Pansy was looking defensive now, her eyebrows pulled into a frown over the chameleon blue eyes, and a trace of hurt lingering about her vulnerable, flower-like mouth.

'I'm sorry. It's just that ... you didn't look or behave as if you belonged together.'

Belonged together? How Oliver would hate that, Helen realised. She was giving Pansy the wrong impression, making her undefined relationship with Oliver seem too formal, but it was too late to backpedal now.

'I don't want to tread on anybody's toes,' Pansy added, with such clear sincerity that Helen's anger faded as quickly as it had come. After all Pansy had done nothing yet, except exist.

'It's all right,' she said wearily. 'You aren't. Nobody belongs to anybody. Forget it.'

'Forget what?'

Chloe had come up the stairs without either of them hearing her. Now she was standing in the open doorway, almost striking a pose. She had one hand on her hip and the other was raised to coil the dark red hair into a knot on top of her head. The stance emphasised her height and slimness and for a moment as she stood there, it was Chloe who was the beauty and not Pansy.

Pansy's sharp stare missed nothing.

'Hello. You were at the audition too, weren't you?'

'Pansy,' said Helen, 'this is Chloe Campbell. Rose's third tenant.'

There was a little, wary moment as the two women looked at each other. Then, immediately after the practised appraisal of attractive women confronting one another, came the answering smiles of complicity. To Helen, watching, it was as if they belonged to a desirable club from which she would be forever excluded. She was oppressed by a sense of her own plainness and dowdiness.

'Forget what?' Chloe was asking Helen again.

'We were talking about Oliver Mortimore,' Pansy said, before Helen could frame an answer. 'Helen was kindly warning me off.'

Helen wished she could find something as lightly dismissive to say, but nothing came. Chloe felt the tension vibrating in the room and tactfully turned her attention to dispersing it.

'Really?' she said vaguely, feigning a lack of interest as she wandered round Pansy's room. There were arched windows with views of the river and Christ Church, and panelling and furniture similar to her own, but here everything was fresher and there were thick new carpets. Chloe peered through the adjoining doors. One led to a bedroom with a glimpse of a bathroom beyond, another revealed a tiny, compact kitchen.

'You've got a whole flat,' she said to Pansy enviously. 'Mine's next door, but it's only a room and a bit.'

'What's yours like?' Pansy was asking Helen, and Helen knew that it was a peace-offering. She was being drawn into the conversation as a means of calling a truce in a skirmish that had never really started. It was generous of Pansy, she thought. More generous than she was herself – but then Pansy could afford to be.

'My room's a small, square cell on the floor above,' she said, managing a smile. 'Servants' quarters.'

Chloe and Pansy both laughed, relieved. The tension was ebbing away.

'How rotten. My father found this, I've no idea how. I suppose it is rather stylish. He's good at things like that.'

'Is your father Masefield Warren?' Chloe asked.

'That's right.'

Of course. Pansy's father's name was almost synonymous with ruthless success. He was a self-made man with an iron reputation who now controlled an empire that embraced oil, newspapers, property and films. And Pansy was his only child. One day she would be very, very rich, as well as startlingly beautiful.

Poor Helen, Chloe was thinking. I can't see her gilded Apollo resisting all that. And Helen was staring down at her clasped hands, not wanting to think at all. To shut off the dull ache of anxiety, she turned to Chloe.

'Nice lunch?' she asked politely.

Chloe laughed, pleased with the chance to talk about it.

'Extremely nice. I'd almost forgotten how delicious it is, meeting someone and realising that you're attracted to him. Then guessing that he feels the same and waiting to see how you're both going to play it.'

She had released the knot on top of her head and her hair came tumbling around her face. It made her look much younger, and her features were alight with an excitement that was almost childish.

It had been a very satisfactory lunch. Stephen Spurring had achieved just the right inviting blend of intimacy and remoteness. Chloe hated pushy men. She wanted to know him better now, and her head was full of the way he had looked and the way his mouth had lifted, crookedly, into a smile of invitation.

When it had been time to leave, Stephen had put his hand over hers.

'Will you dine with me one night at High Table? It might amuse you.'

'I'd like that.'

She was responding to this quiet, subtle man in a way that she hadn't done for years. The recollection of it made her smile again.

'Be careful,' Helen warned her. 'Stephen eats girls. And ... did you know that he's married?'

'I know he's married because he told me,' Chloe said coolly. For an intelligent woman, she thought, Helen could be very prissy. 'And I think I can look after myself. In fact, Dr Spurring had better be careful that I don't eat him. He's quite appetising enough.'

All three of them laughed, a little uneasily, before Pansy asked, 'Who's this Dr Spurring?'

'He's an English don,' Helen told her. 'He was watching you audition too.'

'Him?' Pansy said, a little absently. 'I thought he looked interesting.'

For a moment nobody spoke. Chloe's voice was firm when she answered. 'He certainly interests me.'

In the silence, a little quiver of reawakened tension whispered at them.

Helen collected herself. Now was the time to escape. From the doorway she said a muted goodbye and then climbed heavily up to the deserted box of her room.

There was nothing she could do. Pansy was here, and there was no point in making an enemy of her. All Helen could do was wait, first of all to see whether Oliver would be true to his word and come to look for her here at Follies House. Helen walked over to her window. With the height of the extra storey she could see over the rooftops to the outline of Canterbury Quad and, she imagined, even the windows of Oliver's rooms.

Only wait. Already it felt like the beginning of a vigil. And from downstairs, only just audible, she thought she heard the murmur of conversation and a burst of laughter from Chloe and Pansy. What had once felt to Helen like the unassailable Gothic calm of Follies House, now seemed heavy with vague threats, and half-formed mysterious alliances that excluded her.

Suddenly Helen felt cold, and lonely. She shivered. She needed Oliver's warmth and assurance badly, but he wasn't there.

CHAPTER FOUR

Helen drew up her knees and rested her chin on them. It was cold in her room, and colder still sitting on the window seat against the misted glass, but she didn't think of moving to turn on the heater. Instead she went on staring out at the height of Tom Tower and the smooth stone front of Christ Church. It was a grey, cloudy November day with a vicious wind that whipped the black branches of the trees. On the pavements below Helen could see passers-by shrunk into their winter clothes, their faces raw in the wind.

Very faintly she could hear the river and the hum of traffic but inside it was completely silent. Follies had the ability to swallow sound and spin a sense of isolation around the listener.

Once Helen had relished the peace, but lately it had oppressed her.

Work, her faithful remedy, was no longer any use. For days she had stared blankly at her books, watching the lines of grey type jumping meaninglessly in front of her eyes. Then she had given up the struggle. All she had in its place was the persistent whisper of guilt, chafing her painfully but doing nothing towards driving her back to her desk.

Helen knew that if she wasn't working, she had no justification for staying in Oxford. That knowledge was the most difficult thing to live with. If she wasn't working, then she should be at home where she was needed.

Last time they had talked, Helen's mother had struggled to keep the anxiety out of her voice, for her daughter's sake, but Helen had heard it anyway. Her mother was lonely, there was so little money, and the two of them had nobody to turn to but each other.

Helen winced and pressed her forehead against the cold window pane.

What's the matter with me? she asked herself again, knowing the answer all too well.

She had done something she would have believed impossible.

She had fallen in love, awkwardly and painfully, and whichever way she turned, there was no escaping or forgetting it.

In the days since Pansy had come, Helen had seen Oliver a mere handful of times, but each time she had wanted him more. He seemed to have the power, simply by existing, to blot everything else out of her life. When she saw him sitting at the table in Rose's kitchen, she was oblivious of Rose's sly watchfulness. At the few play rehearsals she had been to, the rest of the cast – even Pansy – shrank to grey shadows beside him.

She found that her eyes followed him when he moved, even though she hated her own slavishness.

Pansy's arrival seemed to have made no difference. Pansy herself gave no more of her attention to Oliver than to anyone else. She simply laughed and joked from day to day with everyone's eyes on her, from Oliver to Gerry Pole who watched her with dog-like devotion. Whether Pansy was present or not, Helen's relationship with Oliver was as puzzlingly tenuous as it had been from the beginning.

But it was still there.

His arm would drop around her shoulders and pull her close to him, or he would kiss the top of her head and draw her hair up to reveal the fragile whiteness of her neck. She would turn blindly to him for a second, and then he would be gone again.

Once, a little while after the auditions, he had come to find her in her room. He had leant against the door, smiling down at her, and from the brightness and distance in his eyes, she guessed that he had been taking drugs again. But it was unthinkable to resist when he reached for her, and pulled her down beside him on to the narrow little bed.

Blindly, she pressed against him, thinking here, now, he's with you. Nothing else matters.

Afterwards, when he lay in her arms and she was secure in his warmth, Helen studied the curves and angles of his face. She thought she saw in them the gentleness of the other Oliver, the half of himself he must feel compelled to hide for some reason that she didn't understand.

Oliver had drifted off to sleep and Helen had gone on lying beside him, her mouth against his hair, lost in the pleasure of possession.

When he woke up again, he seemed to be listening for something in the quiet of the house.

Then he had rolled away from her, his lazy, assured manner

making her doubt the existence of another Oliver after all. When he was dressed he had refused her offer of a cup of tea, kissed her briefly, and gone away.

Helen had quickly learned to accept that.

He came and went as he wanted, and up until now she had seized gratefully and unquestioningly on the few times that they were together without asking for anything more.

It occurred to her that she wouldn't have known what else to ask for, anyway.

Helen frowned. Up until the last few days, that was how it had been. But this afternoon was different. She was not simply numbed by his absence, she was hurt by it. She hadn't seen Oliver for four days, and her need for him was growing acute. Part of the grey afternoon's discomfort was the way her body ached for him. I was so self-controlled once, Helen remembered. Is this what sex is like for everyone? So potent as to rub out everything else, and so bitterly painful when it isn't gratified?

The other sensation that troubled her was a dull sense of foreboding. The room was heavy with it and for a moment Helen imagined that the clouds outside the window bulged with it. Then she rejected the fancifulness of the idea with irritation. The rational Helen whose voice was still sometimes just audible told her that she was being a fool, and that she should go back to her work and forget Oliver until he appeared again. But the emotional Helen who ruled so capriciously now knew that she couldn't do it.

She was sunk in irritable apathy, hurt and impatient and powerless to do anything. The solitude and silence pressed around her, almost tangible.

Suddenly Helen jumped up. She couldn't bear to sit here any longer. Someone to talk to, that was what she needed.

There was no response to her knocking at Chloe's door. Along the panelled gallery at the head of the stairs, Pansy's door was open. Helen looked in at the jungle of record sleeves, empty cups and discarded clothes and half smiled. Pansy was always out somewhere.

Helen leaned on the carved banister and looked down into the body of the hall. The panelling seemed to absorb the light. It was numbingly quiet. Then, astonishingly, Helen heard a babble of voices. Almost at once she realised that it was a radio play. Rose must be listening in the kitchen, probably squashed into her battered armchair beside the Aga. Helen was still a little afraid of Rose, but her need for human company now was so imperative that she didn't hesitate.

'Come in, love', Rose said easily. She was indeed in the armchair, with the massive shapeless tubes of her legs propped up on a stool. 'Sit down somewhere. Move that pile of stuff off the chair.'

Helen tried not to look at the overflowing ashtrays and smeared plates on the table. Rose lived complacently in a ripe, untidy web like a fat spider. Helen came in here rarely, and mostly in the hope of seeing Oliver. When she did meet him, it always surprised her, because he looked bored and irritable and faintly disgusted by the mess.

As she sat down Helen saw Gerry leaning against the dusty dresser behind the door. He was unshaven and his clothes were filthy. He was clutching a teacup and, as he stared at her with unfocused eyes, he lifted it and took a gulp, smacking his lips. There was a strong smell of whisky.

Helen moved uncomfortably. When she met Gerry on the stairs or along the deserted gallery, his hands invariably reached out to touch her while he joked, disconcertingly, in his cultured voice.

'Don't mind him,' Rose ordered. 'He's having one of his bad days.'

Pansy and Chloe had joked about that. Gerry's 'bad days' were the ones when he got drunk. Good days were the ones when he stayed sober, despite his failure to write a word of the non-existent novel promised to follow his single, long-ago success.

'Tea in the pot', Rose told her.

As she lifted the teapot, Helen noticed that there was a crusty dribble of dried egg yolk down the side of it. She poured dark brown tea into a mug, resisting the impulse to wipe the inside of it first with her handkerchief.

'Well, it's not often that we see you, dear. What is it, feel like a chat?' There was an avidity in Rose's eyes that Helen chose not to see. Instead she nodded, grateful for the sympathy.

'It's my work, I suppose. I have to...'

'Work?' Rose's chuckle was derisive. 'No-one looks like you do because of work, darling. Oliver, is it? Take my advice. Give as good as you get.'

In his corner Gerry gave a short, hard laugh. 'Always Oliver. He's too damned lucky by half. Got the lot, he has, and acts like it isn't worth tuppence.' His voice was blurred and bitter, but there was a note of grudging admiration in it too. 'If I was younger, if I could have my time over again...'

'You aren't. And you won't.' Rose interrupted him wearily.

Helen turned to watch him go and then looked away sharply. Just for an instant she had caught an echo of Oliver's voice, and glimpsed the mint-brightness of his features distorted in Gerry's. Surely their relationship was too distant for such a startling likeness, however fleeting?

Rose picked up a long greasy straggle of knitting and attacked it vigorously. When she spoke again, she seemed to have forgotten Oliver.

'You may think he's a wreck now, poor Gerry. But you should have seen him years ago. Handsome, and talented. Women fought to get at him. And he was so sure that he was going to be famous and rich. I used to be asked everywhere just because I was his half-sister. Ha, those were the days.' She was laughing wheezily.

'What happened?'

'Bugger all. A little, early-flowering talent, that was Gerry. He had too much, too easy and too early, and he frittered the whole lot away. He's been trying to get some of it back ever since.'

'How sad,' Helen said absently.

'Sad? Not at all. Pathetic, perhaps.' Rose's voice was harsh. 'He's luckier than most. At least he had something, once. You know,' she said, meditatively, as if it had just occurred to her, 'I think perhaps Oliver's a little like him.'

'No, he isn't.' It was Helen's turn to sound harsh now. 'Oliver's nothing like that.'

Rose's white face hung expressionlessly in front of her like a pasty moon.

'Oh, Oliver's got money, of course. Not a lot, but enough to keep him going even at the rate he spends it. Gerry never had that. And there's Montcalm, and the title, and all that aristocratic rigmarole. But if you took all that away, you'd see the same thing in them both. Self-destructiveness.'

Helen remembered the inner, secret Oliver that she wanted so much to believe in. Perhaps his cool arrogance was to protect that. Not destructive, but protective. 'I'm sure you're wrong,' she told Rose, as humbly as she could. There was a little, bitten-off smile at the corners of Rose's mouth. 'Perhaps. Tell me, love, are you serious about him?'

'Yes. No. Does it matter?'

'Only to you, love.' Rose smoothed her knitting with an air of having finished the conversation. 'Did you come down here hoping to find him?'

'No,' said Helen bleakly.

'Because, as you see, he isn't here. He only comes when he needs something. He's at the rehearsal rooms. If you want him, you should go straight out and get him. Just like he'd do himself.'

Yes, thought Helen. She's right.

Without moving or saying any more, Rose watched her leave. Then, very slowly, she shook her head and turned back to her knitting.

It was even colder outside than it had looked from her window. Helen shivered and plunged forward. She was thinking of nothing, not imagining what she would find when she reached the address that Rose had given her, except that Oliver would be there.

She was breathless when she reached the disused warehouse that was used as a rehearsal room. A blank grey door in a side wall had a rainwashed notice on it reading 'PLAYHOUSE.' There was no bell or knocker, but the door opened when she pushed it. Inside was a little windowless lobby with a heavy steel sliding door blocking one wall. A flight of stone steps faced Helen, and as she ran up them, there was still no thought in her head except Oliver. At the top of the steps she groped in the airless darkness and then caught a breath of clearer air. Following it, she came out on to a catwalk that looked down into the main body of the warehouse.

In the middle of the bare concrete floor below her, lit by a single desk light, was a battered table covered with notes. On hard chairs drawn up to the table, Pansy and Oliver were sitting facing each other.

Helen heard Pansy's voice first. It was soft but penetrating, filling the warehouse to the remotest corner. She was reading a scene and Oliver was following the lines, waiting for his cue.

Helen started forward to call out to them, then stopped herself. Don't interrupt. She would let them finish the scene. She leaned back against the wall to watch, folding her arms patiently.

Oliver and Pansy were completely unaware of being watched. Pansy kept starting her speech and then stopping, trying new emphases. Oliver watched her face intently, and when Pansy looked up to meet his eyes, there was a ripple of laughter between them.

'Perfectionist,' Oliver murmured.

'It will be perfect,' Pansy whispered back. 'It must be. When we stand up there...'

'If you want it, then it will be.'

She was looking across at him, serious-faced. 'What do you want, Oliver?'

The warehouse was a pool of silence. Helen's spine crawled, icy with sudden dread.

As she watched, incapable of moving, Oliver's hand reached out. Pansy's was resting on the table and Oliver took it and touched each of the fingers in turn. Then he traced a circle in the palm.

'You,' he said simply.

The sudden, shocking clatter was his chair overturning as he stood up. Both his hands grasped Pansy's and he lifted her from her seat to face him. Slowly, as if she was frozen, Helen's fist went to her mouth. She bit into the clenched fingers and tried to force her eyes to close, but the scene refused to disappear. They were standing close together now, the gold head bent over the silvery one, their hands still locked together. Neither of them spoke, but their eyes explored each other's faces, waiting.

Then Pansy smiled. It was unmistakable, both an invitation and a challenge to him. At once Oliver dropped her hands. His fingers went to her face, combing back the points of hair so that her cheeks were left exposed and vulnerable. Then, with her dazzling face cupped in his hands, his mouth moved to hers. For a second they hung there, motionless, then Pansy reached to pull him closer. At once their kiss was open, hungry and self-devouring. Their two bodies were glued inseparably together.

Helen was hit by a wave of physical jealousy so naked and powerful that it almost choked her. It swept over her simultaneously with a surge of shocked self-disgust. *I want him to do that to me*, her body told her imperatively. *I need him, and he was mine.* At the same time she thought, why am I creeping and spying like this? I must get out of here. Stop humiliating myself. The realisation unlocked her frozen muscles. She wrenched her head away from the sight of Pansy stretched on tiptoe to reach Oliver's face and stumbled back against the door to the catwalk. As she moved, her foot caught against something hollow and metallic and sent it rolling and bouncing away from her.

In the circle of light below, two heads jerked upwards.

'Who's there?' Oliver's voice was sharp, angry. In spite of the gloom, he saw her almost at once. 'Helen? Oh, Lord. What the hell are you doing here?'

'I'm sorry, I'm sorry,' Helen's voice was unnaturally high and shaky. 'I didn't mean . . . I just came to see you.' Trembling with shock and with tight bands of panic spanning her chest, Helen groped for the door, opened it and fled. She had just had time to see Pansy staring after her, her eyes and mouth three circles of surprise and concern.

She was outside in the dreary, early dusk before she realised that someone was running after her. There was time for her to have a wild, surging hope that it was Oliver, coming to explain and to make everything all right again, before a hand gripped her shoulder and pulled her round.

It was Tom.

'Wait', he said. His face was dark and angry, and his mouth was compressed into a thin line. He looked round swiftly, then guided her into the sheltering angle of a building. As she backed against it, Helen felt crumbling mortar and little cushions of moss beneath her fingers.

'You look terrible,' Tom told her. 'Don't go and . . . just don't be stupid, okay? I saw it too. We were both spying, and we saw what we deserved to see. Finish. Forget it now.'

Helen struggled to focus on what he was saying. What was he doing, intruding into this?

'I'm not stupid,' she told him mechanically. Then the thought struck her that he must feel for Pansy as she did for Oliver. Of course Tom loved her. Even this detached, accomplished man was vulnerable to her. He must be stinging from what they had just seen as much as she was herself.

For a moment sympathy flickered in her, drawing her to Tom in spite of herself. He didn't look angry any more. His eyes were hooded and unfathomable in the fading light, but his face had relaxed and there was even a twist of wry amusement around his mouth. He must already be thinking that their mutual exclusion was funny, Helen saw. How cool he was. Yet he was generous enough to look out for her too. Tom Hart could be a valuable friend, she remembered. And she felt that she needed one now more than she had done in all her life. He stood between her and the bleak street, like a refuge.

Then she stiffened. Tom was no refuge. His sympathy and understanding, however real, was useless to her because of his love for Pansy. That made him hers, just like Oliver. That in itself divided him from Helen like a curtain of steel.

Behind her eyes she saw the scene in the warehouse again, with Pansy's pliant body bent like a bow against Oliver's.

No-one could help exorcise that. All she wanted was to be alone, as far away from here as possible.

'Come home with me,' Tom said gently. 'We'll do something English, like have a cup of tea. Then perhaps we'll follow it up with a lot of bourbon. All this is quite funny, when you come to think of it.'

Helen shook her head. His amusement, and even his kindness, suddenly grated unbearably. She gathered her strength to push past him, staring deliberately over his shoulder.

'I'd rather be by myself. I don't want any tea, or any bourbon.'

The sob rising in her throat made her voice sound harsher than she had intended. Tom stood back at once to let her go and she stumbled away.

His half-smile had vanished. When she had gone he picked up a pebble and threw it sharply against the angle of the wall. It clattered dismally and then rolled away into a bed of sodden leaves.

All the way back to Follies House, she held herself rigid, as if she was afraid that something inside her might split and spill, messily, in front of the strangers who were passing by.

At last she reached the house. There was no-one there, and not a sound to be heard. As she went up she counted the stairs, numbering them off in her head to stop having to think about anything else. Only when she had unlocked her door and bolted it behind her, did she feel safe enough and private enough to cry.

She stumbled to the bed and, almost gratefully, let the tears come. Helen rarely cried, but now she abandoned herself to it.

The storm of weeping that overtook her was not just for Oliver, but for herself too. Disjointed images and phrases flitted through her head with the shaking sobs. She saw Oliver's face in the firelight at the Montcalm cottage.

He was so beautiful, and so gentle then.

She remembered the exhilaration of being driven at speed in his Jaguar and the prickle of champagne in her mouth.

Nothing like him has ever happened to me before. And never will again.

The excitement she had felt at simply being close to him was still with her.

I didn't make demands on him.

But she had not been brilliant enough to keep him.

How could I, after he'd seen Pansy?

And, again,

It isn't fair.

Alone in the dark, Helen cried as if she could never stop. But at last no more tears would come. Still in the same position, cold and cramped, she stared unseeingly upwards and forced herself to think.

She knew that she had walked into this loss with open eyes. She remembered thinking *I don't care what happens. I just want him now.* She had relished the reckless thrill that the thought had given her.

So what had happened, had happened.

She saw now that it had been inevitable from the moment that Pansy had walked into the audition. The only surprising thing was that the scene she had just watched hadn't happened before. It was unlikely, she thought bitterly, that they had held themselves apart for her sake.

Helen shrugged hopelessly.

What now? Somehow, however bleakly, life would have to go on.

Suddenly, and with eerie vividness, she saw her father's face.

'If this is the very worst thing that ever happens to you,' she heard him saying in the flat, familiar voice that she missed so much, 'you'll be a very lucky girl.'

'Poor Dad,' Helen whispered out loud. 'Poor all of us.'

At once, just as if she had been able to step outside herself for an instant, the enormity of Oliver shrank and slipped away from her. She saw him almost as a stranger, a blond young man with the features of a medieval knight and the easy smile of an indulged child.

She was able to hold him at that distance for no more than a moment before the hurt of losing him swept back, but it helped her. Her eyes were dry and hard now as she watched the darkness. She knew what she would have to do. Grimly, Helen recited her plans for the future. First, her neglected work. There would be lectures to catch up on and papers to write. The rhythm of it would be soothing, the intellectual demands a kind of painkiller.

She could, perhaps, find somewhere else to live so that there would be no need to see Oliver and Pansy any more. It wouldn't be long until the summer. Then she would get her degree and find a job, and be able to look after her mother and brother as they deserved. After a few weeks, she told herself with determination, the sight of Pansy and Oliver that was burning into her eyelids now would be forgotten.

It would be as if Oliver Mortimore had never been in her life.

All she had to do was to get through the next few days, and weeks, until that happened.

I won't feel sorry for myself any more, she vowed. There isn't really any reason to. The decision even brought her a kind of exhausted tranquillity.

Faintly, Helen heard the telephone ringing in the stone passage that led to the kitchen. At last it stopped and after a long pause she heard footsteps and someone tapping gently on her door.

'Helen?' It was Chloe's husky voice. 'Helen, are you there?'

She lay rigid on her bed. She couldn't bear to see anyone now, not even Chloe. Tomorrow it would be different, but not now. Outside the door Chloe hesitated and then turned away.

Helen breathed out a long sigh of relief, but moments later she realised that the footsteps were coming back. This time there was the whisper of a note being pushed under her door.

Leave me alone. The words pulsed silently in Helen's head. Then Chloe went away again and this time she really was alone.

Around her the evening sounds of the house, doors opening and closing, music and laughter from somewhere a long way off, settled into silence. At last Helen stopped counting the hours as the Oxford bells struck them and fell into an exhausted sleep.

She had no idea how much later it was, or what had woken her up, but suddenly she was wide awake again. Out of the blanket of silence she heard a sound, and then another. She recognised them immediately. There was Oliver's low moan, the small secret sound of pleasure that she treasured herself, and then Pansy's answering cry as clear as a bell in the night. Downstairs, in the room below her, they were making love.

Helen rolled her face into her pillow and clenched her teeth so hard that she thought her jaw would crack. Her hands twisted on the folds of sheet and she drew up her knees in a spasm of pain. Then she lay, waiting like an eavesdropper again and hating herself for it, to hear if there was any more. But there was nothing. Whether she had really heard those two secret cries or not, the rest was silence.

Helen didn't sleep again that night. When it was fully light she got up, wincing at the stabbing pain in her head. Her eyes felt gritty and so puffy that she could barely open them. As she reached for her dressing gown, she saw a folded slip of white paper on the carpet, and remembered Chloe's note. Her fingers felt thick and clumsy as she opened it.

> Your mother rang. Will you call her as soon as you
> can? She sounded anxious. C.

Helen was still wrapping her robe around her as she ran down the stairs. Anxiety throbbed with her headache.

Early though it was, her mother answered the telephone at once.

'Helen, is that you? Why didn't you call last night?'

'I ... couldn't. Mum, what is it?'

'Oh, darling, I don't know how to tell you. I had notification from the Authority at school yesterday. They're cutting down on supply teachers. Permanent staff will have to fill in instead. Helen, there isn't any work after this week. Nothing. I don't know what to do. I've met this month's mortgage, but...'

'Wait, Mum, let me think.'

Helen leaned her head against the varnished panelling. There was a warm smell of polish and the grey shape of the payphone looked bleakly familiar in a world that threatened to turn itself upside down.

'I'll come home', she said at last, surprised at the firmness in her voice. 'I shouldn't have come back here anyway. Don't worry. I'll find a job.'

'No, Helen. Your father...'

94

Helen broke into her mother's protestations as gently as she could. The undertone of relief in her mother's voice made her want to cry.

'I want to come home. It's where I belong. Oxford ... isn't the same as it was, anyway. Listen, will you be all right for a little while? If I come home right away, I'll have to come back again to arrange things, and I don't want to do that.'

'Yes, we'll be all right. Helen – there's enough money for this month. And there's the possibility of a permanent part-time job in the New Year. But it's only a possibility, and there's Christmas in between, and some bills that must be paid, and everything else is such a price ...'

'Don't worry,' Helen said again. 'Between us, we'll manage.'

When they had said their goodbyes, Helen slowly replaced the receiver and leaned back exhaustedly against the wall.

Fate, she thought bitterly, had made a neat intervention. There was no need to worry about Oliver any more. She would be removed from Oxford altogether. In her mind's eye she saw a picture of the city and what it meant to her. There were the towers and meadows ringed by rivers, the long, sepia shelves of books in libraries and her own handwriting covering pages of blank paper. That was all over.

There would be no more Oxford. It was a pity that last night had to be the last one here, the one she would remember.

Sadly, Helen pulled her robe tightly round her and set out to face the day. First she went to see her tutor. Helen found her, as usual, in her College rooms. The walls were lined from floor to ceiling with books, and french doors looked out over the water meadows. Miss Graham's hair was knotted in a neat bun, and her face was smooth and unworried after a secluded lifetime of academic life.

Helen explained awkwardly that she would have to resign her place and her scholarship. Her mother and brother needed her financial support, and she must go home.

Miss Graham folded her hands and sighed.

'This is a great pity. You know we regard you as a strong candidate for a First. Is there no other way? I wish the College could help. There are funds for students in difficulty, but a whole family ...'

'Thank you, but I don't think there is anything anyone can do.'

'Well. We'll keep your place open, of course. Next year, perhaps, your position will be happier.'

Helen remembered how she had sat in this room as a wide-eyed schoolgirl on her first day, full of excitement and awe at the great institution she was part of, and had to blink back the tears that started into her eyes.

She had reached the door before her tutor asked, almost as an afterthought, 'What do you really want to do with your life, Helen?'

From nowhere, unconsidered and unexpected, the answer came out at once. 'I'd like to marry, and have children.'

Miss Graham smiled. 'You don't need a First for that.'

'No. Goodbye, Miss Graham. I'm sorry about the First.'

A moment later Helen was walking back over Magdalen Bridge towards the High. Why, she asked herself, did I say that? Had she been cherishing some half-baked notion of herself and Oliver, married, filling the back of the rakish Jaguar with blonde babies?

The idea made her laugh in spite of herself. No, her dreams of Oliver had never been to do with marrying him. Why then had she made such a heretical confession to her learned spinster tutor? She had wanted to needle that secure academic complacency, perhaps because it no longer had any bearing on her own life. But perhaps too she had been expressing a much deeper longing to have and to provide security, faced with the crumbling of her own family.

Perhaps.

Helen paused in the middle of Magdalen Bridge and looked upwards. Against the pale sky soared the height of Magdalen Tower, perfectly beautiful and timeless above the stream of cars and cyclists. It was Helen's favourite sight in Oxford and it reminded her that she was leaving.

On one side of her, the river curved around the formal lawns and beds of the Botanic Gardens. On the other, between separate arms, it enclosed the mysterious tangle of dark trees called Addison's Walk. Quickly, Helen crossed the road and ducked through into the cramped porter's lodge of Magdalen College. She would make the circuit of the walk for the last time as a way of saying goodbye.

She passed through the vaulted stonework of Magdalen Cloisters, her feet echoing on the worn stone flags, came out into the light again through an arch of iron gates, then slowed her pace again under the tall trees. The river was slow-moving here, reflecting the bare branches back at the sky. The banks were bare now, but in the spring they would be vivid with crocuses and daffodils. Later, in the summer, the punts would slide past here loaded with noisy parties or with silent, absorbed couples.

Sadly, she wouldn't be here to see any of it.

Yet as it always did the quietness of the setting soothed her. Even though it lay in the middle of a busy town, the place felt utterly remote.

Helen walked slowly, drinking in the cold air and letting the clamorous voices inside her head subside. Later she would have so much to arrange, but now she had her moment of peace.

She was at the outermost point of the circuit where there was no sound but for her own footfalls on the path, when she saw someone leaning on the low wall to stare into the water. At first she didn't recognise him, but then she saw the black hair ruffled by the wind and a dark frown of concentration.

It was Tom Hart.

He looked up and saw her at once, leaving her no chance of slipping by unseen. 'Are you all right?' he asked, unsmiling.

'Yes. Are you?' She noticed that there were creases of tiredness around his eyes. He was unshaven and the dark stubble emphasised the leanness of his face. Helen suddenly saw how good-looking he was, in a way that couldn't have been more unlike Oliver's clear, classical beauty.

Tom shrugged impatiently. 'Of course. It's nothing. They're made for each other, after all.' His sardonic smile failed to conceal from Helen that he had wanted Pansy very badly.

He feels as bad as I do, she thought. Worse – he's probably almost as used to getting what he wants as Oliver and Pansy themselves.

'May I walk round with you?' he asked, formally.

Helen nodded, a little unwillingly, and they began to pace slowly under the arch of trees.

'This is my way of saying goodbye to Oxford. I have to leave at once,' she told him at last.

'For Christ's sake', Tom stared at her incredulously, 'not because of Oliver?'

She laughed. 'No. He means ... meant a lot to me, more than I realised until yesterday, but I wouldn't run away for that reason.' She took a deep breath, and glanced sideways at Tom.

He was looking away from her, into the slow drift of the river. 'My father died in the summer. We aren't very well off now, and I heard from my mother this morning that she has lost her job. She needs me to go home and help her. Neither of us is qualified to earn very much, you see, and there aren't many jobs for anyone in the Midlands right now. But between us, we can probably manage to keep going.'

Tom had stopped, and now he looked down at her with his dark eyebrows pulled close together.

'I'm sorry,' he said simply. 'Can no-one help?'

They were standing in such a way that his shoulders sheltered her from the wind. He was wearing a coat of some soft, thick tweedy material with the collar turned up against his cheeks. It was very warm, standing so close to him. For a stupid moment Helen longed to press her face against his shoulder and murmur *yes, please help me*.

Instead she swung away from him and started to walk again, more briskly now. 'No. No-one can help. I've just told my tutor the same thing.'

They hardly spoke again until they were standing under the arched gateway once more.

'I'm going that way', Helen said dismissively. 'I'd better say goodbye.'

Tom's hand rested on her shoulder for a second.

'Goodbye,' he said, his penetrating dark eyes on her face. 'I'm sorry you're leaving. We might have been friends. We've got at least one thing in common, after all.'

They both laughed, without much humour. Then Helen lifted her hand in a brief wave and walked away.

Back in the bustle of the High she began to count off the things that must be done before she could go home. She would have to pack, give notice to Rose, take books back to the library, say too many goodbyes.

Goodbye. Would she have the courage to say it to Oliver? It would mean walking in under Tom Tower, crossing Canterbury Quad and climbing his staircase, knocking at his door. She longed to see him one last time, but doubted that she could find it in herself to go and look for him again.

Then, as she came down St Aldate's, she saw him. He was with Pansy, of course. The low black shape of the Jaguar was drawn up half on the pavement beside Follies. Just as Helen noticed it, Pansy came running up the steps from the island, two at a time. Her white fur coat was swinging round her like a cloud and she was laughing delightedly.

Oliver raced up the steps in pursuit and Pansy ducked behind the car, feinting another dash as he tried to catch her. Then she vaulted into the driver's seat and groped for the ignition. Oliver's hand seized her arm and held her, triumphant. They looked as happy as children.

Do it now. Just say it and go. Helen braced herself.

She stepped in front of the Jaguar and smiled levelly at them.

'I want to say goodbye. I'm leaving Oxford.'

She saw the laughter fade from Pansy's face first.

'Not because . . .'

'I'm going home to help my mother. It's a question of money.'

'Money?'

How unintelligible that must be, for both of them, Helen thought.

Involuntarily, she turned to Oliver and their eyes met. He stepped towards her, blocking out Pansy for a moment and his arm came lightly round her shoulder again. A familiar tremor shot through Helen at his touch, but she knew that Oliver wanted something different now. He wanted her to bow out, conceding gracefully and making everything all right for him. But Helen held herself rigid and her eyes never wavered. Something like shame showed in Oliver's tanned face before he dropped his arm and looked away again.

Helen lifted her chin and looked at each of them in turn. 'Oliver . . . Pansy . . .' she said lightly. Then, 'I hope the play's a success.'

She was walking down the steps to the island when she heard the car doors slam, and the throaty roar of the exhaust. Just as she had heard it after the magical evening with Oliver at Montcalm. It seemed years ago, now.

She looked up to see Follies House looming above her, a dark red mass of Jacobean brick set solidly on the tiny island in the tumbling water.

I wish I'd never come here, Helen whispered. No, that isn't true. I wish I was staying, staying with Oliver. I wish he wasn't driving away now, with Pansy beside him. I wish he really had been mine. I love him.

And the hopelessness of that settled around Helen like a mist.

Suddenly she longed to be at home. Once she was away from Oxford, it would be easier. If she tried hard enough, she thought, she would have everything done by this evening. Then she could catch a late train and sleep tonight at home, in her own bed. Quickly she ran down the steps towards the house.

One by one the day's disagreeable tasks were slowly accomplished.

Helen hated saying goodbye at any time, and now the word seemed dinned into her brain.

At the end of the afternoon, she made her way down the dark kitchen passage to the telephone. Her luggage was almost ready and she was going to ring and arrange for a mini cab to take her to the station. But first, she thought, she would telephone her bank and ask for her account to be transferred back to her home branch. There was no point in keeping it in Oxford.

To the bored clerk at the other end of the line she recited the details of her request while he took them down infuriatingly slowly. Helen breathed deeply in an effort to keep her patience. With her thumbnail she picked at a blister of paint on the coinbox and repeated her account number yet again.

'And you wish to close this account, Miss Brown?'

'That's right.'

'And the credit balance?'

'Will be transferred to the reopened account at my home town. Could you give me an exact figure for the balance, please?'

The question was no more than a formality. Of necessity Helen always knew exactly how much money she had. At last the clerk came back with the answer.

'With today's deposit your balance is eight hundred and sixty-two pounds, seventy-two pence.'

'What?'

'Eight hundred and sixty...'

'Yes, I did hear, but there's some mistake. I have only about a hundred and ten pounds.'

'That was before today's deposit.'

Once again Helen drew a deep breath.

'I haven't made a deposit. There must be a mistake.'

100

After another long pause a different, slightly older-sounding voice came on the line.

'Is there a problem here, Miss Brown?'

'Not really. Just that a large sum of money has been wrongly credited to my account.'

'Not wrongly. I have the slip here. It gives your name, address and account number quite clearly. And the seven-fifty was quite definitely paid in, in fifties. The only thing that I can't make out is the signature. It's one of those that starts with a big loop and goes on in a straight line with a few bumps in it. Does that mean anything to you?'

'No,' said Helen, utterly bewildered.

'Nor to me,' said the voice, with a trace of irritation. 'Usually we only get complaints when it's the other way round'.

'Just leave things as they are for the time being, then,' Helen said as calmly as she could and slowly replaced the receiver.

Who? Who could have given her so much money? And done it with such surgical coolness that she had never touched it, just found it magically lying in her account?

Helen thought back to the shame in Oliver's face this morning as he had failed to meet her eyes. It must be Oliver. Oliver, trying to make some kind of amends. Oliver was the only person she had ever seen unthinkingly spending a hundred pounds on a single lunch. Oliver would be able to command that kind of money.

He had wanted to help her in some way, as unobtrusively as he could, and this was his way of doing it. What a collection of contradictions he is, thought Helen, before a host of questions came crowding in on her.

She must give the money back, of course, but how could she do it without embarrassment? Without answering tact with bristling pride? Evidently he had found her account and number without difficulty, but however could she find his so that she could slide the money back? She winced at the thought of pressing the pile of notes back into his hands.

What else could she do? Push it under his door? Leave it in his pigeonhole? Write him a cheque with a grateful note? Or wrap it round a brick and lob it through his window? A spurt of laughter bubbled up inside Helen. After the pressures of the day this last shock had left her feeling slightly hysterical.

Another uncharacteristic idea popped into her head. A drink, she told herself. That's what you need. I'm sure Chloe's got a bottle in her room that she'd be glad to share.

Chloe called out reluctantly in answer to her knock. 'Ye-es?'

A moment later Helen saw why. Her hair was wound on heated rollers and her face was a stiff white mask. The rest of her was swathed in a vivid kimono. Through the face mask Chloe attempted a tiny grin and beckoned her inside.

'All stops being pulled out, as you see. It's dinner with Stephen on High Table tonight.'

Helen nodded. She wished her friend wasn't so interested in Stephen Spurring, but she dismissed it from her mind at once as none of her business.

Instead, trying to match the light-hearted tone, she told her, 'I need a stiff drink. Can you help a friend in need?'

'That's not like you,' said Chloe, 'but yes, sure. Gin?'

The drink did indeed make her feel better. The hysterical desire to laugh went away, and her hands stopped shaking.

'What's up?' Chloe's question was casual and her face was invisible, bent over the slow manicuring of her fingernails.

'Trouble,' Helen answered softly. 'My mother's lost her job. There's no money coming in, so I'm going home to help out. No more Oxford. I was stupid to have come back at all.'

Chloe shut her eyes, horrified. Once again the difference between Helen's life and her own leapt out at her like a reproach.

'Then,' Helen's gentle voice didn't change its tone, 'this afternoon, I discovered that someone has put seven hundred and fifty pounds in my bank. Just like that, with no word or explanation. Someone I've told about all this must want to help, but doesn't want to be thanked. Or refused, I suppose.'

'Who?'

'It has to be Oliver.'

Chloe's first instinct was to say No, surely not, but she checked herself. Helen, after all, knew the beautiful but unthinking Oliver better than she did.

'Chloe, how do I give it back to him?'

Chloe was unwinding the rollers from her hair and she teased a long, shiny red strand in her fingers before she answered.

'Must you give it back? Think. Whoever it was made a considered decision. No-one has that kind of money just sitting in a pocket waiting to be handed out in a reckless gesture and then regretted. Whoever gave it to you, wanted you to have it, and probably went to quite a lot of trouble to present you with it in the least embarrassing way. Have you got to reject it out of hand? Would the money help?'

'Help?' Helen considered it for the first time. 'God, yes. It would see us through to the New Year. There's a possibility of another job for Mum then.' She stood up, suddenly excited as the realisation dawned on her. 'It might even mean that I wouldn't have to leave.'

'Well, then', said Chloe.

'You think I should take it?'

'Yes.' And Chloe poured another generous measure of gin into Helen's glass as if to clinch it.

Helen grinned, the brightness breaking through the shadows in her face.

'But I've spent the whole day saying heartrending goodbyes to people. I'm all packed, ready to go. I can't just reappear, can I?'

Patiently, Chloe knelt down in front of Helen's chair and took her small, cold hands between her own.

'Look. People who care about you, will be grateful that you're still here after all. And those who don't, why should you care about them? Just go home for a few days. See your mother, talk about what's happened, make some plans, and then come back. I'll explain to whoever needs to be told, if you like.'

Helen nodded, grateful, knowing that Chloe was right. She was beginning to feel warm and comfortable again, and the brave face that she had worn all day wasn't needed any more.

She wasn't ready, yet, to think about what Oliver's absurdly generous gesture meant to her. Or where it left the two of them now. But it rubbed away a little of the hurt and loss to know that he had done it.

'I even said goodbye to Pansy and Oliver,' she said suddenly, and laughed. 'Very crisply and coolly. I felt rather pleased with myself.'

Chloe eyed her sharply. 'You know about it?'

'It's only just happened.' Helen was quick to defend Oliver. 'He didn't . . . you know, deceive me. Not that he even owed me that,' she added quickly. 'Tom Hart says they're made for each other. I suppose he's right.'

Chloe was making her face up now, deftly stroking colour on to her eyelids.

'And you deserve better.' Without allowing a contradiction, Chloe swept on. 'Now. Let's get organised. When's your train?' Meekly Helen told her. 'Perfect. I have to be with Stephen by seven, so I can drop you at the station on the way there. Hurry.'

Half an hour later they were both ready.

Helen said, 'You look lovely.'

Chloe was wearing a discreet black silk crepe dinner dress, the long sleeves and high neck buttoned with dozens of tiny covered buttons. It was a perfect foil for her beautiful hair, falling in a mass of rich waves around her face. Her only ornament was the diamond studs in her ears.

'It'll be your turn next', said Chloe and then frowned inwardly at the clumsiness of that. She had only meant that it would be Helen's turn next to have as nice a time as she was having herself.

But Helen's mind in any case was on her train, and home.

Chloe left her in the station forecourt, a slim dark girl with a determined face and a bag that looked too heavy for her.

As she swung her car back into the traffic, Chloe bit her lip reflectively. Lucky. You're so lucky, she told herself. Then she thought of Stephen waiting for her and the prospect chased everything else out of her head.

CHAPTER FIVE

'*Benedictus, benedicat.*' Into the echoing quiet in the Hall, the Senior Student delivered the endpiece of the Latin grace from his high lectern. Chloe dropped her hands from the tall chairback in front of her and let Stephen settle her into her place. Around her, in a flutter of black gowns, the dons and their guests sat down. From where she sat, at the Master's right on the low dais, Chloe had a perfect view down the Hall. The sight made her shiver slightly. Stephen's College was an ancient foundation, and this Hall was the jewel amongst its fine buildings.

Over the heads of the undergraduates at their long tables, the roof arched away into dimness, the magnificent hammer beams only just visible. There were glimmers of gold in the dark, from the ornamented bosses and shields. Beneath the elegant tracery of the Gothic windows set high in the walls, the double row of portraits of past Masters in their gold frames stretched back into the sixteenth century. Under so many calm pairs of eyes even the present generation of irreverent diners seemed quieter and more sober in their gowns. The arch of the roof and the solid stone walls muffled the clamour of talk to a low murmur.

Chloe's gaze shifted to the table in front of her, a massive slab of black oak polished like a mirror. It was heavy with thickets of glasses, silverware and crested china. Behind her, white-coated College servants were preparing to serve the first course. She glanced sideways and met Stephen's eyes.

'Sure you wouldn't rather just have an egg?' He was gently mocking the magnificence for her, and a quick smile flashed between them. Then Chloe inclined her head to listen respectfully to the Master. He had seemed very old and forbidding, an expert in classical antiquities, but now Chloe saw that his faded eyes were quick with interest.

'So, Miss Campbell, you must tell us something about advertising.'

In other words, Chloe thought, here you are ... so entertain us. Deliberately she shook out her heavy linen napkin and began to talk.

The conversation was measured and highly polished – like a

rare art-form, she told herself. Over the savoury soufflé and the rare roast lamb, Chloe's opinion was sought on Piero della Francesca, co-education, and a Snowdon photograph of the Master that had just appeared in one of the colour supplements. Everything she said was listened to as gravely as if she were a great authority.

Beside her, Stephen seemed just as courteously formal, but when the hawk-faced linguist opposite Chloe said 'We are so fortunate in having Dr Spurring, who brings such interesting people to enliven our High Table', he breathed in her ear, 'He means women. The old bastard's notoriously jealous. And watch he doesn't pinch your bottom when we get upstairs.'

Chloe stared hard at her plate to stifle the laughter. She was impressed in spite of her worldliness by the ancient Hall and the civilised brilliance of the talk, and it gave the experience an extra little edge to have Stephen close to her, mildly poking fun at it.

The food came and went, unambitious but good. It was the wines that were remarkable. Stephen kept signalling for her glass to be refilled with the fragrant claret that accompanied the lamb. Leo Dawnay had taught Chloe what she knew about wine, and she remembered him saying that the finest wines he had ever tasted came from the cellars of Oxford Colleges.

'Drink as much as you can of this,' Stephen told her. 'We're not likely to see much more of it. The Bursar sold almost the last few cases to pay for some dreary new flooring in the Library. Terrible fuss about it in College Meeting.'

At the end of the main course, long after the last undergraduate had left the Hall, the Master collected the table with a practised eye. Everyone stood up. How odd that there was no pudding, Chloe thought.

Two by two they filed out of the Hall and up a shallow spiral staircase.

'What now?' Chloe whispered to Stephen.

'Wait and see,' he told her.

The Master stopped at a low wooden door under a pointed Gothic arch. Outside the door was a row of hooks, and the fellows took off their gowns and hung them up. Then the Master stood aside from the door.

'He has been presiding up to now, of course,' Stephen told Chloe. 'But this is the Senior Common Room, to which the Master doesn't belong. So the senior fellow present takes over, which happens to be boring old Puffett this evening. Don't worry, I'll see you don't get stuck with him.'

'Won't you come in, Master?' asked old Puffett.

'Thank you, Senior Tutor.'

Together they went in through the low door.

Chloe, following on in her turn, gasped faintly when she saw the room. The focus of it was a stone fireplace with a new fire crackling in it. Over the fire hung the portrait of the College's Royal founder that Chloe had often admired, in an inferior later version, in the National Gallery. The room was lit by the blaze of candles in three silver-gilt candelabra and beyond the rich glow the corners were shadowy with carved oak panelling and velvet curtains.

In front of the fireplace was a horseshoe of table, its arms towards the fire. And the table shone and sparkled with more glasses, crystal and silverware. But this time there was no china. Chloe saw incredulously the dull gleam of gold plate. Between heaped bowls of fruit, nuts and petits fours stood fat crystal decanters of plummy port.

'According to the rules,' Stephen murmured, 'I can't sit with you up here. I have to let you go now, so that my colleagues can enjoy your company too. Who would you like to be put next to?'

Chloe glanced round wildly. 'You know them. You choose for me.'

When she was escorted to her place at the opulent horseshoe, she found herself between an urbane economist with a practised smile and a young man with a shock of blond hair and a worn black leather jacket.

'This is Dave Walker,' Stephen told her. 'Our token Red.'

'Piss off,' said Dave good-humouredly. 'She's mine now, and I'll do my own political introductions. Go and talk to Puffett about your building fund', he turned to Chloe with a grin, 'while your beautiful guest and I discuss life, love and literature. Steve likes to have his little joke because ten years ago he was a Marxist, and he feels bad now because he's sold out.'

Has he? Chloe wondered. When did the cool, cynical don take over from the young idealist? She wanted to know Stephen better, much better, she told herself. They sat down and Chloe asked wickedly, 'How do you manage to be a Marxist and still sit up here surrounded by all this, eating off this?' She tapped her gold plate until it rang, the very sound of privilege.

107

Dave laughed merrily. 'Terrible, isn't it? They only bring the best stuff out in secret up here in case the poor deprived masses of undergraduates see it and decide to rush the defences. Have the trifle, by the way. It's wonderful.'

The trifle was wonderful, a perfect concoction of cream and fruit and nuts, accompanied by a fine white bordeaux.

'No,' Dave was saying mock-seriously. 'I reckon I can change things best from the inside. See that everyone gets gold plate to eat off as soon as possible. Port, madam? Do have it, then it'll give me the chance to pass it round the wrong way. It throws them all into such a fury I can't resist doing it. Any more than I can seriously resist all this booze and grub. I put this on', he tugged at his shred of a tie, 'come in from Cowley on the bike, and enjoy it for what it is – one of life's bizarre little anachronisms. It won't be going on for much longer anyhow,' he added darkly. 'Don't miss the petits fours, whatever you do. Chef's a celebrated *confiseur*.'

Now Chloe's other neighbour was claiming her attention. Warmed and mellowed by the wine and port, she embarked on a spirited argument about the economics of advertising.

The economist flirted outrageously. He watched her mouth and eyes as she talked, leaning forward occasionally to fill her glass or to take the silver nutcrackers from her fingers to crack the kernel out of its shell for her. 'You're very lovely,' he told her seriously, 'and you talk such beautiful nonsense.'

'Not nonsense,' she responded, indignantly. 'I know my business.'

The economist laughed and put his hand over hers. 'Don't talk about business. Tell me about you.'

From the opposite arm of the horseshoe, Stephen winked at her.

When the port had made its last circuit and the last crumb of Stilton and sweetmeat had been eaten, Puffett stood up again. His face was deep crimson and he swayed very slightly as he delivered the Latin benediction that marked the formal end of the evening.

'Is that it?' Chloe asked Stephen when he rejoined her at the door.

'Certainly not. Upstairs again, for brandy, coffee and cigars. Everyone finally lets their hair down, if you relish the spectacle of us old gents doing that. They'll all be groping madly for you.

I think we'll just have a quick nightcap and then make our adieux before the fights break out.'

He took her arm as they wound up the spiral stairs together.

This evening is like some kind of formal Elizabethan dance, Chloe thought. It starts out very slowly and stately, then gets faster and faster until finally everyone falls over. I shall certainly fall over myself if I have any more to drink.

'I didn't catch the economist's name,' she whispered to Stephen.

'Edgar France,' he told her, and Chloe clapped her hand to her mouth with a horrified giggle. 'Oh God, not *the* Edgar France? The world expert, no less. And I was treating him to a lecture on the fundamentals of economics in selling.'

'I haven't seen old Edgar enjoying himself so much in months.'

They both laughed delightedly and went on up the ancient stone steps arm in arm.

The setting for the last measure of the dance was a low room whose dormer windows looked out across the leads to the stone crenellations ornamenting the roof edges. When Chloe glanced out, she saw them standing out black and lacy against the dark blue sky.

In this room there were deep leather sofas and armchairs, another huge log fire, and a rich smell of coffee. The fellows were grouped around a loaded tray of drinks, pouring themselves liberal measures of brandy and coffee in thimble-sized cups. Chloe shook her head at Stephen's offer of brandy.

'Not if I'm to walk out of here on my own two legs.'

He brought across a cup of coffee and made himself comfortable beside her on her sofa. Dave Walker was hovering nearby but Stephen waved him away.

'Do you dine like this every night?' she asked Stephen.

'Of course not. Think of our poor livers. This is a special guest night, and we only have a few of them a term. Usually I'm at home with Beatrice having a bowl of soup and a sleep in front of the television. Just like everyone else.' He smiled at her, and Chloe saw the fine wrinkles at the corners of the bright blue eyes.

Lucky Beatrice, Chloe murmured to herself. I'd share my bowl of soup with Stephen any day. Or night.

She forced herself to look away from him and glance round

the room. There were more red faces and slurred voices than old Puffett's, and an atmosphere of irritation coming from some of the little groups. Chloe had a sudden insight into the pressures of living in a closed community like this, eating with the same people night after night and rubbing along with them like the members of an awkward family. She suddenly understood Stephen's throwaway remark about fights breaking out. But she thought that it was probably up here after a good dinner that the real business of the College was done too. The Master was deep in conversation now with two of the senior fellows, and she had the impression of plots being hatched elsewhere in the room as well.

'I should think this is the real nerve-centre, isn't it?' she asked Stephen and he looked at her admiringly.

'You spotted that? Yes. The College is governed from here, in the odd half-hour or so after dinner. All those formal meetings we sit through are so much wasted time, after this.'

They sat quietly together for a few more moments, watching, then Stephen squeezed her hand.

'I don't want to spend any more of my time with you up here. Come back to my rooms and have a last drink.'

Chloe met his enquiring eyes coolly, levelly. 'Yes. I'd like that.'

They said their goodbyes. The Master bent to kiss Chloe's hand. From behind one of the sofas, like a barricade, Dave Walker gave her a clenched-fist salute and a broad grin.

With Stephen's hand guiding her, Chloe negotiated the twists of the spiral stairs once more and they came out into the clean, cold air of the Quad. It must be very late, Chloe noticed. There were hardly any lights to be seen anywhere. Above the fanciful stonework of the chapel, the stars looked white and brilliant in the thin winter dark.

'I enjoyed that', Chloe said softly. Stephen's hand kept firmly hold of hers.

He chuckled. 'I thought it might amuse you. It's like a complicated game, isn't it?'

He led the way through the dark tunnel of some cloisters and unlocked a door.

'Home from home,' he murmured beside her.

Stephen's College rooms did have the lived-in look of a home. There were books everywhere, filling the shelves and overflowing on to the solid desk, the window seats and floors. There was

110

a white marble bust of Shakespeare, wearing Stephen's mortarboard rakishly over one eye, a dish of alabaster eggs on the low table in front of the fire, and the air was scented with the dusky warmth of potpourri. The walls were hung with tranquil English watercolours. On another table was a huge bowl of chrysanthemums, gold and deep bronze. Chloe put out a finger and touched the waxy curled petals.

'From our garden,' Stephen said absently. His eyes followed Chloe as she prowled around the room. She was quite at her ease, picking things up and putting them down before moving on as though she wanted to fix the whole room in her memory.

'I'm so glad to be here,' she said at last.

'At Oxford?'

Chloe smiled quickly. 'Yes, that of course. But I meant here, with you, in this room. It's just like I imagined it would all be.'

For a moment Stephen said nothing. Chloe stood in her silky black dress with her hair tawny in the firelight, watching. She lifted her hand to push the hair back from her face and as she moved, the diamonds in her ears shot light at him.

'I'm glad you're here,' he whispered. 'Come to me.'

Chloe came, her green eyes alight. Stephen's hands reached out for her and slid from her shoulders to her narrow waist. Then he took one of her hands and slowly, carefully, undid the tiny black buttons at the wrist. He lifted it and pressed his mouth against the warm skin where the pulse throbbed. It was silkier than the black dress, and fragrant with the scent that clung about her.

As they stood together, Chloe looked down at Stephen's bent head and saw the fine grey threads at the temples. She had a sudden sense of all his life, radiating outwards from the centre of this room, all unknown. She longed to change that, to know everything about him that there was to know. Suddenly she ached to possess him, to make him belong to her and no-one else. Her hand brushed against his hair.

Stephen lifted his head. His blue eyes were very clear.

'Yes?' he asked, softly.

'Yes.'

His hands went to her throat and slowly again undid the long line of buttons. Chloe's dress slid from her shoulders and the light shone on her bare skin. Under the black slip she was naked and Stephen's fingers traced the hollow beneath her ribs under the slippery silk and then the outline of her breasts. Chloe's eyes never left his face. She was smiling through parted lips. With a whisper the black slip dropped away and she stood in front of him, creamy pale skin against the tumble of red hair, naked except for the sheer black stockings. 'Leave them', he commanded, his voice very low.

Teasingly, Chloe stepped back against the desk and swung herself on to it, her long legs crossed. Her outstretched hand met the heavy folds of Stephen's gown and suddenly she shook it out and slipped her arms into it. The black stuff half masked her body, transforming her into part schoolmistress, part pin-up. When she turned away from Stephen, the gown billowed behind her in a black cloud.

Stephen half laughed, half groaned.

'That's very sexy.'

He reached out to catch her before she could slip tantalisingly out of his reach. He lifted her up effortlessly and laid her on the low sofa. The gown fell away as he knelt beside her and buried his face between her breasts. Chloe's eyes closed as his tongue began to travel, exploring relentlessly. Blindly now her fingers fought with the folds of his clothes.

At last he was naked beside her and they stretched together, glancing down at the length of their bodies, before he came on top of her. His hands and mouth were insistent.

Chloe's hands found him in response and as she guided him inside her, he whispered, 'Chloe, Chloe, Chloe.'

She drove him insistently, expertly gauging the movements of his response until he lost himself and arched back in her arms, his eyes sightless and his fingers tangled in her hair. Chloe's face was soft with satisfaction as her mouth explored his cheeks, the faint prickle of beard along his jawline and the fringe of lashes that lay dark against his skin. Her hands smoothed over the bunched muscles in his back and shoulders, then returned to stroke the damp hair back from his face.

For a long time there was no sound except for the hiss and crackle of the fire. Then she opened her eyes and looked into his.

'Again. Please,' she said, and at once she felt him move against her. She smiled, teasing, until he pulled the folds of his gown away from her.

'Just you, this time', he ordered and her answer was to slide on top of him and then bend forward, so that he was blindfolded by the curtains of her hair.

Stephen laughed back into the wide eyes and reached up, further and further into her soft heart.

Suddenly Chloe's face changed. Her fingers dug into his arms and the challenge faded from her face as her mouth met his.

'Stephen.'

He had found her now, and it was his turn to play her. He did it unrelentingly, until there was nothing in Chloe's world except his flesh against hers and the image of his face inside her eyelids. Then even that was gone and she wound herself around him, lost, drowned. Without breaking the rhythm of his movements, Stephen turned her so that she lay beneath him once again. When she opened her eyes, she saw his face over hers, dark, and with a twist to the mouth she had never seen before. There was a kind of cruelty in his face, and an exultation in his total power over her. Chloe didn't care. The change in him excited her and she lifted herself against him, hungry for her own release. Still Stephen held her back, changing the pace and depth of his thrusts until she moaned out loud and dug her fingers into the tense muscles of his back.

'Stephen. Please.'

For an instant he stopped, holding her poised on the very edge. The world hung in silence around them. Then one single thrust tore a low moan out of Chloe and she shuddered in his arms for long obliterating seconds. As the waves slowly receded, she clung against him with her eyes glued shut. Gradually awareness crept back to her. Something had happened. Subtly, in the course of their love-making, Stephen had reversed their roles. Before, Chloe had felt like the leader and the instigator. She had been very confident with her own experience and the certainty of what she wanted from him. Now, after that glimpse of his pleasure in his mastery over her and the sheer expertise of his lovemaking, Chloe was not so sure. The gentle, clever don with the suggestive mouth had become someone else, much bigger.

What did she want from him, after all?

Chloe sighed and turned her face into his shoulder to block out the light. She wouldn't think about that, not now while he was still so close.

Beside her, with her head pillowed on his shoulder, Stephen drifted quietly into sleep.

The sky was dirty with the grey light of dawn when they woke up again. Stephen frowned for an instant at the mass of red hair spreading over him, then smiled in satisfaction.

'Chloe,' he whispered. 'Time to wake up.'

She blinked at him and then stretched luxuriously like a cat. Whatever had happened, it felt good.

'It's nearly morning', she said, and a little twinge of anxiety immediately nibbled at her. 'What will ... Beatrice say?'

'Beatrice is quite used to me,' Stephen said smoothly. He was dressing, knotting his tie and looking away from her to the spread of daylight over the Quad outside.

I see, Chloe thought. 'I enjoyed my evening,' she said lightly to cover the little awkwardness. Stephen caught her from behind and kissed the nape of her neck.

'So did I. Shall we do it again soon?'

Questions hovered in Chloe's mind but she dismissed them. Wait, she warned herself. Wait and see.

'Yes, I'd like that.'

Stephen fastened the last two buttons at the neck of her dress for her, and then Chloe bent down to pick up his gown. She shook it out, and tried vainly to smooth out the creases. Stephen watched, one eyebrow raised, and they both laughed. It made the atmosphere between them easy again, and left them feeling pleased with their new intimacy.

'Come on,' Stephen said. 'I'll drive you home before it gets properly light and all the world can see us tiptoeing across the Quad.'

And so in the early morning light, Stephen drove Chloe back to Follies, then turned his car around and headed for the stone rectory where his wife and children were asleep.

For a week of evenings, Helen and her mother sat in their armchairs on either side of the gas fire in their small sitting room and struggled to keep one another cheerful.

Helen had been disturbed to see how thin her mother had become. Her plain tweed skirts hung loose from their waistbands, and her shoulders looked shrunken under her home-knitted cardigans. Her hair looked greyer, and when Helen hugged and kissed her goodnight, she felt her mother's bones knobbly under her skin.

'I'm perfectly all right,' her mother kept saying. 'We can manage. But it's lovely to have you here to talk to, darling.'

And Helen would nod, keeping her heaviness of heart to herself. She had discovered very quickly that it was easy to talk bravely about getting a job, much less easy actually to find one. An abandoned degree in English Literature from Oxford was a positive drawback. The supermarket managers and factory personnel officers eyed her with suspicion and chose someone else from dozens of applicants. Helen had never learned to type, and although she was sure she could learn the rudiments of bookkeeping quickly enough, there was no-one who was willing to give her the chance. She was beginning to despair of ever finding any work, however menial.

The ugliness of the offices she visited depressed her unreasonably, and her head throbbed from the neon lighting and cigarette smoke.

This is what life is like, she kept telling herself. Dad worked in places just like this, and so do millions and millions of other people. Your own existence up to now has been utterly unreal. But still she ached for the beauty and calm of Oxford. The peace of Addison's Walk, on the morning that she had shared it with Tom Hart, seemed to belong to another world.

She dared not think about Oliver.

At the end of a week's job-hunting, she was no nearer to becoming a wage-earner. Desperation was beginning to take hold, in spite of her continued promises to herself that so long as she kept trying something was sure to turn up. Then, late one afternoon, the telephone rang for her mother. After the call Mrs Brown came back into the kitchen where Helen was chopping the vegetables for a stew. Her daughter saw at once that her face was lit by a rare, real smile.

'That was Mr Leigh, the headmaster,' she said. 'There's a part-time permanent job from January, if I want it.'

'And do you?' They were smiling at each other, foolish with relief.

'I may just deign to accept it.'

Helen put down the knife and wrapped her arms around her mother's shoulders. Magically, the load was lifted. They would be able to cope after all. She felt a pang at her own failure, and a double sense of gratitude to her mother, but most strongly of all a thrill of pleasure at the thought of going back to Oxford.

Then she saw her mother frowning again, creases deepening between her eyes. 'But there won't be any salary until the end of January. That's two months. I could ask for an advance, I suppose, or try the bank again.'

Helen took her hands and rubbed them between her own.

'There's no need, Mum. I can help, this time. I've got money in the bank – seven hundred and fifty pounds. I'll write you a cheque for it tomorrow.'

'Where did you get so much money?'

Helen saw a different anxiety in her eyes, and for a second her carefully rehearsed explanation eluded her. Then it came rushing back and she was lying convincingly.

'The College. There's a special fund, a sort of charity, for students in difficulty and the money's a loan from that. I don't have to think of paying it back until I'm established in a proper job. It's almost a gift, really.' She was relieved to see that her mother was prepared to accept this story without question.

'I can't think of anyone who deserves their help more than you do,' she said, as proud of her daughter as ever.

Resolutely Helen squared her shoulders under the double weight of the lie and the knowledge of where the money had really come from, and why.

Their supper that evening was a more cheerful meal than any they had shared since before the terrible summer. Helen went down to the off-licence and bought a bottle of white wine. Her mother pursed her lips at the extravagance, then got pink and giggly after a single glass. She looked happier than she had done for months, proud of her ability to provide for the three of them after all. Helen glanced from her face to her brother's, round and solemn behind his glasses, and struggled against the lump in her throat.

Later, after she had cleared away the meal, Helen went upstairs and tapped at her brother's door.

'Graham? Can I come in?'

He was lying on his bed reading. Helen turned the book over to look at the title and saw that it was *Heart of Darkness*. The adult choice startled her, then she grinned at him.

'You're grown up, aren't you? I suppose I still think of you as being about eight, with pockets full of fruit gums.'

'Yes,' he said, not smiling. 'I'll be able to take care of Mum soon, not the other way round.'

'You don't have to worry about that yet,' Helen told him lightly. 'She's got me as well, you know.'

'Helen?'

116

'Mmmm?'

'Will you be going back to Oxford now? Now that Mum's got a job again?'

'Do you think I should?'

'Of course. But something's happened, hasn't it? Something important? You look different. Sad.'

It took Helen a moment to find an answer. 'It was important, yes. It isn't any more.'

Graham frowned, but he was old enough to see that she wouldn't answer any more questions. After a moment Helen ruffled his hair, as she had often done when he was a little boy, and went away. In her own room, she stared at her reflection in the small mirror and tried to see how it had changed. Graham's only thirteen, she thought. Is it so very obvious, even to him? For the first time since she had come home, she let herself think about Oliver and the sense of loss hit her like a blow.

It was going to take a long time to forget him.

Helen slipped back into Oxford after a week away.

From the train window, just as she had done at the beginning of term, she caught the brief glimpse of the distant spires. But this time, instead of glowing with reflected light, they were curtained with grey rain. Helen tried not to read significance into it, but it seemed an apt enough symbol. Compared with today the beginning of term lay brightly in her memory, promising everything.

It had brought Oliver, and a glimpse of happiness that she had never guessed at. But the light had faded, and the rain came to shroud the Oxford pinnacles.

The greyness was appropriate, she thought sadly. Oxford was still the same, and she was grateful to be coming back to the work she loved. But losing Oliver had extinguished the brilliance of the place for her. Extinguished it, she knew, except for a spark that refused to die. Her logical self told her that she should forget him, but she went on defiantly hoping that he might come back, and set everything alight again.

Helen tried half-heartedly to find somewhere else to live, but it was impossible at mid-term. And Follies drew her back, its square red bulk holding its own fascination as well as the promise and threat of meeting Oliver.

Even now, she longed to see him again.

117

Helen discovered that Rose had not re-let the little room at the top of the house, and so she took it over again. Then she threw herself with deliberate intensity into her work, vowing to make up for the time she had lost. For a few days she saw no-one but Chloe, who welcomed her back with real warmth. Then one morning she met Pansy in the shadowed gallery outside her room. Impulsively Pansy came running to her, put her arms around Helen and hugged her. Helen caught the scent of summer gardens again.

'I'm so glad you're back', Pansy told her. 'Helen . . .' her face was unusually serious, 'are we still friends?'

Helen stepped back and looked at Pansy's glowing face and tousled hair. She was wearing a very short flared skirt and layers of bright woollens, so that she looked like an ice-skater still flushed from frosty air and exercise. It was impossible not to respond to her. Helen had thought of asking, *Why should we need to be friends?* but instead she said very quietly, 'Of course.' She stifled the impulse to ask about Oliver, anything, just to know what he was doing and perhaps whether he ever mentioned her.

Pansy hugged her again and went away humming.

In the end, she asked Chloe. 'Have you seen him?'

Chloe frowned, concerned at Helen's hopeless eagerness.

'Them,' she corrected her. 'Don't think about him any more, Helen. They're always together.'

Pansy and Oliver.

Helen's grey eyes didn't flicker. 'I'm not. Not in that way, anyway. But I want to see him so that I can thank him for what he did. The money. To let him know that I know, and how much it matters. But I don't want it to be a big performance. I just need to meet him somewhere, casually.'

Chloe thought for a moment.

'Look, why don't you come on Sunday? There's a pre-production lunch party for the *As You Like It* people at Stephen Spurring's. You'll be able to see Oliver, and there will be hordes of other people as well, so it'll seem quite natural. Do come. I need some support too.'

Chloe had agreed to help backstage with Tom's production. At first it had seemed an easy way to see more of Stephen, and then she found herself enjoying the work for its own sake. She ran about willingly as the director's dogsbody and proved herself invaluable at handling all the tedious little tasks that no-one else wanted to take on. Part of her reward was to be caught up in the enthusiasm that Tom generated around him, the rest the chance to be near Stephen and to slip off afterwards with him for a drink, or even for a snatched hour in his rooms.

'Please come', she urged Helen again, and at last Helen nodded. It would not be the first party she had been to at the hospitable Spurrings,' nor the first time she had seen one of Stephen's girls covertly appraising his wife and home. The thought of Chloe in the role disturbed her, but she put it out of her head as far as she could. Loyally, she told herself that Chloe wouldn't do anything damaging or dangerous.

On Sunday morning Chloe and Helen drove away from Follies together in Chloe's smart little Renault.

They were very quiet, and not entirely at ease with each other. Helen was too preoccupied with rehearsing over and over what she wanted to say to Oliver to talk much. Chloe longed to talk about Stephen because she could think of almost nothing else. Since the first night in his rooms, he had taken possession of her. The more she glimpsed the inexorable pleasure in dominating her which lay behind the urbane exterior, the more she needed and wanted him to go on doing it. Her obsession with him grew and grew until she felt it threatening to explode inside her. As she drove out into the country she tried to find some way of talking about him that wouldn't sound too heavy-handed. But she couldn't think of a single one, and she sensed some of Helen's disapproval and disinclination to be involved in her affair.

In the end she said nothing, and concentrated instead on following Stephen's directions.

Soon they turned in through a pair of stone gateposts with stone eagles perched on them. There was a short, pot-holed drive between some oak trees and then they pulled up in front of a low, pleasant grey house. There were deep windows looking out over the lawn and the walls were laced over with the winter skeleton of a Virginia creeper. A child's red tricycle lay overturned on the paving in front of the open door. In the line of cars beside Stephen's mud-splashed Peugeot was the shooting brake that belonged to Tom and, at the end, the shiny nose of Oliver's Jaguar. Helen's eyes went to it at once and, as she walked towards the house at Chloe's side, she had to concentrate hard on keeping her breathing even and regular.

Chloe tapped on the stained glass panel in the front door, then they peered inside across the black and white tiled hall. Stephen was standing at the bottom of the stairs with his hand on the shiny mahogany newel-post. He was talking to the girls who were playing Celia and Audrey. Beatrice was beside him with a fair, fat child tugging at her hand.

They came across to meet their guests at once. Stephen kissed them both on the cheek. He had never greeted Helen so warmly before, and she hid a little smile at it.

Beatrice held up a big glass jug. 'Buck's Fizz?' she asked.

Although there were grey streaks in her dark cap of hair and a fan of fine wrinkles around her eyes, she looked younger than her husband. She was very slim, almost like a young girl, and her movements were quick and unthinking as she poured their drinks.

'Come and see the house. And the kids, if you like that sort of thing.' Stephen led Chloe away, and Beatrice seemed deliberately not to watch him go. Helen wondered how much she knew about her husband and whether she was speculating about the svelte girl beside him. There was no sign in Beatrice's calm face and the hand resting on her child's head was quite relaxed.

'How old's Sebastian now?' Helen asked, wanting to break the silence.

'Five. Getting quite civilised, really. Oh good, here's Tom.' She pushed the wings of hair back behind her ears like a schoolgirl.

Tom came across the hall. He was wearing a bright blue sweater, and a pale grey flannel shirt and trousers that were worlds away from his actors' uniform of faded denim. To Helen, he looked very elegant and assured. He smiled at Beatrice and held out his hands for the jug of Buck's Fizz.

'Let me do that.'

'Tom, will you? I've still got things to finish in the kitchen. No good asking Stephen.'

'Leave it to me.'

They like each other, Helen thought at once. Odd, really, when Stephen and Tom so obviously have no time at all for one another.

When Beatrice had gone, Tom poured another measure of Buck's Fizz into Helen's glass and smiled quickly at her.

'Good to see you back. Is everything okay at home?'

Helen nodded, not wanting to talk about it. It would be difficult enough to say what she had to say to Oliver.

'Where is everyone?' she asked conversationally, looking round the empty hall.

'Depends who you mean by everyone.' The underlying humorousness in Tom's face suddenly broke through and he laughed. 'Pansy and Oliver are outside, playing football with Stephen's kids and their friends. Want to come?'

'No, I don't think so.' Not yet, Helen thought. Not until after lunch, when I've got my courage up. Dutch courage, if necessary. 'I'm going to see if I can help Beatrice.'

Stephen's wife was in the sunny kitchen with a red and white striped apron wound round her waist. Helen sniffed appreciatively. There were warm, rich smells of garlic and roasting meat. Gratefully Beatrice handed over her knife and Helen sat down at the scrubbed pine table to prepare the ingredients for *salade frisée*. Beatrice stood over the bright red Aga, slightly flushed with its heat, stirring something in a heavy iron pan.

An organ fugue was rippling through the speakers mounted in the corners of the room and the sun was making bright squares between the rag rugs on the stone floor. How peaceful, Helen thought. There was even a ginger cat asleep in a rocking chair beside the Aga and a plain-faced clock ticking loudly on the wall. There were wellingtons beside the back door, creased Sunday newspapers piled on the battered sofa, needlework and children's paintings and seed catalogues stacked on the oak dresser.

How beautifully peaceful, Helen thought again, to live with your husband and children in an old stone house, cooking and gardening and inviting friends for Sunday lunches. From outside she could hear the shouts and occasional shrieks of laughter from the football players. I want to live like this, she thought. Then Beatrice, coming from the larder with a jar in her hand, stopped in front of the window. A shadow fell across her face. Except for Stephen, Helen remembered. There must be a hollowness inside all this domestic comfort. What kind of peace could there be, living with a man who did what Stephen did? She thought briefly of what Chloe had told her and then suppressed the memory. It was indecent, somehow, here in Beatrice's kitchen. She put down her knife and went to stand beside Beatrice at the window.

The kitchen faced over a wide expanse of rough lawn dotted

haphazardly with fruit trees. People were running across the grass, a black and white ball bouncing between them. A yellow retriever was barking frenziedly. Oliver burst out of the crowd and raced across to shoot at the two apple trees that stood for goalposts. He was a head taller than anyone else, and he stood out like a beacon. Pansy, muffled in scarves, was dancing up and down in the goalmouth, taunting him. Oliver kicked and she dived to the ball, rolling over and over with it in the wet grass. In front of them Joe Spurring leapt up and down yelling encouragement.

Helen glanced sideways at Beatrice, and then followed her gaze.

Stephen and Chloe were standing under the bare trees at the edge of the pitch. There was a careful distance between them, and it was that little space that gave them away. They looked too aware of being watched, too intent on the progress of the haphazard game.

Beatrice suddenly looked her age. Her mouth sagged and the creases deepened around her eyes. Helen wanted to lead her away, or to pull down the blinds and block out the sight of her husband with Chloe.

Then Beatrice shook herself imperceptibly. She turned to Helen and the youthfulness came back into her face. They saw Oliver running across the grass again and Beatrice waved. 'He's very beautiful, isn't he? Is he quite real?'

Helen was caught off her guard by the defencelessness of the moment which had just passed.

'Oh yes,' she said sadly, unthinkingly. 'He's real all right. Too real.'

Beatrice looked sharply at her and their eyes met with the beginning of sympathy. Gently Beatrice touched her sleeve, then they turned away from the window together.

'Let me fill your glass,' Beatrice said firmly, 'and we'll finish the bloody salads, then we can go and enjoy ourselves too.'

Helen was laying the long table in the dining room, when the footballers came bursting in. Their faces were pink from the cold air and they were laughing and pushing each other.

'Oliver, you were a demon. You should be a soccer blue.'

'Too proletarian. I'd have to wear an anorak and carry one of those bags with Adidas on the side.'

'Wonderful smells. I'm starving.'

'Mum, can I have wine?'

Helen put the last fork in its place. At last she had to look up. Her face felt hot and her chest tight with the strain.

Oliver was there, across the room.

When their eyes met, he grinned at her. Friendly, casual.

It was no good, Helen knew. Pansy was beside him, pink and silver like an exotic flower. Still Helen felt just as she had done on her first day with Oliver. She wanted to run across to him and bury her face in his warmth, feeling his arms come around her. She wanted to drag him away from everyone and keep him for herself.

How stupid, she thought bitterly. It was a mistake to have come here. Now she was trapped. She would have to sit and watch them together, listening to the grating conviviality around her. Waiting for the right moment to thank him for his generosity.

Suddenly Helen was possessed by the thought that it wasn't generosity at all. He had bought her off, or handed out a ridiculous tip to satisfy his conscience. She remembered the suggestion of shame in his face when they had met on Folly Bridge.

How horrible. She would give the money back. Then she remembered that she couldn't. It was all made over to her mother.

More people were crowding into the room now. Dully, Helen let herself be guided into a chair. Someone was filling her wineglass, dishes were being held out to her. Mechanically she spooned food that she didn't want on to her plate. Beatrice was sitting at one end of the table with Oliver and Tom on either side of her. Stephen sat at the other, directing the passing out of plates.

'Can I sit here?' someone asked. Stephen looked up to see Pansy slipping into the empty seat beside him. Chloe stopped short on her way towards it and immediately found herself another place between two admiring young men.

'Please do,' Stephen said. 'I've barely had a chance to talk to you yet.'

'Just what I thought.' Pansy's chameleon eyes were bright with satisfaction.

Conversation welled up around the table and the wine passed round and round. Helen ate almost nothing but she let her glass be filled again. It seemed to take the edge off the unhappiness of having to sit in her place and pretend to feel at home. She listened uncomprehendingly to the talk and jokes passing to and fro around her and tried not to look across at Oliver. If she had, she might have seen him watching Pansy and Stephen down the length of the table. He was drinking faster than anyone else and his blue eyes took on an ominous dull glow.

Tom raised one eyebrow at him across the table, but Oliver scowled back belligerently.

By the time Beatrice brought in the coffee, her elder children and their friends had all wandered off elsewhere, bored with adult company. Only Sebastian stayed and he had attached himself to Pansy. He was sitting on her knee, playing with her earrings and the points of her hair. Over his fair head, Pansy smiled at Stephen and went on talking. She was telling him funny stories about her father and his entourage of wives. Stephen looked amused and faintly impressed.

'Coffee, Oliver?' Beatrice asked gently.

He accepted a cup but left it untouched, reaching out instead for the brandy bottle that had appeared on the table. He looked all set to empty it himself, and his scowl deepened.

After a burst of laughter from Pansy and Stephen, he leant forward.

'Can't we all share the joke? Or are you going to monopolise each other for the rest of the day?'

'Shall we, Pansy? What do you think?' Stephen's voice was very smooth.

Pansy jumped up and went to Oliver, wrapping her arms around him from behind. 'Nolly, don't be such a bear. Are you getting pissed?'

'If I am, it's out of boredom.'

Tom put down his cup with a rattle of irritation. Beatrice stood up and began collecting empty plates. The silence was broken by Sebastian who ran after Pansy and pulled at her arm.

'Pansy, Pansy, come and play in my shop. Now.'

Pansy smiled around the table. 'He's so lovely I can't resist. Leave my share of the clearing up and I'll do it later.'

The atmosphere at the table had changed perceptibly. Oliver, leaning back in his chair, swirled the brandy in his glass defiantly.

'You leave it too, Bee,' Stephen said. 'You've done enough. Who'll give me a hand – Chloe?'

She pushed back her chair at once and went to take the tray from Beatrice.

'Of course. That was a wonderful lunch, Beatrice.'

'I'm glad you enjoyed it.'

In a moment Tom, Helen and Oliver were alone in the dining room.

'I can't stand that self-satisfied Romeo,' Oliver said irritably. 'Who does he think he is?'

'Your host, among other things.' Tom's voice was sharp. 'Why don't you knock off the bottle if it makes you so unpleasant?'

Oliver's flush deepened. 'Why don't you just get lost?'

Tom jammed his hands deep into his pockets as if to stop himself hitting out and left the room without a word.

After a long pause Oliver looked across at Helen as if he was surprised to see her. Then he let out a little snort of laughter.

'I know. Don't you say anything. Tell you what, come and have a walk. By the time we get back, everyone will have forgotten and I won't have to do a big apology scene.'

Helen's heart began to thump uncomfortably, but she kept her face expressionless. However badly he behaved, nothing seemed to affect his power over her.

They picked up their coats from where they were draped over the banisters and went out. A sharp wind was blowing and the sun was low in the grey-pink sky. A flock of rooks lifted noisily from the oak trees as they passed and flapped overhead.

'Warm enough?' Oliver asked. Helen nodded and they struck out down the lane away from the house. Oliver set a brisk pace, as if he wanted to put as much distance as possible between himself and the lunch party. After a moment he began to whistle, the same handful of notes over and over again.

Helen clenched her fists inside her pockets. She had barely spoken since they had left the table but there was a jumble of words inside her. She struggled with what she wanted to say. It was important to thank Oliver for his money, and to do it without letting her obstinate feelings for him distort anything.

In the end it was Oliver who spoke first.

'You're not angry are you? It'd be a shame to let it stop us liking each other.'

Liking you? I'm not sure about that, Helen thought, amongst all the other things I feel about you. I love you, and you do make me feel angry, and sometimes ashamed for you. Because of all that, I'm not sure if I do like you.

'No, not angry', she answered, keeping her face turned away and her eyes on her breath clouding in the cold air. 'Surprised. Relieved. And grateful, once I'd worked it out.'

'Grateful?' Oliver raised his eyebrows humorously. 'I suppose that's one way of looking at it. Lucky escape, and all that.'

'Not so much an escape. It just means that I can go on doing what I want to do in peace, without having to worry, and that means a lot to me. I came today because I wanted to say thank you.'

'Well, how very clear-sighted of you. I shall stop feeling guilty at once.'

For a hundred yards they walked on in silence. Something nagged at Helen, making her want to go on questioning him.

'Why did you do it?'

Oliver sighed impatiently. 'For God's sake, I hate post-mortems and heart-to-hearts about who did what and why. Can't we just leave things as they are?'

He's as embarrassed as I am, Helen realised, and subsided at once. She had said what she needed to, however awkwardly it had come out and however awkwardly it had been received. There was no point in pressing him.

Oliver resumed his whistling, then broke off and pointed across an open field. 'Look. We've set up a fox. Can you see him go?'

Helen followed his finger and saw a tall red-brown shape plunge into the shelter of a little copse.

'I've never seen one before,' she told him, and he laughed incredulously.

'You've never hunted?'

Now it was Helen's turn to laugh. 'Of course I've never hunted. Do I look the type?'

They had reached the top of a little hill and they looked back the way they had come. The chimneys of Stephen's house were just visible among the trees.

'Well, you're missing out on the second most exciting experience in life.' He grinned at her, then pulled her arm comfortably through his as they began the walk back. Helen's fingers tightened imperceptibly on his arm. She was barely listening to what he was saying, the effect of being close to him again was so potent.

'Hey, I've got an idea. What are you doing after Christmas? Come to Montcalm for a couple of days, help me face out the family party. You can follow the New Year meet, and there's the Hunt Ball at the house as well. Yes?'

Helen's first instinct was to say no, she couldn't possibly. She had only the vaguest idea of what Montcalm could be like, but she was sure it would be terrifying. Then a thrill of bemused excitement shot through her. He was asking her to stay with him. He wanted to see her. Illogical, irrepressible hope bubbled inside her.

She would go.

Helen swung round to face him and skipped a few steps backwards down the lane. 'Shall I? I will if you promise to brief me very carefully first so that I don't put every foot wrong. My experience of stately homes is limited to lining up between the red ropes.'

'Darling Helen, what can you be expecting? Footmen in powdered wigs and carriages at the door?'

She nodded so vigorously that the curls swung around her face. 'Oh yes, at the very least. And four-poster beds, and tweenies bringing up hot water in enamel jugs.'

'Too much television, my girl. So you'll come?'

'Yes.'

Oliver took her hand again and pulled her into a run. 'Wonderful,' he called over his shoulder. 'Pansy'll be there, of course, and Hart. You can make up the foursome.'

Helen almost stumbled and fell. She wished that the muddy lane would open up and swallow her.

How stupid. How absurd of her to have hoped for anything else.

Of course there was no point in hoping. Oliver wouldn't come back to her. She had amused him for a little while, perhaps just because she was naive and ignorant of his world. And now that was over, and he was held by his fascination with Pansy. Helen was just part of the scenery for him, another figure to populate his crowded landscape. For a moment dislike overcame her, together with contempt for his self-preoccupation and complacency. And yet that wasn't all of Oliver. He was much more complex than that.

Oliver ran faster and faster with Helen's hand still caught

firmly in his. Their heels rang on the metalled road and their breath clouded in the cold air. Helen felt a stab of pain in her chest and began to flag, but still Oliver drew her on.

Even caught up in her instant of dislike, her palm was glued to his. His electricity had never failed to arouse her, and she couldn't have let go his hand to save her life.

Then they were at the stone gateposts and under the arch of oak trees. As soon as Oliver saw the house he stopped, with Helen gasping beside him. 'Thanks,' he said, not looking at her. 'Come on. I'd better go in and make myself agreeable.'

He was just Oliver again, as full of faults as she had always suspected, and she still loved him because something within her always would. But loving him would no longer obliterate everything. Sometime, no matter how far off it was, she would belong to herself again.

Those of the party who remained were sitting around the fire in the drawing room. Teacups and newspapers were scattered comfortably between them.

Stephen, both hands moving expressively to make a point, was talking about the conflicts of love within the play.

Chloe sat a little apart, apparently engrossed in a newspaper.

Oliver went straight to Beatrice and kissed her on both cheeks.

'Sorry I was so rude,' he said penitently. 'Does it mean that you won't ever ask me again?'

'Of course not. It's a pleasure to see you all. We're always here, Stephen and I, and you must come whenever you like.'

Across the room, Chloe folded up her newspaper and put it down. Then she stretched, cat-like, and looked at her watch.

'If you're ready, Helen, I think I'd quite like to get back.'

It was the cue for the party to break up. People began saying their goodbyes.

Stephen and Beatrice stood side by side in the lighted doorway to wave. They were laughing and Beatrice had taken her husband's hand. Stephen hoisted Sebastian up on to his shoulders and the little boy flapped his hands excitedly. They were neatly framed by the dark shape of the house with its warm yellow windows.

Chloe spun the wheel sharply and her car shot forward, the headlights raking a long tunnel through the dusk to the gates. Only when they were past the stone eagles did she breathe out a single long breath. She had been gripped by a pang of jealousy so acute that she could think of nothing but getting away from the house. Everything in it spoke of Beatrice and Stephen's fifteen years together. Its walls were lined with pictures they had chosen, the worn, comfortable furniture had accumulated around them, and the rooms were full of the clamour of their children.

In her mind's eye Chloe saw Beatrice sitting calmly in the middle of it all, her dark head bent over her sewing.

Suddenly it seemed that she had everything Chloe wanted.

Even though Stephen's fingertips had touched hers as he guided her around the house, even though he had held her in his arms and murmured into her hair in the deserted kitchen, it meant nothing. He belonged to Beatrice.

Chloe thought of her own life without pleasure. Before it had been all self-indulgence, leading nowhere. Now, at Oxford, it was lonely and empty – except for Stephen.

And she wanted Stephen even more, now that his inaccessibility had been revealed. Suddenly he seemed more attractive than anyone else in the world, and more important.

Then there was Beatrice.

Chloe's fingers tightened on the wheel and she stared intently ahead into the darkness. Could she . . . would she take Stephen away from her? Like a little dark fish the thought flicked out, then darted back into the sea of her subconscious. Gratefully, Chloe let it go. There was no point in pursuing it now, she told herself easily.

Beside her, Helen sat immobile. Chloe put her own preoccupations aside for a moment.

'Did you say what you wanted to Oliver? You were gone a long time.'

'Yes. He said I was very clear-sighted, and he would stop feeling guilty at once. And he said he hated post-mortems. He didn't want to talk about it, either, I suppose.'

'Simple for him.'

Helen sighed. 'Then he asked me to stay at Montcalm, after Christmas.'

Chloe looked round, surprised. 'No, really? Helen, you've just got to go. Think of how grand it'll be.'

Helen smiled sadly. 'I'd rather not. Chloe, I'm such a fool. I thought he was asking just me. But it's to make up a party. With Tom . . . and Pansy.'

Chloe's face flooded with sympathy, and her hand closed over Helen's and squeezed it.

'I told you,' she said, trying not to make it sound too harsh, 'not to think about him any more like that. Don't hurt yourself.'

'I know.'

After a moment's silence Chloe said, 'So you won't go?'

Helen looked out at the hoardings and street lights of the city's outskirts.

'Oh yes,' she said, almost to herself. 'I've got to go. I can't stop myself. But I'll be okay. I think I understood something this afternoon. But for now, just to be near him is better than nothing. Can you understand that?'

Chloe's thoughts sped back over the afternoon. 'No,' she said softly, 'I don't think I can. I couldn't bear to stand meekly by and watch the man I wanted being possessed by someone else. But if you want to go, then go. Don't let anything stand in your way. You must do what you want in life, Helen. You yourself. Believe me, it's important.'

Helen was startled and faintly alarmed by the vehemence in Chloe's voice. She could find no satisfactory answer.

Silence separated them once again as the walls and towers of the city closed around them.

CHRISTMAS

CHAPTER SIX

Christmas that year was the saddest that Helen had ever spent. As always she and Graham decorated the tree on Christmas Eve, and then arranged the family presents beneath it. When they stood back to admire the effect, Helen saw too clearly that there were only three little piles. She slipped away to her room, but not before Graham had seen the tears in her eyes. That saddened her too, because she had been determined to stay cheerful. But there was a hollowness about the Christmas rituals that was impossible to varnish over. Too often the three of them found themselves sitting in silence, staring at the incongruously festive food and drink. At Christmas dinner only Graham wore the paper hat from his cracker and afterwards, instead of playing the word games which their father had enjoyed, they sat subdued in front of the mock-jollity of the television.

Helen had repeatedly put off the real decision about whether or not to go to Montcalm. She had thought that she could always invent an excuse at the last minute. But as the flat days after Christmas trickled by, she found herself thinking of it more often as an escape from the sad claustrophobia of home. Helen watched her mother carefully, and thought that she was beginning to recover. She was preparing eagerly for her new job, and some of the lines of tension had vanished from her face. Graham, more resilient, was busy with his own friends. But for Helen herself the house was too full of memories of her father, and it was empty now of anything of her own life.

It was with something like guilty relief that she looked up the train times for Montcalm, and then telephoned the number that Oliver had given her.

A suave male voice answered the phone and said, 'I will find his lordship for you, if you will be good enough to hold on.'

Helen made an awed face at herself in the mirror of the hallstand as she waited.

'Helen? You are coming, aren't you? It'll be an errand of mercy. This year's family party surpassed even last year's in awfulness.'

She smiled quickly at hearing his familiar drawl again.

'I'll be there. Can someone meet me off the train?'

'Sure thing. Looking forward to it.'

Helen packed her suitcase in a state of nervous anticipation. She had very few clothes so it wasn't difficult to decide what to put in, but she was afraid that nothing was appropriate for a Christmas house-party at Montcalm.

Twenty-four hours later she was stepping down from the stopping train at the little local station. At first sight the platform seemed empty except for a fat ticket-collector, then she saw a dark figure leaning against the wall of the tiny station house. The anticipation, which she had been trying to curb all the way from home, died in her at once when she saw that it was Tom Hart. He took his hands out of the pockets of his svelte cashmere coat and hugged her briefly before swinging her suitcase out of her reach.

'I'll take it. Welcome to Montcalm. Oliver's hunting, so he asked me to come and collect you.'

'Is Pansy here?'

'Not till this afternoon.'

A flicker of acknowledgement, half humorous and half rueful, passed between them.

Tom's car was out in the station yard. They drove along wintry lanes between black hawthorn bushes that gave occasional glimpses of frost-hardened fields. 'What's it like?' Helen asked.

Tom sketched a quick gesture with a ramrod back and an imperious hand. 'Very grand. Just wait and see. I've no idea what to call anyone, whether it's Oliver's old man or the under-butler. I just adopt the role of the bizarre American, so they're all agreeably surprised when I know what fork to use and don't drink the fingerbowls.'

'That's no help to me,' Helen groaned. Suddenly she felt acutely nervous.

All too soon they were driving beside the long wall that enclosed the park of the great house. Tom turned in at the gates that Helen remembered from her visit with Oliver. She saw that there was a shuttered wooden hut and a turnstile beside the lodge and Tom nodded towards it.

'Not open to the great public today.'

Ahead of them, strikingly defined on its low hill, was the house. To Helen, it seemed a threatening mass of windows, turrets and crenellations. It was an eighteenth-century monument to family pride, vast, assertive, and very slightly mad.

Tom seemed entirely at home. He spun his car sharply on the

gravel approach and shot through an arch into a square paved yard. As he backed into an empty garage Helen saw a fleet of other cars similarly housed. Amongst them was Oliver's black Jaguar.

Somewhere near here must be Jasper Thripp's domain, with his basket of squirming beagle pups and his tack-room full of lovingly polished saddles. 'An old ally of mine,' Oliver had called him. Helen's throat contracted as she remembered the day, and her stunned excitement at finding herself with Oliver.

Don't think about that any more, she warned herself. Don't think about it, or you won't be able to endure this visit.

'This way,' Tom said easily, then smiled at her. 'Don't look so frightened. It's all surface, you know. Doesn't make any difference underneath.'

They were walking along a stone-flagged corridor, frugally carpeted, with bare white walls. Servants' quarters again, Helen thought.

Finally Tom stopped at an open doorway and a rich Gloucestershire voice called out to them.

'You've never brought her in the back way, Mr Hart?'

'Quicker,' said Tom and beckoned Helen in to meet a broad, rosy woman in a flowered overall. 'Mrs Pugh's the housekeeper. Wouldn't you expect a Mrs Danvers figure, all black bombazine and massive key rings? You're wrong for the role you know, Mrs Pugh. Luckily Mr Maitland is more the thing, or our whole expectation would have been dashed.'

Mrs Pugh grinned like a girl.

'That's enough. Mr Maitland is the butler, dear, and he's one of the old school. He's been with the family since he was a boy, and his father before him, and he doesn't care to see standards dropping. But what can you do, with half the country traipsing through the house every other day?' She looked up at the clock on the mantelpiece. 'Now then, Mr Hart, don't keep us here talking again. The Countess is waiting to see you both for lunch, and Miss Brown will want to go upstairs first.'

After a regretful backward glance at the cosy clutter of the housekeeper's room, Helen followed Mrs Pugh through what seemed like a maze of corridors. At last a heavy door swung open and as they passed through Helen's fingertips brushed against the green baize.

It's really true, she thought in amusement, and then, do I belong on this side of the door?

The difference was obvious at once. The carpets here were thick and swallowed up their footsteps. The walls were hung with pictures, portraits and landscapes and sporting scenes all together, and there were carved oak chests and chairs with tapestry seats ranged like sentinels down the length of the lofty corridor.

The room that Mrs Pugh showed Helen into was high and awash with elegant pale shades of blue and pink. There was a little chaise longue upholstered in blue watered silk at the foot of the wide, heavy bed. Even Helen could see that the furniture was Chippendale, but it was well used, with none of the stiff formality of museum pieces. There was a faint but pervasive smell of lavender.

'Would you like me to send someone to unpack for you?' asked Mrs Pugh.

'No. No, thank you, really', said Helen, backing defensively towards her case. No tissue paper, she thought. No monograms, and no expensive labels either.

'Right you are. I've put you next door to your friend, the other young lady. You'll be wanting a good gossip, I expect.'

Helen thought fleetingly that Pansy would indeed be a welcome sight in this intimidating house.

'I expect Mr Hart will come and show you the way down for lunch. If you need anything, just ask me or Mr Maitland.'

When she was alone, Helen smoothed her clothes and combed out her black hair. She could think of nothing else to do to make herself ready so she wandered to and fro, touching the cotton wool and cologne laid out on the dressing table, feeling like an intruder in the dignified room.

On the table beside the bed *Vogue* and *Country Life* lay with a copy of the day's *Times* and a crystal glass and decanter. Helen picked up the newspaper and began to stare unseeingly at it. This is Oliver's home, she kept thinking. All this – those gates, and the house practically filling the horizon, the servants and pictures and beautiful things – this is ordinary life for him. How could I ever have imagined ...

Restlessly she stood up and went to stare out of the window. Parkland, landscaped in the grand style, rolled away from her. There was no other building to be seen. Just grass, and ancient trees, and in the foreground terraces dropping to the geometry of formal gardens.

She turned away in relief when she heard Tom at the door.

'Ready to come on parade?' he asked.

'Don't make me any more nervous than I am already,' she begged. 'Who's going to be there?' Helen noticed that he had toned down the slight eccentricity of his clothes for Montcalm. He was wearing a grey vicuña sweater now over a cream shirt, much more Princeton than Broadway.

'Oh, very much a family party,' he teased her. 'Just you, and me, and her ladyship. Everyone else has gone hunting. The really big meet of the year is held here, tomorrow, before the New Year's Eve ball. But I suppose they want to keep their eye in, or whatever it is you're supposed to do on horseback.' Tom had led them a different way from her room. Now he paused with his hand on her arm.

'Hold on to your hat,' he whispered, then steered her forward. 'Just look at this.'

Helen gasped.

They had come to the centre of the house.

Above them was the bell of a great dome, slotted with light from the windows beneath the cupola. Helen tilted back her head to look at the painting. There were billowing clouds edged with silver, blue-robed attendants lifting a canopy over a chariot and a massive golden figure poised with sun and moon in either hand. Fat, pink putti and garlands of flowers tumbled from the central group to the edges of the dome. It was magnificent; florid and fullblown and unforgettable. Underneath it even the huge gilt and crystal chandelier, the shallow sweep of the great staircase and the tall portraits in curlicued gilt frames seemed understated.

'I've been considering getting one done at home,' Tom murmured. 'What do you think?'

'Perhaps in the guest bathroom?' Helen giggled.

But awed in spite of themselves they were still gazing upwards when they came to the head of the stairs.

The hallway beneath echoed forbiddingly. The floor was tiled in an elaborate mosaic, and huge oriental jars stood guard on either side of closed double doors. At the main door a hooded porter's chair reminded Helen that a footman would have waited in this draughty space to see the last members of the household safely inside. Discreetly hidden beside the chair she saw a rank of little posts, and lengths of coiled red rope.

'Nobody really lives here,' Tom said, following her eyes. 'It's sad, in a way, isn't it? The wing we've just come from is the private one.'

'Oliver told me that they retreated there,' Helen remembered. 'Like survivors in a sinking ship.'

'Some ship,' he said quietly, 'but survivors must be right. How else could a single family keep going from strength to strength for so many hundreds of years?'

Helen looked up at the family portraits that lined the stairs. There, in one face or another, were Oliver's medieval-knight features. Hands, clasped on the pommel of a sword, or a bridle, were Oliver's too.

Helen's mouth set in a firm line.

'Come on,' she said. 'Take me to her ladyship before I lose my nerve completely.'

At the door of the countess's drawing room, there was an impressive figure in a black coat.

'Good morning, sir. Welcome to Montcalm, Miss Brown. Her ladyship will be pleased if you will join her.'

Helen saw that Tom's expression was unchanged, but she thought that the humorous lines at the side of his mouth had deepened.

Maitland showed them into the room.

The long, dove-grey drawing room was dotted with comfortable sofas. There were bowls of hothouse flowers on fragile inlaid tables and a great many photographs in silver frames. Most of them, Helen saw, were of horses and dogs. Over the fireplace was a fine painting of a horse that she suspected must be a Stubbs. The windows with their heavy swags of curtains looked out over the frosty park.

The Countess of Montcalm was sitting beside the fire with an open book on her lap. She was quietly dressed in grey country tweeds, but her face was immaculately made up. She had fair hair, greying now, pale blue eyes and a small, firm mouth. Helen thought that she looked like a rare china doll, the showpiece of some collection.

The countess looked sharply at her, then shook her hand so perfunctorily that their fingers barely touched. Helen recognised at once that their hostess was completely uninterested in her. It was, in a way, a relief. She subsided into a corner of one of the sofas and let Tom make the running.

'Shall I fix you another of my martinis, Lady Montcalm?'

'Definitely not, Tom. Do you know, I had to go and lie down after yesterday lunchtime? I'll have just the smallest sherry. Would you be an angel, to save bringing Maitland back again?'

She spoke with the upper-class inflection of the thirties debutante. Tom moved efficiently at the laden silver tray on one of the tables. As he handed Helen her drink, there was the faintest trace of a wink.

'I'm sorry we are such a small party,' Lady Montcalm said to Helen as they moved into the dining room. 'My elder son won't be back until tomorrow night, and Oliver insists on hunting at every opportunity.' She sighed faintly. 'But he's been so impossible this Christmas that it's a relief to see him doing something with enthusiasm.'

Tom's black eyebrows drew together in a frown.

After the formal little lunch, Tom and Helen gratefully put on their coats and escaped for a walk across the park. They set out at a diagonal from the house, the short grass crunching with half-melted ice beneath their feet. 'What did she mean', Helen asked at last, 'about Oliver being impossible?'

Tom stopped. They both turned round to look at the fantastic façade of Montcalm. Blank windows stared impenetrably back at them.

'I think he hates it,' Tom said. 'You know what Oliver's like. He's almost obsessive about being free to do what he likes. That's hardly possible here. He's expected to behave in a certain way by everyone from his old man to Maitland's underlings. As far as I can tell, he just about manages to contain his boredom and irritation by anaesthetising himself with whisky. And worse. The only time he smiles is when he's been snorting coke.'

They started walking again, by unspoken agreement making for a belt of trees that would take them out of sight of the house.

'I think that's why he's so insistent on you and me, and Pansy, being here. Friends from his own world only emphasise how stuck he is in it.'

Helen thought for a moment. 'He told me once that as he's the younger son he doesn't have to concern himself much with all this.'

The wave of her hand took it all in, the house and the park and the estate stretching as far as they could see.

'No,' Tom said slowly. 'Perhaps that's a pity. He's quite powerful, isn't he? With all his natural advantages he'd have made a good heir. I haven't met the older brother. But have you noticed, nearly all the photographs are of Oliver? Even though there's some dog or horse in the foreground as well?' Helen had noticed, and it had struck her as odd.

'So even though he's impossible, he's still the favourite?'

'I should guess so.'

'That must make it harder still for him', said Helen, very quietly.

They looked at each other for a moment, thinking about him.

'Yes.'

Tom shook his head, then took hold of Helen's arm. 'Let's go back. Maitland wheels in the most wonderful tea tray round about now. I do feel sorry for Oliver, but life isn't all bad around here.'

Lady Montcalm was back in her place beside the fire, but she had exchanged her book for *petit point*.

Maitland brought in the tea at once, and Tom cheerfully lifted the covers off the silver dishes to exclaim over the array of muffins and hot scones and rich fruit cake.

'I love tea. So civilised.'

As he spoke there was a sudden murmur of voices outside and the door opened. The first person to come in was Lord Montcalm. Not a big man, he held himself so straight and his head of fine silvery hair so erect that he looked inches taller than his real height. He was followed by two middle-aged men and then, a little behind, by Oliver. All four of them had taken off their boots but they still wore their white breeches, stocks and waistcoats.

Helen's gaze went to Oliver at once. He was flushed from fresh air and exercise, and his hair was tumbled after pulling off his riding hat. There was dried mud on his white breeches and his stock had come untied to leave his throat bare. He looked handsomer than ever. Helen felt her fingers clasped so tightly round the fragile cup that she was holding that she quickly put it down.

'Hello, Helen', he said, as if he had seen her that morning. 'Did you get here safely?' Then, casually, he bent to kiss the top of her head. 'Pansy's not here yet? I thought she would be.'

'How d'you do?' said Lord Montcalm, and his friends shook her hand too. Then they turned their attention at once to the tea tray.

'Tea, Oliver?' asked Lady Montcalm.

'No, thanks. I'm going to have scotch.' He poured a large measure into a tumbler and took a long swallow.

'Is that appropriate, at four in the afternoon?' His mother's voice was very cool.

'Appropriate at any time of day, as far as I am concerned.' Equally coolly, Oliver went across to one of the windows and held back the heavy curtains so that his view was unimpeded. The exhilaration of the day's sport had faded from his face, to be replaced with irritation.

But a moment later he said 'Here she is,' and there was so much enthusiasm in his face that they all looked round.

A curve of the main driveway was visible from the window and they saw the white Corniche drifting towards them.

Oliver was on his way out of the room at once. Helen and Tom put down their plates and followed him. Pansy, as always, would have a warm reception.

In the shadow of the great main doors, Masefield Warren's chauffeur walked round to open the door of the Rolls. Pansy was out of the car before he could reach it. She ran up the sweep of steps to meet them, then flung back her head to look up at the façade.

'Nolly, it's bigger than Buckingham Palace.'

'Considerably bigger, bloody mausoleum.'

Pansy was laughing and kissing them all.

'Masefield was so pleased that I was mixing in the right company at last that he sent me in his car. Will somebody look after Hobbs?'

'Of course,' Oliver said. 'Maitland will see to it.'

Helen breathed in Pansy's familiar summer-garden scent and felt the soft fur of her white coat brush her cheek as they kissed each other. Very deliberately, she made herself smile. They're made for each other, she repeated to herself. Maitland ... Hobbs ...

For a moment, Helen's smile was genuine.

It was obvious from the moment of her arrival that Pansy would be a big success at Montcalm. When she walked into the drawing room, she was met by the same little silence that greeted her everywhere. Then Lord Montcalm took both her hands in his and led her across to be introduced to her hostess. Lady Montcalm made room for her beside her on the sofa and Lord Montcalm's friends elbowed each other over the tea-things for the privilege of handing her her cup. Oliver's eyes followed her movements with a kind of bemused pride. And in Tom's face, just for an instant, there was a flash of pure jealousy that was replaced almost at once by his habitual air of ironic detachment.

Helen sat quietly in her corner, not minding being overlooked in this company where she felt unable to think of the right things to say.

Pansy was perfectly poised. She was telling them about her Christmas in Masefield's entourage at Gstaad. Even Lady Montcalm's china face split into a smile.

I don't envy her for what she's got, Helen thought. Not the Rolls, or the furs, or her lovely face. Or even Oliver, really, however much I still long for him myself. But I am jealous of her for what she is. She's so natural, and funny, and warm, that it's impossible not to like her. She just goes on being herself. She'd be just as much at home in our front room at home with Mum and Graham, and they'd like her just as much as these people do.

That's what makes me jealous of her. *Why can't I be like that?* What makes me sit here, stupid and silent and resentful?

Then Tom strolled over to her and took her cup out of her hand.

'You look kind of sour,' he murmured. 'Is anything wrong, apart from the obvious?'

Helen flushed uncomfortably.

'Nothing at all,' she told him with defiance.

For the rest of the day Helen felt more as if she was walking through a film of a country house party than real life.

The guests soon drifted away from the fireside to change for dinner. Helen, in her plain knitted dress, came down with Pansy who was wearing a black velvet St Laurent smoking jacket. She had brushed her silver-gilt hair flat to her head so that she looked like a wicked boy. The eyes of the three older men fastened on her greedily as soon as she walked in.

Oliver and Tom lounged on either side of the fire, utterly unlike in spite of the uniform of their dinner jackets. Tom was very dark and sleek and correct, while Oliver's black tie was askew and his blond hair remained uncombed. He was on his third whisky and his face was slightly reddened, but it was obvious that he was in a good humour. He kissed Pansy, and his hand slid down her velvet back. One of the middle-aged men cleared his throat very faintly.

At dinner Helen counted fewer people at table than servants to wait on them. Oliver kept signalling to Maitland to fill his glass. His father frowned at him and he stared challengingly back.

Without Pansy's sparkle, the conversation would have been hard work. Lord and Lady Montcalm were not animated talkers.

At the end of the meal, Lady Montcalm looked from Pansy to Helen and raised her eyebrows. Obediently they stood up and followed her. Before the door closed, Helen heard Lord Montcalm say, 'Care for a rubber, George? Which of you boys will make up a four?'

Oliver said sharply, 'I hate bridge. And Tom, like a sensible man, doesn't play. We're going to the billiard room.'

The door clicked shut and the women made their way back to the drawing room.

Lady Montcalm drank her coffee with an air of weariness and then stood up with a little sigh.

'Will you forgive me if I desert you both? It's our biggest day of the year tomorrow, with the Meet and the Ball in the evening. It means a very great deal of work, so I must allow myself the luxury of an early night.'

'Of course,' they murmured.

As soon as they were alone, they grinned at each other in relief. Pansy threw herself back against the cushions and waved her arms.

'Phooeee, talk about stiff. No wonder Nolly hates it, poor love. It was like having dinner in a fishtank, wasn't it? All those people standing against the wall with their hands folded, waiting for you to put down your fork.'

Helen laughed.

'D'you think they eat like that when there's just the two of them?'

'But of course. One has to keep going somehow, doing what's expected of one.' She had caught Lady Montcalm's vowels to perfection.

Oliver put his head round the door.

'All clear?' he said. 'Right. Off duty time.' He was carrying an empty glass and he picked up a brandy bottle from the drinks tray and swung it by the neck.

The billiard room was in darkness except for the long light over the smooth green cloth. It was warm, but it smelt of dust and disuse. Helen smiled to herself, imagining how the room must have been when it was full of over-fed Edwardian gentlemen, puffing on cigars and placing bets with each other.

She wandered down the length of the table, running her finger along the polished mahogany and thinking how pretty the rolling, clicking coloured balls looked against the green.

The billiard room felt a long way from the rest of the house, and so somehow safe.

Tom had taken off his jacket and was meditatively chalking his cue between shots. Oliver poured brandy and balanced his glass on the corner of the table.

'Do you play, Pansy?' He held out a cue.

Pansy slipped off her velvet jacket at once and took the cue from him. Frowning, she walked around the table and then her face cleared as she saw her shot. She leaned forward and her fingers expertly formed a bridge for the cue. The polished wood snaked to and fro once or twice as she measured the shot. Then *click,* the balls ricocheted and scattered. The pink rolled and plopped softly into a pocket.

'Not bad.' Oliver and Tom both nodded their approval.

'I play with my father sometimes. Kim won't, she thinks it's frightfully unfeminine. Anyway, she's no good.'

'Helen?' Oliver turned to her.

'I've no idea what to do.'

'Look. Like this.'

He guided her to the table and put the shiny cue into her hand. Then he lifted her arms into the position she had seen Pansy adopt so nonchalantly. His body bent over hers, heavy along the length of her back, and his hands closed over her own.

'Brace your left hand like this. Then look along the cue ...' His face was against her hair. Helen struggled with herself, trying to ignore the effect of his closeness. But it was an impossible effort to breathe evenly, and her fingers felt like melting wax.

'Relax,' he murmured, and for a moment the flood of memories threatened to engulf everything else.

Dazed, she drew back her arm and stabbed the cue at the nearest ball. It spun sideways and the cue leapt and then juddered against the green cloth.

Helen dropped it as though it was red hot.

At once Oliver straightened up. Helen had to clench her fists to stop herself reaching after him. She turned her head away and so didn't see him running his fingers over the baize. The other two leaned forward anxiously.

'Okay,' he said casually. 'No damage. But I think you'd make a better spectator. Here, have a drink.'

He might have been talking to one of the anonymous figures who had waited on them at the table. Unseeingly Helen took the tumbler from him. Humiliation welled up inside her. Silently she turned away and groped to a hard leather seat against the wall. At least it was dark beyond the table.

'Can you keep score?' someone was asking. She looked up at the complicated mahogany board with its heavy brass sliding markers.

'No.'

I wish I was at home, she thought helplessly. I can't ride, or play billiards, or even make the right sort of conversation. It was a mistake to come.

'I'll do it.' Tom stood over her and flicked the markers. His hand touched her shoulder, very gently, before he turned back to the game.

Helen drank some of the brandy. The spirit burned her throat, but it comforted her too and so she drank some more. In front of her, incomprehensible, the game went on.

She concentrated hard on not thinking, or not admitting Oliver to her mind at all. It was as if the central figure had been cut out of a canvas, leaving a background of unimportant detail and a gaping, tattered hole.

She had no idea how much later it was when the game finished and they dispersed.

At last Helen lay in the wide bed in the unfamiliar room. The deep silence was doubly oppressive because Pansy had not come back to her room next door. Helen twisted her head on the pillow, grateful that she had drunk enough of the brandy to blunt her consciousness a little. She shut out the reality of Montcalm, towering and stretching all round her. Instead she imagined herself going home. She made herself walk up the path to the front door, heard the exact sound of her key in the latch. There was the worn strip of rug protecting the hectically patterned carpet. It was three paces to the sitting room door, the high metal handle, then the door opening on to the three-piece suite, the photographs of her brother and herself in matching frames on the upright piano, and the *Radio Times* beside the china posy in the little china basket on the coffee table. Piece by familiar piece Helen took herself through the little house until at last she fell into an exhausted sleep.

The last day of the year was very bright and clear. There had been a hard frost overnight and the park was white rimed under a pale blue sky.

When Helen found her way down to breakfast she was aware at once of an atmosphere of excitement. Even Maitland's impassive face bore a tinge of animation. He was presiding at the sideboard over an array of silver chafing dishes, filled with the essentials of an English hunting breakfast. At the table, Lord Montcalm and his guests, as well as Oliver, were fuelling themselves for the day. Helen saw that there was kedgeree and kidneys beside the eggs and bacon but she shook her head at Maitland's enquiry. The brandy of the night before had given her a slight, dry headache.

Tom was sitting a little apart, reading a newspaper. Helen slid into the chair next to his and he nodded briefly, then went on reading.

There was no sign of Lady Montcalm. Pansy appeared when everyone else had almost finished. She had protested that she had never hunted and only rode occasionally but she looked perfectly the part now in jodhpurs and an immaculate black jacket. Lord Montcalm himself took her plate and chose her breakfast for her.

'Looking forward to the day, eh?' he said. 'Best kind of weather. I hope Thripp's got you mounted properly.'

Oliver looked up. 'She's taking Madam Butterfly.'

'Good, good.'

For once there was no sign of tension between father and son. Pansy sat down beside Oliver and they smiled at each other, the unmistakable intimate smile of recent lovers.

Helen stared down into her coffee, hating the corrosiveness of jealousy.

As soon as breakfast was over, everyone seemed to have a great deal to do. Helen aimlessly followed the bustle of people across the great hallway and under the dome. The low winter sun streamed through it, filling the space with misty light and gilding the voluptuous draperies and twining limbs of the painting. The main doors stood open and as she came level with them, Helen looked out at a sight that might almost have been another painting.

Against the winter-sharp landscape were horses, brown and white and chestnut, groomed until they shone. They wheeled and stamped with impatience, and when they snorted their breath plumed in front of them in the icy air. The riders were

146

straight-backed women with their hair caught up in nets under bowler hats, and men in flaring red coats against white breeches. Their black peaked caps were pulled down over florid English faces.

Between the legs of the horses were milling hounds, brown and white and black, tongues lolling, keen with anxiety to be off.

For a moment Helen stood and took it all in, then she let herself be drawn closer, out into the thin sunlight. The air was full of crisp greetings, the jingle of stirrups and the creak of leather.

The excitement was almost tangible now.

Between the horses, Maitland passed to and fro with a heavy tray, handing up silver stirrup cups.

Around the wing of the house that hid the stable block came Jasper Thripp. He was leading two huge hunters. Behind him came a second groom with another pair, and behind them came a lad with a sleek little brown mare. As they came up to the steps, the Montcalm party emerged.

Helen was watching quietly on one side and suddenly she saw the resemblance between Oliver and his father. They stood together looking out over their land and she became aware of the identical shapes of their skulls under the silver and blond hair, and the same set of their heads on their shoulders. Then they pulled on the black top hats and the fleeting likeness was gone.

Jasper Thripp cupped his hands together and Lord Montcalm heaved himself from them into the saddle. Oliver swung unaided into the saddle of his huge chestnut. Jasper turned to beam toothlessly at Pansy. She accepted the same cupped-hand support as she mounted her mare.

'Easy on her, miss,' the old groom said. Pansy gathered the reins in her hands, then leaned forward to stroke the horse's glossy neck and whisper encouragement. The mare pricked her ears forward, happy. expectant.

Lord Montcalm broke away from the mass of riders.

'Morning, Master.'

The Master of the Montcalm Foxhounds was an impossibly upright figure with a brick-red face and a silvery moustache.

'Morning, my lord.'

The stirrup cups had been replaced on Maitland's tray. The babble of talk died away and even the restless hounds were still for a moment.

147

Then Lord Montcalm nodded to the Master and the Master raised his hand to the huntsman. The huntsman lifted the silver horn that hung at his saddle and blew the insistent call. The notes shivered in the air and the hair prickled at the back of Helen's neck. Then the horn fell again, the huntsman wheeled away and the hounds streamed after him in couples. The Master and Lord Montcalm followed side by side. The hunt began to move off with the jingle of harness and the impatient clopping of hooves.

Helen caught sight of Oliver. The vivid pink of his coat made his face look pale, more like the marble knight again. His face was intent under the black peak and his eyes were very blue. As he passed her, he flashed her a single, brilliant smile.

Then he was swallowed up again into the mass of riders and the colours, scarlet and white and rich brown, fanned out in front of her into the grey-green landscape.

Tom was standing beside her, and she turned to him with the breath catching in her throat.

'It's beautiful, isn't it?'

His face was dark and almost foreign looking after so many pink English complexions. When he answered, he was at his most sardonic.

'Beautiful? Let's hope the fox sees it like that.'

Helen was stung, but she answered mildly. 'I don't care for that aspect of it either. But can't you appreciate it just as a spectacle?'

Tom stared after the riders. The rising clip-clop of hooves came sharply back to them on the clear air. There was no sign of Pansy on her little mare.

'Not really.' Then he shrugged dismissively and with an attempt at good humour said, 'You can keep the country. Too much grass. Give me billboards, cab drivers, newsvendors. Neon. I'm a city person.'

Helen saw that he too felt excluded from Pansy and Oliver's closeness, and she understood that he was as out of place here at Montcalm as she was herself. But because he was confident he could dismiss it, the whole impressive structure, as not of interest to him.

'I'm going to do some reading,' he called back over his shoulder as he went up the steps.

All day, Montcalm was a hive of activity. Men in green overalls were putting up lights, and armies of caterers were unloading from Harrods vans. A large Christmas tree was put up and decorated in the entrance hall under the dome.

Helen wandered through one pair of double doors from the hall and was rewarded with a vista of state rooms along the main façade of the house. Here, there was a dining room, hung with dark tapestries, where a man in a green apron was putting the polished silver candelabra out on the long table. Beyond that were formal rooms with brocade sofas, bow-fronted cabinets and rows of heavy pictures. At the end was the long salon that was to be the ballroom. Two men were at work on the floor with electric polishers, and there were musical instruments in cases in one of the corners. A girl in a smock was arranging spikes of holly, evergreens and glittering silver balls on tall stands.

Evidently the Montcalm Ball was to be a grand occasion.

Later Helen put on her coat and wellingtons and walked down the driveway to the lodge and the turnstile at the gates. Then she wandered for a long time along the high-hedged muddy lanes. The clear air was invigorating and restored some of her calm equilibrium. She even found it in herself to laugh a little at the way Montcalm obliterated her. But she wouldn't think about Oliver. The black hole still brooded in the middle of the canvas.

At the farthest point of her walk she was overtaken by a stream of mud-splashed cars, and then a string of children on ponies. When she rounded the next corner she saw cars and a knot of people at a gateway, and stopped with them to watch.

Across the skyline came a quick river of colour. The hounds were running and behind them was a flying column of horsemen, poised for a moment against the light before they plunged over the brow of the hill and down a long slope towards the watchers. A sharp gust of wind carried the confused thud of hooves on hard ground and suddenly a rising cadence from the silver horn. Helen shivered a little. Then the sound was wafted away again, the hounds veered and streamed out of sight in a fold of the hillside. In a moment the landscape was empty again.

Helen turned away and began to walk back to Montcalm.

She was lying in the bath when Pansy tapped on the door. Her face was glowing and her eyes shone.

'Good day?'

Pansy perched on the edge of the bath. 'Wonderful. It was wildly exciting. We had one marvellous gallop, right across

149

about fifteen fields. The hedges were huge, but Madam Butterfly sailed over them...'

'Pansy. You sound exactly like dinner last night.'

'But now I know why they all go on about it. Oliver was hugely reckless. He flung himself over everything as if he was daring anyone else to follow him. Hardly anyone did.' There was a note of amused surprise rather than affection in her voice. 'Oh dear. D'you think I'll turn into a hunting bore? I'd better go and put on something frilly and Kim-like at once, to counteract myself. What are you going to wear?'

Helen's face fell. She owned only one long dress. She had bought it a year before, to wear to a dance with her first lover, and at the time she had been perfectly satisfied with it. But this evening when she had shaken out the limp blue crepe folds she had seen at once that it wouldn't do. The fabric hung badly and had an unattractive sheen, and there was a pulled thread in the bodice. But she knew that she would have to wear it, and the prospect depressed her unreasonably.

Pansy, watching, picked up Helen's sponge and squeezed it absent-mindedly. 'Helen, it would be very boring of you to be prickly about this. But I brought two dresses with me, and I'm sure that subconsciously I put one in because I've always thought it would look better on you.' She dropped the sponge back into the bathwater. 'Look, I'll go and get it.'

When she came back she was carrying a mass of Zandra Rhodes silk chiffon. The dress was a dazzle of squiggles, pleats and drifting tatters, witty and clever in sharp greens and lemons like a child's paintbox. Helen knew that she wasn't going to be able to say no.

'Yes?' said Pansy.

'Yes.'

'Good girl. I'll be back later to check you out. Don't go down without me.'

Pansy was almost out of the room before she stopped, and without turning round said something else, in such a low voice that Helen had to strain to hear her. 'Do you mind very much about me and Oliver?'

In the silence that followed a tap dripped insistently.

'No,' Helen said. 'I mind about being jealous. I mind about missing him so much. And wishing pointlessly that he was mine. But I can see that it was never very likely that he would be mine, for more than a little while. So it wouldn't do any good to mind specifically about Oliver and you. I've tried not to, except right at the very beginning.'

Pansy was still looking away.

'You know, it isn't very important. It's nice, and I like him, but it doesn't mean much. But I've never had women friends before, not women like you, and Chloe. Proper people, not appendages to men. Do you see? I admire you both, especially you, and I don't want to cut myself off from you just because of Oliver.'

Helen had never heard Pansy say anything in such a serious voice.

'You admire me?' she repeated, nonplussed.

'Yes. Do you remember that day when you said goodbye to Oliver and me, outside Follies? You were so clear-cut, and definite. I thought you were being brave, too.'

Helen smiled a little. 'It didn't feel at all like that.'

'But that was how it seemed, and that's what matters. Helen, I'd like us to go on being friends. What's happened to us both with Oliver won't get in the way of that, will it?'

Helen could barely understand. Oliver had meant so much to her, and then Pansy had come along and scooped him away. Yet here she was dismissing him as casually as if he was a temporarily interesting acquaintance who would have lost his appeal by next week. Dismissing him in favour of Helen herself. She appreciated the irony of that, but a faint sick feeling of apprehension gripped her at the same time.

She was certain that Oliver didn't feel so casually about Pansy.

Mixed with the apprehensiveness was a twinge of guilt. She liked Pansy, but she had never begun to think of her as a friend. Helen looked up at the lovely face, uncharacteristically anxious now, and smiled as convincingly as she could.

'No. He won't get in the way,' she said.

She had never thought of Pansy as a friend but, in spite of the odd relationship they found themselves in, perhaps she could try.

Helen stepped into the Zandra Rhodes dress. The chiffon slid erotically over her bare skin and as she turned to Pansy the dipping points of fabric drifted behind her.

Pansy whistled. '*Tu es ravissante.*'

Helen had let Pansy make up her face and do her hair. Her black curls were caught up on one side of her head and fell on

151

the other in a shiny mass. Pansy had shadowed the huge grey eyes to make them look even bigger, and added colour to Helen's cheeks and mouth.

It was a deft transformation.

Helen was a glowing, gipsyish figure without a trace of the sadness that had marked her for so long.

'How do you feel?'

Helen spun round again to make the chiffon float.

'Extrovert.'

'Quick.' Pansy smoothed the blue moiré silk ruffles of her own dress and caught up the billowing skirt. 'Let's get you downstairs before the mood evaporates.'

Lord and Lady Montcalm were giving a big dinner party before the Ball. Most of the guests were assembled in front of the fire in Lady Montcalm's drawing room. When she came in with Pansy, Helen faltered. There were too many unknown faces, men in white ties and black tailcoats and women with heavily powdered faces and old-fashioned jewellery.

Then she felt Pansy drawing her forward, and saw that not all the eyes were fixed on Pansy. Some were on Helen, and there was admiration in them too. Helen lifted her chin and sailed forward. The first person to greet her was Oliver, who bent over her and murmured, 'What a surprising girl you are.'

His eyes had the unnatural glitter that she had seen before, and he was smiling a shade too brightly. Helen knew that he had been fortifying himself for the evening.

Instinctively she looked to Tom, and his tiny frown was a warning before he kissed her.

'You look beautiful,' he said, with his mouth against her hair.

'Is he all right?' Helen asked in a low voice. Tom made a quick, dismissive gesture.

'So far. He can take care of himself this evening. I'm tired of being a buffer between Oliver and life. I've been doing it for a week. I want to enjoy myself tonight. You should stop thinking, just for a few hours, and do the same.'

His dark eyes held hers for a moment. There was a question in them, but she had no idea what answer was expected of her.

She smiled at him. 'I shall. Watch me.'

Helen felt suddenly buoyant, free of a black cloud that had hung about her for months. It was New Year's Eve. The end of a dark year, bringing the hope of a better one to come.

Montcalm's state dining room was a blaze of candlelight. Points of light darted from Lady Montcalm's diamonds. At the head of the table, Lord Montcalm had a duchess at his right hand.

Helen had been placed between one of the red-faced military gentlemen, and a young man with straw-coloured hair and very big ears.

'What do you do?' he asked her as soon as Maitland had eased their chairs forward.

'I'm at Oxford.'

'Oh God,' the young man groaned, blushing to the tips of his ears. 'You can't possibly be clever as well as beautiful. What am I to say to you?'

Helen was enjoying herself. 'Well, what would you say to anyone else?'

'I'd ask – were you out today?'

'Yes, it was beautiful. I had a lovely walk, right across to . . .'

The young man stared. 'I meant out. Hunting.'

'Oh, that.' They both dissolved into laughter.

This is perfectly all right, Helen thought. Here I am, sitting in the midst of the diamonds and the duchesses. Perhaps I can deal with Montcalm quite well after all.

Across the table, she saw Oliver draining his wine at a single gulp. He looked drunk, she thought, and just a little dangerous. Determinedly, she looked away again. Tom was right. It was time to enjoy herself for a few hours.

'May I have the first dance?'

She smiled back at her dinner companion. 'Of course.'

Guests were already crowding in through the great doors and the space under the dome echoed with laughter and music. Lord and Lady Montcalm with the Master and his wife stood under the glittering tree to welcome the arrivals. The long driveway was a string of lights as the cars rolled up.

Helen's partner took her arm and led her through to the ballroom. The band was playing but although the empty, shining floor beckoned, no-one was dancing. Then, through the groups of guests came Oliver. Helen followed his blond head with her eyes. Pansy's hand was in his but Helen sensed that she was holding back a little. Oliver was not to be deflected. In the middle of the floor he stopped and made a mocking little half-bow, not to Pansy but to everyone else. There was something uncoordinated about his movements that told Helen he was drunker than he looked.

Every face in the room turned to them. Pansy, as pretty as a flower in her blue ruffles, looked apprehensive.

Then Oliver raised a hand to the bandleader. The music faltered to a stop and there was a surprised moment of suspense before he lifted his hand again. The bandleader raised his baton, obedient as a clockwork toy, and a waltz began to ripple over the sudden quiet.

Oliver took Pansy in his arms and flung her in a wide, flamboyant circle. Then Helen saw him stumble on one of the cascading blue ruffles. For a split second he swayed and she felt a stab of fear.

Don't, Oliver. Whatever it is you're trying to do, don't do it here with all these eyes on you.

Oliver recovered himself almost at once and smiled. Perhaps only Helen saw that it was, again, too brightly. Then they were moving, waltzing over the wide floor in curving arcs, almost a blur of black and blue and gold. They danced beautifully, instinctively, as if they were one body.

A voice somewhere behind Helen said, 'They make a beautiful couple.'

The music swelled and couples began to flood on to the floor. Laughter and talk broke out again.

But for Helen there might have been no-one there but Oliver and Pansy, waltzing, and herself. She was transfixed by a sudden sadness, brought by the certainty that she must let him go. The Oliver that she had created in her mind drifted away. All that was left was the beautiful, faintly desperate man now holding Pansy in his arms. He was nothing to do with Helen, she understood that at last. Perhaps the other, hidden Oliver that she had glimpsed and fallen in love with was no more than a reflection of the tension within him. And for all the gilded exterior she knew that something was wrong, badly wrong. Helen could only guess at what it was, but as she watched him dancing her sadness for him was mingled with fear.

'Come and have some champagne. I can't do this sort of dancing, but there's a disco somewhere.'

Her pleasant, dull partner looked imploringly at her. Very slowly, Helen turned her back on the bright blond head and the classic perfection of the face that had filled her dreams for so long.

It was time.

As they left the ballroom the gaping edges of the canvas in Helen's head began to knit together. The landscape that was revealed was flat and unremarkable, but at least it was whole.

Champagne, Helen thought. Why not? Froth and sparkle to drown the last few hours of a year she was glad to be leaving. Perhaps next year would be like life had always been before, calm and monotonous.

The discotheque, in sharp contrast to the ballroom, was hot, noisy and almost dark. Helen surrendered herself to the music and the tide of champagne. The faces here were much younger, some of them were familiar. Different people kept asking her to dance, and she was happily drawn deeper and deeper into the party. The chiffon points of her dress floated as she danced.

It's easy, she thought. *There's nothing to be afraid of.*

At eleven o'clock one of the procession of pleasant and flatteringly attentive young men took her to the supper room. The little round tables were candlelit and crowded with laughing faces. Maitland and Mrs Pugh were in charge at the long buffet and Maitland himself prepared her plate for her with the greatest care.

At the table her partner led her to, Helen saw Flora and Fiona.

They made room for her at once. 'Hel-lo', Flora said. 'You look knockout.'

It's easy, Helen thought again, and drank another glass of champagne.

Candlelight blurred the faces, making them look warm and friendly. Helen began to feel a little as if she was floating somewhere outside the old, awkward Helen who had felt so out of place at Montcalm.

She was laughing, leaning forward to catch the end of a lengthy joke, when she heard some confused shouting, pounding feet and then the shiver and smash of breaking glass. There were a few ironic cheers in the supper room but no-one looked round. Then Helen saw Tom slipping past and the laughter faded in her. She murmured a brief excuse into the air and followed him.

Outside was a milling hubbub of people, nearly all men, some of them still laughing uproariously while others looked faintly shamefaced. The floor was covered with broken glass and dark with spilt wine. Then the crowd shifted a little and she stared downwards. At once the ugly little tableau burned itself unforgettably into her head.

Oliver was lying in an awkward heap with the smooth stuff of his tailcoat twisted round him. His face was white with red patches on the cheekbones and he was breathing noisily through his mouth.

Tom was kneeling over him, and the sharpness of his dark, intelligent face made the grinning heads around him look bloated and coarse.

Tom loosened Oliver's white tie and turned his head to one side. Then he looked up at Helen.

'Will you ask Maitland to come out and help me with him?' he asked quietly. Helen whirled round but Maitland was already beside her with a white-jacketed waiter.

'Leave it to us, please, sir', he said calmly to Tom. They bent down and took Oliver's arms, then hoisted him between them. Oliver's head rolled and he murmured something thickly. As they half-carried, half-dragged him away his feet tangled and bumped as if he was a huge doll.

Helen looked away, full of humiliation for Oliver.

Someone in the crowd brayed with laughter.

'Whoops, there goes Mortimore again. Poor bugger's getting past it.'

Guffaws broke out all round and the crowd jostled restlessly, uncertain of where to turn next.

'What are we waiting for?' someone else said. 'The lake.'

They crunched over the broken glass and pounded away like clumsy dogs.

Helen became aware of curious faces peering out of the supper room.

Tom straightened up. He looked tired. 'Come on,' he said, very quietly, and led her away.

They crossed the mosaic floor of the hall in silence and wound up the shallow curves of the great staircase. In the gallery above they found a semicircular niche with a little padded seat between two marble busts.

For a moment they sat and stared at the light welling up from below. Helen could just see the silver star on top of the Christmas tree.

'What happened?' she asked at length.

'I didn't follow the course of his evening,' Tom answered grimly. 'Mostly because I was dancing with Pansy.' His voice softened at her name and Helen looked away. 'But I can guess. Booze, plus whatever cocktail of pills and dope he fancied. Then

156

I suppose he passed out. Quite inconspicuously, really. Only about five hundred people saw him. Christ, what a fool.'

'What was he doing with all those horrible, crass people?'

Tom laughed humourlessly. 'They're upper-class hooligans. I've seen him with them before. It amuses him in some perverse way, egging them on to run riot and break the place up. Doing it in his own home is just the latest development, I guess.'

Helen felt the last vestiges of champagne elation ebbing away. She remembered the crumpled guy of Oliver, and the feet bumping as he was taken away and fear stabbed at her again. Poor Oliver. Tom had been dancing with Pansy, and she had been basking in the glow of strangers' attention, while Oliver was filling himself with whatever lethal concoction it was that had left him in a pathetic bundle outside the supper room door.

If he had asked the three of them here to save him from himself, they had made a poor job of it.

Sorrow and foreboding crawled icily under her skin. She shivered a little and the folds of her dress whispered around her. In the shadows Tom's brooding profile shifted and he shrugged, as if to dismiss his own uncomfortable thoughts.

Then, to her surprise, he took her hand and began to trace the shape of her fingers with his own.

'Helen. Mysterious Helen,' he said in a lighter, teasing voice that startled her. She realised that Tom had been drinking too. Now that the crisis was over there was no need for him to stay sober any more, and she thought he was retreating gratefully behind a screen of tipsiness. Just the opposite of me, she thought, and remembered with fleeting regret her elated mood of the early evening.

'Helen?' Tom said again.

'What?' she asked, stupidly. Her voice was shaky and as she shivered again the folds of her dress rustled between them. Suddenly she became acutely conscious of his hand still holding her own.

'This,' he answered and bent his head quickly over hers. He kissed her once, lightly, then pulled her close to him. Then he was kissing her again, forcing her head back so that the breath caught in her throat and surprise lapped through her. His fingers felt like iron on her bare arms and for a moment she could have let herself fall against him.

After the shock of his kiss came bewilderment, and then

157

anger. 'Don't,' she said sharply, and pulled away from his hands.

Tom raised one eyebrow and his mocking smile came back.

'Whyever not? Don't be so Victorian.'

'It's not that.'

A half-thought, like a fish moving in deep water, stirred briefly within Helen. Even in that instant the implications of it made her giddy. The idea was so extraordinary and so dangerous that even before it was wholly acknowledged her mind was struggling to suppress it.

'What, then?'

She couldn't look at Tom. She stared up into the voluptuous curves of the dome, and her thoughts were racing.

Oliver, her inner voice said, and then she remembered. Oliver was gone, changed into someone different who no longer belonged to her at all. It wasn't Oliver whose kiss still stung her mouth.

Out of the whirlpool of emotions Helen seized desperately on one. Anger came back to her. Of course, that's what was happening. Tom couldn't have Pansy and so he was making do with herself. She fanned her anger deliberately. Tom was amusing himself. He was tight, and making a casual pass at her. Not only that, he was choosing the worst time.

She had taken him for a friend, and after all he had mistaken her.

The strange giddiness was no more than shock, and disappointment, and too much champagne.

The dark, threatening idea slipped away back into her subconscious.

'What then?' Tom persisted. He hadn't taken his eyes from her profile, as if he was seeing it for the first time.

At last Helen said, 'I don't want to be a substitute for Pansy. If you can't have her because of Oliver, then you'll make do with me, just for this evening. That's it, isn't it?'

His anger suddenly matched hers. 'No, it isn't. Don't be a fool.'

Helen drew away from him and wrapped her arms protectively around herself. After a long moment Tom stood up and stared down at her.

'Helen, you're too clever for this. You can't go on for ever selling yourself short as a dull little mouse that nobody wants. It gets boring, and it's not the truth.'

He put out his hands to pull her to her feet and closer to him.

'I want you.'

Helen believed herself certain of her ground now. He was patronising her, and she let his words sting her.

'That's too bad. Perhaps I don't want you. What right have you got to think you know who I am, or what I need? You, Pansy, Oliver – none of you knows anything about the real world. Or about me.'

Tom looked down at the sudden colour in Helen's face, the hard set of her mobile mouth and the furious light in her eyes. At once she seemed much more important than a way to forget Oliver unconscious on the floor. Involuntarily he put his arms round her again and tried to turn her face up to his.

Helen reached back with her free hand and slapped him as hard as she could. Tom lurched back a step, hand to his face.

'Don't ever touch me again,' Helen whispered. Then she turned and walked away, along the gallery and down the stairs with the greens and lemons of her dress floating around her like a summer morning.

Tom's fingers smoothed the red patch on his face. 'Bitch,' he murmured under his breath. Then he thought of pliant, flowery Pansy in her blue ruffles, and after Helen's dark fury, the beautiful face in his mind's eye looked dim and vacuous.

As soon as Helen knew that she was out of Tom's sight, she almost broke into a run. The hall was crowded with people, talking and laughing and gathering round the Christmas tree ready for the stroke of midnight. Blindly she pushed through them, wishing she had turned the other way for the sanctuary of her room.

She was shocked by the violence of her reaction to Tom. He had seemed an ally. Yet a few moments had changed that irreparably. As she forced her way through the revellers Helen had a vertiginous sense of everything peeling away, running out like the last moments of the year, and leaving her standing alone.

Unthinkingly, she was following the route that she had taken with Oliver and Pansy last night. Now she found herself standing in front of the billiard room door. The solid panels offered a secure retreat. She had pushed the door open and closed it behind her before she saw that the room wasn't empty. Someone was sitting on the corner of the table, turning a billiard cue to and fro in his fingers. With the room lit only by the long light behind him, it was impossible to see his face. She groped again for the handle but he called after her.

'You don't have to run away.'

When she looked back he had moved, and she could see him clearly. He had a homely, rubbery face and colourless hair that fell untidily over his forehead. She guessed that he was about thirty. From the weathered but capable hands wrapped round the cue, she thought he might be a farmer, or perhaps a vet. When he smiled, his unmemorable face lit up with quiet good humour.

'Good,' Helen said. 'I can't think of anywhere else to run to.'

The man made room for her on the corner of the billiard table and she swung herself up to sit beside him. He looked at his watch.

'A minute to twelve. If I'd brought some glasses and a bottle of champagne we could have toasted each other.'

'But you didn't...'

'So we can't.'

They broke into laughter. The seconds ticked by and then they heard the long, sonorous strokes of a clock chiming midnight. At once there was a gale of clapping and cheering and then the raucous singing of 'Auld Lang Syne'.

The stranger smiled again at Helen.

'Happy New Year', he said, and she answered, 'Happy New Year.'

Surprisingly, in the dusty remoteness of the billiard room, the rest of the evening was forgotten. She felt quite calm, and perfectly happy.

'My name's Darcy,' he told her.

'Helen.' They shook hands on it, formally, but still smiling at each other.

'Who were you running away from?'

Helen reflected for a moment. 'Myself, mostly.' To deflect him, she asked, 'Are you hiding in here?'

'Not exactly. I don't like parties, that's all. I suppose you don't play billiards, do you?'

Helen winced as she remembered the night before.

'No.'

'Shall I show you?'

'No. I might tear the cloth.'

Darcy frowned, then said vaguely, 'Oh, I shouldn't worry

about that.' At once another idea occurred to him. 'Look, now we know each other, would you like to dance?'

Helen peered around, bewildered. 'Here?'

'Well, no. I meant in the ballroom. We needn't talk to anyone else.'

Helen was laughing again, surprised by the agreeable bizarreness of their encounter. After a moment of looking puzzled, Darcy laughed with her.

Then they left the billiard room and slipped through the crowded rooms to the ballroom. The party was at its height and the floor was packed with dancers. In an inconspicuous corner Darcy held out his arms and Helen came into them. She saw that his face was serious, concentrating as he danced. He did it well enough, but with none of the instinctive fluidity that she had glimpsed in Oliver at the beginning of the evening. But their movements suited each other and Helen let the music carry her, closing her eyes on the crowded room. They drifted unthinkingly from dance to dance. Sometimes, with his cheek against her hair, Darcy would say something inconsequential about the band or the dancers around them. Helen would answer equally inconsequentially and then they settled back into comfortable silence again.

She was amazed when, with a final flourish, the band stopped playing. There was a patter of applause and Helen looked around her. The floor was almost empty and the musicians were putting their instruments away. She turned Darcy's wrist to look at his watch. There were fine bleached hairs on the back of his hand, she noticed, and darker ones at his wrist.

'Ten to three.' She became aware of his hand in hers and dropped it at once.

'I enjoyed that,' he said seriously.

'Me too.' Helen stretched a little and realised at once that she was exhausted. Then she remembered Oliver, and Tom. 'I should go to bed now,' she said sadly.

'May I see you home?'

'Thank you, but I'm staying in the house.'

Darcy looked mildly surprised. Then he said, 'In that case, I'll walk you to the stairs.'

At the foot of the great sweeping curve, he paused and looked upwards for a second.

'Goodnight,' he said softly. 'Thank you. You made an impossible evening enjoyable.'

'I'm glad', Helen told him, 'because you did the same for me.'

She turned and began to climb up the marble steps. If she had hoped that he might want to know more about her, perhaps ask to see her again, then she was disappointed. When she glanced back, Darcy was walking slowly away across the mosaic floor.

Helen came down late to her last breakfast at Montcalm. She had a blurred impression that the room was full of people, house guests staying over from last night, she supposed. The first face that she saw clearly was Oliver's. He stood up when he saw her. He was pale and the bright blue eyes were bloodshot but otherwise he looked none the worse.

'Apparently I was really bloody last night,' he greeted her, his smile as irresistible as ever. 'Not that I remember anything about it. Should I be apologising to you for anything?'

'Not a thing,' she said uncertainly.

His smile broadened. 'Well, thank God there's somebody I didn't insult. Come and sit by me. No-one else will speak to me. Hart has cut me dead.'

Helen looked and saw Tom at the end of the table. He was wearing a very bright blue shirt and a narrow scarlet tie. Theatrical again, Helen thought. He must be leaving Montcalm too. Their eyes met for a second and then slid past each other. Helen felt a little, uncomfortable stab of self-dislike.

Oliver settled her beside him and poured her coffee from the ornate silver pot.

'Eggs? Bacon?'

'No, thank you. Just...' Helen looked up and her voice faltered. Sitting immediately opposite her was Darcy. He was wearing an old, darned pullover and a frayed shirt open at the neck.

'Hello,' he said.

Oliver looked from one to the other.

'D'you know my brother?'

Oliver's brother? The realisation took her breath away. Darcy? The quiet, solid man who had helped her to enjoy last night in the face of everything else was no local farmer or hardworking vet.

He was Viscount Darcy. That was his title, not his Christian name. And this great house was his home even more than it was Oliver's. Helen looked back at the pleasant face with new eyes. Now there was something in the set of the features, the play of expression, that reminded her of Oliver. There was none of the clear-cut beauty that had mesmerised her for so long, but nonetheless she saw that they were alike.

Perhaps, she thought, that's even why I warmed to him so quickly. He was already familiar.

'Last night ... I didn't know you were Oliver's brother.'

'I guessed not,' Darcy said equably.

'Why didn't you tell me?'

'Was it important?'

Helen felt a slow, hot flush spreading across her face. Oliver's faintly raised eyebrows made her collect herself and summon up a smile.

'Not at all.'

As soon as breakfast was over, Helen went back to her room and hurriedly packed her belongings. She wanted to leave Montcalm now, and go back to the unconfusing tranquillity of Oxford.

Just as she was finishing, Pansy came in. Hobbs was coming to collect her to take her to London, and she had insisted that she could perfectly well make the little detour necessary to drop Helen off in Oxford.

'Enjoy the Ball?' Pansy asked.

'Yes, in the end. I met Oliver's brother.'

Pansy brushed the fine hair back from her forehead in a weary gesture. 'My head. Did you? It seems a pity, really.'

'What?'

'Well, that they weren't born the other way round. He's not exactly a match for Oliver, is he?'

Helen chose not to pursue that.

'Did you have a good time?'

Pansy shrugged. 'Oliver set out to be impossible, and duly was. But there were other people who weren't just country hearties, and it was nice to be with Tom.'

'Yes,' Helen said a little shortly. 'I'm sure.'

Friends, she thought grimly, we hardly seem to speak the same language.

Pansy was going. 'Hobbs is already here. I'm ready to leave when you are.'

Their bags were carried down and stowed in the white Rolls. Hobbs was standing at the door in his peaked cap.

Helen was amused by the finely-gauged difference in the farewells which Lord and Lady Montcalm gave to herself and Pansy. Helen was dismissed with the briefest handshake and the

163

suggestion of a smile. For Pansy there was almost an embrace, and a cordial invitation to come and stay again. She winked at Helen from the cover of the door.

Oliver and Tom were standing on the steps. Oliver wrapped his arms round Pansy and rubbed his cheek against her hair.

'Forgiven?' he murmured. Pansy looked faintly impatient.

'Sure thing.'

He kissed her and she smiled at him, but Helen had the impression that her mind was somewhere else.

Helen turned to Tom. She wanted to murmur 'sorry,' but he was watching Pansy too. In the end, when he did look at her, she simply said 'Goodbye,' surprised at the coolness in her voice. Their eyes didn't meet.

Hobbs was holding the door open and Helen was almost into the car when Darcy ran down the steps. His hand touched her arm.

'Where do you live?' he asked abruptly. Helen paused, half in and half out of the Rolls. Darcy's homely, stolid face was almost eager. Behind him she could see Tom, imperviously ironic, and Oliver's amused stare.

Deliberately, she said, 'At Follies House. Beside the river in Oxford.'

He nodded. 'Yes. I know it. I'll ... come and see you.'

Helen ducked into the car and the door closed.

In a moment they were whispering down the drive. Helen glanced back at the towering house and the little group on the steps. Then she sank back into the padded upholstery and suppressed a sudden giggle by staring hard at the back of Hobbs's neck.

Follies, she thought. Follies dragged me into all this, and here I am.

The car turned out of the gates by the lodge and Helen saw a man in an overall taking the shutters down from the hut beside the turnstile.

Then Montcalm was out of sight and they were on the Oxford road.

HILARY TERM

CHAPTER SEVEN

Chloe tapped her fingers absently on her sheaf of notes. She tensed her neck muscles to stop herself looking round again to where the EXIT sign glowed over the curtained door.

Stephen was late. He had promised to be at this rehearsal and she had rushed to the theatre, too early, in her eagerness to see him. Chloe knew that she was coming to need Stephen more and more, and the knowledge disturbed her. Shrewdly, she hid her need from Stephen himself. When she was with him she managed to stay teasingly non-committal, provocative and amusing, but it was turning into a struggle and a pretence. She wanted more of him, the security of a real place in his life, but however closely she watched him she saw no sign that Stephen wanted anything more from her than he already had.

They saw each other often enough, stealing afternoons and evenings from Stephen's teaching schedules and, she imagined, from Beatrice. They had even, in the Christmas vacation, managed four days away together when Stephen was supposed to be at a conference. But Stephen never spoke of his wife or his children and Chloe knew that he was deliberately not admitting her to his thoughts and feelings about them. She was nagged by a sense of being on the periphery of his life, in spite of the passion of their hours together, and she was at a loss to know what to do to change that. She knew quite well that to turn demanding and possessive could be fatal. But what then?

Perhaps she should try another tack. Be less the responsive and good-company Chloe that Stephen had come to enjoy as his right. Perhaps she should make herself less available. Perhaps even needle him a little with a little healthy jealousy. Jealous? she thought. Now, who could I ... Chloe stared down the aisle towards the stage. Tom Hart was standing centre front, rubbing at his black hair with the towel draped round his neck. In his grey tracksuit he looked more like a dancer or an actor than the director of the show. He had been taking his cast through a movement workout before beginning the rehearsal and he had shown himself to be fitter than any of them.

Now, even after the strenuous workout, he was issuing

instructions in a clear voice that didn't betray even a quickening of breath.

'You're stiff, Pansy, and it shows. Go through the basic programmes on your own every day.'

'Oh God, all this bend-stretch is so boring.' Chloe smiled at Pansy's clear voice.

Tom didn't even look at her. 'Too bad. Now let's get on.'

Cocky bastard, Chloe thought, not for the first time. But she saw the dark hair at the throat of his unzipped tracksuit top and the cool authority in his face and thought, yes, he's attractive. But there was something detached in Tom's response to her that told Chloe that he did not find her as interesting as she would have expected. Her gaze shifted to Oliver's windblown hair and Plantagenet features.

Yes, Chloe thought, and then No. There was something wrong about beautiful Oliver, something minutely off-key that warned her away. And anyway, just now he belonged to Pansy.

There was a slight movement behind her and she looked round. Stephen was sliding into the seat next to hers.

'Sorry,' he murmured with his mouth close to her hair. Then, safe in the darkness against the blaze of lights on stage, he kissed her. Chloe's eyes closed and warmth flooded through her as it always did when she was with him.

'What's going on?' Stephen drew back and nodded towards the stage. Oliver's and Tom's heads were close together, light and dark, opposites in the spotlight.

'Not much. Look at those two together. Almost good enough to eat.'

As soon as she had said it, Chloe realised that Stephen was not going to be jealous. He shrugged. 'Depends on your particular appetite.' Then his fingers touched her thigh. 'Come back with me afterwards.'

Chloe knew that he meant to his College rooms where they would bolt the door and reach avidly for each other. She nodded, all thought of making herself unavailable chased out of her head.

But when at last Tom left his seat in the front row and shouted 'Okay everyone, that's it for today,' Pansy jumped down from the stage and came towards them.

'It all sounds too exciting,' Pansy had said when Chloe, needing to talk about her new love, had described her snatched hours with Stephen. 'But why does he lurk in the shadows so much at rehearsals? Is he afraid that we won't be discreet about you two? Bring him to Follies so that the rest of us can get to know him too.'

But Chloe had hugged her times with Stephen closer to herself, and she was glad that they spent the hours he could spare for her alone together.

Now Pansy was kneeling on the seats in front of them, smiling at Stephen. Her hair was freshly washed and her face was bare of make-up. She looked very pretty and very young. Suddenly Chloe was aware of the difference in their ages and the two or three fine lines, still invisible to everyone but herself, that were showing at the corners of her eyes. 'Come back to supper at Follies, won't you, Stephen? Everyone else is. Bring him, Chloe.'

'Well, no ...' Chloe began, but Stephen cut her short.

'Why not? Thank you, Pansy.'

Chloe felt a protest rising in her throat but she bit it back.

'Wonderful.' Pansy's smile was for Stephen alone, and his eyes followed her as she ran back to the stage. He saw nothing of the irritation and the quick flicker of anxiety that showed in Chloe's face.

'You don't mind, do you?' he asked easily.

Yes. Yes, she longed to say. I can't bear to share you with anyone. But she only said 'I suppose not,' and knew that her sulky expression didn't suit her.

Pansy's elegant little flat in Follies House was crowded with people. The scene was familiar to Chloe. Pansy hated to be alone and it reassured her to fill empty rooms with noisy people. Almost invariably she prevailed on someone else to do the cooking in her compact little kitchen, and tonight it was Rose. Her bulk was pressed against the oven as she stirred a bubbling pot of goulash.

Chloe had often joined in these informal suppers but tonight the atmosphere grated on her. Stephen didn't belong in this free-for-all.

Pansy jumped up as soon as she saw them. In her jeans and striped sweatshirt, she looked like an excited boy.

'She's perfect for Rosalind,' Stephen murmured. 'Hart's luckier than he knows.'

'I'm glad you've come,' Pansy told him simply as soon as she reached them. Her vivid face was serious for an instant and

Stephen's conventional greeting died in his throat. He saw the unblemished apricot skin and the exotic palette of blues in her eyes. She was perfect. Unthinkingly he leaned forward and kissed her cheek and for an instant he could have bitten into her as if she was a ripe summer fruit.

Beside them Chloe went stiff and cold. Her careful, expert make-up felt like a mask and her expensive suede tunic weighed on her like a vulgar declaration.

Pansy took Stephen's arm to lead him away but Chloe cut in, her voice unnaturally sharp.

'I'll look after him, Pansy. We can't stay long anyway.'

Pansy half-turned and the two women looked at each other. The complicity that Helen had once seen and envied evaporated. In the new appraisal there was a challenge, and defiance.

'Of course,' Pansy said very softly. Then she was gone, and Chloe shivered as she saw that Stephen was still watching her across the room.

'What's the matter?' she heard him say. At once he was the Stephen she knew again, faintly smiling and with one eyebrow raised. Love for him hammered in her head like an affliction and a panicky desperation made her mumble, 'Stephen. Let's not stay here. Let's go back to your rooms.'

His hand touched her sleeve.

'Chloe, we don't own each other, you know. We can't. Don't we have enough together to make you happy?'

'No. I love you. I need you.'

She could have bitten out her tongue, but it was too late. Stephen's face changed. He looked sad, but not before Chloe had glimpsed the irritation too.

'I thought we understood each other', he said, very gently. Longingly she waited for him to say something else, something to convince her of her own importance to him, but there was nothing. At last he made a tiny gesture. 'I think we're making ourselves a little conspicuous here. Shall we find somewhere to sit down?' He glanced around the room and Chloe knew that he was looking to see where Pansy had gone. Her own gaze travelled across the blur of people. Then, like a film camera focusing to pull one face out of a crowd, she saw Oliver. He was staring at Stephen as if he wanted to hit him. For some reason the memory of the uncomfortable lunch at Stephen's home came back to her.

It was Beatrice she had been jealous of then, Chloe recalled. Why? she asked herself bitterly. Why can't it be simple, this time? I'm tired. The others hadn't mattered, not like this. Even Leo. But Stephen ...

He was already moving away from her, threading his way across the room.

'Find us somewhere,' she managed to call after him, not wanting to admit the feeling that he was abandoning her. 'I just want to talk to Oliver.'

Chloe sat down on a fat velvet floor cushion beside Oliver. He nodded her a brief greeting and then went on staring over to where Pansy was beaming up at Stephen. Her hand was resting lightly on his arm.

Chloe felt little cold fingers of anxiety pressing at her. There was something in Stephen's expression, fascination mingled with a kind of awe, that Chloe had never seen before. He's practically old enough to be her father, she thought. Perhaps that's what she wants. A Masefield-figure that she can actually go to bed with, as well. Hurriedly she put the thought out of her head. The thought of Stephen touching, kissing Pansy's glowing skin made Chloe feel physically sick.

Just let her try, she thought. I won't give him up to her. Never.

Chloe glanced at Oliver. His anger had faded and he looked sullen now. 'What's up?' she asked lightly.

Oliver pointed. 'Look. Look at Spurring, grabbing at Pansy as if she's some kind of merchandise. Smirking, and no doubt spouting some kind of pretentious literary crap. Jumped-up little toad.'

Chloe couldn't help laughing. 'Oh, I think the grabbing's the other way round. Pansy knows what she's doing.'

Suddenly, painfully, she felt a wave of tenderness and love for Stephen. He looked older beside Pansy's brightness, tired and a little bewildered. The mixture of awe and uncertainty in his face as he looked at Pansy touched Chloe, and her anxiety evaporated. He's human, she told herself. How could he resist? She's so lovely to look at, and how could he know yet that she's vain and superficial as well? He needs me, she thought protectively. For all his cleverness, he can't see very straight.

Beside her, Oliver flung himself back against the cushions.

'Stupid bitch, then. Oh Christ, what does it matter anyway?' He poured red supermarket wine from a litre bottle into his glass and made a face as he drank it. 'Talk to me instead, Chloe. Tell me, d'you ever get the feeling that you're in one of those horror-movie rooms where the walls and floor and ceiling creep inwards to crush whoever's inside? D'you ever feel that's what life is?'

'No,' Chloe said, half-joking. 'More like a wheel in a hamster's cage.' But Oliver wasn't listening. He had seen Gerry peering round the door and then sliding into the room.

'For God's sake, that's all I need.' Gerry came over to them, smiling hopefully at Oliver.

'Hello, dear boy. You've been neglecting us lately. Not surprising though, with so much better scenery to look at.'

His wink acknowledged Chloe, and she thought again as she always did how handsome he must once have been and how dissipated he looked now. His blond hair had faded to pepper-and-salt and there were stubbly patches on his cheeks that the razor had missed. He groped for the litre bottle and sloshed the thin red wine into a glass. Oliver was eyeing him with distaste.

'You drink too much, Gerry,' he told him.

'Just like you, dear boy.' Gerry's voice was good-humoured but there was an anxious, uncertain look in his face that told Chloe he was frightened of Oliver as well as admiring of him.

Oliver frowned. 'At least I do it with some sort of style.' He looked restlessly around the room. 'God, how boring everything is. Why is everyone always the same? Even Pansy.'

Pansy was sitting cross-legged in front of the fire with a plate of goulash balanced on her knee. She was waving her fork as she talked, surrounded by a ring of admiring faces. Stephen, on the edge of the group, had recovered his quizzical poise. He beckoned complicity to Chloe but she shook her head.

'Even Pansy,' Oliver said again. Then, abruptly, 'Where's Helen? She makes me feel so calm, and then when she's not around, I forget.'

Chloe shook her head quickly. Oliver was bad news for Helen. And anyway, his job was to keep Pansy occupied. As far away from Stephen as possible.

Upstairs in the room above Pansy's, Helen pulled her reading lamp down to concentrate the circle of light on the page. She was reading Sir Philip Sidney's *Astrophel and Stella*, and the hopeless love of the sonnet sequence saddened and depressed her. Fron Pansy's room the noise of talk and laughter grew

172

louder, and then swelled with music and vague thumping. They must be dancing, she thought, and leaned more deliberately over her work. In the past she had sometimes gone with Chloe to Pansy's impromptu parties, but no longer. It disturbed her to see Oliver. Helen still loved the man she had known, and she missed him almost as much as she had done at the beginning. When she was apart from him, it was easier to live stoically with the loss of him, and the poignant pleasure that her memories of him still brought.

When he was near, in the same room or lounging unthinkingly beside her, it was much harder. He had the same physical effect on her that he always had done. Yet even that she could have dealt with. It was something else that made her uncomfortable. His brilliant, reckless smile was just the same, but Helen thought that the man behind it was changing, and slipping away from them all. He was more capricious, moodier than he had ever been, and the dark moods lasted much longer. His charm was less apparent, and his selfishness more so. Within herself Helen was fiercely loyal to him, but she couldn't help seeing that he was becoming daily more difficult. She sensed that he was struggling, somewhere that no-one could see or reach, and that he needed help. She loved him, but she knew that he would reject whatever small support she could have offered him. The knowledge was painful so, reluctantly, Helen kept away.

There was another reason, too, why Helen kept away from Pansy's rooms. The reason was Tom Hart.

The evening at Montcalm had come awkwardly between them. Helen would have given much for it never to have happened. She knew that her reaction had been absurdly violent. He had kissed her, and he had told her a truth about herself. That was all.

Her anger had been out of proportion, and now in retrospect it puzzled her. It was as if she was protecting herself with it, but that cast Tom in the role of the marauder, and he was far too subtle for that.

On the two or three occasions since when they had met at Follies House, Helen had caught herself staring covertly at him. She felt how well she knew the decisive lines of his face, and then she saw afresh the amusement that lurked around his mouth. She thought his amusement masked the calm assumption that she would apologise, and his determination not to make the overture himself. Annoyance would well up inside her and she would turn away, more stony-faced than she had intended.

The breach was not healed, and though she told herself it didn't, it mattered to her more than she dared to admit. It mattered, because in spite of her resolution to avoid him, her eyes raked the crowded streets for his dark head, and she listened for his voice in the clamour that rose from Pansy's room.

Helen's floor was shaking with the vibrations of the music now. She sighed and pressed her fingers against her forehead, staring at the words in front of her.

There was yet another reason for staying away from Pansy's party, although if this noise went on she might as well go and join in. There was very little time left between now and the Final Schools in June. Helen fought the panicky feeling that she was behind with her work. So much had happened. Her father. Oliver. Her mother's job, and her own fear of having to leave Oxford. Then Oliver's wonderfully tactful present. Helen sighed. There was that; he had done that, even if he refused to let her acknowledge it.

So much had happened, and now it was over. Now she must work to make up for lost time. Helen read on, her shoulders hunched as if to cut herself off from the din downstairs.

When someone knocked at her door, she frowned quickly before calling, automatically, 'Come in.'

Then she turned round in her chair to see Darcy.

'The downstairs door was open,' he said mildly. 'People were teeming in and out.'

'To see Pansy Warren,' she smiled back at him.

'Oliver's girl?'

'The same.'

'Ah.' Darcy wandered in and began picking up books, examining the titles with an expression of bafflement before putting them carefully back in their places again. 'She looks like a picture in one of the glossy mags. Just about as much substance, too. You don't mind, then?'

Helen reflected that her visitor didn't look much like a Viscount. His clothes were shabby and definitely muddy around the edges, and his colourless hair needed cutting. His homely face was anxious, with none of Oliver's hauteur showing in it.

'Mind?' Helen couldn't help smiling. Darcy was so appealingly vague, so obviously good-natured. 'Mind what?'

'Well, me turning up to see you. I could have phoned, but I was passing and ...'

'No, I'm pleased. You're a wonderful reason for not struggling to work any more with all this going on.' She pointed at the floor, laughing.

'What is going on?'

'Pansy's having a party. It happens quite often. Oliver's probably there. D'you want to go down and join in?'

'No,' Darcy recoiled. 'Let's go for a walk instead.'

'At eleven at night?'

Darcy looked surprised. 'Why not? What else shall we do? The pubs will be shut. If you like, next time I take you out, we can go to one of Oliver's flash restaurants, if I steal his address book first. But it's a beautiful night tonight. We can go along the river.'

Helen snapped her book shut and reached for her coat. Together they slipped down the stairs, by unspoken agreement making a wide detour around the open door of Pansy's room. A couple of people were sitting on the stairs with their arms around each other, but neither of them looked up as Darcy and Helen stepped past. Then the heavy door banged shut behind them and Darcy breathed deeply in the sudden quiet. He steered Helen up the steps from the island, across the orange-lit ribbon of road and down again to the towpath. They began to walk together, side by side, hands in their pockets. The silence between them was companionable. Once past the bridge the river ran slow, and there was no sound except the occasional gurgle and slap of a ripple against the bank. Lights from a group of moored barges made wavering patches of brilliance on the black water. The sky was overcast and as black as the water but the air was surprisingly gentle and still. Along the bank under the willows were the pale-bleached splashes of crocuses. Although it was only February, Helen thought she could smell the first warm sweetness of spring.

'I walk a lot at night,' Darcy said. 'There aren't enough daylight hours for a farmer just to wander around looking. I can see things at night that I wouldn't be able to during the day. There's a badger colony in one of my woods.'

'Do you farm at Montcalm?' Helen asked, curious. She

remembered the manicured parkland, but no ploughed fields or untidy cows.

'No. We've another working estate, about twenty miles away. I ... prefer to spend most of my time there. I have to be at Montcalm sometimes, like the evening when I met you. And one day I'll have to live there because that's what I'm for, in a way. But just now I'd rather be at home on the farm.' There was a resigned wistfulness in his voice. Helen guessed that he was no more in love with his ancestral home than Oliver, but for different reasons.

As if his thoughts were following the same track Darcy asked, 'Do you know my brother well?'

Helen answered as honestly as she could. 'I don't think I know him at all well. I suppose I was "Oliver's girl" for a while. An extremely short while.'

'What happened?'

'Oh, he turned his attention elsewhere. To Pansy, actually.'

'Mmm. Were you hurt?'

'Yes. But it doesn't matter now.' Helen was lying, she hoped convincingly.

'I don't think I know him either,' Darcy said, very softly. 'My own brother. I wish I could do something to ... make things easier for him. But I can't. I don't understand his world any more than he wants to live in mine. We barely inhabit the same planet. I wish we'd been born the other way round. I think if Oliver had been the elder son he'd have felt less of an anomaly.'

Don't, Helen thought. Don't you think that too.

'Let's not talk about Oliver. Tell me about something else. Farming. Badgers.'

'I'm sorry,' he said gently. 'Funny, isn't it? People always talk about Oliver. It's something about him. Like your friend Pansy, too.'

They were quiet for a moment as they walked, and then hesitantly Darcy took Helen's arm. Unthreatened, she let herself be drawn against him and lengthened her stride to fit his. Darcy began to talk about the antics of the badgers in the wood.

When they reached the point where the river curved back on itself and into the town, and the lit-up façades of student residences began to lean over them, Darcy stopped and firmly turned around. It was as if he was reluctant to slip by them even in the dark. They retraced their steps to Follies House.

Darcy led her down the steps to the island and watched gravely while she groped for her key. With the door open into the square height of the hall, Helen stopped and asked impulsively, 'Darcy, what's your first name? Your real name? Do I have to go on calling you by your title for ever?'

Darcy leaned against the door post, watching her face.

'John William Aubrey Frederick Mere,' he recited. His smile was lopsided, rueful. 'You can choose whichever you like. But I'm always called Darcy.'

'I'm not surprised,' Helen laughed. 'Goodnight, Darcy, then.'

Before she turned away Darcy reached out and brushed her cheek with his fingers. 'Goodnight, Helen. Can I come again?'

She nodded in the darkness. Just in that instant, in the tilt of his head and the timbre of his voice, she had caught a flicker of Oliver.

'Flash restaurant?'

'Absolutely not.'

No, he wasn't Oliver at all. He mustn't be.

Darcy watched to see her safe inside the house and then walked away, whistling softly, towards his muddy, battered little car.

Helen ran up the stairs. Confronting her in the narrow space of the gallery was a little knot of people at the door of Chloe's room. Tom was there, and her gaze went straight to him. Forgetting herself in the sudden pleasure of seeing him, she smiled a question at him. Then his sombre face and the stillness of the group struck her. She looked over Tom's shoulder into Chloe's room. Oliver was innocently asleep on Chloe's bed. Her exotically patterned oriental bedcover was rucked up around him.

Looking from Chloe to Stephen, Helen saw that Chloe looked anxious, almost imploring, and that Stephen was impatient.

'He asked me for a proper drink, came down and had a couple of brandies, and then just fell asleep,' Chloe said. 'Now he seems dead to the world.'

Pansy had been apparently intent on making intricate pleats in the sleeve of her sweatshirt, but she lifted her silver-gilt head now and said coolly, 'Passed out, more like.' Her eyes fixed on

177

Stephen and she shrugged, making a little, pretty, regretful face. 'Shame,' she whispered.

Stephen moved forward an inch, then collected himself. With an effort he looked at his watch.

'Thank you for supper, Pansy. I can probably find you an hour if you really think you need some Shakespeare background. There's a new feminist book on his heroines that might be useful for your role.' But his little speech didn't sound quite right. For once Stephen wasn't entirely the confident don. He was tentative, not quite certain of his ground, and the whisper of diffidence suited him. He seemed younger, vulnerable.

Chloe's eyes glittered as she watched him.

'Goodnight, Chloe, love,' he said, more smoothly, but Tom's hand caught his arm.

'You might help me get him back to the House,' Tom said sharply.

'If I must,' Stephen responded.

The curious little scene had held them all so intent that only Helen had noticed that Oliver was awake. He smoothed the dazed expression from his face with one hand and then stood up.

'Kind of you both, but not necessary. And I don't care for being talked about as if I'm incapable.'

He was prickly with anger.

'Why act like it then, darling?' Pansy's voice was languid. Oliver took her arm and tried to turn her away towards her room but she shook him off.

'Perhaps you'd be better in your own little bed tonight.'

Oliver stepped back. His face went white and deep vertical lines showed in his cheeks. Then, abruptly, he turned and walked away down the stairs.

Helen looked away, suddenly cold. The tension in the air was ugly, vibrating threateningly among them.

It was Pansy who broke the silence. She laughed a little, then said, 'Well. Sorry everyone. It's not like this at Follies every night, Stephen.'

With evident relief, Stephen said a brief goodnight and went. Pansy leaned over the carved gallery rail and called softly after him, 'Can I ring you in College about my tutorial?'

'Of course.' His voice carried up through the vaulted space, then the door thudded shut behind him. Chloe hadn't moved a muscle. Her fists were clenched, creasing the soft suede of her dress.

At last, Helen met Tom's eyes. They looked at each other for a long moment. She searched her mind for the right thing to say, aware that Pansy and Chloe were watching too. But the phrases that tumbled in her head all sounded too flippant, or too revealing, and she was silent.

At last Tom said, 'As Oliver doesn't appear to need an ambulance service after all, I think I'll go home. Remember your exercises, Pansy.'

The ghost of a smile which he gave them included Helen too. She watched his dark head retreating with a sadness that she couldn't have explained.

The three women stood facing each other in the splash of light from Chloe's doorway. Very slowly, Chloe unclenched her fists.

'Must you acquire him, too, Pansy?' she asked, tonelessly. Pansy's eyebrows went up, almost into the tousled fringe of hair.

'What?' She couldn't have looked more innocent. 'What do you mean?'

'Oh, I think you know what I mean.' Chloe's voice was dangerously low. 'I mean Stephen. I mean your teeny little flirtatious gambits, and your worming your way into his rooms for some totally irrelevant coaching. You took Oliver from Helen. Isn't that enough? Stephen belongs to me. Don't you understand?' With the last words the control ebbed out of her voice. She was too close to tears, and she bit her lip savagely to hide the humiliation.

Helen watched numbly. She put out her hand to Chloe, then drew it back. There was nothing she could do.

'Don't be a fool,' Pansy said, suddenly steely. The flowery innocence melted away and her little pointed face turned pitiless.

Masefield Warren's daughter, Helen thought.

'To start with, I didn't take Oliver from anyone. He came, tongue hanging out. And if you think Stephen belongs to you, you are a fool. He's poor old Beatrice's, if he's anyone's right now. And no, if you want to know, Oliver isn't enough. I don't need a doped-up boy. Stephen is different.'

Chloe turned sharply on her heel and gained the sanctuary of her room. With the door safely shut behind her, she sank on to the stool in front of her dressing table and stared into her reflection. Her mascara had smudged into dark patches beneath her eyes, red-rimmed with the threat of tears, and her skin was flat and chalky. With an exhausted gesture, Chloe swept the surface clear of bottles and jars, laid her head down on her arms, and cried for Stephen.

Never, she thought. He had never let the suave mask drop, never in all their times together, and she had never seen him look as he had looked at Pansy tonight. Yet she had wanted and needed him more than anyone else before, and she had tried so hard to give him what he wanted.

Chloe screwed her eyes tight shut but the tears still streamed out, and there was no shutting out the sight of Stephen kissing Pansy's cheek as if he wanted to devour her. And there was no muffling of Pansy's voice, saying over and over, 'Stephen is different.' Pansy would get what she wanted, there was no doubt about that.

The hopeless tears burned Chloe's cheeks and the sobs clogged her throat. At last she lifted her smeared face and pushed the heavy, damp hair back from her cheeks. In front of her she saw the pretty, inviting lettering on the sachet of a face pack. Savagely Chloe screwed up the pack and flung it at the waste-bin. It bounced off the edge and lay on the carpet, unfurling with a tiny crackle. She stared at it, then stirred uncomfortably.

With a deep breath, Chloe met her own eyes again. The swollen, streaming face was pathetic, and the habits of years were too deeply ingrained. Forcing herself to breathe evenly, Chloe reached out for her jar of cream. Gently, methodically, she began to remove her ravaged make-up. Her eyes were blank with misery.

Pansy had followed Helen upstairs. She came into the room behind her and lay wearily down on the bed. With her hands clasped behind her head, she stared up at the ceiling.

'Won't you make me a cup of coffee?' she asked pleadingly.

'Only instant,' Helen said discouragingly. She didn't want Pansy here.

'Anything will do. God, how I loathe scenes.'

Helen stirred the uninviting liquid in a mug. 'Plastic milk?' she asked coldly and then handed the mug over. Neither of them spoke. Pansy sat up to drink her coffee, one arm wrapped around her knees.

'Pansy,' Helen said at last, knowing that she must say something. 'You said that you liked Chloe. And that you'd never had women friends before. Don't . . .'

'Don't what?' Pansy asked challengingly.

Helen changed her tack, groping for words. 'You said that Oliver isn't important. Perhaps he isn't, to you. But Stephen is important to Chloe. What is it that you want?'

'Not Oliver', she answered softly. 'Oliver's turning into a wreck. But why is it me who has to back off? Don't you think I might be looking for someone, needing someone too?' For a second her face crumpled. 'It's lonely. All this.' Helen knew at once that she meant her lovely face, Masefield's money, the endless, effortless command of centre stage. She felt a bewildering stab of sympathy for her.

'And Stephen's different,' Pansy repeated, almost to herself. 'I don't know why, but I want to find out.'

He's no different, Helen thought. He's a pretence. Don't you fall for it too. And then poor Chloe. But she was silent, watching Pansy drain her coffee.

'If you've finished,' she murmured. 'It's late . . .'

At once Pansy was on her way. But she paused in the doorway. 'You probably won't believe me. But I wish it wasn't like this. Oliver. Chloe. You. A mess, isn't it?' Then a little sardonic half-smile came back. 'But you know what they say. All's fair . . .' night.' With that, she was gone.

Helen sat staring into space, left with the thought of Oliver. Not the dream-Oliver she had fallen in love with, but the real Oliver. A wreck, Pansy had said dismissively. Helen saw the clear features, smooth as marble, which still lived with her even though the man behind them had become someone else. And the dazed expression as he woke up this evening came back to her.

If only she could help him; she would do anything to save him from himself. But there was nothing she could do. Pansy was right. It was a mess, horrible and tangled. And it was going to get worse. 'Stephen. Stephen is different,' she heard again. Pansy could save Oliver, but she wouldn't. Helen could see no solution and she felt cold with apprehension.

Then, with a little sound of helplessness and frustration she stood up and began to make herself ready for bed.

'If you want to know, that stank. You're a bunch of fucking

181

amateurs and it stands out a mile. Now get back in your places and we'll do it again. And we'll go on doing it again until it's how I want it.'

Tom's anger was impressive and more than a little frightening. Even Pansy looked faintly cowed and Oliver straightened up and ran his fingers through his hair with an air of desperation.

'Jesus Christ, we'll be here all night. Can't we knock off?'

Tom rounded on him, his face dark with fury.

'You will be here twenty-four hours a day until we open, if necessary. I'm the director of this shitty play, and I want it done to the best of your admittedly limited capabilities. Try to listen to what I'm saying now, and I'll have notes for every single one of you afterwards. Now move.'

Tom threw his script down and slumped back in his place. He looked exhausted and there were dark, damp patches under the arms and across the back of his tracksuit.

There were only seven days to go before the opening of *As You Like It*. Half-finished bits and pieces of the Forest of Arden set gave the stage a cluttered, makeshift air. The cast sat dispiritedly in the stalls or lounged in the wings, waiting to work through a scene for the umpteenth time. Tom Hart had proved a hard taskmaster, but he was driving his uneven bunch of students into a performance that was beginning to look impressive.

Chloe watched dispassionately as the actors regrouped themselves for the opening scene.

Oliver shook himself, the disenchanted air vanished, and he was Orlando again.

'As I remember, Adam, it was upon this fashion bequeathed me by will but poor a thousand crowns . . .'

Tom leaned back, intent, not missing a single syllable or gesture. Once or twice he scribbled a brief note, but his concentration never wavered.

Intimidatingly professional, Chloe thought. He'll make a good job of this, whatever's going on backstage to wreck it.

There was no doubt, with his mixture of asperity and cajolement, that Tom was getting the best possible performance out of Oliver. Onstage his bored cynicism dropped away and Oliver almost magically became the fresh, idealistic lover. He was best of all in the scenes with Pansy as Rosalind. The tension

182

between them was tangible and it gave the lovers a vivid dimension that Chloe had never seen in the play before.

And Pansy herself was remarkable. The wistfulness in her 'O, how full of briers is this working-day world' brought the tears to Chloe's eyes, even in the prosaic clutter of the half-built set and the anxious, fractious atmosphere of the late rehearsal.

An unspoken truce had reigned at Follies House since the day of Pansy's party. Pansy and Chloe skirted carefully around each other, and Stephen was never mentioned. Pansy absorbed herself in rehearsals and her spare time was spent with Oliver, just as it had been since the autumn. She was as evasively quick to joke as ever, and as difficult to pin down, but she treated him affectionately and he seemed happy enough with that. Chloe knew that Pansy had seen nothing of Stephen. And Chloe and Stephen went on just as before, meeting each other whenever they could. Cautiously Chloe made no mention of Pansy, and worked hard at being as witty and beguiling for Stephen as she knew how.

Away from the feverish pitch of rehearsals, they were quiet, calm days. In a break between scenes Tom came back and sat beside Chloe. She felt at once as he stretched his legs next to her that he was physically tense with concentration. She knew that this production was a very small deal for him, and she admired his absolute dedication to whatever he had in hand, however unimportant it might seem.

They worked well together now. Early on Tom had recognised Chloe's efficiency and had promoted her from dogsbody to informal production manager. Now he came to her to discuss whether a prop needed changing, or to beg her to produce coffee and sandwiches, or to think aloud about how to make a curtain line more effective.

Chloe was used to the discipline of her own world and found it interesting as well as easy to do what he needed.

'You're a godsend,' he had told her once. 'I think I'll take you back with me. How d'you fancy fame and fortune on Broadway?'

'It's you who'll be getting the fame and fortune', she told him coolly. 'I don't see myself as a jewel in the back room. Anyway, you couldn't match my salary. Don't top copywriters earn more than directors' gofers?'

'I expect so,' Tom had said imperturbably. They had

laughed, but their relationship had never settled on an easy personal footing.

Chloe would have liked Tom to respond to her as most men did. She was used to being found attractive, and being treated with the little, flattering extra attentions that went with it. But there was nothing of the kind from Tom. He was impeccably polite and unvaryingly businesslike. Too obviously, the play was their only interest together.

Could he, she wondered, be gay? Would that explain his exasperated but still fascinated loyalty to Oliver? No, she thought. Tom Hart was straight. She decided at last that he was simply frigidly professional, and wondered idly what he would be like when the professional mask dropped.

'Now,' he was murmuring, 'I think we'll just do the last scene once more before letting them go. Looks like they're getting to rebellion point.' Tom worked his cast hard, but he was sensitive to the moment when they would do no more.

Under his direction the play's four pairs of lovers formed up and struck a pose as if for a wedding photograph. The men stood stiffly with their wives-to-be on their arms, smiling against an imaginary sun into an imaginary camera. It was a pretty final tableau. Chloe nodded her approval once again with a slight sigh.

'How neat. Four happy couples, ready to live happily ever after.' The tangles of the plot were all unravelled, neatly plaited and tied off. 'Pity it's not real life.'

Tom grinned. 'Oh, I don't know. Real life has a way of working itself out, perhaps not quite as pat but just as satisfactorily. Anyway, who says anything about happy ever after? Not Shakespeare. Remember "Men are April when they woo, December when they wed"?' He was shrugging into his canary yellow jacket, smiling. 'You're too romantic, Chloe dear. Very dangerous.'

Easy to say that, she thought bitterly.

Tom was strolling away, whistling. As an afterthought he turned and asked casually, 'Where's Helen?'

Helen's occasional visits to rehearsals had completely stopped.

'I don't think she can stand the offstage drama.'

'How sensible.' Tom was wry.

'And she's seeing quite a lot of Darcy.'

There was a perceptible pause before he spoke again. Then

he said, 'How nice.' Tom was on his way again, still smiling faintly, to distribute acerbic notes to each of his actors.

The time before the opening of Tom's *As You Like It* was a happy one for Helen.

Spring came early that year. The crocuses along the river bank were rapidly followed by sheets of daffodils, and then by faint dustings of green on the trailing willow branches. Along the river the air often smelt of fresh paint as the long, flat punts were brought out and cleaned up for the start of the summer season.

Oxford was very beautiful in this early spring light. The pale sunshine penetrated into Follies House, putting a tinge of warmth into the red brick and throwing fantastic shadows from the carved banisters on to the dusty oak boards of the gallery. Helen felt the sense of truce in the house and it comforted her. She walked to and from the libraries or her tutorials with a calm she had imagined that she had lost for ever. Her work was going well, and the days had something of the old, orderly quality of life before the savage upheavals of the last year.

Anxious to preserve her tranquillity, she stayed away from play rehearsals. If she didn't see Oliver she could hope that he was happier, and she could believe that the pain of losing him was fading at last. She had no desire either to witness any more of the feud between Chloe and Pansy.

Helen's self-imposed solitude meant one other thing too. She was denying herself the chance of seeing Tom, and she was unnerved to realise how much she wanted to. She felt that her liking for him had deepened and was still changing, in a way that she didn't quite want to account for. She told herself that her reluctance to confront her feelings sprang from shame at her own silliness on New Year's Eve, and it would all be all right again when she had told him she was sorry. But she held back from going boldly to find him. When they met again, she wanted it to be by accident. Perhaps then she could apologise light-heartedly and their differences would be forgotten.

So Helen went on trying to spot his decisive stride in the ambling crowds of students, and telling herself that she simply missed the stimulating crackle of his company.

Then, one evening, she heard him. The timbre of his voice was unmistakable. It was one night not long after Pansy's party, and he was in Pansy's room again. Helen lifted her head instinctively and cocked it to the sound. In the breathless moment that followed she heard him sounding impatient and exasperated. Then Pansy answered him, her voice raised too, and tinged with petulance.

Don't listen. Helen sprang out of her chair, galvanised by her desire not to hear any more. Whatever Tom wanted from Pansy tonight, whatever – even – he still felt for her, Helen didn't want to know about it. None of my business, she tried to tell herself. I don't care about Pansy or her pretty face or her long tentacles.

Damn it.

Helen clicked off her reading light and went downstairs to Rose and Gerry, rather than stay in her own room and be forced to eavesdrop. Down in the kitchen she half-listened to Rose's talk and remembered the books on her desk with a longing to immerse herself in them again. At least work kept the more uncomfortable realities at bay. I'll stay in Oxford for ever, Helen thought. I'll turn into an old maid and my biggest excitement will be the discovery of a forgotten footnote somewhere. I'll have a smooth, unlined face and literature will be my life. What could be safer than that? Yet the prospect was less inviting than it had been a year ago. Made irritable with herself, Helen went back upstairs.

She had barely reached her room before she heard Pansy's door slam and then the front door. Relief mingled with disappointment gripped her. Whatever Tom had wanted, it wasn't going to keep him with Pansy all night. The house was comfortably silent again, but it was also very empty.

Helen told herself that she was sorry to have missed another chance of telling him how much she wished that New Year's Eve had happened differently.

True to his promise, Darcy came again. He came so often that their outings together started to fall into a pattern. Usually they would walk somewhere, quite often in the quiet corners of the town itself. Darcy had not been at Oxford. 'Agricultural College. Much more my line' he had told her, but he displayed a surprising knowledge of odd, out-of-the-way treasures of the city. Together they visited the mournfully erotic statue of the drowned Shelley hidden in a corner of his one-time college, and the Epstein Lazarus at New College. Once Darcy took her hand as they stared up at the Burne-Jones stained glass in Christ

Church Cathedral. When they turned away again, he gently released it.

On other days he drove them out into the country and they walked quiet lanes and footpaths almost obliterated by brambles. Afterwards Darcy took her to unfrequented pubs and bought her halves of malty, hoppy real ale with such enthusiasm that she began almost to enjoy them. When they ate together, it was ploughman's lunches, or curries in odd little restaurants on the city's outskirts.

Wherever they went, no-one seemed to know Darcy. Once or twice a barman nodded at him, or an old man in wellingtons sitting in a corner beside the dartboard might murmur, 'Evening to you.' But that was all. It couldn't have been more different from going to places with Oliver. Everywhere Oliver went, heads turned after him, and nudges and whispers made ripples in his wake.

Oliver would never have bothered with the quiet pleasures which Darcy enjoyed. Helen tried and failed, amused, to imagine him in a public bar somewhere, watching a darts match with a pint mug of beer in his hand. No. Oliver belonged in his Jaguar, driving too fast to a chic restaurant where the waiters leapt to attend to him and where the other diners tried discreetly not to stare.

Helen remembered her own brief times in the Jaguar beside him, or in the casually expensive disarray of his rooms, as if from another life. She hoarded the memories, but the knowledge that it was over came more easily.

And unlike Oliver, Darcy was the most easygoing companion she had ever had. He liked to hear Helen talk, and she told him happily about her work, her family, the small events of every day. All the things that she had thought too dull or too humble for Oliver. Darcy would listen and nod, walking alongside her with his hands in the pockets of his corduroys. When he put forward his own opinions, he did it mildly, almost with an air of surprise that he should find himself expressing an opinion at all.

Almost by accident, Helen found that she was fond of Darcy and beginning to rely on the steady calm of his company. He wasn't exciting, but he was utterly dependable. She discovered that his range of interests was limited – he cared about farming, the countryside, animals and his few friends – but his feelings for those were deep and genuine. Helen thought that he worried

187

about Montcalm and his intimidating role there, but he was reticent about it and she tactfully avoided the topic.

Then quite soon, Helen saw that Darcy cared about her too. He was very gentle, almost tentative in suggesting places that they might go together, diffident in asking when he could see her again. But there was no pressure from him. Only once or twice, from the look in his eyes, did she see that she was more to him than just a friend to share his walks and meditative pints in country pubs.

The implications of that stabbed Helen with anxiety.

I shouldn't let this happen, she told herself. It isn't fair to him. But when she half-resolved to see less of him, she missed his company at once. Why? she thought. Why cut off something that gives pleasure to us both out of some vague, groundless fear? I don't want not to see Darcy any more. And so they had gone on together.

Without having talked about it, they had both accepted that their relationship was an exclusive one. They never saw anyone else. Helen never mentioned Darcy at Follies, and now they usually met in other places.

They're all busy, Helen thought defensively. After the play is over, perhaps then we can all meet together. But the prospect was not an inviting one, and she put it quickly out of her mind.

One day Darcy took her to Mere.

The working half of the Montcalm estate was centred on a low-lying Cotswold village, honey-coloured stone cottages lying in a fold of rich farmland. As they drove through Mere village, Helen noticed that the pub sign was a brightly painted coat of arms with the name 'Mortimore Arms' above it. Almost simultaneously she saw a pair of farmers talking by the roadside. They touched their caps in greeting to Darcy as he drove past. Of course, she told herself. Darcy would be known and liked here, in his own home. It was only the rest of the world that didn't care about him any more than he cared about it.

Mere House itself looked different from the rest of the village. It was a low, grey house, very old, set slightly forbiddingly against a belt of dark yew hedges. There was nothing of the stately home about it. It was solid, square and functional, a country landowner's home without architectural frills or unnecessary decoration. Darcy told her that it had been the original family seat before the eighteenth-century Mortimores became gradually more powerful and, with the power, hugely wealthy. They had built Montcalm and settled to a fashionable life amongst their terraces and parterres, away from the business of the land. But the sons of the family had traditionally lived at Mere before inheriting, overseeing the business of the estates and the comings and goings of the tenant farms.

Darcy led her round to the front of the house. The paving under the small, heavily leaded windows was cracked and lined with dark green moss. Under the yew hedges were great clumps of daffodils, palest cream to brazen orange. The land dropped away in front of them towards the village, newly-ploughed, dark soil alternating with clipped pasture. In the quiet Helen could hear the steady chug of a tractor and, carried on the wind, the high bleat of new lambs.

Darcy's eyes were on her face, turned slightly away from him as she looked at the view. From the placid, well-ordered landscape under the spring sunshine she turned back to the house. It looked as if it had been standing there for ever. Back into her mind's eye came Montcalm with its fantastic turrets, pinnacles and balustrades.

'Why did they bother?' she murmured to Darcy, laughing.

'My feelings exactly.' There was clear approval in his eyes. 'You like this better?'

Helen hesitated for a minute, then said softly, 'Yes.'

Darcy looked out across the fields again. 'I love it', he said simply. 'I shall miss it when I have to ... leave.'

'Not yet,' she said.

'No,' he agreed. 'But one day, just the same.'

The wind carried birdsong, and the noise of the tractor as it trailed evenly up and down the long field.

'Come inside,' Darcy said at last. 'We'll have some lunch, then I'll take you round the farm.'

There was no exquisite antique furniture or fragile porcelain here. Mere was furnished in heavy dark oak that looked as old and solid as the house itself. The rooms were shadowy, making the sunny patches that fell through the small windows look startlingly bright.

In the big, square, low-beamed dining room there was only one place laid by the carver chair at the head of the table. A silver tankard stood ready with a bottle of beer beside a copy of *Farmer's Weekly*.

How lonely he must be, Helen thought, with a sudden shock

189

of sympathy for the quiet man beside her. The solitary place setting looked so isolated in this silent, sombre room. Mere House would have to be filled with the noise and activity of a huge family, she reflected, before it would feel homely.

'I didn't tell Mrs Maitland that you were coming,' Darcy confessed. 'There'd have been a huge to-do of preparation. I'll call her and tell her now.' He pressed an old-fashioned bell. From the time that it took Mrs Maitland to arrive, Helen guessed that the kitchen quarters were miles away. While they waited, Darcy poured her a glass of sherry. Helen noticed that the bottle was slightly dusty. Evidently Darcy had few visitors.

'Mrs Maitland?' she asked, interested.

'Mmm. Sister to your friend Mr Maitland at Montcalm. See how inbred we are? Not married, actually. The "Mrs" is a courtesy title, you know.'

When the housekeeper arrived, Helen saw that she had the same imperviously correct exterior as her brother, but her manner was noticeably friendlier.

'I've brought a guest for lunch, Mrs Maitland,' Darcy said. 'Bit short notice, I know, but I'm sure you'll manage something.'

'Well, my lord,' she said, after only the briefest surprised glance at Helen, 'we'll rustle something up. It won't be anything very smart, you know.' They smiled at each other, evidently the best of friends. The 'my lord' had startled Helen for an instant. It was hard to remember who Darcy really was, and for a long time now he had been just 'Darcy' in her thoughts.

When they sat down together at the long table Mrs Maitland served them with dark pink cold beef, tiny new potatoes and a crisp salad, and an impressive selection of home-made pickles. Everything was perfectly simple and very good.

Helen looked at Darcy over her last spoonful of rhubarb compote and said, 'I enjoyed that.' They both knew that she meant more than just the food. It had felt very different, being with Darcy in his home rather than in the anonymity of the places they had visited together, but she was just as comfortable with him.

He leaned back in his tall chair. Against the light from one of the windows in its deep embrasure she couldn't see his face, but she heard much more than conventional politeness in his response.

'I'm glad, Helen.'

Be careful, Helen warned herself, and then countered it. Why? Darcy was her friend, a close and valuable friend now.

In the mild afternoon sunshine, Darcy took her over the farm. The stone outbuildings rambled behind the main house. There were tall, mellow barns with steeply sloping roofs, long open-sided sheds displaying gleaming yellow and scarlet farm machinery, scrubbed pens with white-painted rails and busy farm-workers who greeted Darcy respectfully, and with obvious liking. Even Helen's unpractised eye could see that Darcy ran Mere with loving efficiency.

Around one corner they met a man in muddy wellingtons who was climbing into a Land Rover. Darcy shook his hand enthusiastically and introduced him as 'Tim Oakshott. Best vet for miles around.' Helen stood aside as the two men worried over a sick ewe, thinking with amusement how alike they looked. She recalled how she had thought at first, in the billiard room at Montcalm, that Darcy himself might just be a country vet.

'I see a lot of Tim,' Darcy told her as they waved at the disappearing Land Rover. 'More than anyone else, I suppose. Except for you, now.' And he gave her an odd, half-defiant sidelong glance.

After their tour they had tea together in Darcy's sitting room, a dark little bachelor den that doubled as an office. There was an old-fashioned desk in one corner, heaped with an orderly pile of papers.

At last, in the early evening, Darcy walked her back through the house and out to the sheltered corner where he had left his car. The farm seemed deserted now. Helen supposed that the farmhands had gone for the day, back to their honey-stone cottages in Mere village.

It was very quiet.

Darcy leaned past her to open the passenger door for her. Dimly, Helen heard the rooks calling in the tall elms two fields away.

Then Darcy bent his head and kissed her. His mouth was gentle and his skin against hers was very soft. She saw that there was a tiny piece of yellow straw caught in the wool at the neck of his sweater. Then as her eyes travelled she saw his hair with the sun shining through it, and it was exactly the same gold as Oliver's. A spasm of loss and longing, the more breathtaking because it was so unheralded, hit her so sharply that she almost doubled up.

Then, just as quickly, it was gone. It was Darcy who was kissing her, in the sheltered angle of a stone wall with the sun on crumbling yellow lichens and the smell of woodsmoke in the air.

Darcy lifted his head. 'Helen?' he said softly, and his voice was eager. 'You ... didn't mind?'

Helen saw him very clearly then, the plain, good-natured face and the colourless hair, nothing like Oliver's now, falling over his eyes.

She had the sense of standing at a junction, deciding which path to take. The world was very still and silent around them. How could she mind him kissing her, Darcy whom she liked and wanted to be with, just because he wasn't someone else? Someone who didn't even exist.

'No,' she said, so quietly that he had to stoop to hear. 'I didn't mind.' Helen had to turn and duck into the car, away from the joy that leapt into his eyes.

At the same moment that Helen was groping into Darcy's car, suddenly shivery even in the spring-evening warmth, Tom Hart was closing his script on the final dress rehearsal of *As You Like It*. The actors crowded forward on the stage, jostling each other silently, waiting.

Tom stood up and his seat snapped back, startling them with its clatter in the hushed auditorium. He walked thoughtfully down the aisle and stood below the stage, looking up at the circle of faces. The anxiety for his final verdict showed in each of them, from Pansy and Oliver to the non-speaking lords and shepherds. Everyone was fully costumed, and there was a faint starched whispering from Pansy's petticoats under her hooped skirt.

At last Tom's face broke into a wide smile.

'You deserve a huge success. That was sensational. Do it as well tomorrow night and we can't fail.'

A murmur of smiling relief spread round the circle.

'You've all worked very hard. Thank you', Tom said simply.

At once a clamour of talk broke out. Oliver pushed his way to the edge of the stage and looked down.

'Thank you,' he said, grinning. 'If anyone deserves a success, it's you. You're a slave-driving bastard, but you're probably right to do it.'

In Oliver's wake, everyone else crowded forward, calling their thanks.

'Don't get excited yet,' Tom told them coolly. 'It's tomorrow that counts.' He turned away and picked up his jacket. He felt, as he always did when the direction of a play was as good as over, drained and exhausted. It felt like a very long time since he had seen the inside of his home.

'Come and have something to eat,' Pansy called after him.

'No. I want to go home.'

Tom walked through the darkening streets. The trees that lined the quiet roads were knobbed with sticky green buds, but he didn't see them. His dark face was intent, marked by a slight frown.

He had done all that he could do, now, but anxiety still nagged at him.

Then when he reached his front door he shrugged as he took out his key. Just a few more days, he thought. If this fragile balance could only hold for just a few more days.

CHAPTER EIGHT

The theatre foyer was a seething mass of people. They spilled out through the open doors and stood in gossiping groups on the pavement. The constant new arrivals peered with interest at the production photographs in their glass boxes on the theatre walls. Oliver and Pansy as a pair of wistful boys in the mock wooing scene, jerkins and white open-throated shirts over breeches, stared out at the world.

'Ve-ery fetching,' someone said. 'That's Lord Oliver, but who's the girl?'

Inside, in a discreet corner, Tom looked at his watch. Seven-twenty. Another ten minutes to go. The audience was already beginning to filter into the auditorium, rustling programmes and banging seats and greeting each other across the aisles.

Tom glanced at the heavy red curtains that hung motionless across the stage. Time to go backstage and wish everyone luck. Before he moved away he saw, in the centre front stalls, that two of the seats reserved for the critics were already occupied. The serious national dailies always sent someone to the annual Oxford University Dramatic Society's major production and they would be here with added interest this year to see how Greg Hart's son performed. Tom stuck his hands in his pockets and stared across at them. The bland-looking critics were talking desultorily together. He recognised both of them. They were important names, and he felt a momentary pleasure that the papers had sent their top men.

I'll show you, he thought. And you too, Greg. This may only be half-assed student drama, but by God it's going to be the best.

Now he saw Lord and Lady Montcalm sailing majestically towards their seats in the front stalls. A little flotilla of attendants and subordinates fussed behind them. Tom crossed over to speak to them and was greeted almost warmly.

'So brave of you to cast Oliver,' Lady Montcalm said. 'I can't imagine how you've coaxed anything out of him. He's such a frivolous boy.'

'Oh, I think he might surprise you tonight.'

'And dear little Pansy, too.'

Lord Montcalm's face turned a little redder when he heard her name and he cleared his throat, running his finger around under his black tie.

'Pansy's quite an actress,' Tom said. 'I think she's got a long way to go. I hope you enjoy the show. Will you excuse me now?'

Backstage there were white faces under heavy make-up. Oliver's gold head was bent as he stood already in position, waiting. Beside him the face of the actor playing old Adam was, at this close range, an unconvincing mass of brown and grey lines and wispy tufts of stuck-on grey hair.

Stage hands in jeans and teeshirts were padding to and fro making last-minute checks. Tom saw Chloe in the wings. She winked at him.

Tom went over to Oliver and touched him on the shoulder.

'Good luck,' he murmured. Oliver nodded absently and went on listening to the opening lines which pounded in his head. He would have admitted it to no-one, but he felt stifled with nerves. The noise of the audience, beyond the curtain, sounded a threatening muffled roar.

When he was assured that everything was in its place on stage under the expert eyes of the stage manager and Chloe, Tom went up to the dressing rooms. Pansy was unconcernedly playing Scrabble with Anne, the actress taking the part of Celia. Pansy looked exquisite in her tight-waisted Elizabethan dress with its billowing skirts. The stiff little white half-ruff behind her head framed her lovely face. The heavy stage make-up only accentuated the perfection of her features and made the myriad blues in her eyes shine even brighter.

'Good luck,' Tom said to both of the girls.

When he dropped a kiss on Pansy's forehead, he thought for the hundredth time how sweet she smelled and tasted.

'Thanks, darling,' Pansy said. 'Everything okay?'

'Yes.' Tom stood in the doorway. 'Pansy? Thanks for ... holding off.'

'Not at all.'

A bell was ringing. One of the stage hands appeared.

'One minute to curtain up.'

Tom made his way back down to the wings. In an unoccupied corner he sat down on a bench and waited.

Helen and Darcy arrived at the theatre just as the one-minute bell was ringing. Darcy had held back for so long that Helen was convinced they would be late. But in his loyalty to his brother he was determined not to miss a second, and he timed it perfectly. The house lights were dimming as they slipped into their seats and no-one even glanced at them.

The curtain went up and with it the lights on Oliver. Helen heard the tiny gasp around her as he turned his head. He was beautiful. Even to Helen, who knew his face as well as her own, startlingly beautiful.

His voice was perfectly measured as he spoke the opening lines.

'As I remember, Adam, it was upon this fashion...'

Slowly, very slowly, Helen breathed out. Darcy's fingers, tangled so tightly in hers that it hurt, relaxed a little.

They sank back into their seats, and let the magic of the play break over them.

From her vantage point in the wings, Chloe knew that it was good. She had watched the production through so many times, but still tonight its streamlined fluency startled her. Not one movement or inflection was superfluous or wasted. Clever, clever Tom Hart, she thought.

At the opposite side of the golden-lit arch of stage, Tom sat with his chin cupped in his hands. Around him the technicians worked and the actors waited for their entrances.

The play was out of his hands now.

It's okay, Tom told himself. Oliver was doing fine. His physical presence was enough to hold them, but he could act too. In this role, at any rate. But the moment that Tom was waiting for came when Pansy made her first appearance.

You can do it, the refrain ran in his head. Show them.

And Pansy did.

As soon as she began to speak, she held the packed theatre in the palm of her hand. There were subtle, intelligent nuances of feeling in her acting which never appeared in the Pansy of real life. She moved and breathed the merriment and poignancy of Rosalind as if no Pansy Warren had ever existed. She's a born actress. Tom had known it ever since her first audition, and now he smiled in triumph. And as he listened to her liquid voice, something else sang in his ears.

Silence.

Beyond the edge of the stage there was not a cough, a rustle or a whisper. No-one moved, and no-one thought of anything but the play. Tom had heard that silence only once before, and that was at the opening of New York's greatest hit in ten years.

Got you, you bastards.

When the house lights came up for the interval, there was a second's quiet before the rush and jostle began for the bars. Helen and Darcy smiled at each other through it and squeezed hands again.

'It's good, isn't it?' Darcy asked anxiously. 'Surely it is?'

'Yes. It's very, very good. Spectacular, in fact. If only they can carry the rest of it off.'

Squashed together in a far corner of the bar, they watched and listened. No-one was talking about anything else.

'Greg Hart's son. The impresario...'

'Better than the one at Stratford...'

'Rather clever, wouldn't you say?...'

'Of course, you know who she is? Masefield Warren's daughter. The shady tycoon...'

'I like the whisper of bleakness. The play should be a synthesis of light and shade...'

'Oh, for God's sake. But aren't they pretty?...'

Helen need not have worried.

The production gathered momentum until the last, spellbinding moment.

Pansy spoke the epilogue from a small circle of light on the darkened stage. Helen had forgotten everything, forgotten that this magical Rosalind was the girl who lived downstairs at Follies House.

'When I make curtsey,' Pansy's slow smile embraced all of them, 'bid me farewell.'

The storm of applause broke instantly. Wave after wave of clapping rose to the stage as the cast took their bows. Pansy and Oliver, hand in hand, stepped forward and the applause redoubled.

'Bravo,' someone shouted and the cry was taken up across the whole theatre. They stood side by side, flushed and dazed with pleased surprise at the acclaim. Oliver put his arm round Pansy's shoulders and kissed her cheek, and she leaned against him. They were both laughing now and suddenly the spell of the performance was behind them. They were themselves again.

At last the clapping died away. Helen saw that the only empty seats were the ones left by the London critics who had slipped away to phone in their reviews for the early editions. There had been no stampede for the exits tonight.

Now, with the curtains firmly closed at last, she watched the audience streaming up the aisles and saw that there was a smile on every single face.

Not bad, she thought. Not bad for a piddling student production of the classics, and she smiled at the memory of Tom's cynicism.

The awkwardness between them all forgotten, Helen longed to find Tom and congratulate him.

'We must go backstage. Darcy, we must.'

Darcy looked horrified. 'No. It'll be all people kissing each other and shrieking. You go – I'll wait for you.'

Helen was still glowing with the joy of the play, and for the first time, his reticence struck a chord of irritation in her.

'Don't you think Oliver will be hurt if you don't go?'

'No. Yes.' He looked so miserable that Helen was sorry at once.

'Come on,' she said gently. 'There'll be so many people no-one will notice us. We'll just say "well done" and go away again.'

Reluctantly, Darcy followed her.

The spiral of narrow stairs that linked the dressing rooms was packed with laughing, cheering people. The crowd was thickest in Pansy's room. When Helen and Darcy squeezed in, they found her perched in a sea of flowers. Pansy blew them a kiss. A glass of champagne was being passed to her, hand to hand over the heads of the crowd. Beside her Oliver twisted the cork off another bottle. He lifted the bottle with a flourish and drank from it, and silver foam ran down his chin and splashed over his shirt. He spluttered and laughed and Pansy reached across to ruffle his hair. Helen thought he looked happier than he had done for weeks.

They were, once again, the perfect couple.

Head down, Darcy wriggled through the throng to Oliver's side. He touched his brother's shoulder and, with his quick, shy smile, murmured, 'well done'. Extravagantly Oliver flung his arm out to embrace Darcy and shouted, 'Look everyone. Even my mystery brother came.'

Darcy went scarlet but everyone's attention had shifted to the doorway. A bulky man in an emphatically tailored suit was forcing his way in.

'Daddy!' Pansy shouted over the uproar. 'Weren't we good?'

Masefield Warren kissed his daughter's forehead as gently as if she were a piece of rare china.

'You were great, princess,' he said, his blunt, seamed features suffused with pride. 'Just great.'

The dizzy blonde at his side was draped in furs and perched on the highest, thinnest stiletto heels.

'Even I enjoyed it,' Pansy's stepmother giggled. 'Darling, how did you remember all those words?'

When Helen looked again, Darcy had disappeared. He had narrowly avoided his parents. Even here, in this throng that had nothing to do with their world, a narrow path automatically cleared itself for the Earl and Countess of Montcalm. Even the foursquare bulk of Masefield Warren shifted slightly to one side.

But it was Tom whom Helen wanted to see. At last she saw him outside in an angle of the stairs. He was still listening, but the dark, sharp planes of his face were softened. He looked satisfied, under the habitual ironic amusement.

Stephen and Beatrice Spurring reached him and stopped. Under the greying wings of hair, Beatrice's face wore its usual frown of concern, but it dissolved briefly into a smile of real pleasure as she congratulated Tom. Stephen was more circumspect.

'Dazzling,' he said. 'Perhaps a touch too much loud pedal, but overstatement always pulls the crowds in. Well done.'

Tom smiled very slightly. 'I'm delighted you enjoyed it.'

The long association through weeks of rehearsal had done nothing to improve their liking for each other. Hostility still bristled under the polite façade.

'And where's the star of the show?'

Tom pointed to Pansy's dressing room. Stephen sprang up the steps with his wife in his wake. He looked young tonight, in his open-necked bright blue shirt and with his silky hair flopping over his forehead like a boy's. Much younger than Beatrice.

Tom was on his own again, and Helen waited no longer.

She ran down to him, took hold of both his hands and reached up to kiss the corner of his thin, clever mouth. She felt his start of surprise and then his strength as he pulled her close to him.

199

She thought that the ironical mask had dropped to show real pleasure.

'Well?'

His voice was no more than a whisper. He was asking her something intensely private, here in this impervious crowd. The thought suddenly made her shy, so shy that she could think of nothing to say. And then it made her answer him as if all he wanted was a response to his play.

'You know how good it was.'

'Ah. Oh yes, I know how good it was.' Tom kissed her in return, lightly, like an old friend. His arm dropped from her shoulders, and she felt cold. 'But all this celebrating is a shade premature until we've seen the reviews. And filled the seats for the rest of the run.'

'I'm sure you needn't worry about that.'

Another surge of people coming up the stairs pressed them back against the wall. Tom put out his arm to shield her, perfectly polite. He was cool again, just as he almost always was. She realised that the moment for telling him that she was sorry for New Year's Eve had gone. She would never do it now. But how stupid. Whyever not?

Helen opened her mouth again, groping for the words to say I'm sorry. I'm sorry I slapped you like some affronted Victorian maiden. If only it hadn't been then, Tom. So soon after seeing Oliver ...

But someone else was demanding her attention. It was Darcy. He looked hot and uncomfortable.

'Helen, I must be off. It's too crowded for me. If you would like to stay, shall I find someone else to see you home?'

'Darcy.' Tom nodded his greeting. Then he leant comfortably against the wall with his arms folded, watching them.

'I'm sure Tom would,' Darcy said helpfully.

'Darcy.' Helen broke in as quickly as she could. 'I can manage a few hundred yards on my own.' Affection for his old-fashioned concern, his quaintness, flooded through her. But it was increasingly mingled with mild irritation. There was something pedantic about Darcy too. 'Anyway,' she said hurriedly, 'I'm ready too. Goodbye, Tom.'

She turned and almost ran. Behind her, Darcy looked faintly puzzled, but he followed with relief. Tom stood for a moment looking ahead into emptiness, but then he went away up the stairs to drink champagne with his elated actors.

Darcy and Helen stood together on Folly Bridge. The spring night air was cool and sweet-smelling and filled with the gurgle of water. Helen leaned over the parapet. Beneath her the foam showed creamy in the race around the piers of the bridge. Follies House was in total darkness. Everyone was still at the theatre. She concentrated on the sound of the water, letting her odd, prickly ill-humour slide away with it.

Her mind was almost empty when Darcy lifted her hand and laced his fingers into hers. He began to talk in a low, humble voice. He was apologising for dragging her away from the party, laying bare his own fear and shyness with painful, determined honesty.

'Don't think I like myself for it', he murmured. 'Don't think I wouldn't be different, if only I knew how.'

'Oh, Darcy, Darcy.' Helen rubbed her face helplessly against the familiar rough tweed of his jacket. 'Please don't be so unhappy. Please. I like you so much...' But, she was going to say, but I can't do anything to help you, or make things between us any different from the way they are now.

Darcy denied her the chance. He pulled her to him with a violence that was startling in such a gentle man. His face burned against her cheeks and the bones bruised her flesh as he kissed her.

The soothing splash of the river was drowned. Threat boomed instead in Helen's ears as she tensed, then tore herself out of Darcy's arms.

'Don't ask me,' she mumbled incoherently, 'don't need what I can't give you...' Almost before she knew what she was doing she had reached out to touch his cheek with the tips of her fingers, then fled away down the mossy, slippery steps to the safety of the island.

'I'm sorry,' she heard the desperation in Darcy's voice. 'Helen, I won't...'

'I know,' she called back to him. 'I know. Just let's ... not change things.'

He put his hands on the parapet and pulled himself so far over that she was afraid he would fall.

'Never?' he shouted.

'Oh, please,' she was almost sobbing now. 'What do you want?'

Up on the bridge a heavy truck thundered past and Helen

thought that she missed his answer. But then it came, in his normal voice, so that she barely heard him.

'Just to be with you.'

'You are with me,' she blurted out. 'Much more than anybody else. Please, please let that be enough.'

Her key found the lock and the dark vault of the hallway gaped behind her. Darcy seemed to be satisfied. He had half turned away and now a car, travelling very fast, was racing past behind him. He had said something else, Helen was certain. It might have been I love you. But now he was gone, and she hadn't really heard him after all.

Helen was very tired. She closed the door and climbed wearily up through the close darkness of the house.

Helen went out early the next morning to buy the newspapers. It was a perfect spring morning, with sunlight flashing off the ripples and all the trees visibly misted with pale green. As she came out of the house, an empty pleasure steamer chugged past on its way to the little landing-stage downriver. The rows of seats inside it were freshly white-painted and there was a new striped awning fluttering over them ready for the first tourist river trip of the season.

There was so much light and brightness everywhere that anxiety was impossible. The evening with Darcy had given Helen a restless, dream-filled night but the significance of it all melted away in the brilliance of the morning. They would go on just as they had been doing, making each other undemandingly happy. Everything would be all right.

Helen bought a selection of papers and dawdled back to Follies with them folded under her arm, savouring the anticipation of rave reviews.

Chloe heard her coming back and ran down to peer at the bundle under her arm. 'Oh good, you've got them. Come and have coffee and we'll gloat together.'

Helen perched herself in a patch of light on the window seat. In front of her the pinnacles and towers of Oxford shone a pale, buttery gold. Helen sighed with pure contentment.

Chloe handed over a wide china bowl of coffee and a croissant wrapped in a napkin. She licked her fingers greedily, pushed back the tumble of red hair and said, 'Now. Let's see...'

They opened a paper apiece and riffled through to find the place. 'Here,' Chloe murmured. 'Oxford. *As You Like It*.'

There was a second or two of silence as their eyes skimmed and then they were shouting simultaneously, not listening to each other.

'Helen, just hear this! "A magical evening ... outstanding performances ... see it if you possibly can..."'

'Mine's even better!' Helen shook out her paper and read, "This is, quite simply, the best student production I have ever seen. I would go even further and say it is the best *As You Like It* I have ever seen, and there have been a good many. So far as I know this is Mr Hart's debut as a director in this country. If he can be persuaded to stay here, our theatre will be the richer".'

They made awed faces at each other. 'Who's that?' Chloe craned to see which paper it was. 'Not very often he goes over the top like that. What does the other one say?'

Helen found it. 'Oh, listen. "A star was born in Oxford last night. Pansy Warren is a bewitching, enchanting Rosalind. She has the makings of a great Shakespearean actress ... Umm ... Miss Warren is well served by Lord Oliver Mortimore's suitably aristocratic Orlando, and by the most sensitive direction that I have seen in Oxford for a very long time. Greg Hart, the great name of Broadway, will be proud of his son today". Chloe, how fantastic. How pleased Tom will be ... everyone will be ...'

Chloe rocked back on her heels surrounded by the crumpled sheets of newsprint. 'I knew it was good,' she kept saying, 'but I hadn't a clue it was that good. Not a clue. Who said that about Pansy? A star is born?' Still only half-believing they went back to the notices and read them through again. Then they lifted their cups and toasted the production and each other in cold coffee.

Then, with a jug of iced orange juice and a bottle of champagne from Chloe's store, they went along to Pansy's room. But the door was shut, and there was no response to their knocking.

'Oh dear,' Chloe said. 'I was so looking forward to drinking the health of a new-born star.'

'Absent friends, then.'

They drank the Buck's Fizz together, sprawled in the patches of sunlight that glowed on the faded Persian rugs. The champagne and the play's acclaim made them giggly.

Chloe balanced her glass precariously on the cushion beside

her head and laced her fingers across her chest with a contented sigh.

'Mmm. I think drinking champagne in the sun is my favourite kind of morning. It only narrowly pips attending a lecture on devotional poetry of the Middle Ages, of course.'

'A close-run thing,' Helen agreed.

'And are you happy, Helen Brown?'

Helen squinted at the dust particles spinning in a shaft of light.

'Blissfully,' she said lightly. 'Oh yes, ecstatically. Why not?'

Chloe rolled sideways to look at her.

'Oliver all forgotten, then?'

'No, not forgotten. Just ... gone.'

'Vanished into orbit round the star. And now you've got Darcy.'

'Yes,' Helen said a little shortly. 'I have got Darcy. Tell me about Stephen.' For weeks she had avoided asking. Now, in this moment of cheerful intimacy, she wanted to know.

Chloe rolled back and groaned into her cushion. 'I wish I knew. Heaven and hell. He doesn't act married, but it's there, like a plate-glass wall. I can come this close to him,' and Chloe put her hands together, a perfect match but not quite touching, 'but never any closer. It gives me no pleasure to think of wrecking anybody's life, Helen, but I'd give anything for him to be mine. All of him. No more hole-and-corner afternoons, stolen weekends, furtive phone calls.' With sudden violence she said, 'I'm tired. I want it to be simple and clear, like the way I feel for him. I love him, and I'm scared. I know you think I'm morally wrong. D'you think I'm a fool as well?'

Helen turned her empty glass against the light. 'I don't think either of those things. I do think he won't make you happy,' she said very quietly.

'Oh, but he does.' Chloe's voice was full of tenderness. 'Just by existing he does. And so long as he is here, I shall be here for him.'

The room was silent. Helen was remembering Stephen running up the steps to Pansy's dressing room last night, and Beatrice trailing wearily after him. There was nothing more that she could say.

Chloe jumped up and reached for the jug. With a flourish she dribbled the last few drops of Buck's Fizz into their glasses.

'Let's think,' she said cheerfully. 'What shall we drink to? Not happiness, perhaps. I know . . .' she stood upright, smiling, with the sun bleaching out the anxious lines around her eyes. She looked lean and tawny like a jungle cat. 'To satisfaction.'

Helen raised her glass too. Yes, she could drink to that.

'To satisfaction,' she echoed hopefully.

That afternoon Helen was back at her usual desk in the brown somnolence of the Bodleian Library. In the carrels that stretched all around, other people were industriously bent over their weighty books, sheaves of notes, card indexes. Librarians trundled up and down with trolleys of books that had been ordered up from the vast stacks underground.

Helen loved this library. It had existed for hundreds of years for the quiet academic pursuits which were going ahead now in exactly the way they always had. It was the easiest place in the world to concentrate.

Helen was reading *The Rape of the Lock*. Pope's elegantly frivolous couplets danced in her head, suiting her mood to perfection. She felt calm and secure. Darcy and she understood each other. Her friends had scored a huge success. All was as it should be.

She was so intent on her book that it was a long time before she became aware of someone pacing up and down the aisle, stopping and moving hurriedly on again. Looking for somebody.

Tom was almost alongside her when she looked up and, with astonishment, saw who it was. She couldn't have imagined that Tom, so deeply engrossed in his theatre world, would even know that this place existed. His peacock blue leather jacket looked very out of place among the ranks of crumpled dons and shabby students. And what could be so important that he would look for her here?

He leaned over the partition of Helen's desk.

'Thank God I've found you. D'you really sit in this warren all day?' He was gathering up her books and papers. 'Come on, Helen, I need you.'

'Ssshh.' There was a sibilant whisper from the girl in the seat next to Helen's.

'What's going on?' Helen asked, bewildered. She was delighted to see him because it meant that they were completely friends again. But she saw that he was preoccupied, and serious.

'Will you be quiet?' hissed the girl, desperately.

Tom took Helen's arm and half dragged her from the room. She could hear the tutting of irritation behind them. Tom was hustling her down the steps so fast that she almost fell.

'I know,' she panted. 'Pansy's broken her ankle. You want me to step in and play Rosalind. "A second, even brighter star is born."'

'Don't joke,' Tom groaned. 'It's infinitely worse.'

'Thanks.'

'It's Oliver.'

Helen went cold. The smile froze on her face. 'Tell me. Tell me what's happened. Now, Tom.'

'Can't you guess?'

Helen saw with a rush of relief that Tom was angry. Oliver wasn't hurt, then.

'No, I can't guess,' she answered a little sharply. Then, 'Wait ... yes, I can. It's Pansy, isn't it?'

'Got it in one,' Tom answered grimly. He had steered her across the curve of the High and now they were plunging down the narrow, cobbled lane that led to the back of Christ Church and Oliver's rooms in Canterbury Quad. Glancing sideways, Helen saw that Tom's face was contracted into a black frown. He was very angry and, more than that, he was anxious.

Helen had never glimpsed anxiety in him before.

'What has happened?' she asked again, more gently.

Tom slackened his pace. 'I'd better explain before we get there. Of course it's Pansy. Pansy floating through the world like a piece of thistledown with never a thought in her lovely head. Pansy wanted Stephen Spurring, God knows why.' Tom was contemptuous. 'So she reached out her velvet paw and took him. As if she couldn't have waited. Thoughtless bitch.'

He sounded bitter too. Helen wondered wryly how much of this outburst was to do with Tom still wanting Pansy for himself.

'When?' she asked.

Tom made an impatient gesture. 'Oh, last night. After the show. There was lots of boozing and horsing around. You saw the way it was going, didn't you, before Darcy took you away?'

'I saw Stephen with Beatrice, and Masefield Warren, and Their Royal Highnesses.' This was Tom and Helen's name for Oliver's parents, a joke they had shared at Montcalm. The

Christmas Vacation seemed ages ago now. 'What can have happened with everyone looking on?'

'Much later. Almost everyone had gone. Somehow poor Beatrice had been packed off home. There was me, and Oliver, and a few others. And Stephen sitting beside Pansy on the sofa in her dressing room. Pansy gave Stephen a long look out of those purple eyes of hers. Then, very slowly, she wrapped her arms around him and kissed him on the mouth. I saw his face across the room. He looked as if someone had just handed him the Koh-i-Noor diamond. Then, a minute later, they were gone.'

Helen remembered Stephen springing up the steps to Pansy's dressing room. Then she saw Chloe sitting in a patch of sunlight on the faded Persian rug, drinking a toast in cold coffee.

'Was Chloe there?'

'Chloe? Oh, I see. No, she'd left. But Oliver was, and you can guess how the night panned out after that.' In spite of himself a flash of cynical amusement showed in Tom's face. 'He embarked at once on a binge of epic proportions. He's destroying himself, but he's doing it in the grand style. Champagne, with brandy chasers. I stayed up with him. My naive plan was to see him through the worst in a brotherly way, put him to bed when the time came, and follow up in the morning with Alka-Seltzer and some brisk advice to forget all about her.'

'That wouldn't have worked,' Helen said sadly. There was nothing in the story that amused her, and a heavy, uncomfortable weight of foreboding pressed on her.

They passed through the College gates. It was the middle of a busy afternoon and hurrying people jostled past them. A forest of bicycles stood tangled against a sunny stone wall.

'No, it didn't,' Tom agreed. 'There was a kind of grimness about his hitting the bottle that I've never seen in him before. We've got drunk together often enough, God knows. But last night it was different. He was determined to go on, and on. I tried to get him to talk, but he wasn't interested. He got very aggressive when I tried to take the bottle away. And I wouldn't fancy a fight with Oliver, drunk or sober. In the end it was me who collapsed.'

Helen nodded. 'And today?'

'The same.'

'Poor Oliver,' she said.

'Poor nothing.' Tom's anger flashed up again. 'What Oliver chooses to do to himself is Oliver's business, any week except this week. But tonight, and for the next ten nights, he has to get on that stage and act. Now he says that he won't do it. I'll see that he does, but I won't have him walking through it pissed. Jesus, I hate all this backstage drama. It's unprofessional.' To Tom that was the sharpest criticism of all. Helen almost laughed.

'They aren't professionals.'

'They are while they're working for me.'

Yes, Helen thought. You'll see to that.

'You know,' Tom said, 'I saw all this coming. I had a row with Pansy about it. In the end she told me – promised me – that she would keep Oliver happy until the show was on.'

So that explained the raised voices she had heard in Pansy's room.

'You mean you arranged it between you in advance? Rather cold-blooded, isn't it?' Only last night she had thought that Pansy and Oliver looked the perfect couple again.

'Yes,' Tom said levelly. 'That's the way it often has to be, Helen. Not pretty, but realistic.'

They reached the low doorway in Canterbury Quad that led to Oliver's rooms. Helen read the white-painted name board again, *Lord Oliver Mortimore*. Tom turned in the doorway.

'As it happens I wasn't quite realistic enough. Pansy only understands surfaces. I should have known that as soon as the first night was over, and she was sure of a critical success, she would think that the rest of the run wasn't important. She wanted to go off with Stephen Spurring, and that was what mattered.'

Helen understood. But she was pricked by what she saw as Tom's coldness. Her sympathy was all with Oliver. He had lost Pansy now, and Helen remembered vividly what that loss felt like.

'What do you want from me, then?' she asked flatly. They stood at the foot of the staircase. Tom's hand was resting on the newel-post, very close to her own, but neither of them moved. They looked into each other's eyes, weighing up.

Then Tom said, 'I need your help. I think Oliver will listen to you. He was ... talking about you, last night.'

There was a long silence. Looking away from Tom, Helen could see the corner of Oliver's door, shut fast. If there was anything she could do for him, of course she would do it. And in spite of her irritation with him, she was flattered that Tom had thought of asking her for help.

'Please, Helen,' Tom said, very quietly.

'I'm coming,' she answered. They went up the curve of stairs to Oliver's door in silence.

Whatever chaos of empty bottles and overturned furniture Helen might have been expecting, she was surprised to see that everything looked as usual. Oliver's long, elegant room with its view of the classic proportions of the Quad was tidy, quiet and sunlit. Oliver himself was sitting in an armchair, his clean white shirt accentuating his healthy tan. There was a half-empty bottle of white wine at his elbow, and a glass in his hand. He was unshaven, and his eyes glittered, but otherwise he looked as he always did. Then Helen saw the fan-shape of his key ring, with the little silver propelling pencil, thrown down on a low table beside him.

Slowly, Oliver moved his head to look at them.

'I said no, Hart. I don't want to act in your play. I want to sit here on my own and get quietly drunk. Is that unreasonable?'

Helen realised that he was talking with exaggerated care. He was drunk already, she saw, and her heart sank.

'Yes, under the circumstances,' Tom said crisply. He glanced at his watch. 'Three o'clock. I'll be back at six-thirty to take you to the theatre, and I want you sober. You said you'd like to see Helen. Here she is. Now get a grip on yourself.'

Tom picked up the bottle of wine and went to the door. His face softened as he looked back at Helen.

'Can you cope?' he asked.

She nodded, but she was very afraid that she couldn't.

'Helen, thank you. I knew that you at least wouldn't let me down.'

The door closed behind him and she looked at it until she was forced to accept that he was gone.

'Screw your play,' Oliver called. Then he sank back into his chair and wearily shut his eyes. 'And everything else.' His hand groped for the bottle of wine, then he remembered that Tom had taken it. He laughed, scornful. 'Does he really imagine that there isn't any more? Be a darling and bring us another bottle from the fridge. The kitchen's out on the staircase.'

'No,' Helen said. 'But I'll make us some tea.'

'I don't want bloody tea', Oliver said, but she brought it anyway. Carefully she set the tray down between them and then knelt beside his chair to pour it.

'I'm sorry about Pansy,' she said at last, her head still bent over the teacups.

'Oh, Pansy doesn't matter. Not now, anyway.' He took his cup and wound his fingers around it as though his hands were cold. 'Pansy's going is just a symptom.'

'Of what?'

'Of the awful, repetitive sameness of everything. I thought,for a little while, that Pansy was going to be something special. But no. She turns out to be just as monotonously rotten as everything else.'

Suddenly, Oliver reached out and tangled his fingers in Helen's mass of dark hair. He drew her head towards him until it rested against him. Somehow she felt at once how tired he was. His usual restless energy had seeped away, and now he was simply weary. For a moment they sat quietly. Helen felt charged with sympathy for him, and at the same time impotent to dispel the strange blackness that seemed to be gaining the upper hand inside him.

Oliver lifted one of the black curls and watched it wind around his finger. 'I should have held on to you, Helen Brown, while I had you. You're calm, and reasonable. You almost had me convinced I could be the same.'

Helen sat motionless, not trusting herself to speak. She was only aware of fear that it would all start up again inside her, that Oliver would come back to tear like a storm through the flat, ordered landscape of her life.

Oliver went on, half to himself. 'But I wouldn't have made you happy, you know. What happened was the best thing. I did feel guilty, but I don't any more.'

Did giving me the money help? Helen wondered. The money that was all gone now, but had kept her family for a few vital weeks. She wanted to talk about it, but Oliver's train of thought was moving rapidly, half-connectedly on.

'And now it's too late. I suppose you're Darcy's, now.'

'I'm not anyone's,' she protested gently, but Oliver was not to be interrupted.

'Much better,' he was saying. 'Much, much better. I like him, you know. The trouble is just that he doesn't like me. Not that I've ever given him any reason to. Ever since we were tiny, I've acted as if he was some kind of not very subtle joke. Not calculated to make people like you, that.' Suddenly he shivered violently. 'Christ, I'm so cold.'

Helen stood up and wrapped her arms around him, resting her cheek against his hair. The true gold reminded her of how she had seen the sun shining through Darcy's and, for a split second, confused him with his brother.

'How long have you been sitting here?'

'No idea. Hours. Since last night.' He looked round vaguely. 'Hart got my scout in to clear up. And he made me change my shirt. The other one got muck on it.'

Suddenly, he laughed, and Helen saw thankfully that he looked almost himself. He had drunk two cups of tea, thirstily. 'It doesn't really suit him, playing nursemaid.'

Helen had been hunting in the bedroom, and now she produced a thick cable-knit sweater. 'Come on. Let's go out for a walk.'

Oliver pulled the sweater on gratefully, but he looked out at the bright afternoon unwillingly.

'What for? At least let's have a drink, first.'

'No.' Helen took his arm and began to steer him to the door. At first he pulled back angrily, but then he looked around the empty room, shivered again, and let her draw him away.

Helen walked out into the sunlight with Oliver leaning as heavily on her as if he were an invalid. They crossed the College and came out into Christ Church Meadows, open and inviting under the blue sky. Without speaking they took the majestic tree-lined avenue that led like an arrow to the river. There was a mist of pale spring-green everywhere, and the full-throated gurgle of wood-pigeons in the elm trees.

When they reached the river, they turned to walk past the College boathouses. The big double doors of several of them stood open, and they peered to see the glossy shells of rowing eights stacked inside. The air smelt of varnish and linseed oil.

Oliver paused to watch a couple of eights flash past on the water, sending up rainbowed droplets of spray. The oarsmen strained forward and the coxes sat hunched forward, calling the strokes. A rowing coach bicycled past on the towpath, anxious, his stopwatch bumping against his chest.

'I used to row at Eton,' Oliver said, 'until it struck me that there have to be at least a thousand easier ways of getting from A to B.'

There was a pleasant ordinariness in their laughter that was like music to Helen.

Slowly they made two circuits of the Meadows. Oliver kept his arm firmly linked in hers, but otherwise they might have been enjoying any pleasant afternoon stroll. When they spoke at all, it was desultorily, about their immediate surroundings.

At last they stopped on the wide gravel walkway in front of Meadow Building. The sun had disappeared behind it and the air was suddenly cold.

'Six-fifteen,' she said, as coolly as she could. 'We must go back to meet Tom.'

When she looked up into Oliver's face, she saw that the ominous glitter had faded from his eyes. His voice sounded natural and steady again. She thought that he must be almost sober. She would have to suggest it to him now.

'You will go on, won't you? Oliver, there's no-one else to take your part. You must do it, for Tom's sake.'

Oliver stared back down the long avenue of elms. Helen heard him jingling his key ring in his pocket. At last he shrugged.

'I suppose I have to.' His voice was flat.

Quickly, before he could change his mind, Helen steered him back to his rooms. Tom was waiting for them. His black brows went up a fraction, and Helen nodded swiftly to reassure him.

Silently his mouth framed the words. 'Thank you.'

With breathtaking speed, they hustled Oliver between them to the theatre.

'We can do it, between us,' Tom whispered to her. 'Keep him on the rails, just for another few days. And by then the worst will be over. I've seen him in these black fits before, although never quite as bad as this, and they don't last for ever.'

I hope you're right, Helen thought grimly.

Tom supervised Oliver's application of his make-up, waited as he changed into his costume. Orlando began to appear again out of the white-faced, mechanically-moving Oliver.

Helen sat in an armchair watching, and listening to Tom's brisk instructions. Once or twice she went outside to bring them coffee in paper cups from the vending machine beside the stage door.

Soon a stage hand peered into the dressing room.

'Ten minutes.'

'I must do a quick round of everyone else,' Tom said. 'You're not the only actor in this show.' There was no question that he would betray his anxiety to Oliver.

When he had gone, Oliver's reflection in the wide mirror stared back at Helen. He looked odd with his layer of lurid make-up.

'Don't go, will you?' he said.

'No, I won't go if you'd like me to stay here.'

The head reappeared in the doorway. 'Five minutes. On stage, Oliver.'

He stood up, then slammed his fist down so hard on the table that the clutter of tubes and jars rattled.

'Why in God's name am I doing this? I don't want to go out there and be stared at. And I don't want to act opposite her. How can I?'

Helen jumped to her feet.

'There isn't time for this now. They're waiting.'

'Let them wait. I want just one drink.'

'Afterwards.' Almost bodily, Helen propelled him from the room and down into the wings. There was the faintest stir of relief among the knot of people standing there.

Out on the stage, old Adam was waiting. Oliver half went to join him, then turned back to Helen.

'Where's Darcy?'

Startled, she said, 'I don't know. At home, I suppose.'

'Pity. I'd have liked to see old Darcy.'

Then Oliver took up his position. He pressed the palms of his hands to his temples, as if he was trying to suppress the noise in his head. From beyond the curtain the dull murmur of the audience was quieter but infinitely more threatening than the night before.

Helen fled, unable to watch any more.

She found her way to the green room. By an odd chance it was completely deserted. Helen crossed to the controls of the tannoy speaker, turned up the volume, and waited.

Then Oliver's voice came crackling out with the opening lines. Helen forced herself to listen, critically sharp-eared. But he was all right. His voice was still flat, but it was firm. By degrees she let herself relax. There was none of the surrender to enchantment of the night before, but at least the play was on. Oliver was walking blindly through the part, but he was on stage and that would have to be good enough.

Then it was time for Pansy to make her entrance. Even up

in the green room, listening to the distorted, tinny sound of the relayed voice, Helen sat up. If Oliver's performance was wooden, Pansy's was incandescent. She was playing as she had never done it before.

In the auditorium, the spaces in the wings, even in the lighting box, nobody moved. Tom sat in his director's seat, a half-smile lifting the taut lines of his face. And in Pansy's dressing room, Stephen Spurring stared down at his hands, where Pansy had printed kisses before running down to the stage, unbelieving.

Somebody came into the green room. Helen looked up to see Chloe. Her face was dead white under the careful make-up and her eyes were swollen. She gave Helen a small defiant smile and then, as if intent on giving herself something to do, began to tidy the room. She swept empty paper cups into a wastepaper basket and then began to stack up discarded newspapers. The bundle slipped and pages drifted to the floor. Chloe stared down at them for a second before tears spilled down her face.

Helen put her arm around her shoulders and they sat in silence as Chloe fought to stifle the sobs.

'Listen,' she said at last. 'Just listen to her.'

Pansy's voice rippled all round them, soft with a new velvety warmth.

'I can't even be angry,' Chloe said bitterly. 'They have just fallen in love. Luminously, simply. Just like I wanted it to be for me.' Her shoulders shook with the weight of racking sobs and she buried her face in her hands.

Desperately, Helen searched for a consoling word and could think of none.

'Chloe, Chloe,' she murmured, rocking her as if she was a little child. 'Don't cry like this. He isn't worth it.'

'To me he is,' Chloe said. 'At least he came to tell me. At least he was honest. You should have seen his face when he talked about her, as if she was the most precious thing in the world, as if nothing else would ever be important to him again. I said what about Beatrice? and he looked quite blank, hardly remembering her name. I've never seen anyone fall in love like that.'

'And Pansy?'

'Something has happened to Pansy, too. You know that butterfly quality, the way she's always flitting on to something new and more exciting? Well, now she's calm, and still, and smiling. I saw her looking at him tonight with pure, triumphant happiness. Helen, I want to hate her for it, but I can't.'

Chloe sat up and pressed her fingers to her cheeks. 'I can't stay here. Tom'll be needing me. And I don't want anyone to see me looking like this.' Deliberately, Chloe was pulling herself together again. 'The show must go on, eh?' There was even the glimmer of a real smile, and Helen smiled her own admiration and encouragement back.

Chloe would survive, she saw, because deep down she wanted to. But Oliver was a different question. Helen couldn't guess at the answer, and she knew that she didn't really even understand what the question was. Thoughtfully she went down to the public call box outside the theatre and dialled Darcy's number at Mere.

By the end of the third act, he was at her side.

Quickly Helen told him the story. 'Oliver wanted to see me?' he asked. 'Where is he?'

They found him alone in his dressing room, sitting out the interval.

'Darcy?' Oliver said. 'You are here. How odd. You know, the strangest thing. I suddenly thought how good it would be if we played chess again. Like we used to, at home? Do you remember, it was the only thing you ever beat me at?'

Helen realised gratefully that Darcy knew what was needed of him.

'I'll still beat you,' he said calmly. 'Where are the pieces?'

She left them sitting hunched opposite one another over the board. Outside she bumped into Tom who had run up the stairs two at a time.

'Couldn't get away sooner,' he said. 'What's he doing now?'

'Perfectly okay. He's playing chess with Darcy.'

Tom took hold of both her hands and kissed her cheek.

Helen looked quickly away down the long spiral of stairs.

'You and Darcy,' he said gently, 'are true friends in need.'

'So are you', Helen countered lightly. 'Oliver told me about you nursemaiding him.'

'Ah, but my involvement is entirely due to self-interest.' Tom was suddenly at his most sardonic. 'I've just been down to the box-office. Do you know, we're sold out for the run?'

'I don't believe you,' Helen called out after him, not meaning

215

anything to do with his play. But his only answer was a little, cynical laugh.

It was very late when Helen let herself into Follies House that night. She had waited to see whether Oliver would take refuge in drinking after the release of the final curtain. There had been a bottle of whisky, and Oliver had reached for it with the make-up still caked on his face and with Orlando's white shirt clinging damply to his back after the effort of the last scenes. Helen understood what a toll the long evening had taken.

But Darcy had stepped smoothly in before Oliver could drain his first glass. He had insisted, deaf to Oliver's mocking complaints, that his brother should come back with him to Mere. And suddenly Oliver had capitulated, too weary to resist the decisions that were being made for him.

Helen and Tom had said a brief goodnight. 'Until tomorrow,' he had said. 'Will you come again?'

She nodded her promise. 'Yes.' And had gone home alone to Follies, for once feeling the uncomfortable weight of her solitude. But as soon as the thick oak door swung to behind her, Helen felt a cold shiver running down her spine. Before she could see anything at all in the dimness of the Jacobean hallway she sensed the tension in the air. Then there was a movement in front of her. Pansy was standing like a wraith under the gallery rail. She was wrapped in a dark coat, and with a beret pulled down over her silvery hair, she looked even more like a boy. In one hand she was holding one of her chic leather suitcases and the other was clenched into a small white fist. Her face was turned upwards.

Helen followed her gaze.

Chloe was leaning over the carved baluster.

For a long, long moment the two women stared at each other. Then Chloe said, very softly, 'Won't you at least tell me? You're going to Stephen, aren't you?'

Pansy's fist clenched even tighter. 'I have to be with him, Chloe. Surely it's better to go to him than bring him here?'

Chloe's head bent and the dark red hair swung across her face like a curtain.

'Chloe,' Pansy said urgently, 'I can't help it. Any of it. Don't hate me. Even if you can't forgive me.'

There was no response. Pansy turned away and brushed past

Helen as if she didn't exist. Then there was a sudden harsh gust of cold air and Pansy vanished into the dark.

When Helen looked again, Chloe was walking away. There was no sound except for the soft padding of her slippers on the bare oak boards.

CHAPTER NINE

Between them, as Tom had predicted, they built up a system for seeing Oliver through the days and nights of the play.

Each night Darcy took him home to Mere. Oliver scoffed at Darcy's unremarkable car and insisted on driving the black Jaguar recklessly through the country dark. Darcy reported to Helen that once home, they sat up for hours playing game after game of chess. Oliver drank steadily until he had anaesthetised himself enough to fall asleep. Then he would sleep heavily, clinging to oblivion, until late in the morning. Darcy, as always, was up again at first light and made the rounds of his farmwork, half suffocated by yawns. Then Oliver would drive back into Oxford and Helen would try to persuade him to eat something, and then keep him company through the short, sunny afternoons.

Oliver was irritable and resigned by turns, but he had accepted that he had to go on playing Orlando. He was still drinking a good deal but Helen thought that it was a way of keeping himself going. And she guessed that he was taking other things too, when his moods swung from dull apathy to violent impatience with Oxford, *As You Like It* and Helen herself. Yet Helen found herself growing to like him more, and even to understand him. When they talked and Oliver was not being bitterly flippant, she glimpsed a man who was somehow beleaguered and threatened by all the things that made him enviable to the rest of the world. She remembered how she had seen Oliver's gilded exterior as protecting an inner, sensitive man, and had fallen in love with that twin image. This new Oliver was closer to the one that she had dreamed up for herself, but he was more complex and infinitely more vulnerable.

Her new feeling for him was nothing to do with the old, hurtful romantic love. But in its way it was just as strong. It was loyal, and protective, and increasingly sharp with anxiety.

There were signs that Oliver felt something different too. Once, when they were sitting in his rooms watching the light outside fade from gold to grey, he looked across at her and said, 'I suppose we won't do this any more, when the play's over?

When you've delivered me safe and sober to Hart for the last performance?'

'Why not?' she had asked calmly, staring back into his eyes.

'I don't know anybody else, like I know you now,' he had said. 'Funny, isn't it, how alone we all are?'

Another time he had murmured, almost to himself, 'Darcy's luckier than he knows. Or perhaps he does know, after all.'

She hadn't answered that.

In the evenings Tom took over. He saw Oliver through the long demands of the performance with a careful mixture of asperity and subtle cajolement. Helen sat at her desk and tried to make up the lost hours of work.

And so, at length, they reached the last night.

It was traditional for the director of the OUDS major to throw a party after the last performance for everyone connected with the production, and Tom had taken up the idea with enthusiasm. He had been insistent that Darcy and Helen should be there.

'If it hadn't been for you, there wouldn't have been a show after the first performance. Or at least, there'd have been me stumbling through Oliver's part with the book in one hand. Disaster.' He had flashed them one of his rare, brilliant smiles. 'I'm a wonderful director and a lousy actor. So be there, both of you. Please.'

A little to Helen's surprise, Darcy had agreed. And at his suggestion, they were to see the play again too.

When he appeared at Follies House to collect her, his hair was sleeked down, and he was wearing a velvet jacket which wouldn't have looked out of place on Oliver, with a raffish bow tie, which suited him.

'Darcy,' she laughed at him, 'don't confuse me. This is a theatrical party, remember.'

He looked so pleased that she kissed him, and stood for a moment contentedly with his arms around her.

'Oh, one has to go to these affairs from time to time to make sure one isn't missing anything,' he told her cheerfully. 'And I want to be there, for Oliver. You never know. Besides, you'll be there too. You look very pretty tonight, Helen. You do make me wish we weren't going anywhere at all.'

Helen had been awarded a tiny travel bursary. She was supposed to use the money to broaden her studies with travel abroad, but she had half-guiltily spent some of it on new clothes. Tonight's amethyst silky jacket over a camisole top was part of her extravagance.

'D'you like it?' She spun round for him to admire her. 'I love buying things.'

'Frivolous girl,' Darcy said humorously.

They walked to the theatre hand in hand.

Tonight's audience was very different from the first. In place of the tense expectancy there was an air of celebration. Almost everyone there was a friend, connected with the company, ready to enjoy the play and then to toast its success at the party.

Before the house lights went down, Helen caught sight of Stephen. He was sitting to one side of the auditorium, alone, and looking straight ahead at the stage. It was as if he was willing the curtains to open, Helen thought, so that he could see Pansy again.

The play itself was subtly different too. Oliver was adequate, familiarity having given a kind of polish to his playing that compensated for his interest being so far from it. But Pansy was so good that she carried everything with her. The new warmth which Helen had detected from her hiding place in the green room was still there, even intensified. More, she seemed to inspire the rest of the cast to try to match her.

When at last the curtain fell on her epilogue, Helen turned to Darcy and saw that he too was blinking back the tears.

'She's going to be famous,' Helen said, rising to her feet with the entire audience. 'She must be. She'll be a great actress.'

The applause was deafening. Pansy and Oliver took their curtain calls, smiling at the audience hand in hand, but never once looking at each other. Then Pansy came forward alone. She kissed her hand to the sea of faces again and again, laughing, pleasingly bewildered by the acclaim. Then a single white rose landed at her feet. She stooped to pick it up and stuck it into the bodice of her dress. Almost at once there were flowers all around her and she scooped them up until they spilled out of her arms.

In response to a new crescendo of shouts, Pansy held out a hand towards the wings. Tom ducked into the blaze of lights and bowed, quickly, almost formally. Then he took Pansy's hand and kissed it, turned her to face her audience one more time, and then led her away.

The house lights came up to a long, last cheer of delight. The play was over.

Helen and Darcy joined the throng of people making their way to Tom's party. Helen had never seen Tom's home and she looked interestedly up at it. It was an elegant, flat-fronted house in a North Oxford garden square. The front door stood invitingly open.

'Here goes,' said Darcy, pulling at the ends of his bow tie and grinning at her. Helen squeezed his hand, and was still holding it in hers when they stepped into the warmly-lit hall. Tom was greeting his guests at the door. He saw their linked hands and there was a flicker of something that turned into cool amusement in his face. Helen felt a prickle of irritation and wondered why it was that Tom still had the knack of annoying her, however much she liked him.

Their relationship should have been simple, but it wasn't.

He welcomed them warmly, dropping his arms around their shoulders for a brief instant as he murmured, 'I'm glad you both came. I haven't thought of a way to thank you both properly yet, but I will.'

Helen felt the brief pressure of his hands on her shoulder. He glanced down at her outfit and murmured, 'You look as pretty as you did on New Year's Eve.'

She stared up at him, suddenly wondering, but then he said, 'Doesn't she, Darcy?' The blush that had started to rise in her cheeks drained away again.

'She always looks lovely,' Darcy said loyally.

'Of course. Champagne's through there,' Tom told them. He moved away to kiss a well-known woman television don on both cheeks.

Darcy and Helen wandered through the house, glasses of champagne in their hands. It was obviously rented, but aimed at the visiting-professor level rather than student digs. There were small Victorian button-backed sofas upholstered in velvet, thick pale-coloured carpets and glass-topped tables. It amused Helen to see the few items that emphatically belonged to Tom in this setting of carefully neutral good taste. There was a set of African ivory chessmen, and overflowing shelves of books, most of them to do with the theatre. On one low set of shelves there was a rounded, primitive soapstone carving of a polar bear.

But it was Tom's pictures that interested Helen most of all.

221

Every wall, from the hallway right through the house, was lined with them. There were prints and lithographs by modern artists, some of them famous names and some of them that meant nothing to her. Between these were delicate watercolour scenes and landscapes and sombre portraits in oils, all together in an intriguing, concerted demand for attention. They made the expensively soulless little house immediately Tom's own. Helen smiled at the idea of the organisation needed to get them all crated up and shipped to Oxford. Tom was nothing if not efficient. Even his party reflected that, with the discreetly watchful waiters who kept every glass filled and attended to the exotic food laid out in the dining room.

In pride of place over the fireplace there was a little oil painting. It was of an open window, framed with blue wooden shutters, with a vase of bright flowers on the sill. Beyond the window was the sea, bright turquoise and dancing with reflected light. It was a simple, economical picture, with every brushstroke visible. Helen stood in front of it for a long moment, thinking how beautiful it was.

The rooms were filling up rapidly. There were familiar faces from the cast, and backstage at the theatre. There were others that she recognised by sight from grander Oxford circles than those that touched her own – a couple of College masters and their wives, a sprinkling of novelists and poets, and a celebrated painter in the black fedora he always wore. Tom seemed to know and be on terms of easy familiarity with everyone. Helen was impressed, and she felt a little awe creeping into her feelings for him. But even in this sophisticated gathering there was a little stir of people covertly turning to stare as Pansy came in. She was wearing a simple black dress with her hair combed out in a pale halo around her head. Unusually for her she had painted her eyes with extravagant, theatrical rings of blue which made her face look small and fragile, her colouring more delicate. Half a step behind her was Stephen, the same rapt expression that Helen had seen in the theatre tempered with a kind of defiance.

There was no sign of Beatrice.

Pansy was immediately swallowed up by a hubbub of people. As she accepted the kisses and congratulations, she looked all set for a night of enjoying the limelight. So Helen was the more surprised when she looked up a little later to see Pansy slipping into a seat beside her. Deliberately Pansy set her shoulders against the room and, glancing at Darcy, reassured herself that he was occupied in talking to someone else.

'Are you avoiding me, Helen?' she asked directly.

'Not exactly,' Helen responded carefully. She wasn't sure that she even liked Pansy any more, but she shrank from letting her see it. Suddenly she had a sense that Pansy needed friends too. 'You haven't been around much,' she said, truthfully.

'I've been with Stephen.' Pansy looked down at her thin fingers and restlessly twisted the rings. She was struggling with what she wanted to say. 'He's ... left Beatrice, you know. Left it all behind. His children, that house and all their lives in it ... given it up to camp out in his College rooms, with me.' She bit her lips and Helen saw her knuckles whitening as she pressed her fists together in her lap. 'I love him now, Helen, today. Very much. He makes me happier than anyone else has done.'

'I could see that,' Helen said quietly.

'I won't try to tell you why,' Pansy went on. Her crooked smile was painful, hiding something. 'But I do. Perhaps I've only just discovered that older men turn me on. Perhaps it doesn't matter exactly why, it's enough that we do love each other like this. But I'm trapped, now. How can I promise him that it'll still be there tomorrow? And all the other days to justify what he's given up? I'm scared, you know.' Pansy looked back over her shoulder at the room full of people. 'There's never a simple, finite action, is there? Everything reverberates, messily. Look at us all. Oliver. Beatrice, Stephen, you and me. Chloe.'

Helen looked. Chloe had just come in. She was wearing jaunty, scarlet harem pants and a little sequined top that sparkled when she moved. But her face was tired and drawn. Tom was shepherding her over to a knot of people. He began to make introductions and Helen saw her struggling to smile and listen to the names belonging to the anonymous faces. Then she looked back into Pansy's blue-painted eyes.

'Perhaps you're always presented with too many choices, Pansy,' she said.

I used to envy you, Helen thought, but I don't think I do, any more. She wanted to say that even for Pansy, there were choices to be made that wouldn't hurt anyone, but could think of no way to say it that didn't sound priggish.

Pansy stood up, as supple as a cat now after Tom's autocratic rehearsal regime.

'Oh yes', she answered softly. 'Far, far too many choices. It's

223

rather limiting, in a way, you know. Not to speak of isolating. But I shouldn't have asked you to listen about me and Stephen. You wouldn't have approved, would you?' Then she added, in quite a different voice, 'There just isn't anyone else. But we're not really made to be friends, you and me. We're like oil and water. The trouble is, I'm scared that I'm the water. I just evaporate.' Abruptly, she turned aside. 'Shit, what does it matter? I'm going to find Stephen.'

Left alone, Helen sat very still for a long moment. She was stuck with a sense of having failed to say or do something important. And now she had lost the chance.

Instinctively she moved closer to Darcy. He was talking calmly to a geologist about the land at Mere. Helen smiled a little. In that moment she realised that Darcy was the most straightforwardly good person she knew. Everything he did, at least, was clear-cut and honest, and as dependable as the rounds of the seasons themselves over the carefully-tended acres of Mere. She watched the familiar, undistinguished face and the play of kindliness in it with new affection.

Across the room Chloe drained her glass of champagne, and at once it was refilled. The alcohol made her feel better, less tempted to run away and less afraid of crying. She had dressed so carefully for tonight, and made up her face to hide the ravages of the last few days, then had come tensely to the party. All through the long evening before it, she had been reminding herself that there was nothing to hope for, that all she wanted was just to see Stephen, perhaps talk to him for a few moments. But now she was here she knew that of course she had been hoping, hoping so desperately that it had left her almost breathless as she came up the path to Tom's front door. Her eyes had obsessively raked the crowd as soon as she was inside, and she had seen Stephen at once. He was listening to someone, with his head on one side in his characteristic intent pose. Chloe's heart almost turned over in her chest. It was days since she had seen him and she had been counting the hours up to this second without really knowing what it was that she was expecting and longing for.

The intensity of her gaze drew Stephen's attention. When he looked up and saw her, he made a little, embarrassed gesture that was barely a wave. Then he looked away and tilted his head again as if the conversation he was listening to was so fascinating that he couldn't risk missing a syllable.

Chloe's head swam and the room blurred around her. When it cleared again she knew that she had been absurd. Stephen would never reach out for her again. Even as she watched, Pansy came through the crowd, looking almost a child under the flamboyant make-up. Her hand slipped into Stephen's and they stood there shoulder to shoulder. In his face there was incredulous happiness, and Pansy was defiant in her possession. There could have been no clearer declaration that they were together. Everyone in the room saw it. Chloe felt an added surge of bitterness. It was Beatrice who would have their sympathy.

With unflattering clarity Chloe saw the tiny role that she had played. She was just the last in a long line of girls who had failed to do what Pansy had succeeded in so effortlessly. And more, she understood that Pansy had succeeded because she was more beautiful, richer, and above all hardly more than a child. Clever, learned Stephen had been impressed by just that.

The coldness of disillusion made Chloe shiver. Stephen wasn't clever at all. He was a fool. Anger, bitterness and resentment slowly faded away to be replaced by emptiness. 'Pretty, isn't it?' somebody said beside her. Chloe looked and saw Oliver. His face had grown thinner and some of the boyish beauty had given way to harder lines. Chloe thought that he looked handsomer now.

'Very touching,' she answered, and turned deliberately away from the sight of Stephen and Pansy. 'Well. Shall we go and eat?'

Chloe had always felt that there was something just a little wrong about Oliver, but tonight she was glad to have his company. She even felt, as she looked round, that he was the only other person at the party she could bear to be with.

In the dining room, Oliver heaped salmon mousse liberally on to her plate.

'Christ, I'm so glad it's over. I want to celebrate.'

'The play?'

'The play, of course. What else?' Their eyes met and they smiled, cynical smiles that tried to give nothing away.

'Aren't you eating anything?' Chloe asked.

'No. I'm drinking instead. Let's drink lots and lots together.'

Chloe gave him her glass.

Oliver filled it, and then filled it again.

The party began to blur a little. She left her plate almost

untouched, but she went on drinking champagne. The suffocating hurt dwindled to a little black lump that seemed not quite a part of her, and was easy to ignore. Easy except when Stephen and Pansy swam into view, dancing with their arms wrapped round each other or smiling with their faces almost touching, and then Chloe only had to turn away and look at something else. Increasingly she found herself looking at Oliver. She noticed the set of his head and the length of his eyelashes. She saw the fine gold hairs glinting at the neck of his shirt, and a small scar on his wrist. Behind him, the room was a jumble of pale faces and swirling colours, but Oliver was sharply defined. She saw him so clearly that it was as if she had never even looked at him before.

They danced a little, but they kept bumping awkwardly into each other and Chloe had to avert her eyes from Stephen too often amongst the other dancers. They found one of the velvet sofas in a corner instead. Oliver was drinking whisky now and when he kissed her she could taste it on his lips. She turned her head aside a fraction and he opened his eyes, very blue and distant. She had the sudden, disconcerting sense that he wasn't seeing her at all.

'Why not?' he said sharply.

Chloe knew that she should stand up now, call for a taxi and go home alone to her empty room at Follies. The decision was still within her grasp, but when she tried to make the first move, she knew that it was too late. The simple chain of actions seemed impossibly complicated. She lay back against the velvet cushions again and closed her eyes.

'Why not?' she answered tonelessly. 'Why anything?'

Oliver's hand with the scar at the wrist moved to her breast.

Later, she became aware of Darcy and Helen looking down at them.

'Want to share a cab home?' Helen asked.

'I'm not ready to go yet,' Chloe told her. Oliver's arms were insistently around her. She felt smudged and dishevelled and dimly uncomfortable with herself, but still unable to face the prospect of her deserted room.

'Darcy,' Oliver said, 'you look just like a quiz-master in that bow tie.' He and Chloe found this hilariously funny. They collapsed against each other, shaking with laughter.

When Chloe looked again, the party was over. Tom was

leaning against the mantelpiece under a little blue painting of some flowers and the sea.

He looked very cool and detached, the antithesis of the tangle of herself and Oliver.

'There are spare rooms, if you'd like to stay,' he said politely.

Chloe collected herself with dignity.

'No need,' she said. 'Is there, Oliver?'

'Not the slightest,' Oliver agreed. 'Let's not trespass on Hart's generous hospitality an instant longer. He must be longing for his sober, bachelor bed.'

Tom watched them out through the hallway, one eyebrow slightly raised. As they reached the front door he called after them, his voice sharper.

'Oliver. Don't drive.'

Oliver swung round and there was dull red flush of anger rising from his jawline.

'It's finished, you smug bastard. I've done your play. I don't need to be watched and nannied any more. Now leave me alone.'

Despite the drink and the desperation of her mood, the vestiges of Chloe's normal good sense still clung to her.

'We were going to walk anyway,' she said, enunciating clearly although she was not sure for whose benefit, 'because it's such a lovely night.' Firmly she took Oliver's arm.

'Goodnight, then,' Tom said imperturbably. The door closed and they were out in the night together.

'What a good idea,' Oliver said. 'Clever of you, because I've forgotten where my car is. We'll walk, and by the time we get back to the House, it'll be time for a nightcap. You'll join me, of course?'

'Yes', Chloe answered, 'I'll join you.'

She knew vaguely that Oliver was drunker than she was, and she knew that she should see him safely home and then go back to Follies. But a mixture of loneliness and perversity born of bitterness made her reject the knowledge. She didn't want to be alone tonight, and it didn't matter any longer what she did.

They wandered through the deserted streets, Oliver's arm around her shoulders. 'How deliciously warm you are,' he told her. 'I seem always to be cold these days.'

The trees and street lights appeared to swim around Chloe. She hung on to Oliver's arm, wanting him to be a rock but knowing that he was just as much adrift as she. They reached Christ Church and passed under Tom Tower where the porter's lodge was shuttered for the night. Canterbury Quad was all in darkness. They groped up the dark staircase to Oliver's room, and then stood blinking in the brightness when he turned on the light.

Oliver looked down the length of the room and Chloe saw his face contract with dislike.

'Christ,' he whispered. There were two dirty wineglasses on a table and he poured whisky into them. Chloe took hers from him but she knew as soon as she smelt the spirit that she couldn't drink any more. But Oliver gulped his without even glancing at it.

Then he lifted his head and for a long moment they looked blankly into each other's eyes. Chloe heard her own heart beating, and told herself that it still wasn't too late to say goodnight and go peacefully home. But still she stayed silent. She saw that Oliver was sweating a little, and the gold hair clung darkly to his forehead.

He held out one hand, very slowly uncurling the fingers.

'We seem to need each other tonight', he said. Then he reached out for her and Chloe clung to him, digging her fingers into the solid flesh of his arms, holding his body between herself and tomorrow, and all the tomorrows after that. Oliver stroked her hair.

'Come on,' he said urgently. 'Come to bed.'

He led her into his bedroom and they stared down at the tumble of covers. Oliver fumbled with her buttons and then groaned.

'I can't,' he said. 'You do it for me.'

So Chloe undressed herself. She laid her clothes carefully on a chair and then stood still with the dim light throwing bluish shadows in the curves of her body. Oliver looked, and there was the same distance in his eyes as at the party. It was almost as if he didn't know her. But still he drew her down beside him on to the bed. Gratefully, she turned her face into the hollow of his shoulder, feeling the warmth of their flesh together, ready to be gentled into making love.

Something tugged at her consciousness, something she knew that she should remember.

But it was too late, and there was to be no gentleness. Oliver was brutally fierce. He held both her hands imprisoned in his and rolled on top of her. His mouth bruised her lips against her own teeth and then he was pushing so hard into her that she winced with pain.

'No ...' she started to say, but the weight of him crushed the breath out of her. His fingers knotted and tangled in her hair and their bones ground painfully together. For a few fleeting seconds Chloe felt the pressure of her own response to his violence. 'Oliver,' she half-moaned. 'Oliver ...'

Oliver went rigid. He half drew away from her and there was a long, agonised shudder. Then he fell back against her with his face buried in her hair and Chloe's fingers felt the cold dampness of sweat on his back.

In the enveloping silence, she looked round the unfamiliar room. Even with the solid weight of the man's body in her arms, she had never felt more alone in all her life.

At last Oliver rolled to one side. His eyes flickered open and travelled over her face. There was such blackness in them that she thought it's worse for him. Infinitely worse. Cold fear touched her, colder than the sweat that still stood in beads on Oliver's skin. Protectively she pulled the covers up around his shoulder.

'I'm very sorry,' he said formally.

Then he closed his eyes and fell immediately into a deep, unmoving sleep. Chloe shut her own eyes, wanting nothing more than to blank out the rest of this wretched day. But at once the room lurched and started to spin sickeningly so she forced them open again and focused grimly on the extravagant plaster-work of the cornice.

Grey light was beginning to show at the edges of the curtains before she fell into an exhausted doze.

The light was much brighter when Chloe woke again. For a bewildered moment she looked around, and then remembered. Her head throbbed, and she was excruciatingly thirsty. From the sharp, early-morning quality of the light she guessed that she had slept for only a very few hours.

Oliver was still deeply asleep, frowning against the light with two deep vertical clefts between his eyebrows. His fists were lightly clenched. With the play of consciousness rubbed from his face by sleep, Chloe thought that he looked exhausted.

She slid away from under the bedclothes and stood up. The sight of her neatly-folded clothes on a chair made her remember the night before with a slight shudder. In the time that it took her to dress, Oliver never moved. Chloe glanced down at him. She knew that she wanted to leave this room and close the door on what had happened here, and all the night before, for good. She was almost at the door before she turned back, and with a quick movement pulled the curtains close so that the light no longer fell across Oliver's face. He stirred very slightly, but the frown didn't disappear.

Chloe went, crossing the gold and green expanse of the Quad and turning out into the humdrum length of St Aldate's. It was cold, and she shivered in her thin party clothes. But through the cold and her hangover, even through the sickening sense of having made a bad mistake with Oliver last night, Chloe felt the beginnings of strength beginning to flow back. She would survive all this, and the survival was starting even now on this cold but bracing morning. The thought lightened her step as she walked briskly down to Folly Bridge.

Inside the house she met Rose, mountainous in a stained pink wrap. Rose's little eyes took in her crumpled clothes, missing nothing.

'That's it, darling,' she chuckled. 'You make sure you have a good time. One door closes and another opens, eh?'

Chloe smiled a thin smile and went on up the stairs. There was no sense in falling out with Rose, but the thought of her watching over the comings and goings in her house, like a spider in a web, was faintly distasteful.

Once in her room Chloe stripped off her clothes and bundled them away out of sight. Then she wrapped herself in the comforting brightness of her robe and went to take a shower.

Under the scalding water she felt that it was more than just spilt champagne and the clammy coldness of Oliver which was being washed away. The loss of Stephen still hurt, and she knew that it would take a long time to stop missing him and wanting him. But it was as if the repetitive pattern that had drawn her to him was being washed away.

So here I am, she thought. Just me. She smoothed expensive French soap over her arms and watched the spray carrying the lather away.

I'll work, Chloe thought. It's what I came to Oxford for, and I'll do it. I'll get a wonderful, brilliant degree and then I'll use it to go off and do something fascinating. Stephen won't matter, and neither will Leo or anybody at all.

The thought of her books spread open on her desk was calmly inviting.

Chloe reached out and turned off the water with a decisive flick. The last of the soapy water gurgled away.

Once the play was over, the end of the term was in sight.

Oliver seemed to have recovered his own form of equilibrium. He flung himself back into the world in which Helen had first glimpsed him. By day, he rode or went beagling with red-faced, rowdy young men. In the evenings, he dressed up in the frogged velvet uniform of the dining club to which they all belonged and joined them in anachronistic sprees of drink and broken glasses. A succession of pretty girls passed through his rooms. If there was an air of desperation clinging about him, only Darcy and Helen sensed it and they knew that they could do nothing.

Helen's own sights were fixed on the final Schools in June. Her few hours of free time were spent peacefully with Darcy. Pansy and Stephen were living together, partly in his rooms and partly at Follies, and they seemed to need no other company. Tom was immersed in a workshop production of Ibsen. The darkness of the new play rubbed off on him and the few times Helen saw him she was with Darcy, and Tom seemed preoccupied and coolly unforthcoming. She had a faint sense of missing the closeness that they had shared during the difficult days of *As You Like It*.

One morning in the last week of the term, Chloe woke up with a queasy start. Everything was as it always was in her room, but a black misery swooped down on her at once. For a second or two she lay tensely, then she swung herself out of bed and half ran down the gallery to the bathroom. Then she hung over the basin and vomited, a thin, sour trickle. Chloe groaned and rested her head against the cool porcelain. It wasn't over yet. This was the fourth morning and she knew what to expect. After a moment she retched again and then sighed, her hair falling damply around her face. She felt too drained even to jump when someone put a cool hand around her forehead.

'Poor thing,' said Pansy. 'Again?'

Chloe leaned back exhausted.

'No,' she said weakly. 'That's it, I think.'

'Go back to bed,' Pansy ordered. 'I'll bring you something.'

Chloe went shivering back to her room. Pansy reappeared

231

with a mug of very weak milkless tea and a thin, dry piece of toast.

'Thanks,' Chloe said uncertainly. It was almost the first encounter they had had since the last night of the play.

Chloe sipped the tea and felt warmer at once. The first mouthful of toast was a struggle, but the second tasted wonderful. Chloe found herself smiling at Pansy. The other girl was wearing a knobbly blue dressing gown with a tasselled tie-belt like a schoolboy's. The cuffs of a homely, striped nightdress protruded from it.

'D'you really go to bed with Stephen dressed like that?'

The two women stared at each other. Then they dissolved into incredulous laughter.

'Yes. Would it really get him going if I borrowed some of your Janet Reger?' Chloe was laughing so much that she almost spilled her tea. She looked down at it, remembered herself, and the laugh faded into a groan.

Pansy's smile died too.

'Chloe,' she said gently. 'You're pregnant, aren't you?'

Chloe nodded. 'Yes. I'm pregnant. God, how wretched I feel.'

Pansy looked down, crimping the bedcover between her fingers.

'Will you tell Stephen?' she asked.

'Stephen?' Chloe was bitter. 'Pansy, this will make you laugh. It isn't Stephen. It's Oliver.'

There was a brief silence.

'How do you know?'

'Does it matter? As it happens, I have a cap. None of the other things works for me. After the last-night party I went home to bed with Oliver. I was drunk, and very miserable.' Pansy's face was tense as she listened. 'I didn't even think about it. I don't think I cared what happened. And now ...' she counted off on her fingers and held them up. 'Four weeks later. See?'

'So what will you do?'

Chloe turned violently away. 'I've no idea.'

'I know how you feel.' Pansy was very gentle. 'Because it happened to me. I was very young, and I felt so ill that I couldn't do anything. Sick with myself, as well as just sick.' Her face twisted in a little, wry smile. 'In the end, Masefield fixed it. Of course.'

She took Chloe's hands in hers and squeezed them. 'Whichever course you choose, you know, it isn't exactly easy. Chloe ... there's no reason why you should like me enough to let me help you through, but I could if you would let me.' As their eyes met, the slow flames of liking began to kindle in them again. 'Masefield took me to a place in Harley Street. It was very, very good.'

Chloe shuddered. 'Aren't there ordinary places, that everyone goes to? All those ads on the tube?'

'I don't know how easy that is,' Pansy answered. Then, carefully, 'Is it the money?'

'No. It isn't the money. Just that I haven't thought, that's all.'

Chloe was restless now. She put down her empty mug and paced across to the window. In front of her was Christ Church, ribbed in golden stone. 'I've got to tell Oliver, somehow,' she said bleakly. 'It does belong to him too, doesn't it?'

Pansy looked worried, but she said nothing.

Chloe picked up her hairbrush and began to work rhythmically at her hair. 'Well, it's my problem. Thanks for the first aid. Same time, same place tomorrow?'

With a rush of warmth, Pansy went across and hugged her. 'Tea and sympathy always available,' she told her cheerfully. 'Think about Masefield's place. I'll come and hold your hand, if you need someone. And Chloe ...'

'Mmm?'

'If you're going to see Oliver, talk to Helen first. She seems to understand him better than anyone else.'

Pansy was warning her, as subtly as she could, not to expect to find strength in Oliver.

Helen's first reaction when Chloe told her what had happened was stunned surprise. It was impossible that efficient and sophisticated Chloe could have made such an elementary mistake. She stared at her friend and saw that the tawny, tigerish confidence had deserted her. She was white-faced and shaky now.

'Are you sure?' Helen asked, and then frowned at her own stupidity.

'Yes. I'm quite sure.' Chloe wrapped her arms around herself as if she was trying to keep warm. 'I feel invaded. Not in possession of myself any more. It's ironic. At least I felt, before, that I had me. I keep going around and around in my head, trying to think what to do. Whether to ... *say the words, Chloe ...*

keep the baby, or to have an abortion.' Her words ended in a sob and she turned her face away from Helen. 'I'm only sure of one thing. Before I decide, I have to tell Oliver. Not to ask anything of him, but just to let him know. That's only fair, Helen.'

Helen looked straight into Chloe's eyes, neither encouraging nor dissuasive. 'He's in his rooms now.'

Don't wait any longer, she meant. Decide.

Chloe picked up a scarlet jacket from where it hung over the back of a chair and pulled it on. With a lightness that she was far from feeling she waved to Helen and said, 'Well. See you later, then.'

As she walked up towards the tall finger of Tom Tower, hands in her pockets, no-one could see that her fists were clenched. She remembered Oliver lying asleep, the frown deep between his eyes, and how she had felt that she could shut the door on what had happened between them and walk casually away from it. A sudden wave of nausea threatened to overpower her. Vainly she tried the words out in her head.

'Oliver, I want to tell you something...'

'Oliver, do you remember the night of the party ...?'

'Oliver, I'm pregnant. The baby's yours.'

Chloe bit her lip and forced herself to keep walking.

'Yeah?'

Oliver's voice came at once in response to her hesitant tap on his door. As soon as Chloe pushed it open a wall of noise hit her. Music was playing at full volume. Oliver was slouching in an armchair with a young, very thin girl leaning across him. Her hair was caught up at one side of her head in a sprouting blonde tuft. Oliver's expression of moody boredom lightened a little when he saw Chloe.

'Hello,' he said. 'I've been meaning to come and see you, but somehow life slips by so amusingly. Have a drink. There's wine or...'

'Oliver, can we talk?'

'Sure. Sylvie, will you turn it down?'

Sylvie flounced across the room, her tiny flared skirt lifting as she went. Relieved of her embrace Oliver got up and stared blankly down into Canterbury Quad.

'Bloody Oxford.' He gave a short, harsh laugh. 'Not that I should worry. My tutor's threatening to get me sent down. Something to do with essays. Really, does he imagine that anyone gives a fuck about essays? Schools in June, people keep saying. Like a stuck record. Well, it doesn't matter. I'm off on Saturday. Going ski-ing with some people. Not that I care all that much for snow and schnapps, but nothing can be any worse than staying here.' Chloe heard a new, metallic note in his voice. The lines between his eyes had deepened and there were new ones showing at the sides of his mouth. She was trying to say in private, can we talk in private, when the door slammed open again. There were two young men in grimy white shirts with hair slicked back from pale, unhealthy faces.

'Are you coming, Oliver,' one of them asked, 'or not?'

Chloe shrank back. There was something threatening about Oliver's visitors. 'Yeah. Coming now. Going to London for a party, or something,' he explained. 'Sorry to have to go right away.' Recollecting something, he rubbed his fingers into his eyes and then pinched the bridge of his nose. 'Shit, you wanted to talk. Is it something quick?'

She looked from face to face, vacant Sylvie and the impatient, faintly hostile faces of Oliver's odd friends. Oliver himself was hovering near the door, clearly anxious to be off.

'No,' she said coldly. 'It's nothing quick, this time. But it doesn't matter. Enjoy the party, Oliver.'

He frowned after her. 'Look, I'll be back in ... oh well, a couple of days. Come to dinner.'

But Chloe was already out of earshot, counting the steps down as she went and then out into Canterbury Quad. She walked quickly, as if she was hurrying to keep an appointment, but on Folly Bridge she stopped short. The big square house was rosy-red in the sunshine, with the light reflecting off the windows into her eyes. The sight of it suddenly brought back her early days in Oxford. Supposedly here to study in the warm glow from her desk lamp, meeting new challenges, making changes in herself.

Liar.

Nothing had changed. Chloe's moment of self-appraisal was savage. You ran straight from Leo to another man, and you even had to choose one better at self-delusion than yourself. Everything else has just been a smokescreen for a man-hunt. And now look at yourself. Pregnant by a drunken boy you barely know and care less for. And still alone.

Fool.

A sudden wave of determination washed over Chloe. She squared her shoulders and ran down the steps to the island.

When she found Pansy, Helen was with her. Evidently they had been talking about her. Helen was visibly unhappy, but Pansy looked businesslike.

'Well,' Chloe said flatly. 'So much for that. What's the telephone number, then?'

A tiny silence enveloped the three women. Then Helen and Pansy were at her side. Chloe stiffened, then realised how grateful she felt for their arms around her.

'What did he say?' Pansy asked.

'Nothing. He couldn't have, because I didn't tell him.' Chloe made her voice artificially light, and Helen and Pansy exchanged a glance. 'When I got there, it seemed a little inappropriate. I don't even know what I was expecting. Hardly a wave of paternal delight and the family ring.'

Pansy hugged her fiercely. 'Oliver can't even cope with himself. He's not the person to turn to if you need support, or even a clear insight into anything.'

'No. But he has done something for me. He's made me want to face up to this, and to do it alone. So I'll have your doctor's telephone number, Pansy, please.'

Pansy wrote the number down for her on a scrap of paper and Chloe crumpled it into her fist without looking at it.

'Thanks.'

Helen spoke for the first time, and her voice was hesitant.

'Would you like one of us to come with you?'

Chloe was certain. 'No. I'll go on my own.' But suddenly their support seemed vitally important, and she added, 'You do understand that I've got to do this? That there isn't any other way?'

Helen's face flooded with sympathy. 'Chloe, only you can know what to do. But if it was me, I'd do the same.'

She said nothing of her anxiety for Oliver, or her growing fear that he was creating an impenetrable mess around himself. But she felt it, as keenly as she felt for Chloe.

Pansy's mouth was hard for a moment. 'Yes. It's not ... very easy, afterwards. Helen and I will stick around here to look after you.'

Chloe looked from one to the other, and they smiled at her.

The address which the neutral-voiced receptionist had given her

236

was off Harley Street. Chloe sat in the waiting room and looked around her. It might have been a room-set for a smart design magazine with its black Venetian blinds half closed against the London drizzle, glass and steel tables and black Italian leather sofa. There was not a hint of a white coat or a drawer-file, and the air was heavy with the scent of freesias. Chloe felt sick and cold, and forever afterwards associated the smell with the same sensations. The wait was mercifully short.

Pansy's doctor was middle-aged, prosperous and weary-looking. He never once looked into Chloe's eyes.

The examination was very brief and his matter-of-fact questions took scarcely any longer.

'And you want a termination?'

He was rotating a glass paperweight in his fingers and staring out at the curtain of rain.

Termination. Termination. The word dinned in Chloe's head, ugly and cumbersome and final.

'Yes.'

The doctor glanced down at a leather-bound diary, the only item on the desk apart from the paperweight.

'I can offer you a twenty-four-hour bed at my London clinic on Thursday. My receptionist will give you the necessary details.'

'Thank you.' Chloe stood up, numb. The doctor opened a drawer and slid a discreet little card towards her.

'You will want a private room? This is our ... ah ... scale of charges.'

'I don't care about that. I just want it to be quick.'

The doctor glanced at her, not unkindly. 'Yes. There we do have the advantage over the ... ah ... less expensive channels. Good morning, Miss ... ah ... Campbell.' On her way out, Chloe consulted the receptionist. She learned that the clinic itself was close at hand, and that the hefty bill was to be settled in advance.

Wanting nothing more than to be alone, Chloe stayed in London and waited for Thursday. At last the morning came and she checked in at the discreet double-fronted town house in a quiet square. There were no white coats here either, just muffling carpets, bowls of waxy flowers and two or three white-faced girls who couldn't look at one another.

For Chloe, the worst of it was the very smoothness of the system as it processed her. She was stiflingly aware of being a number, sliding along an elegant conveyor belt towards the disposal of an unwanted burden.

At the last moment as she lay waiting to be wheeled away for surgery, panic gripped her. She struggled to scream No. Wait. I want to ... But the anaesthetic had already gagged her. Her eyes went blank and then fell shut, and she slid into blackness.

On Friday morning, when she came out into daylight, the square looked exactly the same. There were even the same pigeons strutting on the grass. Twenty-four hours, she thought. Is that really all? She folded her hands across her stomach and then lifted them again, clenched. She felt empty, and as thin and dry as paper.

When she hailed it, the taxi drew up with exactly the same rumble as the one that had deposited her on the same spot yesterday. Paddington Station was as grimy and cavernous as it had been days before. But Chloe was afraid that nothing would ever look the same again as she hunched over the black space inside her.

At Follies, Pansy and Helen were waiting for her. Pansy took one look at her face and folded her cold hand in both her own.

'I know,' she whispered. 'You won't believe me now, but it goes away.'

For the first time, tears stabbed behind Chloe's eyes and she made no effort to dam them up.

'That's good,' Pansy said. 'It helps to cry.'

'It doesn't help the baby.' Chloe wept as though she could never stop.

They were black days for Chloe. She was oppressed by a sense of the selfishness of the years behind her, and the pointlessness of the years ahead. The time passed painfully slowly.

Helen and Pansy stayed with her, trying by a mixture of sympathy and determined cheerfulness to bring her back to herself. Chloe was dimly aware that Pansy could have very little time to spare for Stephen.

'Where is he?' she asked once, and smiled bleakly at Pansy's anxious start. 'Oh, don't worry. It all seems a very long way off, now.'

'He's around,' Pansy said airily. Appraisingly they looked at each other, then Pansy's silvery-gold head turned away.

'Pansy,' Chloe said softly, 'thank you for being here. You, and Helen too.'

Very slowly the clouds began to lift. Small, everyday activities began to seem significant again, and then one morning Chloe found herself looking forward to the brightness of summer. The Oxford spring was warm, and the borders in the College gardens were splashed with colour.

The surprising, painful longing for the baby that would never be, faded to the point where it stopped obliterating everything else. The scar would stay with Chloe, but the immediate hurt was over.

One evening Chloe cooked a thank-you supper for Helen and Pansy. It was the last evening of full term. From tomorrow most people would disperse for the vacation, and the crowds on the city pavements would be wandering tourists.

The three women sat in the dusk, looking out at the light fading over the spires and domes.

'I've got an idea,' Pansy said. She had bitten the top off an orange and was sucking it dry with childish enjoyment. 'Come to Venice for the Vac.'

Chloe and Helen stared at her in surprise. 'I must have told you about Masefield's palazzo? No? Well, naturally, he has a palazzo on the Grand Canal. I've got to join him and Kim there for a few days.' She made a face as if the prospect was the gloomiest imaginable. 'Do come. It's just what you need, Chloe. Change of scene and all that. And a break for you before Schools, Helen. We can eat lots, and sightsee if you insist, and you can both go shopping with Kim instead of me.'

'We-ell,' Chloe said, tempted in spite of herself.

Helen felt a stab of envy. She could think of nowhere in the world she longed to see more than Venice, but the idea was impossible. Then, with a jolt of excitement that brought the colour rushing to her face, she remembered the remainder of her travel bursary. The money would buy her a standby ticket to Venice and back, with perhaps even a little left over. That's what the money is for, she told herself. And she would see Venice.

'Helen?'

'Will they have room for all of us?' She tried to sound cool, suppressing the longing that leapt inside her in case Pansy's invitation should be withdrawn as casually as it had been issued.

'Room?' Pansy giggled. 'I expect they'll find you a corner somewhere. Wait till you see the place. That's settled, then.'

Chloe nodded slowly. The last time she had been to Venice was with Leo, who was working. He had proclaimed himself too busy to join her in exploring the city, and they had spent his free hours in bed, or in dark restaurants and claustrophobic bars. Now, the thought of seeing it all in the company of Pansy and Helen was inviting.

Somehow, in the horrible days since the clinic, they had become the best friends she had ever had.

The room was almost dark now, but she could still make out Helen's face vivid with excitement, and Pansy's pleased satisfaction.

Chloe lifted her drink.

'To Venice,' she said.

'To Venice,' they echoed her.

EASTER

CHAPTER TEN

'I'll miss you.'

Darcy was standing with his back firmly turned to the queue at the passport desk. He put his hands on Helen's shoulders and drew her towards him.

'If you must go, come back as soon as you can,' he whispered with his mouth close to her hair. Helen breathed in the familiar scent, wool and leather and the open air, and then grinned up at him.

'It's only ten days,' she said lightly. 'But I'll miss you too.'

It's true, she thought. Somehow, without either of us knowing quite how, we've drawn very close. Watching the broad, undistinguished face and rueful smile, she recognised that Darcy was part of her life now.

He bent to kiss her, brushing the corner of her mouth with his own. It wasn't Darcy's way to be more demonstrative in a public place. He lifted one of the black curls and wound it reflectively round his finger.

'I love you,' Darcy said.

'This is the last call for Alitalia flight 349. Last call for Alitalia flight 349.'

The intrusive announcement brought back the crowded terminal, the disappearing queue.

'I know.' Helen's voice was barely audible. She looked down at Darcy's capable, calloused hands gripping her own, then up into his eyes. 'I know.'

He didn't kiss her again. Instead he gently propelled her forward and into the line of travellers at the barrier. Pansy and Chloe, from their discreet distance, grinned at each other and came to join her. When Helen looked back from the far side of the barrier, Darcy waved once and then turned away.

There was such tenderness in his face that she almost ran back to his side, but Chloe and Pansy were behind her and between them they swept her along the featureless tunnels to the boarding gate.

Helen's love affair with Venice began almost at the moment that the jet dipped and swung round to make its final approach. Beneath her was shimmering pearl-grey water, and wide flat plains shrouded in vaporous pearly mist so exactly the same colour that it was impossible to tell where earth met water and sky.

The airport was identical to all other airports, but for Helen it was magical because the signs all read *Venezia*.

Waiting to meet them with Masefield's Mercedes was the Italian version of Hobbs. But the Italian had quick black eyes under his peaked cap, and he smiled at the three of them with open admiration. His way of handing each of them into the car was a beguiling mixture of formality and flirtatiousness. Pansy flung herself back against the cushions with a sigh of pleasure.

'Oh, it's good to be here. If only it was going to be just the three of us.'

Helen was silent. Her eyes were fixed on the low, misty horizon, waiting. The drive from the airport was only a few miles. Then without warning, they were on the great bridge that spanned the lagoon. Helen drew her breath in so sharply that the others glanced at her rapt face and smiled. The oil refineries and chimneys of Mestre smudged the skyline with dirty smoke, there were sprawling developments of ugly new buildings on either side, but ahead of them, shimmering, drowning in the light between water and sky, was Venice.

They were across the lagoon and plunging into a tangle of cars. The chauffeur wrenched the wheel, jammed his finger on the horn and swore in a muted torrent of Italian.

'This is Tronchetto,' Pansy said. Magically, a space opened up for them. 'The car stays here.'

A string of olive-brown boys appeared and, with the suitcases borne in procession in front of them, they emerged from the oily caverns of the garages. Helen blinked in the pure lemon-yellow light. She was standing on a stone-flagged quay but there was water all around her. It splintered with reflected sunlight and with the crisscrossing of boats of all kinds. At the quayside, bobbing on the wavelets, was a trim little white motorboat.

Masefield's driver pulled off his peaked hat and threw it into the boat. He ran his hands through his hair and laughed at them so that all his white teeth showed.

'Much better, yes?' he chuckled in English as they climbed into the rocking boat. The engine coughed and then with a high-pitched roar, they swung in a wide arc and a shower of spray away from the quayside.

'This is the Grand Canal,' Pansy murmured beside Helen. 'Wrong end.'

Helen was stunned, painfully aware that her five senses were inadequate to take it all in. They were speeding between the chugging *vaporetti* now, and in and out of the black high-prowed gondolas. On either side glowed the marble palaces of the Grand Canal. They were as beautiful in reality as in pictures, fine façades with tall windows and bracketed balconies hanging over the curves of the Canal. But she saw now that the real Venice was quite different from the one she had imagined. In her head, she had pictured it as a series of exquisite images, posed, formal, and deserted. But this city was so vibrantly crowded with life that it took her breath away. There were people everywhere, hurrying as in any city, but here they were smiling as they went. There were gaudy shop signs alongside the finest palazzo and heaped stalls of fruit and vegetables, and there were festoons of washing draped from the ancient balconies. And everywhere there was yellow light shining off the rippling water.

Ahead of them a graceful arch spanned the pageant of the Canal.

'I know,' Helen smiled at Pansy and Chloe on either side of her. 'The Rialto Bridge.'

Past the Rialto the motorboat swung right and into the dense shadows of a narrow *rio*. The cool dimness made the water opaque olive-green. At once Helen was enclosed by the smell that was forever to mean Venice for her. It was damp moss, cold stone and the mysterious deep whiff of the green water. The outboard slowed, the throb of it thrown to and fro and amplified by the high walls at either side. They slid under a colonnade of arches and stopped at a stone quay where the water slapped and sucked at the piers beneath. The Venetian smell was so intense that Helen felt she could almost reach out and touch it.

She looked up to see an ancient metal sign that read *Palazzo Croce*.

'Home,' Pansy said. 'Sort of.'

From the private quay she ran up hollowed stone steps within the palazzo towards another arch where brighter light showed in the dimness. The arch gave on to the inner court of the palazzo. Behind her Helen stopped short, letting the arch frame the scene for her.

The walls were lined with creamy marble and a frieze, faded figures in russet and bronze and grey-green, ran round all four sides. There were sightless calm marble heads carved over the windows and the floor of the court was paved in great marble slabs with an intricate mosaic border. The spring afternoon outside was only pleasantly warm, but Helen could imagine how cool and silent this place would be in the blaze of an Italian summer.

In the middle of the peace and beauty of the court, Masefield and Kim were utterly incongruous. They might have been a tableau mistakenly uprooted from the poolside of some expensive modern hotel. Kim was lying on a flowery, padded lounger, surrounded by glossy magazines. There was a viscous drink full of chunks of fruit at her side, and she was intent on varnishing her toenails. Beside her Masefield was sitting on a matching upright chair at a white wrought-iron table spread with papers. He was talking rapidly into a dictaphone, and there was a cordless telephone at his left hand.

As soon as he saw Pansy he jumped up and enveloped her in a bear-like hug, then held her face in his blunt hands to kiss it. There was no mistaking his pride and pleasure in his daughter.

'Baby,' he said. 'Baby, I love you. Just seeing you makes the whole stinking world look brighter.' He kissed her again and then looked round. 'And where are your pals? Here. Well, introduce them to your old Dad.'

Masefield Warren's handshake was very firm, and his eyes behind the welcoming mask of smile were narrow and shrewd. His glance flicked over Helen and lingered a moment longer on Chloe. She stared coolly back at him. He was impressive, she thought, in a faintly brutal way, and noted the physical power in the bull-like shoulders and neck as well as the lines of domineering authority in his face.

'We're honoured,' he was saying bluntly. 'We don't get to see a lot of Pansy's friends these days. This is Kim, my wife.'

'You're always somewhere else, Daddy darling,' Pansy said mildly.

Kim's welcome to Pansy was distinctly less warm than her father's. She turned up her cheek to be kissed and lifted a fingertip at once to smooth away the damage. 'Darling,' she said in a faint voice. 'Always jeans. I know you're a student, but haven't you got anything else? If you haven't, you must come out with me this afternoon and I'll organise you. You can't dress like that here. We've got the Riccadellos coming for dinner.'

'Kim,' Pansy said gleefully, 'I've invited Chloe specially for you. She likes shopping almost as much as you do. You can go together while Helen looks at pictures and gloomy old churches. And me...' Pansy stretched and pirouetted on the marble, '... I'm going to eat wonderful food, which will be a happy change from Oxford, and watch the boys in the gondolas. Now, is there any tea?'

'Show your friends upstairs first,' Masefield said sharply.

Pansy started and went pink, then nodded gracefully and shepherded them away. Helen thought as she followed her friend that between her authoritative father and her near-contemporary stepmother, Pansy was still treated as a wayward child. She could guess how irksome that must be for her.

The Palazzo Croce guest rooms were on the top floor. Helen almost ran to the windows of hers and opened them outwards on to the balcony. The Grand Canal lay below her, and to one side she could just see the domes of St Mark's Basilica and the top of the slim campanile in the piazza. Enchanted, she leaned over the balcony to drink in more of the glittering city. In her eyrie the loudest noise was the call of the swifts as they soared against the blue-grey sky and then plummeted over the warm rooftops.

'Don't fall in,' Pansy warned behind her and Helen turned back.

'It makes the view from Follies look distinctly dim,' she laughed. 'Pansy – thank you for inviting us here. It means a lot.'

'I can see that from your face,' she said softly. 'It's good to have you here. I just wish it was ... different. You know what I mean.'

Helen did. It was strange that both Oliver and Pansy, the two most privileged people she had ever met, should be so unhappy with it in their different ways.

Pansy was lying on her back on Helen's bed, staring up at the white barrel-vault of the ceiling. Ripples of reflected light chased endlessly over it.

'These rooms used to be the kitchens,' she said. 'Being right

247

up here they've escaped most of Kim's Ideal Home improvements. The proper guest suites are on the floor below.'

The room was simply enough furnished, with spare furniture in dark wood and cool terrazzo tiles. Thin voile curtains fluttered at the windows.

'I thought you'd like to be up here because of the view.'

'I love it,' Helen said.

Pansy looked at her, a half-smile showing although her eyes were shadowed.

'You're lucky, Helen, you know. You enjoy things so much. Don't lose the knack.'

Before Helen could answer Pansy swung her legs off the bed and stood up. 'Well. Better go and clean my fingernails and put on a ribboned frock so Kim will permit me at the tea-table. See you downstairs.'

Helen itched with impatience to walk out into the limpid light and begin her Venetian exploration, but went politely downstairs instead and joined her hosts for tea.

Almost as soon as it was over, Kim was issuing instructions for dinner. Important business contacts of Masefield's were expected. They were to dress, and meet for drinks in what Kim called the lounge. Helen tried to imagine what sort of room a lounge could be in this graceful marble palace, and then had to bite back the laughter when she saw Pansy's eloquently arched eyebrows.

Reluctantly she went upstairs to change her clothes again. Outside the light was softening from lemon to gold and Helen was afraid that she would never be able to escape into it. Turning her back on the panorama she peered into her suitcase, and began to understand Kim's shopping obsession. If guests at the Palazzo Croce were expected to change clothes for every meal, Helen thought, she would have to start shopping for herself.

The lounge turned out to be the long first-floor room that fronted the Canal. It was windowed from floor to ceiling, but the heavy carved shutters were pulled almost to so that the room was shadowed. Helen glanced around in fascination while Masefield poured her a drink from the elaborate trolley in one corner. He had looked faintly surprised when she refused whisky. The proportions of the room were perfect, but they were blurred by the fussiness of the furnishings. There were heavily swagged and tasselled curtains at the windows, superfluous to the intricate shutters. A great many spindly occasional tables lurked between the overstuffed sofas, and there was a predominance of cushions and small objects in coloured glass. The worn, beautiful mosaic floor was covered with expensive bright modern rugs. Evidently Kim disliked it, but didn't quite have the courage to hide it entirely.

On the end wall her portrait, flashily done in oils and prominently featuring the diamond on her engagement finger, was lit with a special strip light. The whole effect reminded Helen irresistibly of Maples.

The important guests had not yet arrived. Pansy, wearing a silk dress that was slightly too old for her, was sitting meekly next to Masefield and talking to him about Oxford. Across the room Chloe looked her most polished. There was a heavy gold chain around her neck and gold bracelets against her black sleeve. She looked amused and more animated than she had done for weeks. From time to time Masefield's eyes settled on her. Kim had attention to spare for no-one. She was darting to and fro moving cushions and rattling the drinks trolley. Her blonde hair was piled up on top of her head and her strapless white dress managed to suggest both the naivety of a Greek tunic and the price tag of a top couturier.

'Well, are you all set to see Venice?' Masefield asked Helen loudly.

'Yes. I can't wait.'

'Helen likes paintings,' Pansy put in.

Masefield beamed at his daughter. 'Good, good. With your studies going so well you should be able to tell Helen all about those -inis and -ettos that everyone makes so much of.' His voice breathed the respect of the self-made man for the idea of 'studies.' Helen, well aware that she knew ten times more about Renaissance art than her friend and that Pansy had not attended a single lecture of her art history course, looked away from Pansy's angelic smile and murmured, 'I'm looking forward to it.'

'I adore Canaletto,' Kim said. 'Don't I, Mase?'

The guests turned out to be two thickset jowly men and their overweight, bejewelled wives. Only one of the men spoke English, and even the most trivial remark had to be translated for Kim, who knew no Italian. The conversation was mostly about money, or about people who had money and what they did with it.

The lengthy dinner, impeccably served, was heavy with creamy sauces. When at last it was over the men withdrew sharply with Masefield. All three faces were suddenly alive, wolfish with enthusiasm for the deals to be made. The six women were left to languish in the lounge. Conversation would have died away entirely without Chloe's light, effortless chatter in her almost fluent Italian. Helen thought it was the most stultifying evening she had ever spent and new sympathy for Pansy sprang up inside her. More and more frequently her eyes turned to the velvet dark beyond the cracks in the shutters. Enviously she heard laughter from the boats and the quays, and the singing of the gondoliers.

Pansy followed her eyes. At once she said, 'Kim darling, as it's Helen's first night here, don't you think Chloe and I should take her out somewhere, even if it's just to Quadri's for a coffee? I'm sure Signora Riccadello and Signora Tronzino won't mind.'

Kim plainly longed to veto the idea, but she was trapped into politeness.

'What does Helen want to do?'

'I'd love to go in a gondola.'

Kim looked puzzled. 'In a gondola? Where to? Guido can take you anywhere you want to go in the motorboat.'

'Not to anywhere. Just to look.'

Plainly Kim thought just looking the most eccentric occupation in the world.

Formal goodnights were said all round and then Pansy hustled her friends out of the room. Glancing back Helen saw Kim mustering a bright smile for the Italian matrons, but the sides of her cheeks were pinched in as if she was swallowing a yawn. So evenings like this were Kim's job, for which she was paid with days in Masefield's European palaces and her Armani and Krizia dresses.

Helen wondered if Masefield's first three wives had found the job not to their liking.

The three girls ran down the stairs as if they were escaping from detention.

'Who were those men?' Chloe asked. 'Didn't they look like mobsters?'

'Chloe!' Helen was shocked, but Pansy only laughed.

'I wouldn't be at all surprised. Masefield knows all kinds of very odd characters.'

They crossed the cool silence of the inner court and came down the stone steps to the private quay. Again the slap and suck of the green water filled the air. From the shadows a white shirt materialised, and the white smile of Guido the chauffeur above it. Pansy explained what they wanted and he put two fingers to his mouth and whistled. At once a dark shape came dipping and bobbing towards them. Once under the arches the gondolier thrust his oar in to steady the boat while they climbed aboard. When he saw the three of them he answered Guido's call with another, rising whistle. Guido gave rapid, curt instructions and the gondolier shrugged. Then there was the whisper of notes changing hands.

Helen sat squeezed in the middle, with the warmth of Chloe's and Pansy's arms against her own. In front of her the lantern swinging from the beaked prow sent wavering splashes of gold over the water. There was a lurch, and then they shot out under the arches of Palazzo Croce and into the Venetian night. The Canal was a forest of gondolas sliding under the Rialto Bridge, faster boats cutting through the water and swaying lights of every imaginable colour. Behind her Helen could hear their gondolier humming, and sometimes calling out to another as he passed. She closed her eyes to listen to the water and snatches of music drifting over it and told herself *Venice. I'm in Venice.*

On either side of her Chloe and Pansy were silent, busy with their own thoughts.

The route took the three of them through narrow, dark cuts where the yellow squares of windows were high up in the walls and where ancient lights flared against the stonework, under high-humped bridges and past little paved alleys that allowed glimpses into busy *trattorie.* Helen lay back against the cushions and thought of the precious days ahead that would give her the chance to wander over these bridges and in and out of the dim, inviting churches.

At length they came into a wide expanse of water where the lights of another island winked at them from the distance. The gondola skimmed forward and then swung to the left where a tangle of others swayed against their tall wooden mooring poles.

Helen looked up and saw that they were alongside San Marco. They scrambled out on to the wooden duckboards and then on to the firmness of the quay.

'Quadri's?' Pansy asked.

'Quadri's,' Chloe agreed.

Firmly linking Helen's arms in theirs they guided her through the piazzetta and into St Mark's Square. The great open-air drawing room was alive with people, music from the cafes and the swarming, fluttering pigeons.

Helen stopped dead. The Basilica dominated everything, floodlit, and crowned with its squat Byzantine domes.

'Look,' she breathed. 'Just look.'

Pansy and Chloe smiled indulgently and steered her on.

'Tomorrow,' they promised her.

The open-air tables had just been put out for the season in front of the cafés, but they were not yet packed with tourists. The Venetians were still in possession of their city and they sat idly over coffee cups and talk. At Quadri's there was a violinist walking between the tables playing a sad little melody that hung in the warm, scented air.

Helen sank into her chair and stared about her, stunned.

The others were laughing at her and she was suddenly swept by a wave of love for them both, and happiness that they were there to share this magical evening with her.

Pansy had ordered ice-creams and they came in fluted glasses, five different flavours.

Helen waved her spoon. 'I feel,' she said, 'as if all my birthdays have come at once. What more could anyone ask? Friends, and Venice, and ice-cream like this.'

'Many happy returns,' they answered.

In spite of her fears, Helen was allowed plenty of time to learn the moods of her new love. Sometimes with Chloe, more usually alone, she went out in the blue-grey morning light and let herself drift along the narrow streets, pausing every so often to hang over one of the high bridges and stare into the water. She had begun methodically, with guide-books and lists of sights to see, but gradually she abandoned herself to unplanned wandering. Her rewards were the discovery of an exquisite altarpiece in a dusty, deserted church, or a sudden perfect vista of a narrow street with a single fruit stall and a child playing unconcernedly beside it. She saw the Tintorettos and the Tiepolos and all the great architectural masterpieces, but it was her own private finds that gave her the most pleasure. Sometimes she was out for the whole day, stopping to buy fruit from one of the stalls in the *erberia* and to drink coffee in shabby cafés among strangers.

She came to know the look of the city in every hour from dawn to dark, and as she learned about it she went further afield, riding the *vaporetti* to Murano and Torcello, and the ferryboats out to the Lido where she wandered among the fashionable rich and enjoyed the contrast with the variegated crowds of the real Venice.

Helen found that the thoughtless idling among so much haphazard beauty affected her strangely. She was overtaken by a dreamy sensuality stronger than anything she had felt since her early days with Oliver. Darcy was often in her mind. His quiet company would be perfect for Venice and she imagined his fair head bobbing among the sleek, dark Italian ones all round her. She remembered his words at the airport and his mouth touching hers, and thought, I do want to go back to him. Then the reality of Venice engrossed her again and Darcy sank back into her subconscious.

In their own ways, too, Chloe and Pansy enjoyed their holiday. Kim immediately adopted Chloe as an ally. They were almost the same age and it gave the visitors much secret amusement to see Kim calling on their few extra years of life experience and appealing to Chloe for help in controlling her stepdaughter. Chloe understood at once that Kim was bored to death, and was lacking the resources within herself to provide distraction. Pansy would do no more than poke sly fun at her, but Chloe went good-humouredly on shopping expeditions, or plundering trips as Pansy called them. They came back and modelled their designer bargains with enthusiasm for the others. Two or three times Kim, generous with Masefield's fortune, came back with 'little somethings' for Helen, and Helen had no choice but to accept them. The frivolous, expensive things looked funny in her cupboard alongside the worn skirts and shirts.

Chloe felt genuinely sorry for Kim and her luxurious dull life, and she felt pleasure in her own contrasting existence seeping back with every passing day. The very timeless tranquillity of Venice eased her unhappiness too by making it seem pitifully small.

They saw little of Masefield. He seemed to prefer the company of his papers and telephone to that of his wife, and even his daughter, even though he was always protesting that

Pansy had so little time for him that he hardly knew her. Pansy herself spent most of her days reading on her balcony, a strange, eclectic selection of books that made Helen look at her with new eyes. One day it was *Under the Volcano*, another it was Ruskin's *The Stones of Venice*.

'Are you enjoying it?' Helen asked.

'Rather dry,' was all Pansy would say. 'Didn't he have a curious private life, or something? Have I got the right bloke?'

Helen suspected that behind her careful smokescreen there was a Pansy that nobody knew at all.

One evening towards the end of their stay Masefield and Kim, resplendent in full evening dress, went out for an important dinner with important people. Masefield insisted that the three girls go out to eat too, at a restaurant of his choice. They heard him booking the table himself, and giving instructions that the bill was to be sent direct to him.

'You'll love it,' he told them firmly. 'Food like you get at Al Pescaor doesn't come your way all that often.'

Relieved of their usual slightly awkward evening duties with the Warrens, they spent longer than usual in dressing up, and then went out laughing in the feeling of a special occasion.

Al Pescaor was special indeed. It was small, intimate, and redolent with wonderful smells. The food when it came was reverently laid on a snowy white cloth. It was exquisite, melting sea-food. They ate until they could manage no more and grew giggly on bottles of golden wine. Then they sat replete over coffee and smooth brandy. Their richly contrasting colourings drew admiring glances, but they were happy in their own company and saw none of them.

Pansy sat back with a sigh of contentment. 'It seems a long way off, doesn't it, damp old Oxford, and Follies with Rose shuffling around, and Gerry leering around corners?'

'Another world,' Chloe agreed. 'But in two days, we'll be back in it.'

There was a sudden, small silence.

For more than a week no-one had mentioned Stephen, but now it was as if he was sitting at the table with them.

'It's been wonderful having you both here,' Pansy said abruptly. 'I get very low, on my own with Masefield and Kim. It's fine to come back and make ho-ho jokes about it, but it's miserable just the same. But with you it's been quite different. I haven't ... missed anybody, or wanted to see anyone else.'

'Neither have I,' Chloe said quietly.

Pansy leaned forward to touch her wrist with one fingertip. 'I'd feel happier still if I thought that was the truth,' she whispered.

'It is the truth,' Chloe answered. 'I loved him, but I've stopped now. It isn't as though he hasn't got plenty of faults.'

'I'll say,' Pansy was grinning. 'The way that whatever happens, he's got a quote to supply to make it even more significant.'

'And the way that he puts on his lecture voice, even in bed, and addresses you like a seminar room.'

They were both giggling, while Helen stared in amazement. The taboo topic had at a stroke become a source of shared laughter.

Pansy dabbed at her eyes. 'Poor Stephen. How mean of us.'

'Stephen will survive. Poor Beatrice, rather,' Chloe said with a touch of seriousness.

'Yes. I didn't ask him to leave his wife, you know. I didn't ask him for anything.'

'That was the difference between us,' Chloe said calmly.

'Perhaps. But he came, for whatever reason, and there we were. It scared me to death, and still does. I tried to talk to you about it once, Helen, do you remember?'

Helen reddened a little under Pansy's clear blue gaze.

'And I wasn't very much help, was I? You thought I was taking some kind of moral standpoint, but it was only because of Oliver, and Chloe.'

Oliver. Without anyone voicing it, they knew that they couldn't talk about Oliver here in this mellow room with the water rippling peacefully outside.

'You're a very loyal friend,' Chloe said, squeezing Helen's hand.

'So you are,' Pansy added. 'And you're the only one of us who's got any sense. Darcy's the nicest man I know, and he adores you.'

He adores you. The words rang in Helen's ears and Venice fell away. She saw Darcy standing in the meadows at Mere, smiling at her.

'Didn't you know?' she heard Chloe asking.

Helen collected herself with an effort. 'Oh yes. I knew.' She looked quickly from one to the other and determinedly changed the subject. 'Why are we sitting here talking boyfriends like

255

three schoolgirls? Isn't there anything else?' They were all laughing again.

'There's us. And *The Stones of Venice*, for a start.'

'Do you think we should have some more brandy before Pansy gives us her critical interpretation?'

'I'm *sure* we should have some more brandy.'

Much later, when they reached the Palazzo Croce again, they found Masefield and Kim waiting for them in the lounge. There were creases of genuine concern in Masefield's heavy face, and he was holding out a silver tray with a little square envelope on it.

'This has just been delivered. For you, Helen.'

It was unmistakably an international telegram.

The glow of pleasure from her evening was torn away from Helen by a cold shock of fear. Oh God, a voice said in her head, not Mummy too. Please, not Mummy too. Her hands shook as she snatched the envelope from the pretty tray and clumsily fought to rip it open.

'Not bad news I hope,' Kim said.

For a moment, as Helen stared at them, the words failed to register. She frowned, her lips framing the short message. Then relief so profound flooded through her that she found herself laughing weakly. The telegram fluttered from her fingers and drifted away.

'What is it, Helen, for God's sake?'

'It's nothing. No, I don't mean that. It's Darcy.'

Pansy picked up the telegram again and put it into her hands.

'Come on,' she said briskly.

Helen looked down at the words again, then read them out aloud as slowly as if they were in a difficult foreign language.

'It says "Helen will you marry me Darcy".'

There was a confused babble of exclamations. Helen found that she was still laughing half-hysterically. 'It's so like him,' she explained to no-one in particular. 'Not to say it direct. Or even to telephone. It's so like him, to do it like this.'

Kim stared around, puzzled.

'Will someone tell me who Darcy is?'

'Kim,' Pansy said, 'he's Oliver Mortimore's elder brother.'

Kim's jaw dropped. '*The* elder brother?'

'The one and only. We have the possible future Countess of

Montcalm in our midst.' She turned the telegram over. 'Reply paid. He means business, Helen.'

It was Chloe who gently took her hands. 'Shall we all leave you alone for a bit?'

Helen started. 'No. Don't go away, please. What do I have to do to answer? He'll be waiting.'

Masefield's hand was on his cordless telephone. 'You want to call?'

Helen shook her head. 'No. I just want to answer this.' She held the crumpled telegram out to him.

'What do you want to say?'

She looked from his heavy-lidded eyes to Kim's impressed stare. Beside Kim Pansy and Chloe were watching her affectionately. And behind them the shutters stood open on the scented night. She thought of the way that Venice had possessed her, mind and body, and the way that its languor had made everything seem sweet and simple.

In painful contrast, her memories of the past months were all struggles and sadness. She had fallen helplessly in love with Oliver, and his loss had cost her a great deal. Even her slow recovery had been shadowed by Oliver's growing unhappiness. Now she was left with tenderness for him, and with protectiveness and anxiety still shot through with some of the old love. Even here, far away in Venice with Darcy's telegram in her fingers, she could see Oliver's face and hear his bitter laughter.

Yet it was Darcy who had changed things for her. He had salved her loneliness with his soothing company, and he had taken away much of her sadness. Darcy wasn't Oliver. He was himself, and she suddenly knew how important. *Helen will you marry me Darcy.*

She remembered her day of goodbyes to Oxford, and how her tutor had asked her what she really wanted. Her answer, 'I'd like to marry and have children', had shocked them both. The thought of it with Oliver was painfully inappropriate. But with Darcy, it was different. He was clear, and faithful, and she knew that he loved her.

Then at Stephen Spurring's house, she had envied Beatrice in the warm clutter of her family kitchen. That could be her own life now, and for her husband she would have Darcy whose goodness was unmistakable.

She could go home to Darcy and the low grey house against

the hillside, and the warmth of his love. And to the invincible security of his great name, however little that had to do with the man himself. She would be secure with Darcy, and she could be free to be happy. Nor would it be just for herself. Her mother and Graham would never have to worry again. She was certain that Darcy would see to that.

Pansy and Chloe and the Warrens were still looking at her, smiling uncertainly. Outside the low music of the Venetian night went on. Life had seemed sweet and simple here. Her heart leapt as she realised that that simplicity could stay with her now.

And do you love Darcy? She answered herself unhesitatingly *yes*. If she was not in love with him, as she had been with Oliver . . . well, that had proved to be suffocating and then agonising. That was to be avoided, surely.

Slowly Helen looked into her friends' faces. They seemed to beam encouragement. Masefield was waiting at the door.

'I want to reply "Yes Helen".'

'I'll get that fixed up for you,' he said.

There, it was done.

There need be no more barely-admitted battle with herself, no more running from the reality of Darcy. That was all that had been needed. Just to be made to decide.

Then without warning another face floated in front of her. She saw Tom Hart's sceptical frown, and the hint of amusement behind it that so often pricked her. Tom would be surprised at her. She pushed aside the unwelcome thought, and with it a tiny, deep-seated fear within her. If Tom was her friend, he would be pleased by her happiness. And if he wasn't pleased, why should it matter to her at all?

None of this was anything to do with Tom Hart.

They were all crowding around her now.

'Congratulations,' somebody said. There were kisses on her cheeks, and arms around her shoulders to hug her.

'This calls for a celebration,' Masefield decreed. He wrenched the cork from a bottle of champagne and a jet of silvery froth shot over them.

'Here's to Viscountess Darcy,' they toasted her.

'No. Just to Darcy's wife,' Helen protested. She had a sudden vision of Montcalm sitting aggressively on the skyline inder its coronet of turrets and domes.

Then she saw Lord and Lady Montcalm smiling thinly on the

steps, watching herself and Pansy as they climbed into Masefield's Rolls.

Did they know? What would they think?

It wasn't the time to worry about that now. Just remember Darcy, gentle, loving Darcy, and the wide acres of Mere.

Helen wrapped her fingers around her champagne glass and drank so deeply that she felt as if the bubbles were exploding inside her head.

Everyone seemed ready to have a party, but before she had reached the bottom of her glass Helen was overcome with weariness.

Unsteadily she put her glass down and blinked around at them.

'I've got to go to bed. I suddenly feel so tired.' Sleep beckoned as the most wonderful prospect in the world.

'Are you all right?' The voices were concerned.

'It's just reaction to the excitement,' Kim said soothingly. 'Just get a good night's sleep and tomorrow we'll go and look for some Venetian glass for your engagement present. Although I expect they've got more than enough wonderful glass at Montcalm.' Her voice was wistful.

Helen found her way to the door. 'Goodnight,' she mumbled. 'Goodnight, everyone.'

Helen knew that she was waiting for someone. She was confident that he would come, and aware that there was no hurry. So she sat patiently in the sunshine, feeling the warmth of the stone wall beneath her, her fingertips stroking the rough blocks. The view in front of her was old-fashioned English pastureland in early summer, dotted with oak trees and laced over with the milky froth of cow parsley.

Then she saw someone coming over the tussocky grass. She knew it was not the person she had been expecting, but there was no surprise. Instead she jumped down from the wall and ran to him. The meadow grass brushed her bare ankles as she went.

Tom held out his arms.

Her face was against his shoulder and she thought that she could hear both their hearts beating. She opened her mouth to say something, but he stopped her.

'Quiet. Listen.'

Over their heads a lark was singing, measuring out his territory against the blue sky.

Tom kissed her. He touched her eyelashes and the curve of her cheekbones as if he was tasting them, and then his mouth found hers. In the darkness of his eyes Helen saw the passion that was so often masked by his cynical smile. His fingers were counting her buttons, white buttons familiar on a dress that she only wore in summertime.

One by one he undid them.

His eyes were closed now and she saw the blackness of the lashes against his cheek. With the tip of his tongue Tom traced the arch of her collarbone and tasted the white skin in the tiny hollow at the base of her throat. His hands rippled over her ribs, spanned her waist and then rested on the points of her hips.

'Gipsy Helen,' he said, very softly. 'Dearest gipsy Helen.'

The meadow was gone now. They were lying face to face on a white bed in a shadowed room. Helen was minutely conscious of the kiss of flesh against her own. With a sudden breeze the thin curtains blew inwards from the open window. Helen half-turned to look. Her body was washed with physical sweetness and certainty. There was no hurry, no fear, and no distance from the loved body alongside hers. The curtains fluttered once more and she turned back to him, reaching out her hands to touch and her mouth to taste.

Her fingers closed on emptiness.

She was alone. The room was the same, her Venetian bedroom with the arched ceiling and the window over the Canal. But she had never shared it with anyone. The dream had been so vivid that she could still feel the warmth of another body hollowing the mattress, but it had only been a dream. No more than that. The lingering happiness that it had left behind was chased away by disappointment, and then dismay.

Helen sat up. She was awake now, but even so she looked down at the pillow next to her own. It was as smooth and plumped-up as when the maid had left it.

Pieces of consciousness began to fit together again to make the flat jigsaw of reality. It wasn't Tom she was looking for, it was Darcy.

Last night she had agreed to marry Darcy.

Helen got out of bed and went out on to her balcony. It was very early. A single gondola wove under the Rialto Bridge and a flat barge full of refuse chugged prosaically past her. A thin veil of mist was rising from the water.

Helen scrambled haphazardly into her clothes and slipped down through the sleeping palazzo. Outside it was cold and she shivered under her thin sweater, then began to walk determinedly. She knew the network of little alleys well now and she moved without hesitation over the worn paving and up and over the sharp summits of the tiny bridges. Her mind was working just as quickly.

She pushed away the uncomfortably erotic dream and the memory of Tom Hart. It clung too closely, and together with the sensuality that Venice seemed to breed in her she was troubled by a physical longing that she had never known before.

Instead she thought of Darcy and the immensity of the promise she had made. She was happy to think of the happiness that it would have given him, but a shadow of uncertainty darkened everything else.

She had never thought of marrying Darcy, yet when the moment came she had agreed unhesitatingly.

Helen clung to that. If she had answered yes without soul-searching, almost without thought, then deep down inside herself she must know that it was right. Yet she was disturbed to find that she couldn't recall Darcy's face. After her dream Tom Hart's was crystal clear, every mysterious and mocking plane of it.

The ripples generated by the shock of Darcy's telegram spread on outwards in her thoughts. Helen remembered her mother, and smiled. Her mother would be delighted with whatever and whoever made her daughter happy, but she would be an unnatural mother if she were not even more pleased because Darcy was who he was. Then there were Their Royal Highnesses.

No. That was what she and Tom had called them.

Lord and Lady Montcalm, rather. Helen smiled again, gleefully this time. It would be amusing to see their faces when Darcy took her to Montcalm again, this time not as an unnoticed friend of Oliver's, but as their future daughter-in-law. She wouldn't be afraid of them any more. She would have Darcy with her.

Helen's pace quickened. She knew that she wanted to see him

again very much. In only two more days they would be together.

She wondered whether he would want them to be married quickly, or whether marrying a Viscount took a lot of fuss and arranging. The idea amused her again. She knew Darcy so well, and she was certain that he would insist on the simplest, quietest wedding possible. For a moment the word *wedding* jolted her a little, and then she collected herself with the thought that it couldn't happen for a time yet.

There were Schools to do first, only two months away. Until yesterday the exams had loomed as the most important hurdle in the world. Now they had diminished a little, but they still mattered. Helen wanted her First.

When she looked around her she saw that she had reached the shabby quarter of the city surrounding the railway station. The houses were patched with peeling paint and plaster here and blanketed with lines of grey washing. At the corner of the street she stood in two painfully thin dogs were tussling over some scraps of food. But in the ripening glow of light Venice still seemed achingly beautiful. Helen stood for a moment drinking it in and then thought *I'll come here with Darcy*. It was hard to imagine what effect the peculiar, melancholy spell of the sinking city would have on his solid Englishness, but she would make sure that he came.

Helen realised that she was hungry and thirsty. In the faded café opposite she ordered coffee and a square of meltingly sweet pastry, then sat down at a little blue tin table in the sun to eat it. A workman in stained overalls came by and smiled suggestively at her.

'Hello, beautiful,' he said in Italian. 'Why are you all alone?'

Happiness suffused her. 'Oh, but I'm not,' she beamed at him. 'I'm not alone.'

The workman went away looking faintly puzzled, and Helen laughed out loud.

Her step was light as she made her way back to the Palazzo Croce.

Everyone was sitting round the table in the dining room, evidently waiting for her. The day was going to be hot, and already the doors stood open on the well of coolness within the inner court.

'Couldn't you sleep?' Kim called out to her. 'I know when

Masefield proposed to me I didn't get a wink for three nights, I was so happy. Wasn't I, darling?'

Masefield looked up briefly from the financial pages, clearly deaf to Kim's talk.

'You bet,' he agreed. 'What have you girls got planned for today? Wish I could join you, but I'm waiting to call London. I should be in London. If it weren't for this Lido development hitch ...' He gathered up his papers and made for the door, kissing the air above Pansy's head as he passed.

'Masefield,' Kim said plaintively. 'Just for once, couldn't you take the day off?'

'Out of the question right now, pet. Next week, maybe. Have you got everything you want? Why don't you go out to lunch somewhere nice?'

For the rest of the day he would be barricaded behind a wall of papers. Kim's pretty face clouded in a pout, then she sighed and leaned back in her seat to nibble at the last quarter of the single apple she allowed herself for breakfast. Staying slim was her religion.

'Be thankful you're not marrying a businessman,' she said to Helen. 'Masefield works so hard, but he does it all for us, doesn't he, Pansy?'

'Of course not.' Pansy was brisk. 'He does it because he's a workaholic. And what could he possibly do if he wasn't working? He lacks the concept of leisure. Poor man.' She laughed merrily and Kim gazed at her blank-faced.

'What does Darcy do all day?' Kim asked.

'Farms, mostly,' Helen told her. 'Worries about rain, and delivers lambs in the middle of the night, and drives round with bales of hay in the back of a Land Rover.' Helen's face softened, and Chloe and Pansy winked at each other.

'Himself?'

Kim looked so disappointed that Helen hastened to add, 'You see, there are so many hundreds of acres in the Mere and Montcalm estates that he feels he could never stay in touch with them without working the land himself. He's responsible for dozens of farmhands and a whole village full of tenants, as well.'

'Oh yes, of course.' This picture of the feudal lord fitted in much better with Kim's idea of Darcy's grandeur. Helen kept her eyes firmly averted from Chloe and Pansy.

'Do you suppose you'll have to open village fêtes?' Kim asked, envious. There was a muffled snort from Pansy.

'I think they ask actors from *The Archers* to do that sort of thing, don't they? Darcy's never mentioned it as a regular feature of life, anyway.'

As she made her light-hearted answer an uncomfortable thought nagged at Helen. Kim's question hadn't been so very far off the mark, for all the amusement that had greeted it. However much she wanted it, she couldn't just be Darcy's wife in the rural haven of Mere. Whether or not it was at village fêtes, they would have to play a role together in the local life. And when his father died, much more would be expected of them. Helen knew that Darcy hated and feared that side of his life, and she knew too that she lacked the particular strength to help him to be a more public person. She thought, a little sadly, that he should have chosen some kindly, confident girl with the assurance bred of coming from the same background as his own. There must be one somewhere. Not all of them could be like Oliver's friends. That's what Their Royal Highnesses would be expecting of him. And instead he would be bringing home Helen.

Some of the elation ebbed away, and a little, dismal premonition of trouble took its place.

She made herself listen to the talk around the table again. Pansy was proposing a last boat trip on the lagoon, and a picnic on one of the distant islands.

'Come with us, Kim,' she invited with unusual warmth. Seeing her stepmother through her friends' eyes had touched her with sudden sympathy.

'We-ell,' Kim said. 'Couldn't we have lunch at the Lido?'

'No.'

'I won't, then. I need some new shoes, and I want to buy Helen a present she can remember us by.'

Pansy shrugged. 'It baffles me how anyone who owns forty pairs of shoes can need another.'

'Unlike you, I don't choose to slop about in flipflops,' Kim said sharply.

Relations had shifted rapidly back to normal again.

'Kim, I can remember you without a present,' Helen protested. Kim swung round in amazement.

'Oh but you must. It's part of it all. I was showered with wonderful things when we got married.'

They let her go to solace herself with shopping, and spent a day idyllic with the first warmth of summer in drifting over the dappled waters of the lagoon.

The last hours in Venice slipped rapidly past. On their last morning Helen packed her case with a sharp mixture of regret and anticipation. She was leaving the city that had affected her more potently than anywhere else she had ever been, but she was going home to Darcy. One day soon they would come back here, together. Carefully she wrapped Kim's souvenir and nested it amongst her clothes. It was a set of Murano glass bowls, slightly too brightly coloured for her own taste.

With the air of a man bestowing a huge privilege, Masefield himself took them to the airport. They were flying standby and seats had materialised at short notice, so he drove with rapid and unwavering determination, just like he did everything else. Kim hung on to his arm all the way, as possessive as a child with a toy.

Their flight was already being called when they reached the airport and their goodbyes were brief.

'Work hard,' Masefield ordered his daughter. 'Any ideas yet about what you want to do when you finish?'

'I want to act,' Pansy said in a low voice.

'You do? I'll call Tony Prescott. It's not one of my companies, but he owes me a favour.'

'No.' Her voice was suddenly sharp, but she modulated it at once and smiled sweetly. 'Let me finish my course first. One thing at a time.'

'Quite right. Goodbye, both of you.' He planted identical kisses on Chloe's and Helen's cheeks. A glance showed him that Kim was twirling a rack of glossy magazines. Helen had turned away, but she heard him say, 'You won't change your mind about London?'

'No,' Chloe said, cool-voiced. 'But thanks.'

Helen hurried away towards the barrier.

When they looked back to wave, Masefield and Kim were standing side by side. They made an arresting couple, the heavy, powerful-looking man and his pretty young wife.

Within an hour they were over the Italian Alps. Helen peered down at the jagged snowy peaks and turned quickly back to Chloe sitting beside her. Across the aisle Pansy was apparently fast asleep. She insisted that it was the only way to deal with aeroplanes.

'Enjoy your holiday?' Chloe asked.

'Mmm. Everything seems almost too good to be true,' she said with a long sigh. 'Venice, and Darcy.' Helen hesitated, then decided she could surely tell Chloe about something that had nibbled continuously at the edges of her mind.

'A funny thing happened. The night after Darcy's telegram, I had a wildly sexy dream. About Tom. I blush to think about it now.'

'Whyever should you?' Chloe chuckled. 'It sounds to me like a classic case of anxiety at the sudden closing of options. Explore the possibilities in dreams instead.'

'You think that's all?'

'Of course. You don't think that deep down you're really madly in love with Tom Hart, do you?'

'No,' Helen said quickly.

'Well then, that's okay, isn't it?'

Was it okay? Helen asked herself. She was disturbed to find that there was no answer.

'Did you enjoy your holiday?' Helen countered. It occurred to her that Chloe was looking her old self again, sleek and tawny as a tiger. The drawn look and painfilled eyes were almost completely gone.

'Yes. I began to think that I shall be able to live with myself again after all.' Chloe glanced down at her hands and then said, 'Something funny happened to me, too. Masefield asked if he could see me in London.'

Chloe had been sitting alone in the inner court of the palazzo, watching the evening light thicken on the mosaics. Masefield came out and looked around at the empty chairs.

'Where is everyone?'

'Changing,' she told him, and instead of going away again he sat down and watched her, his eyes unashamedly exploring her face. She saw that he had blue eyes, not shifting pools of different blues like Pansy's, but solid and piercing.

'You're lovely, Chloe,' he said abruptly, and then, 'Do you think I'm an old man?'

'No,' she said, understanding him.

They were both acutely aware of the blank rows of windows looking out over the court. Masefield lit a cigarette with exaggerated attention.

'I'm often in London,' he said. 'Sometimes alone. Shall we meet there?'

Their eyes met and the seconds of possibility ticked past, then Chloe looked down and away from him. As gently as she could, she said, 'No, I don't think that would be very clever of us.'

'Pity.' Masefield was crisp. 'We might have enjoyed ourselves.'

In the plane high over Switzerland, Chloe saw that Helen was watching her without surprise.

'What did you say?'

'Oh, I turned him down, of course.' Chloe's smile was lopsided. 'I've done enough tangling with married men.'

That was all, but the insignificant little encounter had changed Chloe's mood dramatically. With her refusal, self-confidence had flooded back into her, and a renewed sense of pleasure in controlling her own life. She was free again, and she would make the most of it. Oxford beckoned now, and the disciplines of work that she was beginning to enjoy for its own sake.

Of the three of them, only Pansy behind her closed eyelids felt no pleasure at her return. She was winging away from the restrictions imposed by Masefield and Kim, but in his own way Stephen and his consuming passion for her was beginning to feel just as restricting.

Impatience seethed inside Pansy, but she kept the muscles of her face slack and her eyelids firmly closed.

TRINITY TERM

CHAPTER ELEVEN

Heathrow looked profoundly ugly.

Confronted with the acres of orange and green plastic and submerged in the cacophony of noise, Helen felt depression folding around her. It affected Chloe and Pansy too, and they stood in a silent group at the baggage carousel during the interminable wait for their suitcases.

When they came through the customs hall, Helen saw him at once. Darcy was there, anxiously scanning the crowd of arrivals. He was not as tall as she remembered, and the intent frown made him look short-sighted. A second later he saw her and his face split into a smile of pure delight.

As he pushed against the tide of people towards her, Helen only thought No. I didn't expect him to be here.

I don't want a reunion like this. I'm not ready.

Then he was beside her, seizing her hands and looking expectantly into her eyes.

'How did you know to meet this flight?' was all Helen could find to say. Even in her own ears her voice sounded shamefully unwelcoming.

'I've met every flight since I got your wire. Somehow I ... thought you'd come home at once.' Faint disappointment, and forgiveness, showed so plainly in his face that Helen had to bury hers against his shoulder. Her fingers felt the tense muscles in his forearms.

'I'm sorry', she mumbled. 'I'm just so surprised to see you here. You shouldn't ... no, I don't mean that. Thank you for coming. I didn't know you'd expect me right away.'

At last she looked up at him and his face cleared immediately.

'Don't worry,' he soothed. 'Come on, let's go home.'

Chloe and Pansy had gone their separate ways, so Darcy and Helen drove down from London alone together.

As they went she tried to explain her love affair with Venice and the strange hold the city had taken on her, trying to justify her failing to fly home to him at once. Darcy listened, nodding, his eyes on the road.

'Of course we'll go together,' he promised her, 'for our

honeymoon if you like.' This time he snatched a sideways glance at her, ready to exchange a complicit smile, but Helen's profile was turned a little away, watching the newly green countryside as it flashed past.

When they reached Oxford, Darcy took the bypass instead of heading for the city centre. Helen turned to him startled.

'Where are we going?'

'Home, of course. To Mere.'

She sank back into her seat. She had been expecting Follies, looking forward to seeing the eccentric old house again, and the privacy of her own place. Instead they were heading for Mere. Darcy was bringing home his bride-to-be. It was all going wrong, she realised miserably. None of this was as she had imagined her homecoming during the last precious hours in Venice. There was nothing to be done about the grey opaque day or the hideous tangle of roads and service stations that fringed Oxford. But the scratchiness was coming from inside her, and it was her own fault.

Darcy was exactly the same as always.

He looked at her, kindly and puzzled, and she could have slapped herself for her perversity.

'Tell you what,' he said. 'Let's stop for a drink.'

There was a tiny country pub not far away. Darcy was a connoisseur of the beer and Helen enjoyed watching the sparse mixture of car-workers and farm hands that made up the clientele.

'The Wheatsheaf?'

'The Wheatsheaf it is.'

That was better, Helen thought. Neutral ground for just a little while longer. The bar was unusually crowded with the run-up to a darts match, but they found a table in a corner and sat facing each other. Helen tasted her hoppy beer and grinned at him. 'The flavour of England. Home at last.'

'To stay for ever, I hope. Helen, there's nothing wrong, is there?'

She shook her head. There wasn't anything wrong that she could put her finger on. It was just irritation with the world, and with Darcy, and most of all with herself. She looked around the little room, at dark beams hung with pewter pots and at the polished brass handles of the beer pumps.

This much she understood.

'It's good to think that we'll go on sitting in pubs like this, together, for years and years. Watching the people and not saying much, but together.'

It was the first time she had mentioned their shared future. They stared solemnly at each other, realising what they had promised.

Darcy slid his hand into his pocket. 'I want to give you this.' A little blue velvet box sat on the table-top amongst the rings of spilled beer. Helen gazed at it, knowing and reluctant.

'Go on,' he ordered.

Inside the box was a ring. It was an immense blood-red ruby in an old-fashioned setting of diamonds. 'My God,' she breathed, staring at the great jewel. It was so unlike her that she couldn't conceive herself wearing it. She couldn't even bring herself to touch it.

Darcy took it out of its velvet nest and lifted her left hand. The ring, cold and massive, slid over her third finger and hung loose as she unwillingly held out her hand for them both to see it.

'It's the Viscountess's ring,' he told her. 'I don't know how many generations, but very old.' And then, 'How tiny your hand is. Such thin, little fingers. We shall have to get it altered for you.'

Helen thought of all the proud, splendid women who must have worn this ruby as their right, and her heart failed within her. 'Darcy,' she said miserably, 'I can't wear this.'

'You must, as my wife.' There was to be no argument, and it was the first time that Helen had glimpsed strength of will in him. Nor could she have guessed at the insistence on family tradition, but it was clear to her now. Darcy folded her hand into a fist. 'Wear it for me today,' he said, 'and then I'll get our jeweller to remake it. Don't you see, my darling? I'm proud of you, Helen, and in my own way I'm proud of my family too. I want you to wear our ring. Do it for me.'

She nodded dumbly, but there were tears in her eyes. She could feel the curious stare of the other drinkers on her back. 'Do your parents know about this?' She held up her fist like a challenge.

'Not yet. I want us to tell them together. And I want to talk to your mother first, of course. Or Graham, as the male head of the family.'

He was making gentle fun of his own insistence on form, and she smiled with gratitude and felt herself relax a little.

'Graham will want to make sure that you can keep me in the style to which I am accustomed.' She drained her drink. 'Let's go back to Mere. Back home.' The correction was quick. 'If you've been hanging around Heathrow for two days you must have a lot of things waiting to be done.'

The sight of Mere almost set things to rights again. The low grey house was as solid as a rock against its dense yew hedges. Darcy, with a brief murmured apology, was on his way to see his head man.

'I'll stay out here for a while,' she told him, 'and meet you on the way back.' She leant against the stone wall of a barn and looked out across the farm in the gathering dusk. The orderly yards were empty, but there was a low hum of activity from the long milking sheds.

Helen half-closed her eyes and tried to imagine herself crossing this yard in two or three years' time.

Perhaps she would have been to pick herbs in the kitchen garden, or to visit a sick lamb with a bottle of warm milk.

She would be waiting for her husband to come home, listening for the Land Rover or for the ring of his boots on the well-swept cobbles of the yard. Perhaps there would be a child, an heir for Darcy, with the look of his father and Oliver's gold hair.

No. That was all in the past. The inappropriateness of the thought frightened her. Darcy's wife. The lady of the manor.

Fear and uncertainty swept over Helen and she swayed giddily. At her back the stone barn was solid, but the rest of the world was terrifyingly distorted. Then, incongruously, she remembered her dream. The calm sweetness of it flooded back, exactly as she had felt it in Venice. With it came Tom's face, sharp and clear. Helen was rigid. 'What have I done?' she whispered. 'What am I doing?' She opened her eyes to see Darcy coming towards her, on his way home to her as he would be all through their married life until they were old and tired. She reached out to snatch his hand and clung to the rough warmth of it. His arm came round her shoulders and he led her into the yellow lamplight inside the house.

They ate a quiet, simple supper in the oak dining room. Mrs Maitland served it, correct and non-committal, and Helen kept her clenched fist out of sight in her pocket.

After their meal they sat over their coffee in Darcy's little sitting room. The silences between them were beginning to draw out. 'Helen,' he said at last, 'will you stay here with me tonight?'

She drew her breath in. She knew it was coming. Part of herself wanted to go to him, giving herself as the least she could offer in return for his wholeheartedness. But another, stronger part clamoured for time, and for a chance to think.

She said, gently, with her forehead against his and her eyes lowered, 'I'd like to wait a little. Will you mind that?'

He smiled, but his face was wistful. 'As long as you want. Until we're married, if you need it to be like that between us.'

Unspoken, but acknowledged between them just the same, was the fact that she had slept with his brother.

He doesn't deserve this, Helen thought, watching the tiny muscles move in his face, and his hands as they stroked hers. He's good, and generous, and I'm not.

'When will we be married?' he asked.

'After my Schools.' She heard herself almost gabbling with anxiety. 'When I've done my exams. Need we make any plans before then? It's been three years of hard work you see, and I want to give them all my attention. Then after that...'

'Of course. Of course you must do the exams first. Do you think I can't wait until June? I love you and I want you, but I want you to be happy and sure, and I don't want you to sacrifice anything for my sake.'

Darcy took her face between his hands and kissed her eyelids. 'You look so tired. Tomorrow we'll go to see your family, but now I'll drive you home to Follies. Don't worry any more. Don't worry about anything.'

'Are you happy, darling?' Helen and her mother were washing up the tea-things together. Darcy was in the front room of the little house watching a television football match with Graham. He had displayed an unguessed-at interest in the game that delighted Helen's brother.

Helen stared out at the rectangular garden, less well-kept now than when her father was alive. Her mind was blank. 'Yes,' she answered. 'Yes, of course.' It was so strange, Darcy being here, drinking tea out of the familiar cups and looking at the pictures of Graham and herself ranged on the piano.

Darcy had been determined. He had insisted on coming, and as soon as he and Helen were seated side by side on the sofa, with her hand in his, he said, 'Mrs Brown, I want to marry Helen, and I'm amazed to find that she wants me, too. Will you give us your blessing?' Helen loved him for his simplicity and his will to do what was right, but she felt the lifelines being severed all around her.

After her first stunned surprise, Mrs Brown had reacted just as Helen had imagined. Happiness was mingled with relief. Not only could she stop worrying about her daughter, but her daughter would be in a position to see that none of them had to worry any more. She was awed when she discovered who Darcy was, but she firmly believed that he was no better than her daughter deserved.

Now, alone together in the kitchen, she hugged Helen. 'I'm so surprised, but in a way I'm not, either. I knew you would be someone special. I'm so proud of you, Helen. Dad would have been too. If only he could have been here.'

For a moment they held one another, unspeaking. Then Mrs Brown said cautiously, 'What will it mean, the title and everything? What will you have to do?'

'Just be a farmer's wife, at first. Until he inherits, at least. After that, I suppose we'll work together to keep Montcalm going. It'll be a business, just like any other except for a few trappings.' Helen thought her voice sounded hollow.

'And there'll be your children. They'll expect children.'

'Yes,' Helen whispered. 'Children too.'

Mrs Brown put away the cups and saucers. 'I just want to see you happy, whether you're a countess or a cleaner. I'd rather you were a countess, of course.' She giggled like a young girl, pink with pleasure at the resonant word. 'Imagine it. But I couldn't have hoped for you to bring home a nicer boy. He seems so gentle. And I can see how much he loves you just by looking at his face. I know he'll make you happy.'

'Yes,' Helen said again, unable to escape her dismal sense of being cut adrift.

Later, Darcy took them all out to dinner. They went to an Italian restaurant in the nearby shopping parade. The food was bad, a depressing travesty that still brought back Venice, and the erotic elation of her spirits there. Where has it all gone? Helen wondered, looking around her. No-one seemed to notice the inadequacy of her mood. Darcy was calm and fully at his ease, and her mother opened to his attention like a flower. Graham, owlish behind his spectacles with the effects of the wine, seemed already to regard Darcy as an unofficial elder brother.

On the drive back to Oxford, Darcy said, 'I like your family.'

That's because they're not very demanding, Helen thought, and then recoiled from her own sourness. 'They're not very like yours,' she answered.

'No,' he said carefully. 'You're rather lucky in that respect, aren't you?'

Helen suddenly understood how much happier Darcy would have been to be born ordinary instead of in the flare of family expectation and then under the shadow of golden Oliver. She reached out and squeezed his hand as it rested on the wheel. 'Come and spend the day at Mere tomorrow,' he begged.

'Darcy, I must do some work. Sunday is the very best day, because it's so quiet everywhere.'

And he had acquiesced, so uncomplaining that she had almost told him that she would come out to Mere after all.

In the early evening Helen made her way back to Follies from the brown calm of her library. She felt reassured by the continuity of study, and more certain that the frightening new aspects of her life would all, at last, come right. She pushed open the door of her room at the top of the house, and then stopped short.

Tom Hart was sitting in the window.

'Back at last,' he drawled.

The muscles in her throat contracted so fiercely that she almost choked. There, flesh and blood, was her Italian dream. There was a shadow across his face but she still knew every line of it. She knew the easy sprawl of his arms and legs too, and the quick muscles of his shoulders, and the long line of his back.

He was watching her, and under his dark eyes she felt herself, dream-like, naked too. Somewhere, out of the corner of her eye, she thought she glimpsed the lazy billow of a thin white curtain.

'Why have you gone so red?' Tom asked. The light, ironic voice was unbearably familiar. 'I could have sat outside on the stairs, but it seemed a little pointless as the door was open. And you've been hours.' He looked around the room and as he turned his head out of the shadow she saw the reality of the dark, handsome face and the sceptical downward turn of his sensitive mouth. 'It's quite respectable,' he prodded her. 'I don't see any compromising bits of lingerie scattered around. And I promise I haven't even glanced at your diary, or your letters.' He smiled, teasing charm changing all the angles of his face again.

'I don't think you'd have found them very interesting in any case.' Helen was stiff. 'I lead a quiet life.' Her instinct was to defend herself, and to shore up the walls of separateness that her dream had brought tumbling down.

Tom's eyebrows shot up into mocking peaks.

'Quiet? And newly engaged to a viscount, no less? What would you call exciting, then?'

Helen sat down as far from him as she could.

'Who told you?' she asked.

'Pansy.'

There was a moment's silence. Helen felt uncomfortably that she was transparent, and that Tom could see right into her, more clearly than she could see herself.

'Helen, are you happy?' he asked.

She knew, however vehemently she insisted that she was, Tom would see that it was a lie. She looked back at him, protecting herself but infinitely vulnerable to him.

'I'm very happy.' The words came out sounding thin and defiant. Disappointment in her showed clearly in his face. Helen found herself half wanting to escape from him, and half longing to run to him and tell him no.

The chance was gone.

Tom stood up, and then held out a square package neatly wrapped in brown paper and tied with string. When he spoke again his voice was flippant.

'Congratulations. We can call this an engagement present.'

He managed to make the idea of an engagement sound like an amusing anachronism. Some of the old irritation that he always stirred in her revived in Helen, but she took the brown parcel without comment and turned it in her hands.

'Go on,' he ordered.

Helen pulled at the string, then folded back the paper. The first thing she saw was a hammer, and then a twist of tissue paper that revealed a slim nail and a hook. Frowning now she tore away more paper, and then found herself staring into the turquoise brilliance of the sea behind a vase of summer flowers. It was the little oil painting that she had seen in pride of place over Tom's fireplace.

Helen held it up and marvelled again at how the economical brushstrokes, there for all to see, could conjure up so much dancing light.

Then she turned to Tom. The downward turn had come back to his mouth, and he was watching her sombrely.

'I can't take this,' she said. 'You can't part with anything so beautiful.'

Tom's hand closed over hers so that it tightened on the frame of the picture. 'It's yours now,' he told her. 'I wanted to give you something ... and Darcy ... for everything you did to help the play, and Oliver. I saw you at the party, looking up at my picture, and I knew that you'd love it as much as I do. And what better occasion could there be for a present than your engagement? To Darcy himself. What could be neater?' Again there was the flash of mockery. 'So let's hang it and see how it looks.'

Tom went over to the mantelpiece of the little iron grate and deftly swept it clear of the student clutter of lecture lists and invitations to long-past faculty sherry parties. He held the picture up against the chimney breast, cocked his head to one side to judge it, then put it down to hammer in the picture pin.

They stood back shoulder to shoulder to examine it.

The little picture was perfectly at home on the bare wall. It seemed to brighten the room, and to bring with it a breath of flowers and the salt sea air.

'Thank you,' she said, almost inaudibly. Afraid that he hadn't heard her, Helen put out her hand and met the supple leather of his bright blue jacket, then stretched to kiss his cheek. As she moved he turned his face and her lips were faintly grazed by the prickle of beard on his jaw. Her mouth met the corner of his and she started back, shocked by the electricity that seemed to crackle through them.

Tom's faint smile might have been an acknowledgement of her thanks, or of something else altogether.

'And now,' he said, 'I think we should celebrate by going out to dinner.'

'I can't...'

'You've taken my picture,' he reminded her coolly. 'The least you can do is let me buy you dinner as a way of saying goodbye to it.'

Helen knew that she didn't want to say no.

Tom drove her out to Woodstock, and they sat over drinks in a garden heavy with the scent of lilacs and wet grass. Helen was uncomfortable, but she was also vividly aware that her depression had lifted. The evening scents, and the texture of grass or paving beneath her feet, seemed sharp and precious. Ordinary things seemed significant, whether it was the low murmur of voices from an open window or the arc of a car's lights in the lane beyond.

'Are you warm enough out here?' His voice, too, seemed to have a different timbre.

'Yes,' she said softly. 'It's beautiful.'

Tom leaned across and lifted her hand from her lap. He turned it to and fro in his and then looked at her, quizzical.

Helen resisted her first impulse to snatch her hand away, and let it lie. 'There is a ring,' she heard herself saying. 'The Viscountess's ring. Darcy took it away to be remade because it's too big. It's a ruby, about the size of golfball, and about ten diamonds besides. I don't think it's me, really.' Her voice trailed away into silence. Tom still held her hand in his, but he was looking away across the restaurant garden as if his mind was somewhere else.

'Remember New Year's Eve?' he asked.

Helen snatched her hand away now as if it had been burnt. 'Vividly. Rather a lot of things happened.'

'I haven't been slapped for kissing someone since I was about twelve and tried to grab Ellen Lou Parker at a Saturday morning movie show. It was rather exciting, once I'd got over the shock.'

'I was upset,' she defended herself. 'After we'd just seen Oliver . . .'

'I don't want to talk about Oliver right now.'

Helen was painfully conscious of his dark stare, and behind that the sense that he expected something of her. She retreated further behind a barrier of tumbling words.

'I remember running off to hide in the billiard room, and finding Darcy hiding there too . . .'

'I particularly don't want to talk about Darcy right now.'

A sudden brittle silence yawned between them.

Helen had the feeling that whatever she said to break it would change things for good.

A shadow fell across the table. It was the waiter.

'Are you ready to order now, sir?'

Tom's face showed only the faintest flicker as he picked up his menu. 'I think so. What are you going to have to start with, Helen? The duck terrine is wonderful . . .'

The moment was past.

As Tom escorted her across the restaurant he was greeted by two separate parties. He stopped to kiss one woman theatrically on both cheeks, and to exchange jokes with another group, one of whom Helen recognised as a middlingly famous television actor.

At last they reached their table, discreetly placed in a corner. Tom sighed comically as he sat down opposite her.

'Business, business.'

Throughout the meal they devoted themselves to keeping the conversation on neutral ground. Tom asked her about Venice, and she found herself talking stiltedly at first about the paintings and the frescoes and the Renaissance palaces. Then, her tongue loosened by good food and wine, and led on by Tom's gentle questions, she began to describe the odd, sensual spell that the city had cast over her.

'It was like living in one of those very vivid dreams one has, just before waking up.'

The word 'dream' struck her, but this time she didn't blush.

'It affects me too, in just the same way. It always makes me feel unbearably randy.' Tom was smiling at her, appreciative of the animation in her face. 'Tell me, did you discover that church in a little square? San Zaccaria, I think. There's an altarpiece, a Bellini, the Madonna with Four Saints...'

'Yes. Oh yes, I saw it late one afternoon, and the doorkeeper was standing in a shaft of light with a huge key, waiting to close up, like a Bellini figure himself. I wanted to go back and see it again but I never did.'

'I'll take you. I'd like to see it with you more than anyone else.' He said it very quietly, but perfectly matter-of-fact. When Helen met his eyes she saw the challenge in them, and some of the old mockery. She didn't hesitate.

'That's impossible.'

'Because of Darcy?'

'Of course because of Darcy. I'm going to marry him.'

'Helen...' Tom put his warm hands over hers. 'Are you really going to marry Viscount Darcy? Or is it an elaborate joke?'

Defiance stiffened her. She lifted her chin and looked straight into his face.

'It wouldn't be a very funny joke, would it? Yes, I'm going to marry Darcy. I love him.'

Whistling in the dark, her inner heart said sadly.

Slowly Tom lifted her clasped hands between his and kissed the knuckles of each before lowering them again.

'In that case,' he said, 'I wish you both every happiness.'

He signalled to the discreetly distant waiter.

They must all think we're lovers, Helen thought miserably.

There was nothing else to say, and it was time to go.

They drove back to Oxford in almost unbroken silence. Then, as they approached it past the flat, watery reaches of Port

Meadow, they rounded a sharp corner and at once dipped over the steep bridge over the Isis.

'Look.'

Helen drew in her breath at the sight. In front of them, hidden until the last moment by the curve of the road and the protective willows, were the lights of a travelling fair. The brilliant dazzle lay in the dark, empty space like a mirage. Across the meadows towards them drifted the tinny music and the shouts of the barkers.

Tom stopped at once. They climbed out into the night air and leant together on the five-barred gate to stare. The world seemed utterly deserted, shrouded in darkness and the mist rising from the river, but there in front of them were the diamond necklaces of lights chaining the roundabouts, the flash of scarlet and blue and green, and the distant determined gaiety of the music.

'It's not really there,' Helen breathed. 'It's a ghost fair. Or a scene from a Fellini film.'

'No,' Tom corrected her. 'More like early Antonioni.'

A bubble of laughter burst between them, the tension all forgotten. Tom's face was alive with sudden childish anticipation. 'What are we waiting for?'

They vaulted the gate and ran towards tangled necklaces of lights, with the multi-coloured spokes of the Big Wheel revolving slowly over them like a great star.

The fair was real enough. They wandered between the booths, breathing in the competing smells of candyfloss, hot dogs, trampled grass and oil, and hailed on every side by stallholders eager for custom.

'Come on now, try yer luck.'

'Prize every time. Hit the red and win yer girlfriend this lovely tea-service.'

'Want to try?' Tom was heaping wooden balls into her arms. Gaudily-painted clowns' faces with wide-open mouths rotated in front of her. 'Watch me then.' Laughing at each other they showered balls at the targets. Helen proved to be a much better shot. Her prize was a pink nylon-fur teddy bear and she held it out to Tom.

'Tom, I ... want you to have this.'

'Helen, I shall treasure it for ever. Now, please let me get back some of my masculine pride by winning on the rifle range.'

He led her insistently from stall to stall and they shot, rolled balls and flung hoops. They were almost the only customers and

Helen half-imagined that Tom had laid on the fair for her alone, as a whimsical after-dinner amusement. 'I don't think we need any more coconuts,' he said at last. 'Time for the rides, now.'

At the heart of the fair were the hobby horses. The huge Victorian merry-go-round sparkled with lights, mosaics of mirror and engraved glass and swags of painted flowers. The horses themselves, galloping hooves and gold-painted manes and staring eyes, flew round on their barley-sugar twisted poles to thundering organ music.

Tom and Helen stood at the steps lost in admiration. At last the machine slowed and the music wheezed away into a murmur.

'Which one?' Tom asked and Helen ran to one of the outer horses, cream and gold with 'Prancer' painted around its neck in a garland of painted flowers. Tom handed her up into the high saddle and she gathered the reins into her fingers. When he came up behind her, he steadied them with an arm around her waist.

Slowly the horses began to move again, up and then down, and in a slowly blurring circle of white and gold. Helen felt Tom at her back, and then his mouth against her ear.

'Not quite riding out with the Montcalm foxhounds. But more fun, don't you think?'

'Yes,' she flung back at him.

Helen let the rise and fall of the wooden horse and the wild blare of the music carry her away on the wings of exhilaration. The rest of the world beyond this painted horse and its cocoon of light was, for a precious few minutes, no more than a meaningless blur.

Once she turned around and caught the white flash of Tom's smile answering her own. His hands tightened on her waist as she leaned back against him. There was nothing else that mattered at all.

Yet, all too soon, the carved ripples of Prancer's mane rose and fell slower and slower and the lights beyond the merry-go-round steadied and swung to a standstill. Tom was lifting her back to the trodden grass again and she stumbled, dizzy, and almost fell against him. He hugged her, laughing, as he supported her.

'I think it's got to be the Ferris wheel to finish with, don't you?' The big wheel was at a standstill, waiting for riders. In a moment they were in the little car, and the attendant bolted the safety bar in front of them. The wheel turned and they were swept backwards swinging, and on up into the darkness.

Helen gasped and her fingers tightened on the bar.

At the highest point the wheel stopped and they hung, rocking, high up in empty space. Far below another couple were climbing into a car to balance their own.

'Scared?'

Tom seemed very close and solid beside her in this airy, swinging emptiness. The noise and clatter of the fair sounded far off.

'Don't be,' he said softly. 'There's no need.'

Awkward in the confined space he reached for her. Helen had the confused memory of another dark space where they had once sat together, isolated above a carpet of light. She had rejected him then. Now she couldn't do it. Something like greed rose in her. In the half-second as their eyes met before they kissed, Helen and Tom saw that they came together under the same compulsion. He kissed her lightly at first, tasting her mouth and then her skin. Helen's fingers found the crisp hair at the nape of his neck and she drew him closer, her mouth opening to drink in the taste of him, forgetting herself in her own hunger for him.

'Helen?' His mouth moved against hers and she answered, 'I'm here. I'm here.'

When she opened her eyes again she saw the shadow in the hollow of his cheek, and the dark line of his eyebrows fiercely drawn together. Behind him was the wide open blackness of Port Meadow and beyond, so far off that it scarcely mattered at all, the faint orange glow of Oxford.

The wheel jerked again and they rolled forward, swinging out into space, swooping down past the bored attendant and back into their own world of silent, windy nothingness.

The momentum of the great wheel possessed them as they rocked in one another's arms. The alternating dark of the high-point and confused brightness of the low swept over their closed eyelids. Just once, Tom tried to pull her closer so that their bodies could touch but they were confined by the brutal metal bar.

'Curse this little box', he groaned.

But when the wheel described a slower circle, and their car stopped at the wooden platform at the bottom, Helen said, 'No. I don't want to get out yet.'

'Again,' Tom said, and stuffed the money into the attendant's hands. Helen saw the man's tattooed forearms with bemused clarity before the wheel swept her away again to the place where there was only Tom.

When they were suspended again above their kingdom of space, Tom said, 'We can't stay up here all night, darling. I can't reach enough of you.' She felt the tightness in the muscles of his throat as he spoke, and heard the happiness in his voice. 'I want to take you home to bed.'

Helen was possessed by a delicious sense of abandonment, of being beyond reality suspended here above the mysterious, deserted fair.

'When the wheel stops,' she said dreamily. 'When the wheel stops.'

Almost at once, it seemed, they were slowing again and coming to rest in the intrusive glare of the lights.

'Ready this time, guv?' said the wheel man.

They looked at each other, glowing with excitement. Helen felt that her hair was tangled and her mouth burning, and that she couldn't have cared less.

'I think so,' Tom said.

'Yes,' Helen told him. 'Ready this time.'

The bar swung up and they stepped shakily out into the world once again. Tom's hand clasped hers and he began to draw her away. Helen followed him, willing, lightheaded.

Then a voice called after them.

'Having a nice time?'

They stopped dead, still hand in hand, and turned slowly around. Gerry Pole was standing at the steps up to the hobby horses, and beside him was Oliver.

'Up until now,' Tom said curtly. He had sized up the intrusion at once, and made to turn Helen away again. But she was frozen to the spot. The sight of Gerry and Oliver brought back reality with an icy, threatening blast. She saw that Gerry was drunk, and Oliver drunker still. But they were here in front of them, and she saw how she must look. She was guiltily trapped with her hand in Tom's and her face burning with his kisses. Gerry's face was alive with prurient curiosity.

Oliver swayed forward. 'My darling Helen,' he said very carefully. 'I've been so remiss. I should have come at once to see you and offer my condolences on the prospect of becoming a Mortimore. Are you quite sure? Not too late yet, you know. Sure Darcy would understand.' His glazed eyes travelled away

285

to Tom, and she saw clearly the confused connection of his thoughts.

'Hello, Oliver,' Helen said in a small, flat voice. 'Of course I'm sure. Darcy and I are very happy.'

Oh God, her inner voice whispered, how have I got everything so badly wrong?

'How lovely,' Oliver said, vague now. 'Darcy's a lucky man. I'm an unlucky man, on the other hand. As I've been telling old Gerry here.' He put his arm round Gerry's shoulder and they staggered a little, laughing. As she had been once before, Helen was struck by their physical likeness. Oliver's face was tanned from his ski-ing holiday, but it was thinner, and marked by the beginnings of the same creases that split Gerry's. The gold of his hair seemed to have faded, so that in the garish fairground lights it was closer to Gerry's lifeless grey.

'Don't start all that again,' Gerry said. 'Now that we're all here, why don't we go somewhere for a nightcap? You'll come, won't you love?' He grinned at Helen.

'No thanks,' Tom said coolly. 'Helen and I are on our way home.'

Oliver frowned in belated surprise.

'It is you, Hart. Thank God for someone civilised. I've had enough of Gerry. But what are you doing with my brother's fiancée?' He squared up to Tom in a parody of gentlemanly offence.

'Buying her dinner and a ride on the roundabouts. I delivered a present to her, to celebrate her engagement to your brother, and she is thanking me with an evening of her company. Does that satisfy your curiosity?'

Thank you, Tom, Helen said silently. Thank you for your tact and sensitivity.

Oliver had forgotten his question. He thrust his arms through theirs and said, 'Good job you've turned up. Gerry and I've lost the car somewhere. We'd've had to walk back.'

'Do you good,' Tom muttered, and then 'Come on. I suppose we'll have to drive you home.'

Helen shivered. The mood of the evening had changed so sharply that she felt sick and shaken. Confusion and the first stab of guilt warred inside her as they trailed in silence across the wet grass. The five-barred gate appeared through the mist with the car beyond it. Once inside Oliver slumped in his corner and fell asleep while Gerry kept up a stream of disconnected talk, impervious to the lack of response.

286

Tom glanced quickly at Helen, then his face contracted in a black frown.

'We'll leave them at St Aldate's and then go home.'

'No,' Helen said tonelessly. 'Take me back to Follies too.'

They drove on in silence.

Outside Christ Church they roused Oliver and saw him wander in under the tower. Tom stopped again on Folly Bridge and Gerry hauled himself out.

'So grateful,' he said. 'Can't think how I'd have got Oliver home otherwise. Let me escort you inside, Helen.'

'I will take care of Helen.' Tom was dangerously quiet. Gerry shrugged and went away down the steps.

Alone in the car Helen and Tom looked bleakly at one another. The carelessness that had set them free on the wheel above Port Meadow was utterly gone. They were sombre and apprehensive.

Tom ran his fingers through his black hair.

'Rather a mess,' he said.

Helen took a deep breath. 'It wasn't real, that fair,' she told him. 'None of it really happened. I'm going to go inside now, and we can both forget it all.' She forced conviction into her words.

Tom rounded on her furiously.

'Don't be a fool. Of course it happened. And we both know why, and what it means. How can you pretend that it didn't?'

'I can. I must.' Helen was urgent. 'Darcy . . .'

'Screw Darcy. Oh, I'll bet you haven't. No, forget I said that.'

The door banged open and Helen leapt out on to the bridge. 'I thought you were clever,' she heard him call after her. 'Obviously I misjudged you.'

Helen ran down the slippery mossed steps to the island. Up on the bridge she heard the engine roar and then a scream of tyres as Tom wrenched the car away. It was very dark in the cavernous hallway. She was almost on top of Gerry before she saw him, and had to bite back a gasp of fear. He was sitting on the bottom stair with his hands hanging loosely between his knees. She tried to edge past him.

'Don't worry about me, love,' he said. 'As far as I'm concerned, I didn't see a thing.'

His low chuckle followed her up the stairs.

For once Helen's room felt less than a sanctuary. She had come back to it this evening, so few hours ago, and Tom had been sitting there. Now she felt that he was still with her, dark and impatient. She sat down on the bed and stared at the dim rectangle of the window. Think, she kept telling herself. You know how to think. But all she could manage to focus on was a series of disconnected images. Tom's face close to hers, Gerry's insinuating *Having a nice time?*, the dizzy blur of the hobby horses, Oliver's unfocused gaze, and Tom yet again. 'We both know why, and what it means.' What does it mean? she asked herself helplessly. How could she have forgotten herself so far, and – more – forgotten Darcy too?

At last she shook herself.

It was the fair. An isolated, intoxicated minute. Perhaps it had been prompted by her Venetian dream and then by the mystery of the sparkling mirage in the dark meadow. None of that assuaged the guilt and self-distrust that afflicted her now, but at least it was the thread of an excuse to cling to.

Then she thought painfully, I can't use that as an excuse. It wasn't just the fair. All this began long ago, and it goes back and back.

Back from tonight, when I found Tom here and knew that I was lying when I told him I was happy. Back to Venice, and my dream. Back to the play, and the days when we shared our anxiety for Oliver. Before that, to New Year's Eve. I knew now why I was so angry and afraid when he kissed me. Even after all the pain of Oliver I must have sensed that there was a chance of it all happening all over again with Tom.

Even before that, I must have been drawn to him. In Addison's Walk, when I wanted to hide from everything against his shoulder. Even on the first day, when I saw him in Oliver's rooms, I thought how different from everyone else he looked. If I hadn't been blinded by Oliver then, I would have seen at once how special.

Helen sat motionless, uncomfortably hunched on her bed in the cold room, too shocked by the labyrinths of her self-deception even to move.

And what now?

Darcy, she reminded herself deliberately. When her imagination captured his face, it was with his half-habitual anxious frown. She was aware of the mixture of tenderness, loyalty and unshakeable affection that she felt for him. Love, too. But nothing like the insistent force that had assailed her tonight. She had never felt anything like that before.

Slowly Helen began to understand. She saw that the obscure

irritation and sense of unease that Tom roused in her was rooted in attraction, physical as much as emotional. She admitted it to herself as clinically as she could. But she had made that mistake once, disastrously, with Oliver. She could never, ever, let it happen again.

Funny, she thought, with a wry flicker of amusement. I'd never have thought of myself as particularly hot-blooded. And I once thought I knew myself quite well.

Wrong, and wrong again.

Suddenly Helen felt coldly afraid. She didn't understand or even trust herself any more, and she felt unpleasantly adrift in a dark, threatening sea. A single certainty flashed like a beacon at her. It was Darcy's worth, unchanging and pledged to her with utmost generosity. As she had pledged herself in return. She had promised to marry Darcy, and that remained a single fixed point.

It was impossible, impossible, to think of turning to him now and saying that she had made a mistake. And although the deepest core of herself longed blindly for Tom, the careful, practical Helen who was just as much a part of her told her that she should cling to the security of Darcy. Part of her recoiled from the ferment of her feelings for Tom, and groped blindly backwards to safety.

Time, she whispered out loud. I need time. Time to distinguish between two kinds of love, and to gauge which one is real.

Tomorrow, she promised herself, she would talk to Darcy. She would explain – not about tonight, there must never be a whisper of that – but about needing time, and peace, to think about their marriage.

Darcy would understand, because he always did.

And because she was afraid that she could not trust herself otherwise, she made one other resolution. She must not see Tom alone any more. To see him was to succumb to him, and for Darcy's sake that must never be allowed to happen.

At once a little of her fear abated. Yet at the same time the inner, reckless Helen cried out No. I love him. I need to see him. The voice was so passionate that she almost wavered.

To silence it, Helen reached out and turned on the lamp. The room was lit with the familiar glow, every outline reassuringly the same in spite of the upheaval in her world.

She would stay true to Darcy. She would, because she must.

The other way was to gamble everything, and now the stakes had risen too dizzyingly high.

But even time was to be denied her.

Darcy came early the next morning, and she saw the resolve in his face at once. He took her hands and made her stand still to listen to him.

'I want you to come with me to Montcalm. We must tell them, Helen, and I want us to do it today. I've telephoned, and they're expecting us to lunch. Father was going racing, but I've told him it was important and he agreed to stay. So they will almost know already.'

, Helen went cold.

'I can't, Darcy, we can't do it today. I want to talk to you. It's important and it's something we have to understand between us before we see your mother and father.'

The thought of Montcalm and the cold, surprised faces of Their Royal Highnesses made her feel shaky with fear.

Darcy was immediately concerned.

'What is it? Is something wrong?'

'Not wrong.' Helen searched uncomfortably for the right way to say her piece.

'It's just that I'm ... afraid. All this has happened very quickly. I'm only just beginning to understand what I've promised you. I need some time now, to think about it and to be sure that what we're doing is right.' She was talking more quickly, gaining confidence.

Darcy's face cleared.

'You can have all the time in the world. I've already told you that. And of course you are afraid. Do you think I'm not? And do you think every couple who promise to marry walk blithely into it without a tremor of doubt? I'm happy to be afraid, because it means I understand how serious it is. But it's why I want to tell everyone, too. It will be easier once there is a clear statement between us, no murky areas and nothing to misunderstand.'

Oh, but there is, Helen thought bitterly. And does he really think that announcing our engagement to Lord and Lady Montcalm is going to cement it?

Disconcertingly, the current of her thoughts changed direction. Perhaps it would do just that. There was something to be said for burned boats.

She looked at Darcy, and saw the honest conviction shining in his face.

'We-ell,' she said, knowing that she was being weak. Sensing his advantage, Darcy produced his rare, stubborn expression, all the more effective because she had seen it only once before.

'We must go,' he said. 'They're waiting for us.'

Helen bowed her head and made to follow him. Her legs felt as if they were lifting lead weights. Darcy stopped her at the door.

'And there's this.' The blue box again.

Helen took out the ring, and he slid it on to her finger. The wide gold circlet fitted perfectly now, but the ruby felt too heavy and too obvious.

'Please wear it,' he said. 'I want them to see our ring on your finger.' He hugged her and then kissed her forehead, cajoling.

He's afraid of them too, Helen realised dismally. He's a grown man, but somehow they reduce him to a small boy, who thinks that presenting them with a *fait accompli* will make his disobedience easier to swallow.

Sadness engulfed her as she followed Darcy down to the echoing gallery and out through the heavy door on to the island. For the first time she was struck by the appropriateness of the name of the old house.

The drive to Montcalm was unbelievably short. It seemed they had barely left Oxford before they reached the lodge at the great gates. The ticket booth was open and there was a small queue of cars in front of it. Darcy swung round them and the ticket man looked up sharply, and then straightened into a half salute. Helen and Darcy didn't look at each other.

She saw the house on the skyline again, and now it seemed more threatening than fantastic. Darcy stopped the car at the centre of the gravel sweep between the two towering side-wings of the house. There was to be no momentary shelter in the safety of Jasper Thripp's yard on this formal morning. Darcy ushered Helen out of the car and up the shallow rise of steps to the huge doors. The doors swung silently open in front of them and Maitland, black-coated, stood against the brilliance reflected from within the dome.

'Good morning, my lord. Good morning, madam.'

Helen's breath was coming in short, painful gasps and her heart seemed to pound with audible thumps. Darcy was pale, but he turned at the door to the private wing and smiled at her, then clasped her hand.

'I love you,' he whispered. Helen prayed that she was only imagining the effort at conviction she heard in his words.

291

'His lordship and her ladyship are in the private drawing room, my lord.'

'Thank you, Maitland.'

A few steps, they were at the door, and then inside the room.

Lady Montcalm was sitting at her embroidery, a spaniel asleep at her feet. Lord Montcalm was standing stiff-backed against the fireplace.

Helen saw, just as she had imagined, the cool and distant surprise in their faces, and her flickering courage died inside her. She knew, as fatally as if it had already happened, that she would fail miserably to impress these frosty people as a future daughter-in-law and heiress to the towering pile around them.

For a moment nobody spoke. Then Lady Montcalm put down her embroidery and smiled, a little tired smile.

'What a surprise, Darcy. And Helen too. Come and sit down, won't you?' She patted the sofa cushion beside her, looking at Helen as if she had no idea who this intruder could be. Her ladyship was perfectly coiffed and manicured, and dressed in a grey pleated dress with about a hundred tiny covered buttons. Helen felt shabby, and hot, and awkward as she crossed the pale green carpet.

Darcy's father shook his heavy handsome head. 'What is all this? I should be at Cheltenham.'

Darcy didn't hesitate. Only Helen heard the tremor in his voice. 'Helen and I are going to be married.' He lifted Helen's left hand, keeping it tightly clasped in his, to show them the ring. Incongruously, she felt like a winning prize fighter and had to suppress a wild desire to laugh. A shocked silence spread across the room. The spaniel stirred and sighed in its sleep, the silky fur rippling.

Lady Montcalm said, 'Darling, I had no idea you were so romantic.'

The silence deepened, and Helen wished that she could be anywhere else in the world except where she sat now. But her fear was beginning to ebb away. It was replaced by shame for Darcy for his parents, and a determination to love and support him where they had so clearly failed.

Lord Montcalm said, 'This is very sudden.' His manner showed a stupid man's embarrassed reluctance to confront real feelings.

'It's not sudden at all,' Darcy answered. He seemed more

than ever the stubborn schoolboy, and Helen defensively longed for him to reveal more of the real Darcy that she herself knew.

Lady Montcalm laughed, a light, pretty laugh. 'This is lovely. I'm so pleased for you both, but you must forgive us for being a little surprised.' She stretched her hand out to Helen's. 'The ring, too. What slender little hands you have. Half the size of mine, and I remember thinking how huge the ring was when Aubrey produced it for me. The ruby is much too heavy, Darcy. Couldn't we find something more suitable for Helen? A pretty diamond?'

'No, Mother. I want Helen to wear the proper ring.'

There was another tiny silence. Lord Montcalm looked at his watch.

'This all seems perfectly suitable. There's a great deal to discuss, arrangements and so forth, but I think that can wait. Jane?'

His wife was precise. 'Yes. I think it can wait.'

'In that case, I'll be off. The stewards are expecting me.' Lord Montcalm held out his hand to his son. 'Congratulations, old boy.' And then, to Helen, 'He's a good chap. I'm sure he'll make you happy.' He leant towards her and almost kissed her cheek. Helen understood that Lord Montcalm had no particular objection to her. She was, at least, not quite blatantly unsuitable. Her future father-in-law was too intent on his afternoon's racing to disturb himself any further.

It was Lady Montcalm who was her real adversary. Helen felt her determination strengthening.

After Lord Montcalm had gone, she turned the full light of her attractive long-suffering smile on Helen.

'Well,' she sighed, 'we must have a lovely long talk. I want to hear all about you and your life, and your family. I feel at such a disadvantage, not knowing you at all. Do you know, I thought you were a friend of Oliver's. Weren't you his guest at Christmas?'

Helen lifted her chin. Her grey eyes were very bright, and there was a faint flush across her cheeks.

'Oliver and I are friends, yes. We met at Oxford.'

'Helen lives in Rose Pole's house,' Darcy put in.

'Oh yes. Poor Rose. I should go and see her one day. But I hear . . .' Lady Montcalm's fingers fluttered delicately. Plainly, belonging to the Follies circle was not much of a recommendation for Helen.

After sherry in the drawing room, they went in to lunch.

Helen was reminded of her first visit to Montcalm. Then it had been Tom and not Darcy at Lady Montcalm's side. Helen remembered admiring his suave self-possession. Now Darcy sat quietly. It was Helen who had to bear the steely focus of attention. The questions came one after another, subtly put and charmingly expressed, but Helen knew that she was being grilled. She made her answers as brief and dignified as she could, reflecting that she had nothing to be ashamed of. She was proud of her loving, supportive family. Prouder than she would ever be of her parents-in-law.

Suppressed anger put a bite into her voice. As she talked, Darcy watched her with pride and affection.

'My father died last year. My mother is a part-time schoolteacher and I have a younger brother still at school. No-one else, really. Some cousins in Sunderland.'

'Sunderland?'

Helen might have said Tashkent.

By the end of the meal Lady Montcalm was satisfied that Helen had come from nowhere, knew no-one and had no idea of the world she was marrying into. Darcy's choice was as bad as it could be.

She dabbed at her lips with a napkin.

'This is all wonderful.' Helen knew that she had failed all the tests, and she knew equally that Lady Montcalm was far too clever to let her opposition show. 'Is there any hurry, Darcy?' she was asking. 'Let's all spend some time getting to know each other before putting the announcement in the papers and so forth.'

'I'm sure you'll deal with all that beautifully,' Darcy said. 'Helen wants to sit her Schools first, in June. She's going to get a First.'

'Oh yes. Helen's exams.' They might have been talking about some bizarre ritual engaged in by a remote primitive tribe, Helen thought, trying to raise her own spirits. No wonder Oliver had no interest in his own academic progress.

Lady Montcalm made a tiny gesture and Darcy moved to pull back her chair. As she stood up, she bent her head towards Helen and said, 'I'm so very, very pleased. Darcy must bring you to Montcalm very often. But now, I'm afraid . . .' she sighed again, '. . . I must go up and have my rest.'

A brief kiss was bestowed on the air close to Darcy's head and his mother was gone. 'Take me home,' Helen said. 'Please, let's go home. To Follies.'

She thought that she would never be happier to see the square bulk of the old red house.

They left Montcalm behind them, the dome and turrets leaden against a heavy grey sky.

'I'm sorry,' Darcy said humbly as they drove.

'I don't want you to be sorry.' Helen was fierce. She was thinking of the warmth with which her own mother had welcomed Darcy. But then that isn't quite the same, she thought, struggling to be fair. 'We've done it now anyway.' They smiled at each other, more relieved than triumphant.

You've done it now, she echoed to herself. Today's tense little encounter had had one surprising effect. It had made her want to love Darcy more than anything, and to be a new family for him. And if she wanted it enough, she told herself almost grimly, then she could do it. For Darcy.

And Tom . . .

Helen stared at the Oxford road unwinding in front of them. He still seemed tangibly close, his features vivid inside her eyelids.

There could be no Tom. No more thinking about him, no more seeing him as anything but a friend. In time, the hurt of that would fade until it was no more painful than an old bruise. In time, she thought.

Helen had made her choice.

CHAPTER TWELVE

Summer began in Oxford that year, just as it always did, on the morning of the first of May.

For hours before dawn the streets were packed with surging crowds. They spilled out of parties and continued their celebrations in the cobbled alleys and courts. Under the trailing branches of the willows fringing the river, the punts slid down to Magdalen Bridge. They were packed with more noisy party-goers, heading for the focus of the night's festivity. Behind them empty champagne bottles bobbed in the black and gold-rippled water. As the city's clocks struck five, and then the half-hour, the revellers in the streets were drawn to the river too. They massed on Magdalen Bridge in the brightening grey light. A cold wind blew off the water, more reminiscent of March than the first summer's day.

As six o'clock approached faces began to turn upwards to Magdalen Tower, waiting. A scarlet kite with a tail of streamers dipped in the wind, higher than the tower's flagpole, and was greeted by a hubbub of cheering.

Chloe and Helen had left Follies together in the chilly, early summer dawn. It was Chloe's first May morning, and Helen's last. Pansy had declined to come, saying that even the best party in the world wouldn't tempt her out at five a.m. In the subdued atmosphere that reigned in the house, no-one had felt like staying up all night.

So Helen and Chloe walked through Christ Church Meadows together, and joined the rowdy throng under the tower. It was a colourful gathering in the pale light. Bunches of bright balloons bobbed from the lamp-posts, and gaudily dressed morris men with garters of jingling bells jigged to insistent fiddle music. From the river came screams and rising plumes of water as people pushed each other in. With the shouting and singing and competing bands, the noise was deafening. Helen and Chloe were swept backwards and forwards by the jostling mass.

But at six o'clock the first bell tolled, and was taken up by chime after chime across the city. Silence fell, and the crowd waited.

Helen craned her neck to look upwards and glimpsed a flag of white sleeve. Then she heard the first notes rising, pure and clear, as the tolling bells died away.

The Chapel choir had filed out on to the leads, their surplices fluttering. As they did every year, they sang a spring anthem into the windy space over the tower. Beneath them hundreds of faces turned up to hear the high, thin singing as it was snatched away from them into the grey-white sky.

It was over almost as soon as it had begun. Magdalen bells rang out again, almost drowned by the storm of cheering and singing, whistles and handclapping.

Another summer had been welcomed.

Suddenly Helen was blinking back tears. It was almost all over. It was a bare month until Schools, and then Oxford would erupt in the brief, hectic glitter of Commem week. After that it would be finished. And she herself would be Darcy's wife.

It was in that moment, fighting against the stinging tears, that she saw Tom watching her. He was quite close, sitting on the parapet of the bridge with his back against the latticed pillar that carried one of the white-globed lights. His bright, flippant clothes made him part of the crowd, but he was separate too. Helen thought she saw the detached amusement in his face at the eccentric Englishness of it all. But when his eyes met hers there was no mockery in them. There was simply a question, wordless but no less clear to both of them. His dark eyes held hers insistently, demanding a response.

They hadn't seen each other since their evening at the fair.

Without a glance left or right, blind and deaf to everything except the imperative need within her, Helen began to stumble towards him. Longing flooded through her and she already felt the weight of his arms around her, and the pressure of his mouth against hers.

The rest of the world was forgotten in the surge of pure joy at the sight of him.

The crowds tangled around her, pinioning her arms and keeping her agonisingly apart from him. She saw Tom hold out his hands to her before a long chain of conga dancers twisted between them and he was hidden.

Helen snatched her cold hands out of her pockets to help force her way through the crowds. As she moved she felt the weight sliding on her finger and then heard a tiny clink as the Viscountess's ring dropped and rolled away. She froze in her headlong rush. Slowly she tore her gaze from the point where she had seen Tom and made her eyes quarter the pavement between the shuffling feet. The ring lay a few inches away, as ominously bright as a splash of new blood on the paving. Helen sank stiffly to her knees and reached for it. When her fingers closed over it again, she felt it cold and bulky and almost unbearably heavy.

Darcy. Darcy's ring. Her promise, and her vow not to see Tom any more. I can't trust myself, she whispered, and she knew they were the truest words she'd ever spoken. Desperately her fingers tightened around the ring until the stones bit cruelly into her flesh. She scrambled up and saw that the space in front of her had miraculously cleared. Only a few yards separated her from Tom and he was still waiting for her, one hand outstretched.

'No,' Helen shouted desperately. 'I can't.'

The dancers looked curiously at her and then swirled around to separate them again.

With every bone and muscle in her body aching and crying out against the movement, Helen turned away. She felt Tom's gaze on her back, and knew that she would never forget how he had looked as he sat there with his black hair blown into a peak by the river wind.

Chloe was in the crowd to the right of her. Helen pushed frantically towards her, longing but not daring to look back at the bridge parapet. She reached Chloe and grasped at her arm. The solid warmth of it gave her the strength to look back.

Tom had vanished. The space on the bridge mocked her with its emptiness. The crowds were already streaming away, to breakfast parties or to dance and sing in the streets with the fiddle-players and morris men, and they had engulfed him.

Helen swayed slightly, suddenly icy cold. She was numbly aware of having made a terrible decision; a decision that had left her lonely and hopeless.

'Are you all right?' Chloe's voice was anxious at her side. 'You look ill.'

'Yes.' Helen fought to collect herself. No-one must know, not even Chloe. 'Yes. I'm okay. Just cold, that's all. There are too many people here. Let's walk a little way to warm up.'

They followed the press of people up the High, and were

swept on into Broad Street. There, in front of the Bodleian, Helen glimpsed him again, standing poised under one of the stone emperors. They were separated by a gaggle of morris dancers. One of them capered in and out of the dance with a pig's bladder on a stick. Tom was watching, frowning, with his hands deep in his pockets. This time Helen gave herself no chance to think. She started to run to him, blind to the intricate dance that she would have to cut through, but it was too late.

Much closer, two girls in extravagant twenties costumes and heavily rouged cheeks had seen him too. They pounced on him with cries of greeting, and took his arms insistently in theirs. After only an instant's hesitation, Tom kissed the rouged cheeks and turned on his laconic smile. The girls were pointing, pulling him away, and he let himself be drawn along with them to join their party.

He hadn't seen Helen. She stopped short and then turned blindly back.

'Wasn't that Tom?' Chloe asked.

'Was it?' Helen responded tonelessly. 'I didn't see.'

Chloe looked sideways at her friend and then suggested, 'Let's walk through the Parks. It's too beautiful to go inside yet.'

The grey-white sky had turned eggshell blue, and the wind had dropped. There was a promise of warmth in the still air. Chloe and Helen passed the red and yellow brick slab of Keble Chapel and turned into the University Parks. The trees were still heavy with blossom but the grass underneath was starred with white petals. Helen walked slowly, concentrating on the scent of blossom and mown grass and on the exuberant song of a blackbird.

'Are you sure you don't want to sit down for a while?' Chloe said at length. 'You look a bit better, but you went so white back there, I thought you were going to faint.'

Helen shook her head. 'No, let's walk on. I just want to get away from ... all those crowds.'

The steadiness of her own voice surprised her. She felt that within herself she was running headlong, trying to escape the panicky conviction that she was wrong, all over again. Wronger this time than she could have believed possible.

What do I want, she kept asking herself, and getting back only the numbing answer that it was too late to allow herself any kind of choice.

Helen looked desperately around, at the summer-green brilliance of the empty Parks, and at Chloe's calm profile tactfully turned away towards the river. Everything was as it always was, and yet horribly dislocated too. All the natural rightness of the summer morning was bathed in a lurid new light, the certainty that she wanted to run to Tom.

Fear and apprehension welled up in her. She struggled against it, and at last managed to replace it with Darcy's face. It was suffused with pride, as it had been when she held out her hand for him to see the ruby ring.

Her engagement ring.

Not here, not here. It was impossible to think about anything here. Back home in the safety of Follies, she would face this horrible problem there. In the meantime there was this expanse of petal-covered grass to cross, and Chloe beside her who must not be allowed to guess at anything. With a superhuman effort Helen said, 'I'm sorry. I'm not very good company this morning.'

She saw that they were coming to the river. The bank was lined with willows, and the olive green water tugged endlessly at the trailing branches. Just in front of them a high-arched bridge spanned the water like an iron rainbow.

'Look,' Chloe said, pointing. Someone was sitting huddled on a wooden bench to one side of the bridge. 'It's Beatrice.'

Helen was so lost in the turmoil of her thoughts that she caught herself wondering wildly who Beatrice was. Only when they had stopped in front of the bench did she see that it was Stephen's wife.

Beatrice looked years older. The wings of grey hair over her ears had thickened, and the taut skin of her face had sagged. Her eyes were dark, and dull with watching. She had been feeding the ducks with bread from a brown paper bag, and she held the last crust in her fingers. She was shredding it into grey crumbs that scattered over the front of her raincoat.

When she saw them, she smiled vaguely, unsurprised, and said, 'Stupid, isn't it? Even when the children aren't around, I automatically bring bread to feed the bloody ducks.'

They stood awkwardly in front of her, not knowing whether to stop or move on and leave her to her solitude.

'Sit down,' Beatrice said. 'It'd be nice to have someone to talk to.'

'Where are the children?' Helen asked, grateful for something

– anything – external to focus on. Beatrice flung the last crumbs of bread across the water and brushed away the crumbs.

'Staying with my mother for a while. It's supposed to give me a chance to think, but in fact I can't find anything to do to fill the time. Have you seen Stephen?' The abruptness of the question betrayed her anxiety. Helen and Chloe glanced at one another, not sure of what to tell her.

'Yes,' Chloe said at last. 'I saw him at Follies.'

'He was with her, I suppose?'

'Yes.'

Beatrice ducked her head and the wings of hair fell forward across her cheeks. She was looking down at her hands, the fingers splayed out flat against the dark stuff of her raincoat. They were faintly roughened with gardening, and the only ring was her thin gold wedding band.

'Strange, isn't it?' she said, 'How fifteen years, three children, all those days and hours and minutes together, awake and asleep, seem to count for nothing now?' Her voice was muffled and she kept her head bent to hide the tears behind her veil of hair. 'Stephen's always been in love with being young. Being young himself, and proving it with endless girls.'

Chloe listened, wishing that she didn't have to hear. She didn't care for the image of herself glimpsed through Beatrice's eyes. Beatrice sensed her stillness and said, 'I'm sorry. You were one, weren't you?' She was sad rather than bitter. 'He probably hurt you, too.'

'I deserved it,' Chloe said grimly.

Beatrice's attention had already shifted to the thought that was preoccupying her. 'Pansy Warren is different. I wasn't afraid of any of the others, but I'm afraid of Pansy. I can cope with her being so beautiful, and likeable, and having all the things she does. It's her carelessness that frightens me. It makes her invulnerable. Stephen is vulnerable, and God knows, so am I.' She spread her fingers further apart in her lap. 'What can either of us do? And how can I compete?' Beatrice was crying openly now. 'I don't want to have to compete for my husband. Do you know, they say that children keep you young? They don't. They make you old, and then you find that your husband doesn't want you any more. He's gone to live with a lovely child who trails him around like an emasculated shadow.'

The bitterness was clear now. Helen and Chloe sat numbly, at a loss for anything to say or do.

So that's marriage, Helen thought. The exquisite freshness of the morning seemed to turn dark and chilly around her. Once, briefly, she had envied Beatrice at home in her family-warm rectory kitchen. Helen was going to have just that sort of life herself now, in the pleasant security of Mere. And Darcy would never be like Stephen Spurring. She knew without a flicker of doubt that once his promise was made, Darcy would be honest and faithful to her until the day he died.

But still there was no glow in the sunlight, and the breeze felt cold at her back.

What is the matter? Helen asked herself. Is it really true that I've promised to marry the wrong man?

Unseeingly she watched the ragged flutter of pink and white blossom as it drifted down around her.

Beatrice stood up stiffly. 'I'm going to walk on,' she told them. 'Give my love to Stephen, won't you, next time you see him?'

'Beatrice,' Chloe said quickly, 'if it's any consolation, it won't last for ever. Pansy is already looking over his shoulder.'

Beatrice laughed without amusement. 'It isn't any consolation. Do you suppose that Stephen will want to come back when Pansy has finished with him? Or that I should take him back? What would you do? No.' She answered herself. 'There isn't any point in asking you that. You couldn't know what fifteen years of marriage is like without having lived it.' Beatrice pulled her raincoat more tightly around her, ready to walk on, and then remembered something. 'Helen, I heard about your engagement. I wish you both every happiness. Don't take Stephen and me as an advertisement for marriage. At least, don't take what you can see now.' Suddenly she smiled, and the years fell away from her face. 'Anyway, one survives. Somehow one survives. Women are much better at that than men, you know.'

In that moment they glimpsed her mettle. Beatrice was brave, and she had the enviable clear-sightedness of experience.

'Goodbye, Helen, Chloe. Come out to the Rectory and see me sometime. I could do with the company.' Then she turned and walked away along the river path, a slight figure in a black raincoat with her head held up.

There was a long silence before Chloe said savagely, 'He doesn't deserve her, does he?' And then, with the anger giving way to weariness, 'Why are we all such fools? Except you, Helen.'

'Oh, I'm the biggest fool of all.' Helen's voice was so low that

Chloe turned to her, uncertain of whether she had heard correctly. Helen gave her no chance to press her any further. 'Come on,' she said, with a pretence of briskness. 'I really need a cup of coffee. Let's go to the market.'

The indoor market with its rows of close-packed shops and stalls was beginning to fill up with people in search of breakfast after a long night. The taxi-drivers' café in the middle was packed with a motley crowd of people, porters in overalls and impatient cab-drivers and jostling students, some of them still wet from the river, and a sprinkling of faintly defiant people in evening clothes. The atmosphere was thick with frying bacon, and the windows were running with condensation.

'Can you stand this?' Chloe asked.

'Just about.'

They found themselves two seats and wrapped their hands gratefully round thick white pint-mugs of coffee. Helen had barely tasted hers before there was a crash behind her, a roar of warning and then someone fell against her so that coffee slopped over her fingers. Protestingly she turned around and half recognised the four reddened faces scuffling together.

'I'm frightfully sorry,' one of them said. There was no mistaking the intonation. They were Oliver's hearty friends from Christ Church. In the same instant she saw Oliver behind them, and she was struck cold by his air of being a spectre at a particularly jolly party. His face was almost gaunt, and the fresh-minted quality of his golden good looks was fading fast. Once again, Helen thought of Gerry. His friends were boisterously merry, but Oliver was sober for once. Only his unnaturally wide eyes gave him away.

'Hello,' he said carefully. 'You keep catching me at the real high points of my dizzy social life. This,' and he gestured at his friends who now had the air of looking around for bread rolls to throw, 'is the Christ Church Commem Ball Committee. We started out last night with the definite intention of discussing marquee hire and cloakroom facilities. Somehow the night has slipped away, and we are no further forward. But don't worry. We shall keep on trying. You'll come to our Ball, won't you, darling Helen? Oh, of course you will. Darcy will escort you and see you safe home afterwards. What about you, Chloe? Shall I fix you up with one of my friends here? Or you could always risk it with me.' Chloe looked away from him, trying not to remember.

Helen rounded on him, white-faced. 'Why, Oliver? What's the matter with you? Have you got to fling everything away, and with people like those?'

Oliver mimed a travesty of surprise. 'But they are my peers, darling. The so-privileged few with whom I am supposed to spend my time. The others, the ones with dirty white shirts and pale faces and little phials full of fascinating things, they're the ones I'm not supposed to know.' Oliver put his arms around their shoulders and bent so that his face was close to theirs. 'But the funny thing is that they're all, all of them, equally and disastrously fucking dreary. So what can one do in this waste of dullness but soldier on, taking one's enjoyment where one can? I'm only sorry, sweet wholesome Helen, that it incurs your disapproval.' Oliver's mouth twisted uncomfortably as he stood up again.

'I'll leave you to your breakfast. I'm sure that you'll want to hurry off soon to make sure that no-one has taken your special seat in the Upper Reading Room.' Before Helen could collect herself, Oliver had slammed away, without a backward glance at her or at his oblivious companions.

Helen buried her face in her hands. 'I didn't mean to say it like that,' she whispered. 'It just came out too quickly. I didn't mean to be priggish, and pompous, and all the other things he recoils from. Chloe, all I wanted to say was Look. You don't have to make yourself like this. Why can't he see? I just wanted...'

'I know,' Chloe told her gently. 'But he can't hear that.'

Helen's sleeve was soaked with cold coffee and she tried vainly to roll it back. There was a leaden, stifling weight inside her chest and a taste of metal deep in her throat. There seemed to be nothing in the whole world that she could focus on that was clear, and sweet, and straight. Then she thought again. There was Darcy, in all his goodness and devotion. And there was Tom, with his uncompromising clear sight and the sharp weapon of his intelligence. Two opposite sides of the same truth, she thought. But which of them was the truth that she needed for herself?

Helen pushed back her chair with a sharp scrape. 'This is a horrible day,' she mumbled to Chloe. 'I'm going to do just as Oliver said. I'm going to go away and work. That's easy to understand, at least.'

She turned away in the same direction as Oliver, and Chloe watched her go with a deep frown marked between her eyes.

'I hate this house.'

Stephen Spurring was looking up into the shadowy height of Follies' hall.

Chloe smiled faintly. 'Why? I should have thought it was right up your street.'

They had come face to face one evening at the steps leading down to the island, where it was impossible for either of them to turn aside. Although they had barely spoken since the play, they managed to put a casual gloss on this awkward meeting. Stephen asked politely about her work, and Chloe responded with equal formality. Now she was surprised by the sudden vehemence in his voice.

He shrugged, irritable. 'Not the shell itself. That's very fine, of course. Just the atmosphere. I wish Pansy would come and live somewhere else. I've tried to persuade her, but she won't hear of it. I could rent us a place, at least.'

Chloe couldn't resist a tiny pinprick.

'Surely Pansy could buy a house? Or Masefield would set her up in anything she wanted.'

Stephen flushed uncomfortably. 'There wouldn't be any need for that.'

Poor Stephen, Chloe thought suddenly. Married, and in love with a mercurial girl half his age. And a rich man's daughter, at that. He must know he can't give her any of the things she's used to.

Chloe saw that her old lover looked weary, and diminished. The air of confident, pedagogic authority that had once attracted her was gone. Even his feminine good looks had turned faintly seedy. He wasn't the man she had fallen in love with at the beginning of the year, and that must mean that he was no longer the man that Pansy had so unerringly reached for either.

Poor Stephen.

'Come and have a drink,' she said warmly. His eyes met hers in a surprised stare. 'Don't worry.' Her voice was softer. 'It's all right. I'm all right.'

He followed her up the stairs but at her door, he hesitated.

'I don't want Pansy to come back and find that I'm not here. She'll just go off somewhere again.'

'Leave the door open then. You can see her coming up the stairs. Where is she?'

Stephen took a glass of wine, and sat down where he could see along the gallery.

'London. For an interview. She won't say any more ... you know what Pansy's like.' He seemed to crumple in front of Chloe's eyes. 'I thought at first I understood her, and now I see that I don't at all. All I do know is that I need her.' Stephen collected himself with an effort. 'Chloe, I shouldn't be talking like this. To you, of all people.'

'Don't worry,' she murmured again. 'I had a bad time, but that was more to do with my own mistakes than you.' She remembered sharply the aching days of *As You Like It*, Oliver's clammy desperation, and then the clinic off Harley Street and the void inside her. That void was still with her, and always would be, and beside that Stephen was irrelevant. He was as small as if viewed through the wrong end of a telescope. I've survived, she thought. I've learnt. Gratitude swept over her, and through it, she looked calmly at Stephen. 'Talk about it if it helps,' she said.

Stephen was wry, a flicker of his old self showing. 'Nothing helps much, except being with her. I've never longed to possess anyone so totally before. I've always found possessiveness rather a shortcoming. As you know.'

Neither of them smiled.

'What about your ... what about Beatrice?'

He looked away.

'Beatrice is very unhappy.' There was a long silence before he went on. 'I'd give anything not to be hurting her like this. But it's too late. I can't be without Pansy now. I'm like an addict, Chloe. Waiting around Follies for my fix.' Crumpled in Chloe's armchair with his head in his hands, Stephen looked just that. Chloe watched him helplessly. There was nothing to say. There was no point in telling him that Pansy was the last woman in the world to be addicted to. She was too quick, too changeable, and most of all too private. Stephen, from the defeated lines in his face, knew that already.

The silence was broken by the sound of someone running up the stairs. Stephen jerked upright, already smiling at the doorway. Then Pansy was there, bright as a flame. She swooped in on them. Her greeting was for both of them, impartial. 'So. Having a party without me. Am I invited now, or shall I go away?' Belatedly she kissed the top of Stephen's head and he reached out for her, but she was already whirling away again.

'Stay, of course,' they told her.

'Don't ask me how it went,' Pansy ordered. 'I can't talk about it till I know. But . . .' her face broke into her enchanting smile, 'I feel lucky.'

'Did you go dressed like that?' Stephen asked. Pansy was wearing a tiny skirt, two tiers of scarlet ruffles that made her legs look endless. The tight blue teeshirt with a trail of glitter over the shoulder showed every line of her small breasts. There was glitter on her eyelids too, and her hair was combed into a peak at the front and close into the nape of her neck. She looked like an innocent child playing at being street-wise; an irresistible combination. Stephen swallowed, dry-mouthed.

'Sure. I'm not asking to be a curator at the British Museum, you know. Or a lecturer in palaeontology.'

Wherever Pansy had been, it was somewhere that was already carrying her far beyond the narrow horizons of Oxford. Her words showed no more than an amused affection for Stephen's academic world. Her Oxford don, once captured, wouldn't hold her for very long. Chloe saw the beginnings of impatience with him in her face. But when he pulled her into his arms, she still capitulated. She let her pliant body bend against his, and his hands slide down the length of her back to the scarlet ruffles. Chloe saw that Stephen was still partly in possession. Abruptly she looked away, remembering the pleasure that his love-making had given her, too. Even now, after all that had happened, she didn't want to think of him doing that to Pansy.

'We must go,' Stephen said huskily. Chloe watched them, unspeaking. Some of the old, satisfied glow showed in Pansy's face. They murmured their goodbyes and went along the echoing gallery. Pansy's door closed fast behind them.

Chloe's face set in new, determined lines and she sat down at her desk. Briefly she thought of Pansy, imagining how she would go on through life just as she did now. There would be the steely, unwavering concentration on getting what she wanted, followed by the intense, fruitful period of radiant satisfaction when she had achieved it. Then the focus would shift to something new, whether it was a different lover or a mysterious job. Pansy would be a success, there was no doubt about it, because Pansy always got what she wanted. It was no real concern of hers that she left a trail of wreckage in her bright wake.

The thought floated away from Chloe as she looked down at her work. Pansy and Stephen were forgotten as the waters of concentration closed over her head.

Helen, too, closed herself off in her books. She let herself sink deeper and deeper, living in the worlds created for her by Elizabethan poets or Victorian novelists in preference to her own.

Every morning she woke up to the weight of the same unanswered question, and every day she pushed it aside. After Schools, she repeated to herself. When it's all over, I'll confront it then. But not now, not yet. Instead she read more and more avidly, and sat up late under the green-shaded library lamp writing with a compulsion that she had never experienced before. She was working well, better than she could have hoped, and she clung tenaciously to the coolness of academic discipline. Here at least, in this dry world, emotions were at one remove safely between book covers. Helen knew that with every day she allowed to pass, she was making the tangle worse, and part of her detested her own cowardice. Yet she let herself go on hoping that when the right time came she would somehow know what to do, and how to do it without causing pain. The weeks of May and brilliant early June slipped by.

Darcy's patience both humbled and chafed her. He never complained at the long hours she spent working, and he developed a knack of coming to meet her at the right time, and knowing whether she needed to be left with her own thoughts or to be jollied with cheerful talk. Almost as if she was ill, he coddled her with translucent pink curls of smoked salmon sent by Mrs Maitland, or half bottles of luscious dessert wine that they drank under the willows beside the river.

Just once, sitting on the shaded white seat where they always picnicked, Darcy turned to her and said, 'You aren't very happy, are you?'

A motorboat passed, ploughing a green-white furrow of water that fell away into long ripples licking along the bank.

Helen looked at him, her eyes travelling over his sun-reddened cheek and the square line of his jaw. She could almost hear the seconds ticking past.

Love, fear, and a sudden optimism flared inside her. Maybe it would work.

'I'm trying to be,' she said humbly. 'I'm sorry to make it seem so difficult.'

Darcy's eyes were still on the river but he took her hand and wound their fingers together. 'Do you want to change anything?'

The sun warm on her head and shoulders made her uncertainty seem colder and even more threatening.

'No,' Helen whispered, hoping.

He turned his head and looked straight into her eyes.

'Come home to Mere with me for the weekend.' Prove it, he was saying. Prove us. The shadow was there in his face before she could even reply.

'Not yet. I can't yet, Darcy.'

Usually it was Helen who looked at her watch and insisted that she must go back to work. Today Darcy stood up first and began to repack the picnic things. He drove her to the library without speaking and left her with a kiss that barely brushed her cheekbone, yet she felt that it had burned into her skin.

But the next day he was waiting for her again, and the old gentle intimacy between them resumed.

Helen began to number the days left until Schools with painful anticipation. Eleven left, then seven, then only four.

In all this time she saw Tom only once. She had written him a stilted little note to thank him for the sea picture, without mentioning the fair or May Morning. It had gone unacknowledged and she had taken the picture down and hidden it away, rather than let it confront her mutely with his absence, and yet his closeness. Now, in the last week before the deadline of exams that she had set herself, she had been out walking directionlessly through the streets. The close library air had begun to oppress her. Passing the Museum of Modern Art she slipped inside on impulse, thinking that it would help her to empty her mind if she sat in front of a picture. The word set up reverberations, almost a premonition, but she dismissed them.

Inside the gallery was the confused babble from a private viewing of a new exhibition. Helen began to back away, then a lazy voice behind her said, 'Going already?'

Tom was instantly so sharply there, so physical and important to her that his nearness shut off the noisy party like a glass wall.

'I should stay a little. The pictures are worth a look, and the wine's really quite good.' He held out a glass to her but she

309

shook her head. She couldn't trust her fingers to hold it, or her legs not to melt underneath her.

'What are you doing here?' she asked foolishly.

'Waiting.'

As he said it, Tom's mask slipped. He looked at Helen's candid grey eyes and the mass of black curls that she had tied severely back from her cheeks. It made her look fragile, and touchingly determined. Tom put his hand out clumsily to reach her and he thought he saw answering hunger leap into her face. They moved together like robots in the empty space that they had created in the crowded room. Her hand came up to his, but she was fending him off instead of pulling him towards her.

'Don't. I don't want you to wait for anything, do you hear?'

That was so like her, so much the paradox of reserved English Helen denying the sensuality inside her like fire within marble, that he almost laughed out loud. Then anger at her wilful stubbornness possessed him. They both snapped upright, almost spitting at each other.

'Ostrich,' he taunted her.

'Leave ... me ... alone.' Helen bit off each word, her voice as sharp as a knife.

Then she turned and walked away from him. Her shoulders were square and her back absolutely straight. Even Tom couldn't have guessed at the effort it cost her just to keep on walking.

Three days, two days.

There was no more work to do. Helen knew that she should be resting now, hoarding her energy for the physical effort of writing exams six hours a day for the next five days. Five short days, the culmination of three years' work. Numbly she sat with Chloe in her room, staring out at the golden front of Christ Church over endless cups of coffee, trying not to think.

Chloe was taut with anticipation too, but she hid it even from Helen. It was Chloe's way to joke about the unimportance of Mods, her first-year exams, admitting to no-one but herself her surprising, fierce desire to acquit herself well.

On the second to last day, Darcy came to wish Helen luck. They had already agreed that she would stay alone through the week of exams, keeping her concentration finely honed. Helen knew that that wasn't the only reason, but she swallowed the guilt. She was becoming quite the expert at not facing things, she told herself wryly.

When the time came for Darcy to leave, he stood uncomfortably at the door. Helen knew that he had something difficult to say and waited, knowing that his directness would force him to bring whatever it was out complete, without prompting.

'Helen. I want to announce our engagement.'

From his pocket he produced a carefully folded piece of paper and showed it to her.

'In the *Times* and the *Telegraph* and so forth. This is the proper form of words. If you don't have any objection to the convention, of course.'

So he was giving her the chance to object to the way it was being said, but not to the announcement itself. Tenacious Darcy, under the diffident exterior.

The engagement is announced between John William Aubrey Frederick Mere, Viscount Darcy of Mere House, Mere, Glos., and Helen Jane, only daughter of . . .

She looked up into the stubborn light in his eyes.

'Why now, Darcy?'

Honest as always, he made no evasion. 'It's Mama. If she won't believe that I'm going to marry you, then I'm going to have to force her by making the rest of her world acknowledge it.' He lifted the square of paper. 'This is the first step.'

It makes no difference, Helen thought. She was suddenly too weary to do battle. The fact of our engagement exists simply between Darcy and me, just as it has done ever since Venice. It doesn't make any difference when a whole lot of people neither of us care about read it over their breakfast coffee.

The Countess of Montcalm's china-doll face floated into her mind's eye, wearing its complacent smile.

Not good enough for your son? Helen asked it. You aren't intelligent enough to see it, but I'm good enough for him in every single way except the one that really matters. I can only try to love him, but I'll be doing it better than you.

Helen rested her head against Darcy's chest and closed her eyes. She nodded her head once.

'I'll ring the papers, then,' he persevered.

'Yes. If you think it will make any difference.'

He kissed her, finding the corner of her mouth and then following the outline with his tongue. 'Soon,' he said. 'I love you. Go and do your exams. Good luck, although you don't need it.'

Helen watched him go with the old mixture of anxiety and tenderness.

One more day.

On the last evening, Tom made a slow detour through the narrow streets towards Christ Church. It was Midsummer's Eve, and the thick stone walls seemed saturated with light and warmth. He circled through New College, walking even more slowly where clouds of scent drifted from the great herbaceous borders. On the still air the chock of a croquet mallet and ball followed by a burst of cheering carried across open lawns. Snatches of music from open windows were amplified and then swallowed up by the dense green of topheavy trees. Tom stopped in the twilit silence of the cloister, his white shirt spectral in the dimness. He leaned against one of the low, ancient arches to watch the shadows deepen on the square of turf within, but his inner eye saw nothing. His mind was elsewhere; working, wondering. At length he jerked away from the pitted warmth of the stone and began to walk with new determination. The light in the curve of the High was too bright and dusty, and the traffic too insistent. He ducked quickly across it and the urban noise was swallowed at once by the little cobbled alleyways beyond. He looked up once at the slit of blue sky overhead and smiled briefly. It brought back a sudden memory of New York. Mid-town Manhattan in the summer heat, he thought, couldn't be farther from the cluster of Oxford around its jewelled lawns and the ring of cool, lush water meadows that shielded it.

But the year in Oxford was ending, and he was ready to go home. He had done everything that he had come to do, but now there was one more thing that had begun to matter more than anything else. One more thing, and without it it wouldn't matter where he was or what he was doing.

Helen.

Fragile, tough-minded, cool and passionate Helen. He wanted her more than anything else. More than all Greg Hart's theatres, more than success and acclaim and the artistic power that had always seemed so seductive. Without Helen he didn't want any of it, and Tom's strength had always been in knowing exactly what he wanted.

The certainty had been growing in him since New Year's Eve. It was then that he had first seen, behind the smouldering anger in Helen's eyes, a strength that fascinated him far more than Pansy's practised appeal. Slowly his interest in Pansy had slipped away as he watched Helen. His friendship and concern for her had deepened into something far more important as the weeks passed. At first he had waited, biding his time coolly until Oliver's potent spell was exorcised and New Year's Eve was forgotten, but almost at once it had seemed to be too late.

Darcy had intervened.

Still Tom had waited, leisurely in his confidence that they would be together in the end. As well as knowing what he wanted, Tom was secure in a long history of getting it. He cursed himself now for overconfidence. He had let Helen drift away to Venice, and she had come back engaged. And he knew that for Helen, a promise was not made to be broken. It was one of the reasons that he loved her now.

And yet, he would have to try to make her do it. Have to, because he was irrevocably in love with her now. More, he was convinced that she loved him. The implications of that, for Darcy more than himself, darkened his face.

Tom was at the gateway with its tangle of bicycles where he had led Helen to rescue Oliver, and the play. Beyond was Canterbury Quad, mellow and majestic. A stone urn filled with marigolds was a shock of colour, hummed over by bees. Soothed by the lazy buzz, Tom glanced up and saw that the curtains at Oliver's tall windows were closed. At once his frown deepened and he was taking the stairs two at a time.

'Oliver?'

The outer door was open and the inner swung to his touch. Tom breathed in hard and then looked around. In the darkened room he saw Oliver's blond head, and then the blue flicker of the television. Bogart's profile filled the screen, then Oliver peered round at him.

'Hart. Thanks for coming.' He rubbed his hands over his face. 'Why doesn't there seem to be anything to do but watch old movies? Where has everyone gone?'

Tom moved to pull back the curtains and light flooded in.

'You don't have to do it in the dark.'

'Suits my mood better these days. I'm glad you're here. I was beginning to feel just a touch lonely.' It was a rare admission for Oliver and they looked soberly at each other.

'Done any work?' Tom was direct.

'None.'

'And are you going to sit the papers?'

Oliver shrugged elaborately. 'It won't make the smallest difference. So. What shall we do?'

Tom had picked up the whisky bottle from the tray and he poured hefty measures into two glasses.

'I think we should have a last evening.'

Oliver stared with dislike at the whisky in his glass, then drained it in a single gulp.

'Last?'

'Yes.' Tom turned abruptly to the window. 'I don't think anything is going to be the same, any more. Whichever way it goes.'

Oliver put down his glass.

'We'd better make it a good one, then.' There was a flare of his old high spirits. 'Lead on.'

When Tom came to remember the evening he recalled Oliver at the dinner table, at his most charming and insistent that they should try another pudding and at least a bottle of Château Nairac to go with it. Afterwards he had led the way to Vincent's, and been comically appalled to find it full of drunken revellers whose exams were already over.

'Bad taste to flaunt it,' he had muttered, and retreated to a darker and more exclusive club where he ordered port, plummy and satisfying and absurdly expensive, and then leaned back smiling behind a veil of cigar smoke.

For the first time in months, Tom found him easy company. He remembered why he liked him so much. Even with the second bottle of port, when his eyes began to glaze and beads of sweat to show on his forehead, Oliver was still the witty aristocrat who had introduced Tom as a wary New Yorker to mysterious inner Oxford.

Tom drank glass for glass with him, but he couldn't achieve Oliver's practised slide into abandonment. Recollection nagged at him, and the alcohol simply accumulated into a knotted headache. The port bottle was almost empty again when Tom half-reluctantly unfolded a newspaper cutting from his wallet. Suddenly he needed to talk to Oliver, but he felt as embarrassed as a teenager. Irritation throbbed with the headache and he pushed his glass aside.

'Have you seen this?'

Oliver glanced at it and saw the crest of the *Times* Court and Social page. He snorted with derision.

'Of course not. Hardly required reading, is it?'

'Look, damn you.'

Oliver squinted past Tom's finger at the first announcement in the list of Forthcoming Marriages.

'Oh, I see. Well, it isn't news. What's the matter, for God's sake?' He looked across at Tom's dark face and surprised comprehension slowly dawned. 'Ah. Aha. How very unHart-like. How difficult for you, but you must admit, how funny too.' Oliver leaned back against the velvet banquette and laughed aloud. Tom cut impatiently through the merriment.

'Why now? Why announce it today? I thought they were waiting. I thought I still had time.'

'Why? Oh, because of Mama, I suppose. She's all agin' it, you know. Darcy must think he'll force her hand.'

When Oliver's laughter had evaporated, Tom leaned intently over the table. 'Listen. I'm asking you, as my friend. And as his brother, and ... Helen's friend, too. Should I just wish them God speed and make a gentlemanly exit? Or should I do as every instinct suggests, and try to take her away from him?'

Oliver narrowed his eyes and chewed thoughtfully on his cigar. 'Unless I'm very much mistaken,' he said smoothly, 'that rather depends on Helen. Doesn't it?'

Through the smoke Tom looked back at him. 'I think I know what Helen wants,' he said, almost to himself. 'And it isn't Darcy.'

There was a small silence. 'In that case,' Oliver answered, 'what are you asking me for? If you're not going to drink any more, I'll finish the bottle.'

Tom's fingers grasped the neck of the decanter before he passed it over. 'I'm not asking you. I've just realised. I'm telling you. And you won't finish the bottle, because I'm going to.'

Oliver yawned. 'Anything you like. So long as you stop treating me like an agony auntie.'

With the laughter, Tom saw that his way was clear. At once his headache lifted. For a single moment everything seemed simple, and he was filled with affection for Oliver, the dark club-room, and the whole world. He would be with Helen. He wouldn't let her slip away, because he couldn't.

'Not time to go yet, is it?' The warm fingers of drunken euphoria began to wrap themselves around him.

'Definitely not.'

Much later, they stumbled back to Christ Church together.

315

There was a lightness between them which had been missing for months. Oliver seemed his old, reckless and cheerful self. If he can still be like this, Tom thought dimly, there can't be so very much wrong with him.

They clattered through the porter's lodge together, elaborately signalling each other to silence and suppressing snorts of laughter like a pair of truant schoolboys.

In the rooms overlooking Canterbury Quad, Tom lurched against the mantelpiece and then mumbled, 'What a long way off North Oxford seems. Think I'll just sleep on your couch here. Sleep, lovely sleep.'

Oliver was leaning crookedly against the bedroom door. 'Be my guest. See if you can drag me to the Schools by nine-thirty. What an extremely funny prospect.'

Tom was already plunging into sleep when he heard Oliver talking as collectedly as if he was quite sober.

'It wouldn't have worked anyway, you know.'

'Wha'?'

'My brother. And Helen. I never thought they quite matched, although I don't envy you the prospect of unmatching them with the full weight of the Court and Social behind them. Darcy's too straight, and Helen's too loyal. Mmmm, Helen. Sorry I missed my own chance. Story of my life.'

'Oliver?'

'Yeah?'

'Go away.'

The morning came. Helen watched the light intensifying at her windows and counted off the hours as they struck.

Her mind was as clear as crystal now. The week lying ahead of her was the important thing. She wouldn't sacrifice that to anyone. Not anyone. Helen and Chloe met on the gallery, dressed in the regulation subfusc costume for sitting University exams. Black stockings, black skirt and jacket, white shirt and black tie, worn with cap and gown.

'This get-up,' Chloe complained, 'does nothing except make me feel rampantly sexy. How can I write exams?' Chloe's sheer black stockings were seamed, and her chic black velvet suit was braided and frogged. At the throat of her white frilled blouse was a black ribbon fastened with a cameo brooch.

'Think of the poor man sitting next to you,' Helen grinned. The severity of her own plain black and white showed off the pale cream of her skin, and the lights in her black hair. The billowing length of her scholar's gown made her look slimmer still, flattering beside Chloe's cut-off commoner's version.

'And this awful hat,' Chloe moaned, pulling the black square down over one eye like a pirate. 'Why can't we have schoolmaster-sketch mortarboards like the men?'

Along the gallery, Pansy flung her door open.

'How elegant and serious you both look.'

'Not like traffic wardens?'

'Not one bit. Just terrifyingly clever. I'm so glad my dear little course doesn't involve anything as serious as exams. Come on, I'm going to make you both some breakfast, poor lambs.'

Pansy was yawning, white-blonde and tousled as she pulled her dressing gown around her, and her room was empty.

'Stephen's staying in College,' she said evasively. Helen and Chloe raised their eyebrows at each other and changed the subject.

At nine-fifteen exactly they were ready to leave the house. Rose shuffled out into the dim hall and planted a moist kiss on their cheeks.

'Every year I see them going off, clutching their caps and nice new fountain pens and looking like they're going to the guillotine, just like you two. And then a minute later it's all over and it doesn't seem to make a scrap of difference afterwards. Still, I'm no scholar. Make sure you do well, now. Keep up the good name of the house.' She winked at them and went away, snuffling with laughter.

Outside the streets were full of black and white figures, walking or bicycling, gown tabs fluttering.

'Oh, God,' Chloe said.

Helen was walking briskly, but her face had gone dead white. At the steps of the Schools, they exchanged a last, apprehensive smile and then filed away across the echoing black and white tiles to their separate halls.

Tom had to haul Oliver out of bed. As soon as he was conscious he looked blankly around him, and then his face contracted with the unpleasant recollection.

'Oh, Christ.'

Tom looked with sympathy and a stab of guilt at his grey face.

'Sorry. Last night was mostly my fault. Here, black coffee.'

Oliver's black clouds seemed to have gathered even more

thickly after the brief light of the evening. He watched in sardonic silence as Tom found him a dark grey suit with a Savile Row label, a white shirt and wing collar, and the dismembered butterfly of his white bow tie. He flung on the clothes without looking at them and then stood looking at the dark-clad groups crossing the Quad.

'Neat, tidy little people,' he murmured.

'Gown? Mortarboard?' Tom prompted. 'It's time to go.'

Oliver rounded on him.

'If you know so much about it, why don't you sit the papers for me? I can get there by myself, Hart. I don't need you to carry me.'

'I'd like to come,' Tom said quietly.

At the steps he didn't see Oliver go. Tom's eyes were raking the muted crowds for Helen's black gipsy hair. Twice he thought he glimpsed her, and then the heads turned to disappoint him with the faces of strangers. He waited until the shrill bells were ringing and the last stragglers ran up the steps. Only when the heavy doors closed did he turn away. He knew where she was, and he would come back again.

Inside Oliver stalked to his place, hating the smell of tension and the serious faces milling around him. He felt unspeakably isolated, and faintly dizzy with the meaninglessness of his presence here. On the rickety little desk in the middle of a long line of identical desks he read his name on a white label. There was a blank script, and a question paper carefully placed face-down so that he couldn't catch a glimpse of the questions until the decreed second. The futility of that brought a bitter smile.

The quiet girl in the next seat glanced up and saw him. Lord Oliver Mortimore looking like an unshaven archangel, she thought, and sighed a little.

'You may begin writing now. You have three hours in which to complete the paper.'

The morning's invigilator was an elderly professor whose mincing delivery Oliver had once enjoyed mimicking. Now he turned over the paper without glancing at him, and looked down the list of questions.

Not one of them meant anything to him.

Oliver unscrewed his pen and wrote in the space provided, *Oliver Mortimore (Lord)*. His own name and the empty title mocked him. He stared down at the blank white space and the sick isolation was slowly submerged under a pulsing tide of regret, so powerful that he almost put up his arms to ward it off.

It wasn't the exams. His father had done just the same, and had been half applauded as an amusing tearaway. It went far deeper. Oliver felt that he was being sucked down into a sterile sea, and had been incapable of striking out against it. The wastefulness choked him.

He pulled a piece of the carefully provided scrap paper towards him and wrote on it in thick, black letters. 'Why am I screwing it up?' Then, underneath, 'No more.'

Then Oliver put the cap back on his pen, crumpled up the paper, and walked out of the examination room. He ignored the smirking professor.

The eyes of the quiet girl followed him with a mixture of guilty fascination and nervous awe.

CHAPTER THIRTEEN

It was like running a race.

Helen felt like an athlete, pacing herself with miserly care for the bursts of intense effort. As each paper finished, she put it behind her and focused unwaveringly on the next. She was exhilarated, forging ahead on the adrenalin that pounded through her. And she barely dared to admit it to herself, but she was doing well. Each answer came to her out of the air, compact and satisfying. Her head danced with ideas and insights, long quotes which she had no idea she knew, as she ran down the long black-and-white tunnel of the week. It was a world of paper, the dry whisper of the question sheet and her own handwriting covering page after blank page. She came alive in the silence of the halls, deaf to the coughs and shuffles of concentration and the crisp instructions of the invigilators.

Between exams Helen slept, gratefully and dreamlessly, ate alone as far from other people as she could, and walked the river banks with her mind working at the next paper.

It was the longest and the shortest week that she had ever known. She felt that she had been living like this for half her life, and that it was finished before it had begun. It was the last day, and she was filing across the black and white tiles and down the long rows to her desk for the last time. She was vaguely surprised to see the grey, exhausted faces around her. Surely she couldn't look like that herself. The familiar face-down oblong of question paper sat in front of her, and the empty answer book. Nearly there. It was nearly finished.

The black gown of the invigilator swished past and something made her look up. It was Stephen. The sight of him stirred submerged recollections of life a long way off and she forced them back again. Not yet. Finish this, first. 'You may begin writing now.'

Stephen unhooked his thumbs from the bands of his gown and strolled to his desk on the raised dais. In his place he unfolded the *Times* and leisurely began on the crossword. Usually he enjoyed invigilating. The contrast between his own restful three hours and the feverish effort in front of him was amusing. But now the empty lights of the puzzle blurred and the monotonous refrain played in his head again.

Pansy, Pansy. Where was she? What was she doing? Pansy was slipping away from him and he was helpless and enraged. Stephen felt middle-aged, unwholesome, and chafed with the sourness of guilt. The counterpoint to the repetitive theme was Beatrice. Home, children, family. Then Pansy again, the silky feel of her and her small firm breasts and the taunt of sex in her eyes. Stephen hunched against the knife that twisted in him. His eyes travelled in search of distraction along the rows of bent heads. None as bright as Pansy's. No-one with Pansy's coltish elegance. He came to Helen, and watched her for a minute. She was writing, not scribbling furiously, but with smooth certainty. He could almost follow the measured length of her sentences. Too bloodlessly correct for his own tastes, Stephen thought, but a clever girl. An odd threesome that, at Follies. Pansy's friends. Pansy.

It was a long three hours for Stephen.

At last, 'Will you stop writing now.'

Helen came to the end of her last sentence and sat back. Suddenly her fingers, her arm and her whole body, felt like lead. She groped to her feet and, robot-like, took her paper to the box on the invigilator's desk. Only half recognising him, she saw Stephen watching her. There were creases in his face, and white specks of dandruff on the shoulders of his gown. Awareness began to creep around her again. Real people. Messy real life, she thought.

The surging crowd was carrying her out of the hall, down the corridors into the daylight. It was five o'clock on a late-June afternoon. The sun was warm on her head, and everywhere people cheering, stumbling against each other and tipping green and gold champagne bottles to their mouths. Colour flooded back into Helen's world as if she was living the end of an old, spellbinding black-and-white movie. She began to move, jerkily at first and then running down the steps. She was looking from side to side, knowing that she was searching for one face.

Tom caught her in his arms.

Tom, in jeans and a white shirt, tanned and smiling, waiting for her. She saw the button at his collar, the line of his jaw and his hand reaching out to her. He was undoing the black bow of ribbon at her throat, and he took her black academic cap out of her stiff fingers.

321

'All over,' he said gently. 'Come with me, now.'

Without taking her eyes off him, as if afraid that he would disappear, Helen followed. His car was in the cobbled closeness of Merton Lane. Briefly they were driving through the stale streets, and then in the open country. Tom took them through green lanes where the hawthorn hedges seemed almost to meet overhead, and then up the slopes of a long hill. At last he stopped in a gateway at the end of a lane shadowed with elms. Tom unhooked the gate for her to walk through. Side by side they came out on to a wide, grassy hillside. Below them lay the Thames valley, moist greens and blues patched with squares of yellow, and the river threading through it like a dull silver ribbon. Oxford lay in the middle distance, a grey hump with a centre of improbable gold.

'Does that put it in perspective?' Tom asked, laughter in his voice.

Helen sighed with pleasure.

'Perfectly. Very beautiful, and a long way off.'

Tom had brought a basket with him from the car. Now he unpacked it; champagne flutes laughably elegant in the rough grass, raspberries in a nest of leaves and a pot of thick yellow cream, and the champagne bottle itself misted with cold beads. When he poured it for her Helen saw that it was pink, and it tasted of flowers and fruit like the distilled essence of the afternoon itself.

'Sustenance for the survivor,' Tom said and they touched their glasses together. The back of his brown hand grazed hers and pink froth spilled over her fingers. Tom propped himself lazily on one elbow and smiled at her.

'Do you know,' he said, 'when you came out of that fearful doorway, you looked as if you'd just won an Olympic gold. Quite intoxicated with your own prowess. Very immodest, with all those shell-shocked faces teeming around you.'

Helen put her head back and laughed, feeling the meadow grass tickling her face. Tom watched the line of her throat against the green.

'I think I quite enjoyed it. What an admission. But I'm so, so glad it's over now.'

'And so am I. Look, eat some of these.'

Tom held a heaped spoonful of raspberries out to her and she lifted her head to reach it. She tasted the smooth bowl of the spoon and then sweetness filled her mouth. Scarlet juice spilled down her chin. With the tip of his finger, Tom dammed the trickle, then he put his finger to his mouth and licked it clean. Helen's breath caught in her chest.

The simple intimacy of the gesture struck closer to her than any kiss had ever done.

She shivered, and her fingers twisted in the sappy stalks of grass. Silence seemed to spread outwards from their grassy hollow until the world hung poised in the buttery sunshine. When at last her eyes were drawn to him, Helen saw past the self-sure, handsome mould of his face, past the ironic detachment that he used as a cloak, to a real question. Plain hope quenched the mocking lift of his smile. His eyes were not just dark but velvety brown, faintly flecked with hazel, and his mouth was stained like hers with the abundant sweet red juice.

Helen knew that she had all the time in the world. Slowly, without taking her eyes from Tom's, she lifted her glass to him and filled her mouth with the last of the prickling bubbles. She wanted to laugh, rejoicing, but she wanted something else first. She let her glass go and it rolled away among the buttercups. Then she reached out and touched the taut skin over his cheekbones, and moved to lock her hands behind his dark head. She lifted herself off the grass to reach up to him.

When their mouths met, they were very gentle. It was the sealing of a pact between them, and Helen felt again the sweetness of her Italian dream. But now when she opened her eyes, he was still there. He was very close, familiar to her but suddenly intensely exotic. She wanted to explore him, setting sail on an inner voyage from which she knew there would be no turning back. As they lay watching each other, Helen began to hear again, the hum of bees over the clumps of meadowsweet and the drone of a light aircraft invisible in the blue above. Around her head the grass was alive with minute rustlings of insects. The world seemed ordered, a rational progression of things large to small, and unbelievably beautiful.

Here and now, Helen thought. This is where I want to be.

But Tom moved back a little and she frowned to focus on his face again. He reached for it, caught her hand in his, and she felt the heavy stone on her finger digging into their flesh.

'So you won't do it?'

For a shaming moment Helen had to search her mind, and then remembered Darcy. They had planned that he would meet her from the last exam. He would have been there in the crowd at the foot of the steps too, craning to see her. But the face that she had lit on had been Tom's, and she had gone with him without thinking.

Worse – she had gone eagerly. She had a sudden picture of Darcy waiting, seeing the last stragglers empty out of the halls and the tide of celebration ebbing away up the High to leave him stranded.

'Do what?' she echoed Tom's question stupidly.

'Helen', Tom said quietly. 'You aren't a fool.'

He would excuse her nothing, she saw. Tom wouldn't make things easy for her, or let her hide from what she must do.

'Won't marry Darcy?' His plain, good-natured face superimposed itself on Tom's for an instant. She remembered the affection and the trust that linked them. Not love, she thought. Not love. 'No,' she answered herself, and looked up to meet Tom's sombre stare. 'I don't think I can.'

Helen sat up and then buried her face against her drawn-up knees. The thought of what she must do repelled her, and in that moment she hated Tom irrationally for bringing her to it.

'What can I do?' Her heart failed her at the prospect.

'You must tell him, of course. It would have had to come sometime. Better now. Better than in a year, or five years.'

Ruthless, Helen thought, but right. That sums you up, Tom Hart, doesn't it? But I need you. Oh, I need you. I can't think of going without you any more. Is this being in love, then? This paradoxical mix of urgency and anger and longing? Not the peace I knew with Darcy at all. Nothing like that.

Something blotted out the sun over her bent head. Tom leaned over her and forced her face up to meet his. This time his lips jarred against hers and his tongue forced her mouth open so that she sank back, and back into the grass where the waving stalks blurred against the sky. He rolled and the weight of him was heavy along her body, but she could have lifted him and carried them both away on the answering strength of her response.

She could do anything, so long as she had him here, like this.

But not now, yet. She hadn't earned that, yet.

'You see, don't you?' He was asking her if she felt it too, and she nodded her head just once.

It was hard to do, painfully hard, but she turned her head

away from him and closed her hands on his arms to restrain him.

Tom groaned very softly, and then they were apart and looking away across the wide valley to Oxford and its crown of tiny spires.

'My director's instinct agrees that this isn't the place or the time,' he told her. His smile came back and he was smooth and certain once again. But he put one finger on the pulse at her wrist to still her for a second.

'But it won't be too long, will it? I'm not Darcy, Helen. I'm not at all a patient man.'

'I noticed,' she shot back at him. 'I know what I have to do. I owe it to Darcy not to ... deceive him. Enough?'

Tom understood that.

'Come on then.' He took her hands and pulled her to her feet. 'There's a stream down there. Nearest thing to the cold shower I'm in urgent need of. Run.' Hand in hand they went flying down the hillside, slithering over the turf and leaping the hummocks with yells of warning and encouragement. Exuberance came back to Helen and she gave herself up completely to the rush of warm, scented air, the pounding of her feet and Tom, pulling her on and down the long slope. There was a wide expanse of lush meadow at the bottom and then a stream fringed with stumpy alders. The pitted marks of cattle hooves stood out in the sun-baked mud. The stream water was clear as glass over the smooth pebbles, and long green fronds of weed rippled like hair. Tom, in jeans and sneakers, didn't even pause at the bank. He plunged straight into the water and spray sparkled up around him, catching the light in rainbow arcs. He bent to splash cold water over his face and hair and then straightened up, gasping and laughing.

'Come on in. The water's fine.'

More circumspect, Helen stopped on a flat stone at the edge. She peeled off her black subfusc stockings and Tom faltered at the pale flash of smooth inner thigh that they revealed.

'Don't do that,' he called out to her. 'Or this cold shower will be wasted.' Then Helen was wading in beside him, grinning in pleasure as the delicious cold water licked around her bare legs. In midstream the current pulled at her decorous black skirt and wrapped it limply against her.

'Too bad if I have to resit the exams.'

'Come here, naiad.'

She came and they stood together in the stream, arms wrapped around each other and their eyes closed against the light off the water.

It was right, Helen thought. She had been blind, and deaf, and hurtful to cling to a notion that a choice made was a choice for ever. Worse even than hurtful – proud. Too proud to admit her own mistake. But after so many mistakes, she knew that she was right now. As she realised it, the sun slid behind a long finger of cloud. She looked away up the slope. The water suddenly felt cold, and her bare legs were numbed by it.

'I must go back to Oxford,' she said quietly.

Shame pulled at her. It was unjust that she should be happy here in this summer landscape, while Darcy was waiting fruitlessly for her.

Without a word, Tom guided her across the smooth pebbles to the bank. They climbed the hill together, slowly, arms round each other's waists.

At last, outside Follies House, he leaned across and kissed her, no more than a touch on the corner of her mouth.

'Don't be afraid.'

Helen looked levelly at him.

'I'm not afraid. I'm ashamed, and I'm hurt at the thought of hurting him. But I'm not a coward.'

'I know that.'

They were silent again, watching each other's faces, learning the nuances of expression with greedy fascination.

Helen felt that she couldn't bear to leave him, even for a few hours, and surprise shook her. She had never felt that about Darcy. He had slipped in and out of her days, compared with this, just like a pleasant shadow.

Lucky. She was so lucky, now.

'I don't want to go,' she said.

'I don't want you to. But you must.' Tom was very gentle, different from the man she had known. Cynical, aloof and sophisticated Tom was looking at her with pride, and love. 'Will you be at this Ball?'

Christ Church Commem Ball, tomorrow night. The year's last fling. Darcy had bought their double ticket with a flourish, from Oliver. Oliver had made fun of his new sociability and Darcy had answered, 'I can do all these things, now I've got Helen.'

'Yes,' she answered painfully. 'I am – I was – going with Darcy.'

'I'll be there too.' He slid the car into gear. He was moving away. She barely caught the words, but Tom said, 'I love you.'

Helen climbed down the mossed steps. Her feet and legs were still bare, and her wet skirt clung to her. Darcy had said just the same words, in almost the same place. She had tried to run away then, but it hadn't been nearly far enough. Helen felt pulled in half by the battle between love and sympathy within her. As she came into the hall the telephone was ringing. With vague irritation she went to answer it. It would be for Pansy, because it always was, and she hadn't seen or thought about Pansy for days.

'Helen? Thank goodness. Are you very angry?'

It was Darcy.

'What?'

'With me, for not being there. It was a real crisis or I'd have come, you know that. I had to get Tim Oakshott out here to the sheep. It turned out not to be what we were afraid of, but I had to hang on until we were sure. Where have you been? I've been ringing and ringing. I was starting to worry.'

'Oh. I just ... went out.'

'How did it go?'

'What?'

'Helen, your exams. The reason why I haven't seen you for a week.'

Practical, prosaic Darcy, sounding just as he always did. A little bothered now because of his sheep, but unchanging. Helen looked at the grey box of the payphone, the dusty floor and the dim light filtering down from the gallery. She understood that he hadn't missed her outside the Schools after all. He hadn't even guessed at anything, yet. What could she say to him now, cold, on the telephone?

'Helen, are you still there?'

'Yes. The exams went fine.'

Couldn't he hear the catch in her voice?

'Will you mind very much if I don't come today?' Darcy was busy with his own anxiety. She pictured him in his office at Mere, frowning and staring out at the grey woolly masses of the sheep moving on the slope across the valley.

'No, I won't mind.'

'Until tomorrow, then. Eight o'clock. We'll go to dinner before the Ball. There's a surprise.' And Darcy rang off, chuckling.

'Will the sheep be all right?' she asked, too late, into the dead receiver. Dinner. She would tell him then, Helen thought. Over dinner, alone together. There would be no need to go through the travesty of partnering him to the Ball with this weight dragging at her.

Slowly Helen climbed the stairs to her room, thinking about the year and the changes and the mistakes. *Follies*, she said aloud, and smiled wistfully. But she had come to Tom at last, and that was all she wanted.

Helen's room looked dusty and un-lived in. She blinked at the piles of books and the notes drifting over her desk. The intense preoccupation of the long week had been obliterated by the happy poignancy of this afternoon. Tom's arms around her and his face against hers were realer than all the three years that lay behind. She could only remember it dimly now, as an irrelevance. The books under her hand might have been in some unknown foreign language.

Helen went across and leaned her head against the window. The view engrossed her as it always did. Magdalen, All Souls,' St Mary's, Tom Tower, she said, counting off the towers and spires as her eyes travelled over them. Oxford peaceful and impregnable under the evening sun. Tomorrow was the last day of her last term. After tomorrow she wouldn't belong here any longer.

And where would she belong?

Helen realised with startling suddenness that she had no idea. Dimly in the past weeks, and with reluctance, she had thought of Mere and a life watching the fields and the slow roll of the seasons. There wouldn't be that, any more. It was as if a sudden stiff breeze, sharp with the salt tang of the sea, had swept through the stuffy room. She felt free, drunk with freedom. Tom had asked nothing of her, and had promised her nothing in return. She could do anything now, but she knew too that if she chose to she could share her freedom with Tom.

Remembering something, Helen went to her cupboard. At the back, hidden behind boxes and suitcases, there was a little square package. She pulled the wrapping away impatiently and looked down into the brilliance of Tom's sea picture. The pin that he had hammered for her was still in place. She hung the

328

picture again and stood back to look at it, smelling the flower scent and the tough, challenging draught of sea air.

Stephen waited in his rooms. Pansy was just over an hour late. Hardly at all, by Pansy's standards. She had stayed with him here only infrequently, but there were signs of her occupation everywhere. There was a paperback novel he had once made a disparaging remark about, which had doubled her enthusiasm for it. There was a bottle of Perrier on his drinks tray because she always asked for it, and through the open door to the bedroom he could see a scarlet sweater tactfully folded and put aside by his scout. In the drawer of his desk, hidden from the inquisitive eyes of students coming for tutorials, there was a photograph of her. She had given it to him in the early, incredible days when she had made him a present of herself. She was wearing her Rosalind-Ganymede costume, breeches and a white laced shirt and a leather jerkin, and she looked vulnerable and mischievous and maddeningly desirable. On the reverse, in her execrable loopy handwriting, she had scrawled 'To darling Stephen, all my love P.' Banal, Stephen tried to tell himself. Under-educated, self-centred and spoiled. But for each of those things Pansy was a hundred others too. He ached for her as he had never stopped doing from the moment when she had leaned forward and kissed him full on the mouth.

Time after time, in the company of his puzzled children or listening to Beatrice's tearful voice on the telephone, Stephen wished that he had never seen her. But it was unthinkable that he could do without her now. So he waited on in his rooms, irritable and anxious, and imprisoned as securely as if she had locked him in.

At last, crossing to the window for the fifteenth time, he saw her coming. Short skirt, long tanned legs and hair bleached even blonder by the sun. She was strolling along without a trace of hurry.

Bitch, Stephen thought. Then he saw the heads of the students lounging on the grass turn as she passed, and a hard knot of excitement formed inside him. He moved to arrange himself and his papers at his desk, pretending to be absorbed in his work.

'Seven o'clock?' he asked when she came in, smiling at her in spite of his anger.

'Sorry.' Pansy was withdrawn, almost sulky. He reached for

her at once but she slipped out of his reach and left him feeling lecherous and slimy.

'Can I have a drink?'

'Perrier?'

'No. Gin, or scotch or something, if you've got it.'

Stephen mixed the drink, his eyebrows raised in faint surprise. When he handed it to her, he smelt her flower scent and the peachy freshness of her skin and the knot in his stomach tightened.

Pansy swallowed the drink straight off and then, at last, she met his eyes.

'I've come to tell you that it can't go on between us.'

The words fell like little drops of ice into the pleasant room. She waited, unmoving, and then Stephen laughed. Of course she was joking.

'It?'

'I can't see you any more.'

Not a joke, but still he tried to laugh. He wanted to be warm and fatherly, dismissing this childish whim.

'Pansy darling, what do you mean?'

Even as he said it, he saw the little, steely face and the cold blue determination in her eyes. He knew what she meant and shock silenced him like a blow in the chest.

'I mean that I'm going away. To the States, as it happens. To work for a while.' Pansy looked down and away from him and for a moment he thought he glimpsed discomfort in her eyes. 'I've come to thank you, Stephen. And say I'm sorry. And goodbye, I suppose.'

Stephen stared at her incredulously. He put out his hands and then dropped them again.

'Thank you?' he repeated. 'To thank me and then go? Just walk out after all the months we've been together and everything we've shared?'

There was a little silence and then she said, 'You did just that to Beatrice, except that it was years, not months.'

Stephen went white. How had this cold little creature replaced pliant, sexy Pansy?

'I left my wife for you.'

'I never asked you to do that, Stephen. I never wanted you to. Listen, please listen. We made each other happy for a while but now it's over. Please, let me go without a scene.'

'A scene? Jesus Christ, a scene?' Stephen was shaking now,

and he realised something else. For the first time since childhood
he was going to cry. His eyes stung and then the tears came,
burning his face.

'Oh no.' Pansy was staring at him. 'Please, no.'

Stephen's hand groped like a blind man's, he found the arm
of his chair and then sat down.

Pansy moved awkwardly to him and took his head in her
arms. She stood looking down at him, stricken, but he never saw
that.

'Don't cry for me. I'm not worth it.'

Stephen pulled himself away from her and said through stiff
lips, 'I'm not crying for you, you little wrecker. I'm crying for
the paltriness of it all.'

'Yes,' Pansy mumbled after him. 'The paltriness of it all.'

She reached the door and then the staircase beyond. Then she
was running, running away without the vaguest idea of where
she was going, oblivious past the curious admiring eyes that had
watched her arrival.

As she ran and a sharp pain began to stab in her side, she was
rolling down the practised steel shutters in her mind.

Put it behind you, her feet pounded. Close it off. It's done with
now. It's too late to change any of it. Perhaps another time it'll
be different. Perhaps you'll be able to feel like everyone else.
Think ahead, now. Think of what's coming and what you want
to do. That makes it worthwhile, doesn't it?

As she ran on Pansy's face was clenched and for once almost
without a trace of prettiness.

For a long time Stephen sat with his head in his arms. Then
he jerked open the desk drawer and looked down into the
smiling, tantalising face. With one savage gesture he screwed
the print up into a glossy cracked ball and sent it spinning away
across the room.

The next evening Helen sat peering into the awkwardly-placed
little square of mirror in her room. It felt all wrong to be dressing
up.

There was nothing to celebrate tonight.

But still her fingers went through the motions of putting up
her hair. As she twisted a few glossy tendrils to frame her face
she stared gravely at herself. Her face was naturally pale but
tonight there were two spots of colour high on her cheekbones.
The grey eyes looking back at her were bright and anxious.

Helen secured the knot of hair with two elegant pearl combs, lent by Chloe. She was ready now. Behind her her dress was hanging against the wardrobe door, white broderie anglaise, ruffled and starched, demure with a low-cut front that belied its own innocence. All she had to do was put it on, but still Helen sat in front of the mirror looking at herself and trying to fathom the churning feelings within her.

In a few minutes Darcy would be here. She would have to find the words to tell him that she couldn't marry him, and the thought alone made her feel sick.

But then, she was dressing for a ball and Tom would be there. Even though she shouldn't be going, probably wouldn't be, she was getting ready with care because it was for him, and she longed to see him. There was satisfaction in her glance at herself because she was looking pretty, for Tom. Guilt, anxiety and apprehension over Darcy warred with her very happiness. She had never felt so confused. It made her light-headed. Everything normal seemed threateningly misshapen, as if she was drunk, or drugged.

Helen leaned forward and began mechanically to make up her eyes in the way that Pansy had shown her, at Montcalm, so many months ago. She remembered herself standing in the pink and blue bedroom, decked out in the brilliance of her borrowed ball dress. It was Oliver who filled her head then. Oliver who made her want to look her best. Even at this distance, the naive futility of those hopes made her mouth twist into a smile. Oliver's dominance over her seemed far away now, diminished by distance and the avalanche of events that had overtaken her since then. But she would never forget the magic of their short days together, and the sharpness of her first love. The urgency of it had driven her, from the moment of meeting him, all through the early wintry Follies days. It had driven her further, when Oliver's brilliance had glanced away to reflect on Pansy, to Darcy. Sometimes there had been enough of Oliver's ghost in him, as when he had first kissed her at Mere, to stir her faintly in response. And he was Oliver's antithesis too, solid where his brother was evanescent. She had clutched at the security he had offered, then found herself imprisoned by it.

How a single year has changed everything, she thought. Helen reflected that she would barely recognise the shy, hesitant girl who had been herself a year ago.

If only, she whispered, if only changing so much means that I'll never make the same mistakes again.

I don't want to be hurt any more. And I can't bear ever to hurt anyone myself. Never again, after this.

Someone tapped at her door. 'Helen?'

'Wait. Just a second,' she called guiltily. Darcy was here already and she was still sitting in her long white slip, staring into the familiar yet frighteningly apart reflection in her mirror.

She let her comb drop with a clatter and reached for the dress. The white ruffles rustled as she dragged it on, but she couldn't reach the little pearl buttons at the back. The colour in her face was heightened as she struggled.

'Come in,' she said, despairing of managing it herself.

Darcy stopped short in the doorway.

'You look stunning,' he said simply. And then, 'Let me do that.'

One by one, his outdoor hands looking incongruous against the delicate fabric, he did up the little buttons. Darcy's face was reddened too. When the last button was secure, he bent and kissed the exposed nape of her neck.

'You look different,' he said, and Helen wondered if she was imagining the sadness in his voice. 'Is it because you've done your hair like that? Helen, I've missed you so much.'

He turned her round to face him and kissed her again. With pain and tenderness she saw his colourless hair damped smoothly down, making his face look rounder and younger, the careful black tie and the smoothness of his dinner jacket showing the developed muscles of his shoulders.

'Darcy. Darcy . . .' she began.

But the sadness that she had glimpsed, real or not, was all gone. Darcy looked like a little boy now with a big secret that he couldn't bear to keep to himself any longer. He was looking round impatiently.

'Are you ready? Come on, we must go. Where's your wrap, or whatever it is?'

She had Chloe's black velvet evening cloak, and he put it around her shoulders. Bemused, she let him lead her down the stairs. The first-floor gallery was empty and dark, but there was a square of light and the sound of voices below. At first sight from the wider sweep of stairs, the high panelled hall seemed full of people. Helen glimpsed Chloe's mass of dark red hair,

Pansy's wand-like slimness, more faces she knew from *As You Like It*, and her College, and others, strangers to her. Everyone seemed to be laughing. They started to clap and cheer as she came down the stairs with Darcy at her shoulder. It was impossible to imagine anything more incongruous with her mood.

'What?' she asked Darcy, blankly. He beamed at her, but there was anxiety behind it.

'To celebrate. Your Schools, of course, and our engagement. We've never had a party. I wanted to give you one tonight.'

Oh God, no, she wanted to say, but Darcy was already leading her into the crowd. Chloe hugged her. Her friend was vivid in dark green shot silk, with long jet earrings dangling extravagantly in her ears.

'Do you mind all this?' she murmured. 'Darcy was so keen to do it.'

'No,' Helen said, hearing her voice coming from a long way off. 'No, of course not.'

Chloe turned back to her partner. She was with Dave Walker, Stephen Spurring's College 'token Red.' Helen remembered that Chloe had struck up an ill-assorted but lively friendship with him. The night was full of surprises, she thought. Dave grinned at her. He was mock-defiant in his leather jacket, his floppy red bow tie a parody of the stiff black of the other men's.

'Mmm,' and '*mmm*, well done.' Pansy theatrically kissed both her cheeks. There was a tough-looking little man with ginger hair standing beside her. 'This is Scot Scotney,' she said, introducing him as if the name ought to mean something to Helen. 'Do you mind me bringing him to your party?'

'Not a bit.' Helen was utterly dazed.

Through a little avenue of people, she saw Oliver at the far side of the hall. He was lounging, detached and negligent, but when their eyes met he blew her a kiss and then beckoned deliberately.

'Hello, lovely,' he murmured and lifted her chin with one finger so that he could kiss her mouth. 'Hart was invited. But he thought, under the circumstances, that it was tactful to refuse.'

Helen leapt back. 'Oliver. If you dare, if you have dared, to say anything to Darcy...'

'Oh, I haven't. Don't look so frightened. None of my business, is it? But your demure exterior does deceive. I don't think Darcy recognises that at all.' Helen shivered. Oliver wasn't safe. There was a wildness about him tonight that scared her, even through her confusion.

'Our last Oxford night,' he reminded her. 'Time to stop playing, and dressing up.' One finger flicked his coat. 'We'd better make it one to remember.'

Oliver was wearing the uniform of his privileged dining club. There was a green braided velvet coat with satin facings over a white waistcoat and starched stock, tight black trousers and buckled shoes.

'How exotic you look,' she said, with an attempt at lightness.

'Not like a pantomime footman?'

No, not like that. With his fading gold hair and the tight-drawn Plantagenet lines of his face he might have been a ghost, a sad apparition allowed to materialise for a single night ... Helen shook herself. She was being fanciful, but there was nothing pantomime about Oliver tonight.

Darcy was marshalling everyone ready to leave. They swept out of Follies House to the line of waiting cars. For his celebration dinner Darcy had booked the whole room of a chic North Oxford restaurant. It was a feat of organisation, Helen realised, in Commem Week when the whole world was dining out.

She had wondered how she would ever get through it, but the meal passed in a merciful blur. She could eat hardly a mouthful of the food that came and went in front of her. She was too painfully conscious of Darcy down the long line of faces at the other end of the table, raising his glass to her in an unspoken toast. She knew what it must have cost him to break out of his shell of reticence to do this for her.

And later she must tell him. Watch his face change ...

The waiter came and lifted away another plateful of barely-tasted food. She was just able to focus on the talk around her, smiling in response to her friends' brightness.

Pansy was alight with vivacity next to her ginger-haired escort. Helen had never seen her look more beautiful. Her dress was a tight-bodiced billow of hand-painted rose silk, worn with a necklace of rose crystal that shot points of light. She looked like a Fragonard portrait.

'That's *the* Scot Scotney', Chloe murmured to Helen, and

335

Helen vaguely recalled that he was something to do with films.

Out of the blur again Pansy was telling her, 'He's the director of *Eyes of Flame*. He saw me as Rosalind, by some immense fluke, and I went to London to do a test for him. His next movie's *Moll Flanders* and he wants me for Moll. It's Hollywood, Helen.'

For a happy moment everything was forgotten as she jumped with delight for Pansy. Scot Scotney, of course. Cinema's Glaswegian *enfant terrible*. He looked more like a street tough to Helen. She had never seen a man so apparently unimpressed by Pansy's beauty.

'Look at hairr,' he was saying. 'Wearring half the budget of ma last picture on hairr barck.'

Pansy was clearly enchanted with him. 'He got that scar on his cheek in a knife fight when he was twelve,' she whispered. Pansy had already left Oxford behind her. Helen thought briefly of Stephen, and guessed that Pansy must have discarded him by now.

Discarded. She was doing the very same thing herself, and Darcy had never deserved it. Miserable recollection flooded back and swamped her pleasure in Pansy's good news.

The meal was almost over. There was no chance to talk to Darcy. She would have to go on to the Ball with him, and all these other people. Tom would be there. Giddily her mood swung from sadness to intense expectation.

If only she could get through this horrible, garish, bewildering night. After this, she could face anything.

In the blur again, she was packed into a car between Darcy and Chloe who were joking across her. They were pulling up outside Christ Church under the height of Tom Tower. As soon as they climbed out they were swallowed up in the stream of people passing through the crowded lodge. Darcy took her hand and she followed him miserably through into Tom Quad.

Helen drew in her breath. Wolsey's College was transformed. The statue of Mercury and the fountain basin basked under a tented dome of laser light, ribbons of blue and green silver that fell away to the four corners of the great space. Facing them was a pavilion lined in the same green and blue and silver, and on the stage beneath it a medium-famous new wave band was already half-way through its set. The walls enclosed and amplified the insistent music, and there were couples dancing on the grass. White laser light playing on the fountain made it look as if it was frozen in silver.

The sky beyond the ribbon canopy of light was dark velvet blue.

Around her everyone in Darcy's party was laughing and clapping. Helen had only the sour taste of apprehension in her mouth. The night was magical and beautiful, and panic was rising inside her. In a minute Tom would appear. Darcy was beside her, his arm heavy around her shoulders. He would see them both, and he would guess. It would be the worst, the cruellest way for him to know.

'Like it?' Oliver had come up behind her. 'My light show?' He was closer, steering her away from Darcy.

'Very clever,' she answered mechanically.

'The committee thought it was right over the top. But the repugnant little man who owns the lights owes me a huge favour, so I thought I'd just make use of them. Darcy, I'm taking Helen to dance. D'you mind?'

'Not a bit.' Darcy was delighted with the success of his dinner. He was leading Chloe towards the dancing now. Dave Walker was laughing.

'For an anachronism, he's not a bad bloke at all,' she heard him say. Then they were out of earshot. Oliver had rescued her, and the moment of panic was past. She followed him under the lights and past the fountain bowl. The huge carp, she thought irrelevantly, must be hiding under the lily pads from this explosion of noise and light.

They passed under an arch and climbed the wide curve of stone steps to the Hall. Helen listened to the hem of her dress swishing on the hollowed treads. It was quiet and dim under the recesses of the great arched roof. The long polished tables were being laid for the Ball supper, and a bar on the dais at the end was stocked with bottles.

A waiter in a white jacket called over his shoulder, 'I'm sorry, sir, the Hall isn't open yet.' Then, seeing Oliver, 'Oh, good evening, my lord.'

'It's okay, Joe,' Oliver said. 'We're just looking for a drink and a quiet corner.' He strolled away down the length of the Hall. Helen saw his assurance and the perfect fit of his green velvet coat across his shoulders. An unformed thought about the unfairness of hereditary privilege flicked through her head. Yet how different Darcy was from his brother.

'Here.' Oliver brought back a bottle and some glasses. 'Let's try to keep our spirits up. Fun at all costs.' He was drinking determinedly hard, with none of the light-heartedness of his evening with Tom.

A flight of wooden stairs 'ed up to the minstrels' gallery at one end of the Hall. Helen guessed from the music cases and stands that there would be a string quartet up there playing through supper.

A beautiful night, she thought painfully, in exquisite surroundings filled with music and light and the faces of friends, and yet a cold, leaden weight pulling at her. She sat down heavily on the lowest wooden step with Oliver lounging beside her.

'Here's to the future.' He tipped his glass and she was shocked by the bitterness in his face.

'What will you do?'

'Without the magic talisman of an Oxford degree, you mean?'

'No, I didn't mean that particularly.'

Oliver's face set in disdainful lines. 'Oh, it's all been fixed up for me. It would be, of course. I'm to go into a bank.'

Helen coughed over her glass and Oliver smiled at her humourlessly. 'D'you think I care what it is I'm supposed to be doing? It's all very suitable. A small but highly influential City merchant bank, the kind of place that loves a lord amongst its minions. My father's on the board, as it happens. They'll find something harmless to occupy me. I shall invest in some natty chalk-striped gent's suiting, and be swallowed up for ever.'

Helen sat up, horrified by the flatness of his voice. The idea of Oliver in a bank was ridiculous, shocking. Impulsively she put her arms around his shoulders, forcing him to look at her.

'Oliver, for God's sake. Can't you think of anything else that you want out of your life?'

The memory of the intoxicating glimpse of power and freedom that Tom had given her came back, and sympathy for Oliver shook her as she realised that some flaw within him denied him the same happiness.

His brilliant blue eyes looked dull and the whites were unhealthily bloodshot, but there was a spark of real humour in them as they held hers.

'Nothing at all,' he murmured. 'Helen, my love. You're such a fighter yourself. Lack of fibre in other people really disturbs

338

you, doesn't it? You can't fathom why I don't pick myself up and become Prime Minister. For you, I could almost summon up the enthusiasm. You know, I like you very much.' He picked up her hand and lightly kissed the knuckles. 'You're worth ten of tiresome little Pansy, if only I'd been awake enough to see it. In every respect, including the obvious one. I wish you were mine. But Hart will make you happy. Good luck to you.' He drank again, defiantly.

'And Darcy?' Helen asked softly.

'Don't worry about Darcy. It will be a blow, but he'll survive because he's interested in survival. His anxious desire for it makes him timid. Whereas I don't give a toss. That's always been the difference between us. Don't you see that?'

Yes, she saw it clearly enough. Helen felt the cold fingers of fear touching her. In the dim light of the arched Hall, Oliver was gauntly beautiful, but grimness clung around him like a pall.

'Look at this place,' he said, staring out at the carved panelling, the ranks of portraits and the arched windows where the intricate glass was blackened now by the night sky beyond. The waiters were lighting the candles down the lengths of the tables, and as the flames steadied reflections from the polished tables made twin points of light.

'It's beautiful,' Helen said. She was already aware of how much she would miss the privilege of living and working in buildings like these.

Oliver turned his head away. 'You think so? I shall be glad to get away from it. It's far too uncomfortably reminiscent of home.'

Helen seized gratefully on the laughter, however cynical it sounded in her ears. Oliver helped her to her feet and then spun her around in his arms so that the candlelight blurred in front of her eyes. In a flash, wild gaiety seemed to have replaced the grimness.

'Dance with me,' he begged. 'Just one more time.'

'As many times as you like,' she promised him.

Tom Quad was a blaze of lights and colour. Couples were spilling off the oval of the dance floor and on to the grass under the ribbons of silver, green and blue. Oliver took her firmly in his arms and drew her into the crowd. For an instant she held herself stiff, and then she relaxed and let the music take hold. Her forehead sank against the velvet pile of Oliver's shoulder and she felt the smooth satin facings under her fingers. For just a little while, she would go on dancing like this.

Then she would go in search of Darcy.

And somewhere here, under these interwoven ribbons of light, Tom was waiting for her. A sudden smile irradiated her face.

She shivered between the intense extremes of feeling.

As they danced, the eyes of other women flicked enviously over her. A girl in the arms of romantic Lord Oliver Mortimore, a girl in a white dress with a light flush over her cheekbones and a dazed smile. A lucky girl, so obviously lost in the magic of an evening.

Helen was blind to it all. In all the kaleidoscopic crowd there were only two faces that she could have had eyes for.

Oliver's mouth moved against her hair. 'Dreadful of me. I'm so caught up in my own enthralling whirl that I never asked you about your Schools. A formal First, I hope?'

Helen drew back a little, wanting to meet his eyes.

'Whatever it is, I owe my degree to you.'

Oliver stopped dancing. 'To me? Whatever do you mean?'

Helen began to say *You gave me the money so that I could stay, didn't you?* Then, over Oliver's shoulder and through a long tunnel of extraneous noise and movement, she saw Tom.

He was sitting on the stone coping of the fountain basin with the plume of frozen silver spray behind him. She took in the smoothness of his white tuxedo that set him apart at once, exotic in the black-suited crowds. There was a red rosebud in his buttonhole. As if he was meeting a stranger, she thought, and needing a signal that would draw her to him. Neither of us needs to do that ever again, she realised with sudden certainty. Tom was watching her, one eyebrow raised in a peak. The saturnine darkness of his face struck her afresh after Oliver's high English colouring. She dropped her hands from Oliver's arms. Love for Tom was overflowing inside her like a flood from a breached dam. Very slowly she was beginning to move to him.

'There's Tom.'

Oliver glanced briefly at her and then let her go.

'Good luck,' he said again, and then turned away. The dancers swallowed him up at once.

Helen crossed the few yards of polished floor that separated them and put out her hands. Tom lifted them briefly and looked down at her fingers. She saw the set of his skull on his shoulders, the dark hair falling across his forehead. He looked back at her face and the Viscountess's ring caught a splash of light between them. They were both immediately aware that Darcy could be anywhere, watching, suddenly seeing them through painfully opened eyes.

'I was on my way to find him,' Helen said. Her voice caught in her throat. Tom smiled a little. He was as uncompromising and as certain as he always was. He was simply waiting for her, allowing her the freedom of her own choices.

'You looked very pretty, dancing with Oliver.' He stood up and drew her back on to the floor. 'My turn now, I think.'

They moved together instinctively. Helen was vividly conscious of his white sleeve against her bare arm. Funny that they had never danced together before, she thought, and yet they were perfectly attuned. She looked up, through the lights, at the intense purple-blackness of the midsummer sky. Hanging over the pinnacles of Christ Church was the rising moon, almost full, pinky-gold and trailing fine wisps of cloud.

Tom followed her eyes.

'Sad to be going?' he asked gently.

'Not exactly. I'm bewildered because I don't know where I'm going to. I'm excited because of you, and because of you nothing else matters. Except Darcy. I'm sad for Darcy.'

Tom's fingers tightened on her arms.

'Do you want me to tell you where you are going? That you must come back to the States with me? Do you want me to decide for us?'

The rhythm between them was broken. They stopped and stood facing each other among the swirling dancers under the summer moon.

'No,' Helen said levelly. 'That isn't how it is between us, is it?'

Tom was looking at her as if she was the only person in the great golden quadrangle.

'And I love you for it,' he whispered.

With a final reverberating chord that hung on the motionless air the music stopped. Under the pavilion the sweating musicians bowed and grinned at the applause.

'I'm going to find Darcy,' Helen said. She was certain now, implacably certain, and it gave her the vital courage that she needed for Darcy.

Tom stepped back, hands in his pockets, detached once more.

'I won't be far away, if you need me.'

Helen began her search. He wasn't among the crowds beginning to ebb out of Tom Quad in search of supper, nor was he already at the candlelit tables. At last she found him under the pink and white ruched lining of the marquee in Canterbury Quad. Another, noisier band was playing here and the dancing was uninhibited.

Helen saw Pansy first. She had the rose-pink folds of her dress caught up in her fists like a little girl going paddling, and the ribbons amongst the silvery points of hair flew as she danced. The dipping hem of her dress showed pink silk stockings. Darcy was partnering her. He was jigging up and down, alternately frowning with concentration and then beaming with delight. He was flushed, and his hair looked darkened with sweat. Helen had never seen him drink more than a couple of pints of beer, but she thought that he looked tipsy now, jovially and intentionally so. A few steps away Chloe was dancing with Dave Walker, whose red bow tie had come undone to dangle in frayed points down his shirtfront. At one of the small tables that fringed the floor, Scot Scotney was sitting with a bottle at his elbow, watching, entertained in spite of himself.

Everyone having a good time, Helen realised with a dull pang.

Darcy saw her and immediately put a heavy arm around her shoulders.

'Where have you been?' he exclaimed. 'We come to the Ball to celebrate our engagement and I don't see you all evening.'

'With Oliver, and Tom,' Helen said quietly.

Pansy, Chloe and Dave were crowding around them. They were exhilarated, laughing and jostling.

'Can't think when I've ever had such a good time,' Darcy was saying. 'Perhaps Oliver's got the right idea after all.'

'Darcy, can we go somewhere quiet?' Helen pleaded. He was deaf to the urgency in her voice. Instead he took her hands and whirled her on to the dance floor. 'Quiet? At a ball? Dance with me first. We haven't danced together since Montcalm. New Year's Eve, remember? I couldn't believe my luck. I still can't, Helen.' He kissed her cheek, and Helen felt as if he was twisting a knife between her ribs. Then she saw Chloe looking curiously at her and forced a bright smile. As his arms came round her and he dragged her into the dance she thought that Darcy was like a huge, affectionate dog. How different from Tom's aloof coolness, with the heat beneath.

The evening drew her on into its bright, frivolous, utterly inapposite tangle. The others seemed to dance inexhaustibly. When she begged to be allowed to sit down, she was passed inexorably from Dave Walker's clutches to Scot's taut grip. She found his stiff-lipped Glaswegian incomprehensible against the roar of the music. When he smiled at her only one half of his face moved, the pucker of scar tissue keeping the other immobile. 'Ye don't look sae happy for a gairrl just engaged,' he told her, and she turned her head away from him.

At last they had apparently danced enough ...

'Supper,' somebody said, and 'Much more champagne,' someone else added. She found herself being drawn out into the moonlight again. The moon was high overhead now, and the colour of beaten silver. Darcy was holding her hand, leading her up the hollowed steps again and into the Hall. Candlelight shone into amused faces all round her, and on pretty, festive food that she couldn't have imagined eating. There was indeed a string quartet, playing Beethoven into the dim arch of space above the clatter, and calling out, and clinking of glasses. Then immediately, it seemed, they were off again. Helen was hopelessly letting herself be carried along with the evening's tide instead of trying to swim against it. Darcy was not to be deflected from his determined enjoyment, and she knew his stubbornness. Wearily, she decided that she was incapable of judging now whether the moment was tactful or cruelly ill-timed.

The evening was interminable, and there were hours to endure yet. There would be more dancing, and then breakfast among the pools of candlewax at the long tables, and then emergence into the incongruous bright daylight and the roar of work-bound traffic.

Helen followed the cheerful babble down the steps again, her heavy feet making her lag behind. She saw the hem of Pansy's dress whisk out through the arch and away under the lacings of laser light.

A hand caught her arm, so suddenly and sharply that she almost cried out. A green velvet sleeve, and then Oliver's hollow, glittering smile hanging over her. His fingers dug into her flesh.

'Let's round off the evening by going on the river.'

'No.' Helen answered instinctively.

'Come with me,' Oliver said. 'I want you to.'

'Not the river,' she persisted. She looked sidelong at Oliver and saw that his eyes seemed to have sunk back into their sockets. They were remote, expressionless. He was pulling her outside, away across the festivity of Tom Quad. His insistence and the vice-like grip on her arm made her think suddenly of the Ancient Mariner. The idea was fanciful but she shivered in her thin dress. She looked quickly around for Darcy, for Chloe and Dave, or even Scot Scotney, but there wasn't one familiar face amongst the revellers.

Oliver was walking so quickly that she almost stumbled behind him. They reached Tom Tower and the stewards in the porter's lodge stood back respectfully to let them pass. The night beyond looked pitch black and empty as the lights closed behind them.

'Wait . . .' she said, but he was deaf to her. They were almost out into the street when someone stepped in front of them.

A white jacket, and a rosebud against the lapel. Tom. Thank God. Helen felt her irrational fear subside. I won't be far away he'd said, hadn't he?

'Oliver wants to go on the river', she gasped at him, breathless with relief. Tom took one look at Oliver's face and the diamond-hard eyes in the deep sockets.

'Why not?' he said calmly. 'We'll all go. Where's your wrap?'

The black velvet cloak appeared and she was hustled off between them into the night. The black Jaguar sat at the kerb directly opposite. Oliver swung himself into it and smiled at them, his teeth showing in white points.

'A last romantic glide along the water and under the willows,' he murmured. 'Just the three of us.'

The Jaguar roared and plunged forward. Helen felt the bite of acceleration pressing her back against the seat and the firm warmth of Tom's shoulder.

A corner, too fast, traffic lights, red, behind them now, another two or three dizzying turns and then a narrower road that bumped towards the black square of the deserted punt station.

Tom helped her out of the car. He was talking across her to

Oliver, laughing, apparently unthinking. She pulled the heavy cloak around her to hide her shivers.

Over the dew-wet grass that soaked her thin slippers, they came to the river's edge. The water was utterly black and still. A line of punts swayed almost imperceptibly from their moorings. Oliver vaulted into the nearest one and the ripples suddenly spread outwards, lapping under the boards of the landing stage. Tom materialised out of the dark with a pole and an armful of cushions.

'You do the work,' he ordered Oliver and passed the tall pole across the water.

She stepped unwillingly down into the punt. Tom slid into the narrow seat beside her and settled her cloak around her ankles. The boat rocked sharply as Oliver stood up on the flat stern behind them. Then the long shell swung ponderously in the water and pointed downstream. Helen heard the swish of the pole as it slid down through Oliver's hands, the plop of it in the water and then the slight jolt as the tip found the river bed. Oliver put his weight to it to send the clumsy boat skimming over the water. He bent to the rhythm, savagely pushing the blunt prow through the water, twisting the pole free from the greedy mud bottom and hauling it up hand over hand in a shower of cold droplets, ready for the next thrust. They began to travel smoothly, faster, with Oliver as intent as if they were racing for their lives.

Tom's hand found hers under the cloak, and Helen leant her head back against his shoulder. She smelt the waterproof reek of the rexine cushions, varnish, and the deep, mud and weed-green smell of the river itself. Away on either side of her the banks and boles of the trees were shrouded in a low white mist. The moon had disappeared and the sky was very black, the darkest hour of the night before the summer dawn.

Tom's hand was stroking hers, gently, and his mouth was close to her cheek. She closed her eyes against the eerie night and the loud slap of the water and listened to Tom's calm, even breathing. She matched her own to it and her anxiety began to melt away. They were isolated together in a cocoon of water and darkness, warm under their blanket of black velvet. Slow currents began to stir inside her. She turned her head to meet Tom's mouth. His light kiss touched the corner of her lips and then her tongue, and she felt the warmth of him beside her.

Across the grass came the din of the Ball at full swing. The music was plangent, distorted by the damp air. It might have been drifting from another world. Oliver was whistling through his teeth like a demonic gondolier. Once Helen looked backwards and saw the familiar shape of his head with the hair sweat-flattened against it. He smiled at her.

Helen was suddenly gripped by panicky disorientation. They seemed to have been surging on for hours, and she had no idea where they were. Out of the corner of her eye she saw a white notice on the bankside. It was gone into the dark behind them, but the jolt of it brought her upright. It was the water authority warning sign. She remembered the red lettering, seen a hundred times before at the point where punts made a slow U-turn in the Cherwell.

Danger. No punts past this point

Up ahead of them the Cherwell joined the fast-running Thames just upstream from Follies Island.

'For Christ's sake, Oliver. Where are you going?'

Tom was almost on his feet but the boat rocked violently and he sank back again. The banks slid away on either side of them. Rushed on by the water as the tributary ran into the river, they were out in the mainstream.

'Tired of pissing about up there. Let's do some real boating.'

Oliver's face was stretched into a wide, exhilarated smile. They couldn't see it, but his eyes had come alive with reckless light.

'The bank. Steer into the bank,' Tom shouted at him.

Ahead Helen glimpsed the square outline of Follies House sitting on its little island, the three arches of the bridge carrying their ribbon of orange light across the river, and the curl of white water licking around the piers.

Tom's arms were steadying her.

'Keep still,' he hissed. 'Lie flat. Calm water past the bridge.'

The white water hurtled towards them, and the bridge.

'Oliver.'

It towered unbelievably high above them.

'Oliver,' Tom was yelling. 'Steer left.'

The central pier was coming straight at them. The noise of the water was deafening. The prow swung sharply and missed the mossed stone by inches. Helen saw water sliding over the varnished wood and lapping down towards her. The punt

346

swung giddily under the arch. Almost before it happened she heard the splintering crash as the stern smashed against the stone. There was a crack and a sound that might almost have been a cry.

The rushing water swallowed it up. The stern suddenly bobbed upwards.

Helen looked back. No-one.

'Oliver,' she screamed.

He was gone.

CHAPTER FOURTEEN

Desperately Helen struggled to climb backwards.

Tom's hand held on to her with a grip like iron as icy water foamed over the sides of the boat and soaked them. The force of the smash sent the punt juddering sideways. Within a second they rammed into the bank beyond the bridge. Instantly Tom flung himself forward and caught at the rough grass.

'Climb out,' he shouted. 'Move.'

Helen felt a useless scream rising in her throat as she scrambled over him to the towpath. As soon as he saw her safe, Tom pushed the punt away and struck out for the bridge.

Beneath it the water was black and white, empty.

She heard another splash and saw a head bobbing in the fast water, swimming like a dog. Blond hair plastered to the skull. Unmistakably shaped.

Relief surged inside her.

'Tom,' she screamed. 'Over there. Swimming.'

She ran along the path and into the booming space under the bridge. Gravel bit into her feet through her thin shoes and her dress clung around her ankles in hobbling folds. The swimmer was circling, dipping constantly under the threatening white foam.

What's the matter with him? Why doesn't he make for the bank?

The questions pounded in her head. Tom was fighting towards him through the ripping current.

Then Helen saw.

Not Oliver at all. It was Gerry.

Oliver was still down there, under all that rush of water.

Oh God. Please. The words wrenched themselves out of her. Gerry's head went down again. Then she saw something else, a flash of white and a dark length like a dead log. Two heads.

Please, God. Inching towards the island. Too slowly. Hardly moving, and Tom still too many feet away. Both heads gone again. She plunged frantically to the water's edge.

'Stay there.' Tom shouting back at her. Impotence choked her. She was too weak a swimmer to hope to reach them.

There, Gerry's head again. And miraculously Tom's beside him. A weight between them, dragging them down. The terrible gap between them and the island closing, so slowly.

Get help. Decision galvanised Helen. She ran up on to the bridge where the road mocked her with its emptiness. There was no-one at all, no-one to shout to. She turned and scrambled down the steps to Follies, down to the tip of the island. Tom's head splashed out of the blackness with Gerry beside him, gasping and choking with his eyes shut. Helen flung herself down and stretched out her arms. With a groaning heave, Tom shoved Gerry towards her and she groped for him, then caught at his icy wrists. For a moment he hung there and the water almost snatched him away again. Helen's arms were burning in their sockets before he kicked feebly and then found the strength to roll and scramble up on to the bank. Once he was clear he staggered and collapsed behind her. But she had no thought for him now. Tom was fighting in the water with the black, unmoving weight of Oliver in his arms.

Again she leant over the mud and swirling water.

'Hold him. Just hold,' he gasped at her.

Sodden velvet and slippery satin in her fingers now. This one was motionless and unbearably heavy. The water pulled greedily at him but she hung on, her eyes shut, ready to be torn in half before she would let go.

Tom pulled himself up beside her, coughing the water up out of his lungs. Together, the pain stabbing in their chests, they dragged the arms, the shoulders, then the long back out of the water. The feet came, unwillingly, as they hauled him out on to the grass. His head rolled back and Helen glimpsed the terrifying whiteness of his face.

Behind them Gerry raised himself on all fours and coughed. River water gushed out of his mouth. Tom didn't even spare him a glance. He was thumping at Oliver's chest with the heel of one hand pressed over the other. He wrenched the white face to one side.

'Ambulance,' he hurled at her, and then with a gulp of air he pressed his mouth down over Oliver's.

Helen was already running. Up the weed-fringed path to the heavy door with its studding of bolt-heads. Mercifully it swung open. The splash of her wet clothes across the pitch-black hall and the corridor to Rose's kitchen. No time for lights. Remembering where, then reaching out and feeling the cold shape of the payphone in front of her. Her numbed fingers reached for the right slot and she dialled.

'Emergency. Which service, please?'

Helen gabbled her message and then ran again. The tableau at the tip of the island was almost unchanged. Gerry was sitting with his head in his hands, tears of shock running down his face.

Tom was kneeling, the only sound the sharp gasp of indrawn breath as he sucked in and then blew precious air into Oliver's motionless chest. Once, only once, he glanced up desperately towards the bridge.

'They're coming,' Helen said. Her face sagged as she spoke. She had seen the dark contusion at Oliver's temple where his head had struck the stone pier of the bridge.

The seconds dragged into minutes, an infinity of time. Helen knelt on the wet grass with her fists clenched, not daring to move. Gerry smeared the tears from his face and crouched wordlessly beside her. The only sound in the world was Tom blowing into the white lips beneath his.

At last they heard the speeding ambulance and saw the blue light flash on the bridge above them.

'Thank God,' Tom said, not looking up from his task.

Helen scrambled to the steps to guide them and they came running, two homely men in blue uniforms with a black bag between them.

A dim hope fluttered inside her.

'Stand aside, please.' One of the men put his hand on Tom's shoulder as he got painfully to his feet. The three of them stood huddled to one side as the rescuers bent to their work.

But as soon as she saw that their attempts to bring Oliver back were grim ritual, Helen knew that it was no use. They seemed so cruelly rough with him, but still he made no flicker of response.

At last, very slowly, one of the ambulance men stood up. He had a round baby-face, with spectacles glinting under his peaked cap.

'I'm sorry,' he said.

The lights in Follies House flicked suddenly on and the door swung open. Rose came stumbling across the grass. She was in her nightdress and her bulk wobbled shapelessly beneath it. Her mouth was open to scream but no sound came out. Instead she fell into a heap beside Oliver and started to stroke his face, pushing the matted wet hair back from his temples like a child's.

'Come back,' she begged him in a high, thin voice. 'Oh please, come back. I will look after you. You know I will.' The scream came now, and one of the ambulance men helped her away.

'Will somebody take her back indoors?' he asked.

Helen put her arms around the cushiony shoulders and led her away. As she went she saw that Gerry was standing stiffly over Oliver, looking down into his face as if he wanted to apologise for something. At last Tom seemed to notice him.

'You can only just swim yourself, can't you?' Gerry nodded numbly. 'You're a very brave man,' Tom said. His voice was breaking and he turned sharply away. He walked like an old man down to the tip of the island and stood staring away into the horrible water. Helen went on up the path with Rose. Fear began to well up through the immediate shock and grief. Tom would take the responsibility for tonight upon himself, and he would take it hard.

Helen forced her own feelings out of her head and set about tending to Rose. The fat woman was utterly distraught. She was babbling through the tears that pulsed out of her screwed-up eyes. 'I loved him. I let him have anything, oh, everything that he wanted just to keep him coming here once in a while. You think that's impossible, an old woman like me, loving a boy like that? But I did. I loved him like a lover. My lovely Oliver.'

Helen couldn't bear to listen. 'We all loved him,' she said gently. It's true, she thought. For his reckless, doomed charm, we all loved him in our different ways.

Mechanically she groped about in Rose's witches' kitchen, making sweet tea and searching for something that would act as a sedative. At last, leaving Rose whimpering in her rocking chair, she went back into the hall.

They had brought Oliver in on a stretcher. The police were there now, burly men flashing silver buttons and chains and talking about statements. Tom was waiting tensely with Gerry beside him. Helen bled for the pain in his dark eyes. A young doctor, his face bleared with sleep, was folding a blanket back over what was no longer Oliver, but simply a cold, sad body. Helen saw how still it lay under the bright scarlet blanket. She looked away, up past the exquisite Jacobean panelling and the fat carved balusters of the gallery to the dim heights above them.

It was just here, she remembered, that she had first spoken to him. So long ago, now.

There was the sound of running footsteps outside and sharp, anxious voices. It was the others, coming back from the Ball. She had a sudden picture of the scene up on the bridge, the white police Rover with the orange and red flashes and the ambulance behind it, doors open, the blue light still revolving futilely on the roof. The grim appendages of every accident and tragedy. How many times had she averted her gaze from the same scene? And seen it too clearly once before, when they came for her father. How must it look now to Darcy and the others, coming back laughing, in search of her probably, and seeing that waiting for them?

Darcy. A cold shaft pierced her. Again, how could she, she had forgotten him. Her thoughts had been all for Tom.

The front door opened and beyond it she saw that the dawn had broken. The sky was gunmetal grey.

Her friends crowded in together, fear in their faces. Darcy's eyes found hers at once and the horror in them melted away. Then he saw her pallor and the muddy, soaking wreck of her dress.

'Helen. What's happened. Are you all right?'

Over her shoulder he saw the stretcher and the long red outline, and the faces of the police, the ambulance men and the doctor.

'It's Oliver, isn't it?' He looked around at them all. 'Isn't it?' he repeated. 'Please tell me what has happened.'

Behind him Chloe's hand went to her mouth. Pansy reached out to Scot Scotney and he held on to her, eyes narrowed in his tough face.

It was Helen who told him, in broken sentences ragged with her first sobs. Darcy listened with his head bowed but his hands were on her arms, comforting her. At the end he looked up, across to Gerry and then to Tom.

'You went in after him?' he asked. Their soaked clothes and uncontrollable shivering even under draped blankets answered him. 'Thank you,' he said simply.

The doctor, younger than Darcy, shifted on his feet. 'He struck his head on the bridge as he overbalanced. His lungs filled with water at once. Death would have been within seconds. No-one could have done anything.'

Helen saw Tom shuddering. Except prevent him from going

352

on the river at all. She heard the words in his head as clearly as if he had spoken them. Her muscles bunched to run to him, but then she saw Darcy's hands, inanimate, still on her arms. She froze and Tom sat down, alone, at the foot of the stairs.

Darcy was talking. His voice was very gentle, but he had discarded his old, diffident self as inappropriate for this ugly dawn. He was their authority now. He thanked the ambulance men gravely and then turned to the police.

'Yes. I am his brother.'

'Your name, sir?'

'John Mortimore,' he answered, and Helen looked at him as if he was a stranger. 'Viscount Darcy.'

'Thank you, sir. Um, my lord.'

The statements, pitifully brief, took only a few moments to collect. Tom and Helen gave theirs. Gerry, by the merest coincidence, had been outside smoking a last cigarette and had seen them coming. He had nothing else to add.

It was all over. The police bent to the poles of the stretcher.

'Do you have to take him away?' Darcy asked.

'I am afraid so, my lord.'

'Will you let me have two minutes with him?' His voice never wavered.

They crowded clumsily away into Rose's kitchen. Rose was still hunched in her chair, and she looked up through swollen eyes at the averted faces of the police. Chloe was crying, black smudges of mascara under her eyes, but Pansy's white face was dry and hard. She simply twisted a shred of handkerchief between her fingers, to and fro, like a snake.

Tom was there too, across the room, but Helen couldn't look at him. An awful realisation was coming to her.

Darcy came back.

'Thank you,' he said. 'Take him now, if you're ready, officer.'

They went out and between them they lifted the poles of the stretcher. The awkward procession bumped out into the grey light. From the hallway the women heard them slipping and sliding on the narrow stone steps, and the little grunts of effort as they carried Oliver's body away. Then the ambulance doors slammed on him, and he was gone.

Darcy slowly retraced his steps into the house. He came straight to Helen, put his arms around her and kissed her hair.

'I'm sorry to have to leave you,' he said. 'But I must go straight to Montcalm. You understand, don't you?' She nodded mutely. 'Try to sleep a little,' he said gently.

One by one the others went away. Helen thought that she was alone with Tom at last in the bleak, empty hall. Then she looked up and saw Gerry. He half-smiled, bitter with grief, and once again there was the cruel flash of his resemblance to Oliver.

'He often said that he didn't want to end up like me. He won't now, will he?' He shrugged his shoulders and then walked away.

They were left to themselves.

Tom was still shaking, long uncontrollable shivers that set his teeth chattering. Slowly Helen went to him and took his hands in hers.

'You must get dry.' The inadequacy made her wonder how she could ever again say anything to fill the silence between them.

She might not have spoken at all.

Tom said, 'I shouldn't have let him go. It's my fault.' The words came out as if they had been circling inside his head for hours. Helen's hands tightened on his.

'You can't blame yourself.'

Tom lifted his head and the misery in his eyes struck into her.

'Can't I?'

'Oliver wasn't stoppable. We both know that.'

Heavily Tom stood up and they looked at each other. A restraint was growing between them, bred out of the horror of the night and the fear that it had changed everything.

'What now?' he asked her, almost whispering.

She believed that there was nothing else for her to say, but it sounded like a knell as she spoke. 'I can't leave Darcy now.' Stiff, cold little words. 'Not now. Because he needs me.'

'And you think I don't?'

Tom looked utterly changed. His shoulders were hunched and the assurance had drained out of his face, leaving it grey and exhausted. Helen made a move towards him, longing to comfort him, but he fended her off.

'Well?' There was to be no kindly pretence. Tom wouldn't have that.

'I don't think that you need me as much.' The truth hurt her physically as if she was being ripped in half. Sympathy, respect, tenderness, she thought, versus love. Painful, inescapable, real love.

But how can I hurt Darcy now? And if not now, whenever?

Bewilderment and hurt seethed around her. She saw that Tom was leaving her. He walked away, in a wide circle around where the red stretcher had lain.

Panic gripped Helen.

'Wait,' she called after him. 'Tom. I love you.'

He didn't stop, or even look around. 'I don't think so.' The door opened, and shut with finality.

'Tom?' she shouted. 'Tom!'

But the silence was unbroken and she felt the weight of the house around her, sombre and stricken with tragedy. Somewhere, Oliver was lying dead. He was alone, among strangers. He was gone, and the little conflicts of their world went on without him. As if it mattered, as if it mattered. Pity for him washed through her like a river.

Helen went upstairs through the brooding house. She lay down and let the tears for her friend come, breaking in long waves until the first tide of grief subsided and she sank into the sleep of exhaustion.

Later in the day Darcy came back. He was calm, and very gentle to her, almost as if it was Helen's brother who had died instead of his own. She watched him as he stood by the window with the curtains looped back in one hand so that he could see the sun-golden front of Christ Church. The brightness of the day was in bitter contrast to the darkness they carried with them. The curtains had been drawn, and the high room was airless.

They spoke very little. Helen was not even sure that she knew this different Darcy, white-faced with shock but still with all his diffidence gone. The burden of making – and she recoiled from the horrible word – arrangements seemed to have fallen squarely on him, and he was meeting it capably.

There would have to be a post-mortem and an inquest, he told her, but he had already spoken to the coroner and there was no doubt that the verdict would be accidental death. There would be no delay to the funeral.

'It will be in the church, at Mere,' he told her. 'Do you suppose that many of Oliver's friends will want to come?'

'I think they all will,' she answered him. We all loved him, she thought again, in our own ways.

'Darcy,' she ventured, 'how are your parents?' Her dislike of Lord and Lady Montcalm was forgotten in her sympathy for them.

'Broken. Especially my mother.' Helen saw it clearly. The beloved, intriguing and wayward Oliver, focus of all those silver-framed photographs, was gone. She understood that for all his difficulty he had been idolised. And she saw Darcy's homely face and self-effacing bearing, remembering how often anger had possessed her at his parents' coldness.

Now, in the midst of this tragedy, Darcy was somehow proving himself. Respect took its place with liking in the complication of her feelings for him.

He came and sat beside her, taking her fingers in his firm clasp.

'I didn't know him very well,' he said sadly. 'We never understood each other. But lately, just lately, I felt that we liked one another better. Like brothers in any other family.' His smile was wistful, with a trace of hunger in it. He wanted her to talk about Oliver. 'You were probably closer to him than I ever was.'

'Perhaps.' She couldn't do it, without uncovering truths that were too close to pain to face today.

The silence settled around them again. Darcy was so close, solid beside her, but Helen felt as alone as she had ever done in her life.

How isolated we are, she thought. And how tenuous the strongest links turn out to be. She had the vertiginous sense that Darcy was a total stranger, and that all the strength of her feelings for Tom had been hallucination. But no. That wasn't true. She knew that she loved Tom with every fibre of herself. And yet she had turned him away so that she could go on sitting here beside Darcy because she believed that it was the right thing for her to do.

The right thing?

With the irony of fate, it had turned out to be Darcy who possessed all the strength. She felt that the tragedy had stripped her of all hers, stripped her of everything except the potential to hurt. And what had it done to Tom? She thought of him, aching with longing, and knew that she couldn't go to him now. Perhaps he would come back. Perhaps he would give her another chance. And perhaps this wasn't all that there was left, sitting in silence beside a Darcy she didn't know, and comparing. The endless, unwanted comparisons ran on inside her head. Even the hand that held hers. Heavy and blunt after Tom's expressive hands with the quick fingers. Stop it. Oh, stop.

Darcy was watching her with the new decisive expression intensifying behind his eyes.

'Would you like me to take you out for something to eat?'

'I don't think I could eat anything,' she answered him lifelessly.

With unbearable gentleness he replaced her hand in her lap. 'I'll go back to Montcalm, then,' he said. 'To be with my mother for a while.'

Helen nodded, and then again to hide the tears that gathered in her eyes. In case Darcy saw them, and stayed. It was much easier to be alone.

Did Tom feel that?

He never came, although she waited for him all through the stifling days before the funeral. The air stagnated in Follies House until she felt that it was almost unfit to breathe. Helen and Chloe saw no-one except Darcy. If Pansy was grieving she did it alone and away from the house, because her room stayed dark and locked. They drew closer together in their isolation, reaching the point of friendship beyond secrets.

'You don't want to marry him, do you?' Chloe asked her in the small hours of one sleepless night. She felt rather than saw the shake of Helen's head. 'It's Tom, isn't it?'

'Is it so very obvious?' Helen's voice was muffled. Her face was buried against her drawn-up knees. 'Darcy mustn't know. Must never know.'

'Oh, Helen. Are you so very certain that he doesn't know?'

I was certain, Helen thought. Now I don't think I know anything, any more.

The melancholy sense of things coming to an end possessed them all. Helen began to pack her things. The books went back into the cardboard boxes that Oliver had carried up the stairs for her, and her clothes into the shabby suitcases. The little white room took on its bare, uninhabited look again, but she left Tom's sea picture in its place over the mantelpiece. She still thought that she could smell the fresh salt air.

Helen's feeling of being cast adrift was heightened by realising that she had no idea where she was going, now. She could go back to her mother's house, and begin to look for a job all over again. Or if Darcy wanted her at Mere, she would go with him. That was what her promise meant and she had chosen to keep it. But in the times that she spent with Darcy, they were painstakingly gentle with each other, and almost formal. Neither of them mentioned it.

Downstairs Chloe was packing too. She would be coming back to Oxford after the summer, but not to Follies House. Too much had happened there.

'I've got my London flat,' she told Helen. 'Come and stay with me until you get your bearings again. I'd love you to be there.' Chloe was going back to do a freelance job, but London seemed to belong to a forgotten part of her life now. Helen's company would be a precious link with reality.

Helen thanked her, but she hadn't said that she would come. She was clinging to Oxford because she knew that Tom was still there.

The day of the funeral came.

In the morning Pansy materialised again. She came with Hobbs who parked Masefield's white Rolls up on the bridge.

When Chloe and Helen found her, she was stuffing belongings into her bags. Hobbs was ferrying suitcases out of the diminishing chaos in her room.

Pansy straightened up from her task and smiled at them. Her plain grey dress showed that she was thinner, and her lovely face looked a little older. The maturity suited her. They hugged each other in turn, wordlessly acknowledging the sadness of their reunion.

'The funeral's today,' they told her.

'Yes. That's why I'm here. May I come with you? I could get Hobbs to take me, but . . .' She gestured out to the ostentatious car with a flash of the old, merry, irreverent Pansy.

'We'll all go together,' Chloe said quietly. Instinctively they turned the talk, if not their thoughts, away from the black tribute of the afternoon.

'Where have you been?' Chloe asked her.

'London. On my own, mostly. Thinking about Oliver quite a lot, as it happens.' Pansy had indeed done her own mourning for him, and it was part of her that she should have done it alone, and in secret. Helen found herself wondering, as she had done often before, about how much more Pansy there was submerged, iceberg like, beneath the frivolous surface. Lightly, Pansy went on, 'I did a bit of work with Scot. Reading the *Moll*

Flanders script with him.' An un-Pansy-like flush of enthusiastic colour came into her face. 'He's a brilliant director. I'm so proud that he's asked me to work with him. It's not just getting into films, and Hollywood and all that, that I'm excited about. But working for Scot. And you know the best thing of all? I did it myself, without any of Masefield's string-pulling or demanding of favours to be returned. Just me, on my own. What d'you think of that?'

They smiled at her.

'I think you'll be a huge success, and far too famous to have anything to do with Helen and me any more.'

'Oh no.' Pansy was serious at once. She put an arm around their shoulders. 'I won't ever forget this year. Or the way that somehow our friendship has survived, in spite of all the things that I did. Whatever happens to us all, I shall still think of you as the best friends I'll ever have.' For Pansy it was a long, serious speech, and they believed her.

It stirred up the muddy waters of memory, and brought them back to Oliver.

When the time came, they made themselves ready to go, feeling the heat of the house in their dark clothes.

As they filed down the shallow stairs, Rose came out to them. They hadn't seen her for days because she had been locked in her room with her grief. Now they were shocked to see how terrible she looked. Her huge face was blotched with purple and her little eyes were almost invisible. Her ragged hair appeared to be falling out, leaving grey patches of skin. She was squeezed into a heavy black coat, and she stared mutely up as they came down towards her.

Chloe put a hand on her arm. 'Would you like to come with us?' she asked.

Rose shook her head. There was a glimmer of the old, defensive malice. 'Gerry is taking me. As family, we are going in a suitable car, even if they have chosen to ignore us.'

Helen felt a flash of surprise that Darcy hadn't made arrangements for them to be driven to the funeral. She doubted, too, whether Gerry would be capable. He had been drunk for a week.

Yet when they came out into the unwelcome sunlight, they saw a big black car with a black-suited driver waiting on the bridge. Gerry was half-leaning against it. As they reached him, they saw that he was practically sober. His black suit was too tight for him, and cut in the style of ten years ago, but it was clean and pressed. He nodded to each of them as they stepped past, and they realised that he was in tears. 'Oliver would be pleased that you are going to say goodbye,' he mumbled, with the drinker's sentimentality.

When they were past, Pansy murmured through tight lips, 'I think Oliver would simply laugh at the whole thing.'

'It doesn't matter,' Helen answered wearily. The sadness of the day was choking.

What did Tom feel? she wondered. Why was she being such a fool as not to be with him? His face flashed in front of her with the vividness of a hallucination.

Because of her loyalty to Darcy.

And Darcy didn't need her after all.

The familiar drive to Mere took them through the luxuriant, high-summer splendour of the countryside. The broad fields were golden yellow or lush green, fringed with the heavyleaved shade of oaks and elms. Cows moved through the pastureland, up to their bellies in the rich grass. Through the opened windows Helen caught the scent of cow-parsley, and the dog-roses that rambled over the hedges. She turned her eyes away and looked down at the black hem of her skirt. The beauty of the day and the tranquil thought of the seasons' slow succession was too painful to contemplate, because it was over for Oliver.

They drove slowly through Mere village, and Helen saw that the curtains in many of the cottage windows were drawn. At the Mortimore Arms, a black pall was hanging over the swinging sign board that bore the family coat of arms. At the end of the village was the square tower of the little Saxon church. Beyond it was the low grey line of Mere House, enclosed by its yew hedges against the sunny hillside.

No-one spoke as they walked from the car to the lych-gate. The road was lined with silent villagers, many of them farm-labourers with ruddy faces and pale foreheads left startlingly bare by the removal of their caps. From the church tower a single bell tolled, the reverberations dying on the still, scented air and then gathering again.

As the cool shadow of the lych-gate passed over her face, Helen looked to the south door of the church and saw Darcy standing in the porch. He had a brief word for each of the dark figures that came slowly past him. She walked heavily on up the path, past the ancient yew tree at the gate and the mossed headstones of long-forgotten Mortimore tenants.

When he saw her, he smiled his grave smile, and his lips brushed her cheek. 'Thank you,' he said quietly, and then he turned to Pansy and Chloe. A word for each of them as they passed into the dimness of the church.

It was packed. Two vergers came forward, and Helen found to her bewilderment that she was separated from Pansy and Chloe. The old man led her down the aisle, past line after line of mourners. At the very front, it felt like a mile away, was a high, carved pew with a twisted red rope across the step up to it. The verger bent to unclasp the brass hook from its round eye, and stood aside to let her in.

The family pew.

Darcy's fiancée in the family pew. Helen knelt down in the empty, carved box and felt the loneliness gathering around her.

When she looked up again she saw the faded rose pinks and violets of the east window, the brass crucifix glowing in the dimness, and the banks of waxy white lilies on either side. Slowly she turned her head. At the foot of the chancel steps was the bier, with white candles in tall holders at each corner. On the big dark coffin there was a single wreath of lilies.

Helen looked away again, and up at the light filtering through the medieval stained glass. None of this, the pervasive smell of lilies or the muted organ music, was anything to do with Oliver. He was nowhere here.

The organ music died away with a single, long chord. There was a moment of whispering silence and then Lady Montcalm came down the aisle supported by her husband and son. She was moving slowly, suddenly aged, and her hand on her husband's black sleeve looked knobbed and stiff. Her face was half hidden by a black net veil. As they came into the pew Lord Montcalm looked at Helen from under his white eyebrows. Grief seemed to have rubbed out the autocratic stare. Darcy came in after his mother, half lifting her into her place. Helen bent her head, saddened to see how tragedy had diminished them. Had she once been so afraid of them?

The rector of Mere was at the chancel steps. He began to read the old, magnificent words of the Burial Service. Helen bent her head and prayed that they would comfort Oliver's family.

After the brief service, Darcy walked out into the aisle again and stood at the head of the coffin. At once five other men joined him, bracing themselves in readiness to lift the weight on to their shoulders. Helen saw that two of them had the unmistakable Mortimore head. Cousins, perhaps. Two more were from the boisterous company of upper-class young men who had filled one part of Oliver's life since early childhood.

The sixth was Tom. It was Darcy's graceful gesture to include him in the tight phalanx.

Simple love for him filled Helen as she watched his dark profile. He was looking straight ahead of him as he bent with the others and they shouldered their burden. Slowly, in step, the bearers moved away down the aisle, taking Oliver out into the sunshine for the last time. Lord and Lady Montcalm followed him together, heads up now. The pews disgorged their dark occupants in their wake. Helen hung back and was swallowed up in the slow press forward. They came out of the cool church and into the light, where the afternoon sun was dipping lower and lengthening the shadows behind the headstones. White butterflies skimmed over the wildflowers that fringed the churchyard.

With Chloe and Pansy, Helen stood at the edge of the solid black crowd. She knew that Tom, and Darcy, and the other bearers were straining to hold the coffin steady on its band as it made the slow descent into the dark hole. Then there would be the scattering of earth, and the last, great, solemn words.

She struggled to hold the reality of Oliver close to her, away from here, as he had once been. She felt the vibrant life in him as he braced himself beside her in the black Jaguar. The curled sheepskin lining of his aviator's coat tickled her throat and wrists. Suddenly, suffocatingly, he was all round her. She remembered his kiss after their first lunch together, and how he had tasted faintly of the rich burgundy.

They had gone to the little house that he called home on the Montcalm estate. He had carried her away, effortlessly out of herself, so that she didn't belong to herself any more, but to him. Remembering his love-making, the natural way he had taken her as if she was a ripe fruit, the days of her love for him came flooding back as vividly as if they had just happened. It had been Oliver's way to take, unthinkingly, with the assurance born of extreme privilege. But he had given too, his vitality and mercurial charm, with prodigal generosity while it was still his to give.

Love for him flowed through Helen once again, against the fierce current of sorrow and bitterness at his loss.

Out of the crowd a face caught her attention. It was Jasper Thripp, almost at the grave-mouth. Tears were sliding down his seamed brown face and falling unregarded on to his ancient, greeny-black suit. Helen jerked her eyes away again, unwilling to witness the nakedness of grief.

At once her gaze encountered someone else. Beatrice was listening intently with the grey sweeps of hair over her ears pinned youthfully back. The ravaged expression that she had worn beside the river had gone. She looked, once again, the intelligent, slightly harried, middle-aged mother and wife. Helen searched for him and found Stephen standing next to her. Their hands were even discreetly clasped behind the folds of Beatrice's skirt. They had made their own compromises, Helen thought. Stephen looked sorrowful, but his attention was elsewhere. Helen wondered what he was really thinking about.

Compromises. The reasonableness of the word mocked her and her own mistaken idealism.

The funeral was over. In twos and threes the mourners were turning away from the graveside and along the flagged path to the lych-gate. It was Lord and Lady Montcalm who stood in the porch now, finding the sombre strength to acknowledge the condolences. Rose Pole came past. She was dry-eyed at last, and with a kind of defiant dignity showing in her blotched face. Gerry was beside her, ginny tears still streaming. Darcy had a gentle word for them, but when they reached Lady Montcalm she shot a glance of such poisonous hatred at Rose that the fat woman ducked her head and shuffled wordlessly past.

Helen's thoughts were too intently fixed elsewhere even to wonder why. The bearers were the last to leave the graveside. She stood stock-still as they filed past. Tom was staring straight ahead again, and she saw how drawn his face was. He walked by without a word, or even a glance at her, and Helen knew that she had been expecting nothing else. There was nothing for them to say to each other, and they were avoiding the pain of pretending that there was.

She stood watching with numbed, patient acceptance as Darcy moved to and fro. He managed to find the right words and the right gestures for everyone. He had become himself, as if the finality of Oliver's loss had set him free from the confines of his own fears.

I wish I loved him. I wish.

He put his arms round his mother's shoulders and led her away to the funereal black Rolls. Lady Montcalm put her white hand up to his cheek as she shrank inside, and he kissed it.

Cars purred away through the village. They were taking people away back into the sunshine, where they would undo tight collars and buttons with relief, sigh, and turn their attention back to the business of life.

Darcy was coming back down the path to where Helen waited for him. They were the only people left in the churchyard except for the sexton and his boy who were bending to their task with the dark, raw earth. The heady scent drifting from the heaped-up flowers was overpowering.

Darcy turned abruptly away.

'Come round to the other side of the church,' he said, and for the first time Helen heard from his voice that he was close to breaking down.

They walked away, the unclipped grass brushing at their ankles. The shadowed north side of the church was cooler. The tombstones here were ancient, leaning crazily over sunken slabs mossed with yellow lichen. Beyond the drystone wall was open pastureland and the bulk of Mere House against its yew-dark setting. 'Come and sit on the wall. I used to spend hours here when I was a kid.' Darcy led her to the place, and they sat on the flat stones with their backs to the churchyard. Ahead of them Mere's acres spread under the lazy fingers of sun.

Helen listened to the superficial silence of rural peace, underscored by the hum of insects and the rustle of grass and leaves.

Darcy said, 'It isn't any use, is it?'

Away somewhere behind them a blackbird launched into a torrent of liquid song. 'I wish it could have been,' she whispered.

The bird sang on, its own exultant fountain.

She turned to look at him, and her eyes travelled over the lines of his open face, exactly as familiar and dear to her as it always had been.

'I'm sorry.' She offered him the honesty of her heart.

'Don't be. There's no reason. It shouldn't have taken me so

long to find the courage to face it. Peculiar, isn't it, that losing Oliver should have given it to me?'

'I think I understand,' Helen told him.

Darcy lifted her hand and surprised her with his old, half-smothered laugh. 'You always hated this, didn't you?'

The Viscountess's blood-red ruby shone in its net of diamonds.

'I'd never have made a viscountess for you. Somebody else will.' She slid the heavy weight off her finger and gave it back to him. He dropped it into his pocket without looking at it. His eyes were on the meadows and the plain grey face of Mere House.

'I hope so. I need that.'

'I know so,' she promised him. 'But it couldn't have been me.'

'No. I was wrong to try to convince us both otherwise.'

They sat for a moment longer looking out at the view. Nothing to do with me, any longer, Helen told herself, these fields and stones and all the centuries of tradition lying behind and ahead. Relief lifted a heavy weight from her shoulders like a stifling blanket. Her hand felt as if it could fly up from her lap, weightless.

She wanted Darcy to know something, a truth that seemed vitally important now. 'I love you,' she said, knowing that he would understand.

He smiled back at her. 'I love you too. I always will.'

Darcy stood up and put out his hands to swing her down from the low wall. There was no more to add. Helen felt that the old, peaceful intimacy had come back between them, and that they could keep it for ever now.

They circled the church once more and stood beside the long mound of fresh sweet earth. Long moments passed and the stillness lapped around them. Helen looked away at the low hillside, believing that Darcy wouldn't want her to see his tears now.

At length he rubbed his eyes with his knuckles, like a schoolboy.

'I'm glad you were here,' he said softly. And then, 'Come on, I'll take you home.' Back to Follies. They turned away together and left the deserted churchyard.

Outside Follies House, neither of them looked at the bridge or the river beneath. Darcy's hands rested on the wheel.

'Be happy, won't you?' he said, uncertainly. Helen looked down at her bare fingers.

'I don't know,' she answered, 'if I deserve that.'

Darcy smiled at her. 'You do. And he deserves you. Tom Hart is a good man.' He leaned across and opened the door for her. Helen stepped automatically out, the shock-wave that his words had set up ringing in her ears. He knew, then. Of course he knew.

'Go on,' Darcy told her. He lifted his hand in a brief salute, let in the clutch, and drove sharply away.

When he had gone, Helen didn't look round at the steps, or up at the big red house. Instead she turned and started walking up St Aldate's. Ahead of her lay Carfax and the ugly jumble of chain-stores and bus stops. Beyond that was the calm spread of North Oxford, and Tom's rented house in the garden square. She walked quickly. The pavements were hot under her feet and drifted over with the litter of the city's summer invasion. Two coaches were parked beneath Tom Tower, disgorging their loads of tourists who streamed into the green space of the Quad. Carfax was wedged with buses and the faces in the shopping thoroughfare beyond had turned suddenly middle-aged. The year was over.

Helen walked under the shade of the tall plane trees in St Giles, and then into the leafy residential streets that fanned out beyond it.

When she came into the little square, her eyes fastened at once on the white-painted house. She saw with a beat of relief that the first-floor windows stood open on the wrought-iron balcony. Tom must be there. As she came through the late-afternoon hush she was almost running.

The front door was ajar. She pushed it open and walked into the hall. The pictures had been taken down from one wall, and were being packed into waiting crates. Tom's year was over too.

Helen felt a surge of panic. Was she too late?

The house was very quiet. She went along the hall and into the neat, white, rented kitchen.

'Tom?' she called. French windows stood open on a little square of brick-paved garden. It was shaded with trailing green leaves, and there were tall terracotta pots bright with splashes of scarlet and pink. Tom was sitting in a white-painted wicker chair, his hands dangling loosely.

'Tom.'

He jerked around, and then leapt to his feet. The wicker chair scraped backwards. Before she ran to him, Helen glimpsed that he had taken off his dark clothes. He was in jeans, and a torn sweatshirt that showed his lean chest. His face was tense. He was still waiting for something.

'It's all right.' She put her arms out, and at once he pulled her to him with a force that frightened her. Her face was crushed against his shoulder and she still pressed herself closer, submerging herself in him.

'What?' he said roughly.

'It's all right,' she repeated, and she was smiling ecstatically into the grey stuff of his sleeve. She opened her eyes and saw a scatter of red petals on the bricks, and the moving patterns of shade under the leaves. She felt that the little corner of view was clearer, sweeter and more significant than anything she had ever set eyes on before.

Without looking, Tom's left hand found hers. He felt the nakedness of it and then clenched her fingers in his. With their clasped hands pulled between them, he kissed her and she closed her eyes on the leaves and the patterns of light. There was nothing now but Tom, and the avenues of freedom that opened out in front of them. Yet he lifted his head an inch from hers, and when she tried to draw him back she felt that his muscles were like iron. She opened her eyes to look into his and saw the fierceness. Her smile faded into anxiety. Was there still, still something wrong?

'Have you told Darcy?' There was the old insistent, uncompromising Tom. Nothing less than the full truth would satisfy him. Helen shook her head and saw the instant flash of anger before she answered.

'I didn't have the courage. Tom, it was Darcy who told me. He knew. He ... he told me that you were a good man.'

She felt the taut muscles flutter and relax under her hands. Tom's mouth was close to hers again.

'I think we will be good for one another,' he said, and she felt the beguiling warmth of his tongue as it traced her mouth.

'And are you all mine now?'

She nodded mutely.

'All mine?'

'Yes.'

Insistently Tom drew her away from the dappled shade of the

367

garden. They walked through the house together hand in hand, not letting go, as if they were afraid that the other could still disappear.

Tom's room was shadowy, and there were thin white curtains lifting in the slow breeze at the windows. He took off her black dress, letting it rustle to a heap at their feet. He unpinned her hair and for a moment he stood with her locked in his arms, watching the black curls uncoiling across the whiteness of her skin. Then deftly he peeled off the last things and she stood in front of him, not proud or diffident, but simply ready to give herself.

Tom took her in his arms and lifted her on to the bed.

Her mouth, her flesh and the inner chasms of herself opened at the insistence of his touch. Tom was a faultless lover that first time. He made her cry out under the gentle brutality of his hands and mouth, and then he bore her away to remote, rocking islands of pleasure that she had never dreamed existed. He was her equal and her opposite half, both knowing and innocent, as gentle as a child and so powerful that even as she cried for him to go on, and on, she was afraid that he would break her in half.

And over himself, his dominance was steely. Only when Helen lay limp in his arms did he release himself, and the cry that he gave was more in pain than pleasure.

When at last he lay still she watched his face and saw it suffused with weariness. Tom had been performing for her, a performance born more out of passion than love.

His dark eyes opened and held hers, and the black lashes were stuck into points with the heat of their bodies. Gently Helen stroked back the damp hair from his forehead. They had taken possession of each other's bodies, but something still held their hearts apart like a thin, cold sheet of glass. She took his face in her hands and forced him to look at her.

'What?' she demanded. Pain came with the weariness into his face, and she felt him shiver.

'I can't cry for him.'

Helen circled him with her arms and drew his head down between her breasts. Her hair fell down across his face like a protective curtain.

'Cry,' she whispered. 'My darling, cry now.'

His tears came with long, shuddering sobs that tore at them in the sweet afternoon silence. Helen hunched over him, the meaningless, murmured words of tenderness swallowed between them. She understood his loss, and his grief, and his crying for the imagined, but still shocking moment of negligence that had lost him his friend's life.

The weeping man in her arms was not the dictatorial and steely Tom Hart of the Playhouse, nor the ironically smiling and impervious man who had angered and unconsciously attracted her all through the Follies year. Magically he had become the equal and exact counterpart that she longed for, but she saw that he was as vulnerable, and as needy too, as she was herself. He was a whole, round person, grief-stricken now but still strong, and so alive that she wanted to seize him, and hold him, and absorb the warmth and solidity of him into herself. He was the man she loved.

'I love you', she whispered. 'I love you more than all the world.'

The crying had stopped. His wet face lay against hers and his fingers fluttered over her skin, and then his hands closed over her breasts. The length of his body tensed and hardened, and he came to her again.

The performance was forgotten now. He arched into her, and moaned, lost within himself, and she rocked him in her arms and rejoiced in the oblivion he had found.

Too soon Tom cried out again, utterly defenceless, and fell blindly against her. The thin, cold sheet had all dissolved away. They were at one, and they had found their own peace at the year's end.

'I'm sorry,' Tom said. His voice was hoarse, but there was the faint lift of a smile at the corner of his mouth.

'Don't be. I liked that much better.'

'Perverse girl. After all my efforts.'

Smiling, they locked their arms around each other. The white curtain blew gently at the window, and they drifted into untroubled sleep.

When they woke up the light had softened to the soft, pale grey of evening. It was deliciously cool and sweet-smelling. It must have rained while they were asleep. Helen heard the high, sharp peet of swallows dipping over grass somewhere nearby.

Tom stirred, smiling, and reached out for her.

'*Again?*' She smiled at him, pretending prim surprise.

'Whyever not? You might as well know that I shall be an intensely demanding husband.'

Laughing, Helen spread her fingers over his mouth.

'Who said anything about marriage?'

'I gave you my favourite picture, didn't I? Marrying you is the only way I can think of to get it back.'

'Oh well, in that case ...'

Tom rolled her over in his arms and they retreated into the intricate labyrinths of their new-found world.

Afterwards, Helen stood dreamily at the long window, wrapped in Tom's bathrobe. It smelt of him and she stretched luxuriously, glowing with the happiness that seemed so strong around her that she felt she could touch it. Behind her Tom lay propped up on one elbow, watching her half-turned profile.

The moment was so perfect that fear touched her.

'You won't go away, will you?' she whispered.

'Never.'

Helen turned back from the window and sat down beside him.

'Do you know what I would like us to do, tonight?'

'Anything in the world.'

'I want us to go out, to somewhere that Oliver especially liked. I want us to go with Pansy and Chloe, and I want us to drink a lot of his favourite wine, and eat great platefuls of all the things he liked. I want us to talk about him as if he hasn't just ... gone away. I want to say goodbye to him like that. I didn't feel that this afternoon, all that sorrow and black ceremonial, was anything to do with Oliver.'

Tom bent and kissed her, and there was a kind of fulfilment in his face that had never shown there before.

'Yes,' he said gently. 'That's just what we'll do. Oliver would appreciate that.'

SUMMER

CHAPTER FIFTEEN

They went to the old pub in the Cotswold village where Oliver had once taken Helen to lunch. She looked up as they went in at the creaking sign with its painted mulberry tree, remembering.

The discreet dining room was full, but somehow Tom had secured a table. Chloe looked doubtfully around at the heavy oak furniture, the dark panelling and the middle-aged diners.

'And this is Oliver's favourite restaurant?'

Tom smiled at her through the candlelight. 'One of them. Look at the wine list.'

They bent their heads over it together, discovering a common language.

'Mmm. Oh yes, I see. Clever Oliver.'

Tom was decisive. 'There's no choice, really. We must have Krug, Oliver's champagne. And then the burgundy. Gevrey-Chambertin.'

Clos St Jacques, Helen remembered. 'Not quite the very greatest, but as good as one can find almost anywhere.' His voice sounded as clearly as if he was sitting beside her. She leaned back in her chair and looked at her friends. Chloe in a pink ruffled shirt that showed the tops of her breasts, her magnificent tawny-red hair pinned back from her face with a jet comb. Flamboyant long jet earrings dangled in her ears. Pansy sat beside her in one of her understated-expensive silk teeshirts. The vivid cornflower blue came nowhere near eclipsing her eyes. And next to her, Tom. Helen didn't need to look at him. He felt as close to her as if he was part of her own flesh. His hand brushed hers as he filled her glass, and Pansy and Chloe saw their involuntary smiles. The happiness radiating from them would have made explanations seem pedantic.

Chloe and Pansy had seized the chance to say their own kinds of farewell. For all of them, the funeral had been so much empty ritual. Now, gathered around the table with the champagne that had fuelled so many of Oliver's nights prickling in their mouths, they felt his loss more sharply. Yet, for all the sadness of the evening, there was no unhappiness. They were drawn together, closer than friends, into a kind of family.

They talked about the shared year that had gone, and about the separate routes ahead of them.

Pansy made them laugh by guying the idea of herself as a movie star. She could mimic Scot Scotney's carefully preserved Glasgow accent to perfection too.

'Ye've got a long way to go, but ye won't du it wi'out harrrd werrk, an' ye won't du it wi'out me.'

Tom put his hand over hers. 'Pansy darling, you're a born comedienne as well. Will you come back to New York one day and act for me again?'

'Oh sure, if the deal's right.' Her eyes narrowed, mock-tough.

'Not just for old times' sake?'

'Certainly not. What do you take me for, an amateur?'

Helen laughed with them, but she said little. She simply let herself slip into the intimacy of the evening, and the champagne's warm glow, without thinking of tomorrow. There were still so many questions; the prospect of her mother's bewilderment at her broken engagement and immediate re-engagement to somebody else ... in spite of herself, Helen's face lit with a smile at the thought. And there was the question of her own future too. Helen had no intention of living as an appendage of Tom's, in New York or anywhere else. But not tonight. After the extraordinary tumult of today, and with these faces around the glowing table with her, there was no need to ask anything at all.

'And you, Chloe?' Tom was asking. The old asperity that had lingered on between them, even through the success of their working partnership, had all evaporated now. Chloe lifted her glass and her green eyes met each of theirs in turn.

'Oh, a long, hard summer of writing body copy for something or other. And then, in October ...' she smiled, conspiratorial, '... I shall just come back to Oxford. Do you know, I can't think of anything else I want to do, or anywhere else I want to be? I think I've just discovered job satisfaction. I shall take over your discarded role, Helen, when Tom has carried you off into the stratosphere somewhere.'

As she spoke, they turned to each other, and their fingertips met on the white cloth. Their oneness was acknowledged, and there was no need for anyone to say any more.

Chloe was laughing. 'I shall fling myself into my books, I shall get my First in due course, and I shall stay on here, growing increasingly spinsterish and set in my eccentric ways, turning out intensely clever articles for the learned journals. Look out for me in *Notes and Queries*, won't you?'

They looked back at Chloe's tawny, exotic glamour and the idea was so preposterous that they dissolved into laughter once more.

When the food came, they found that they were ravenously hungry. There was no game, so they ate rare, tender beef as the nearest substitute and heaped it with the simplicity of summer vegetables. The rich, stylish burgundy lapped them in its generous warmth. When the second bottle came, Helen recalled Oliver joking about the one-bottle lunch being a thing of the past, and how afterwards his mouth had tasted of the wine when he kissed her.

Goodbye, she murmured in her heart. Goodbye.

After the beef came summer pudding, the first of the year, running in its own crimson juice.

'How perfect,' Pansy sighed, as she spooned up the last mouthful.

Much later, over the brandy glasses, it was Pansy who spoke the words that were in each of their minds.

'How Noll would have enjoyed that. Except he would have insisted "At least another bottle".' Her eyes went round the table, almost as though she was measuring the space for another chair. 'It's as if he's sitting here with us. I couldn't think about him at that graveside this afternoon. But now, tonight he's here. Slouching back in his seat, holding his glass up against the candlelight.' Her lovely voice was husky and hardly more than a whisper, but they heard and remembered every word.

Pansy was a little drunk, and she let her guard slip lower than they had ever known it. 'The trick is to be able to forgive yourself, isn't it? Noll couldn't do that. He couldn't be gentle with himself. Funny that someone so outwardly invulnerable should be the most fragile person I have ever known.'

Fragile, Helen thought. Yes, that's what it was. His world had made his hold on reality too fragile, and he distorted it beyond that with drink and drugs.

'D'you think he wanted to die?' Pansy whispered.

Tom stirred a little. 'Perhaps, in the bad times, just once or twice. But not when it happened. He was too alive, then. It was the cruellest accident.'

His voice trailed away and Helen reached and took his hand. They sat in silence, thinking about him and the void that he had left.

'Here's to him,' Pansy said, and swallowed her brandy in a long gulp. In their candlelit circle they drank to him. 'He's here when we meet like this. We'll do it again, won't we?'

Yes, they answered her. Somehow or other, we'll do it.

'Another toast,' Pansy added. 'You two.'

And Helen and Tom exchanged the fleeting, complicit glance of lovers.

'What about Darcy?' Chloe asked gently. Tonight had brought them too close for them to need to keep tactful silences.

'I think Darcy will be all right,' Helen answered her. 'We didn't belong together in that way, you know. I tried to believe that we did, from the very beginning in Venice, but it never was the truth.'

Pansy spoke again. 'I was watching him this afternoon. I think Oliver cast a very long shadow. Darcy will grieve for him, but he'll grow too.'

I hope so, Helen thought. If there were ever to be a fifth in this circle, I wish it could be Darcy.

The evening was over.

They were quiet as they watched the miles to Oxford slide past, but it was the quiet of calm, not sadness.

They came back to Follies House for the last time, down the steps with their faces turned away from the river race.

Hobbs had already taken Pansy's vast load of luggage back to London. Chloe's trunk of books stood corded and waiting for the carrier in the shadows of the hallway.

Helen hesitated at the foot of the stairs, looking up into the panelled heights. Each of them was aware that the moment of separation had come, and they hung back from it.

It was Pansy who broke the silence. Quickly she kissed Helen's cheek.

'Au revoir,' she said, and went on up into the gallery. Her blonde head was a bright spot in the dimness and the scent of summer gardens drifted behind her. Chloe turned back and hugged them both, wordlessly.

Helen wanted to say Wait. Don't go yet. But Tom was beside

her and she knew too that, more than anything, she wanted to be alone with him again.

The year that was gone flashed through her memory, linking her for an instant to her own earlier self. Am I the same Helen? she thought, and answered herself No. The Follies year had changed her beyond recall, and it had brought her to Tom. Her fingers tightened gratefully on his.

It was time to leave Follies, and Oxford, behind her now, and she was ready for that. There was no question that she was leaving Pansy and Chloe, because they would always be with her.

Her smile broke out as she wrapped her arms around Chloe and hugged her until the breath was squeezed out of them both.

'Don't work too hard,' she ordered her. 'All work and no play, remember?'

'Oh no,' Chloe said with her throaty chuckle. 'I don't think I'll altogether lose the knack of playing. I like it far too much. Just hope I hit the jackpot in the end, like you.'

They didn't say goodbye. She blew a kiss down to them over the carved baluster and the silence of the house wrapped round them once again.

Helen shivered a little and said, 'I don't belong here any more. Tom, do I live with you now?'

He laughed at her. 'Try to live anywhere else. Come on. I want you to myself again.'

The plush anonymity of the little rented house welcomed them. It doesn't matter where we are, Helen realised. I live where Tom is, just like he is now, pouring tea into two striped mugs.

The exhilarating sense of freedom returned to her, doubly sweet because it was shared and untinged with loneliness. We can go anywhere, she thought. Do anything. And then, Montcalm would have crushed me with its very weight.

Tom felt her eyes on him and looked up, his dark face suddenly serious.

'No regrets?'

'Not one.'

'You don't feel that you are leaving too much behind? Do you remember the day we met in Addison's Walk? You told me that you were saying goodbye to Oxford, and you looked so sad, and so brave, that I wished there was anything in the world that I could have done to change it for you. Perhaps without knowing it that was when I fell in love with you.'

'You were thinking about Pansy,' Helen reminded him cheerfully. 'And no, I don't care about anything except being with you. I've done everything I want to do here. There are all kinds of things and places I want to do and see, but I couldn't begin without you.'

'Thank you,' he said simply. 'We'll do them all, I promise, together.' He came to her and rested his cheek against her hair. 'I'm glad you're not at Follies any more,' he murmured. 'While you were there I was still afraid that I might lose you. Not like Oliver, and not quite to Rose's malign influence, but something like that.'

'To Rose?' Helen started back.

'You didn't know?' Tom asked her gently. 'That it was Rose who supplied him with the pills, and the coke, and the rest of her stock-in-trade? That was her particular hold over him. And over your unhappy friend Frances Page, who was more loyal to the old witch than she ever deserved.'

Helen leant her head against the solidity of his shoulder again. She saw the unwholesome tangle of Rose's kitchen web, and the whole little history with shadowless clarity.

'No,' she said humbly. 'I didn't know that. I just felt sorry for her.'

Tom's arms tightened around her.

'Don't change,' he said with sudden fierceness. 'Not ever.'

'I don't think so,' she answered, half to herself. If we can stay just like we are now. If we can only be so lucky. 'Tom? Let's go to bed. Now. I need you very much.'

Almost roughly, he lifted her and carried her away.

Helen stood at the high window and looked out, still not quite believing it or herself. The New York skyline was just as she had seen it in a thousand corny pictures, but not one of them had prepared her for the exuberance of the real thing. The flash and glitter of sun on glass and the minutely shaded perspectives of block laid against block receded up town ahead of her, beckoning seductively.

'Can you fall in love with somewhere so quickly?' she had asked Tom. 'And why didn't you tell me it was so beautiful?'

'Would you have believed me? And yes, either you love it or

you don't. Thank God you do. Look at you,' he teased her. 'More New York than the New Yorkers.'

It was true. She had responded to the raucous vigour of the city with an excitement that was infinitely more alive than the languor that had possessed her in Venice. Yet it had the same effect of arousal. Their hungry exploration of each other was fuelled for her by the sleepless energy around them. She felt more positive and more potent than she had ever done, and she understood the ironic detachment that had set Tom aside as a spectator in Oxford. It was all gone now and he was plunged into work again. She felt that without seeing him here in his native city she could never have understood him, or loved him half as much as she did now.

A month separated them from the evening under the mulberry tree when they had made their own kind of peace with Oliver.

Helen's memory of it was still sharp, but it was overlaid with a patina that spoke of more than a month in time and a distance greater than the width of the Atlantic. A different iife. Tom and New York.

Helen shivered a little. She was still unused to the sudden awareness of complete happiness. Anxiously she cocked her head to the silence in the apartment, then heard the splash of the shower. Tom was singing above it.

Helen smiled as she crossed the great white space of the loft and looked south to the peaks of the financial district away down town. If she craned her head downwards, she could see the quiet street outside Tom's warehouse building. Greene Street, SoHo, New York, she repeated to herself. I'm here. And I can be here, with Tom, for ever.

Over her head in the upper loft space, the little painting of wild flowers against the turquoise sea hung over their bed. It looked as if it had been there always.

Tom came out of the shower in his bathrobe, rubbing at his black hair with a towel until it stood in a rakish crest over his head.

'Want to go to the Market Diner for breakfast?'

Helen loved the hubbub of Lower West Side diners, and the intricate permutations of breakfast menus.

'I've made coffee. Let's stay home and have it.'

Tom slung his towel round his neck and reached out for her. 'Mmm. We could take it back to bed.'

Behind them in the lobby, the letterbox rattled and Helen lifted her head away from his.

'Post,' she said, and Tom corrected her cheerfully.

'Mail.' He went out for it, and came back leafing desultorily through the envelopes. He stopped at a square white one and held it out to her.

'One for you. Forwarded from Oxford.'

Helen sat down very quickly.

'It's the exam result.'

The words brought it all back. The black and white week, and the endless leaves of paper under her hands. She had walked out at the end of it into Tom's arms. He knelt down beside her now and held out the letter.

'Open it.'

Stiff-fingered and clumsy, she ripped the envelope and took out the white card with the University crest. A clerk had written on it, in loopy, unformed handwriting, two words.

Class One.

Helen dropped the card and her head flopped forward against Tom's shoulder. She felt how tensely he was waiting and bubbles of delighted laughter erupted inside her.

'I did it. It's a First.'

'Zowie.' She had never seen Tom so delighted. His pleasure in the news eclipsed her own, and anything she had ever seen him show for his own successes. He took her hands and waltzed her in and out of the pillars until she gasped for breath.

'My clever darling. My beautiful, totally un-bluestocking, brilliant first-class girl. This calls for the biggest celebration ever. Hell, where can we go at nine a.m.? Champagne. Let me get at the fridge . . .'

'Wait,' she begged him.

'Wait? What for?' He snatched up the telephone. 'Call Greg. He'll fall in love with you all over again. Or no, your mother first. Ruth'll want to give you a party. "My son's fiancée, the college professor". Imagine.'

They laughed at the thought, as pleased as children at an unexpected treat.

'Wait.' She rubbed her face against his. 'I don't want to share it with anyone else yet. Only you. Celebrate by having breakfast with me here in the sun.'

She set the little table up in front of the window and Tom pulled across the low chairs. He poured her coffee for her, and put the cup into her hands. They acknowledged the touch of their fingers with a glance, then moved back with the luxury of having all the time together that they needed.

Helen looked away at the panorama outside. A long white yacht was making its way slowly up the Hudson.

'There is someone else to share it with,' she said softly. 'Oliver made it possible for me to go on and finish it.'

Tom watched her profile against the light, and waited. He felt a tiny beat of jealousy, and leapt within himself to suppress it.

'You remember when I nearly had to go away? Because of the money?' Her glance flicked around the apartment, from the white space above them to the pictures on the high walls and the uncluttered lines of the few pieces of furniture. It was important not to let the memories of her little room at Follies, or of her home town, slip too far away from her in the midst of this.

'Somehow Oliver found my bank account. He put seven hundred and fifty pounds in it. It meant that I could keep us going, Mum and Graham and me, for just long enough.' Her hands moved, a quick gesture of helplessness. 'He never let me talk about it.'

She was quiet, thinking about Oliver and their odd, improbable friendship. But friends they had been. 'I liked him very much,' she said, almost to herself.

Tom said nothing. Very slowly he leaned forward and put his cup down on the table, then he stared blindly out at the glimmer of river between the grey and brown blocks. In its place he saw the bare trees in Addison's Walk, and the pinnacles of Magdalen Tower. He felt the fragility of Helen's shoulders in his arms, and the determination that held her head up. She hadn't given way to the impulse to ask for his help. He had willed her to do it, but she had preferred to fight alone with her own pride.

Tom recalled how he had gone back to Follies and watched the heavy door until he saw her set out again, pulling her duffle coat around her in the sharp wind. The dusty, close smell of the old house filled his nostrils as he remembered the climb to the top, her unlocked door, and the row of digits that he had copied from her chequebook on the desk.

He had paid the money in notes into her account, and scribbled a meaningless signature.

Then he too thought of Oliver. Charming and reckless.

Generous and thoughtless. A man of impulses, and never of careful, tactful plans. His face came back to Tom, as clear-cut as a profile on a coin. For a second Tom felt a lead weight on his shoulder and saw Darcy's dark shoulders in front of him, bent under the same weight.

Swiftly Tom left his seat and knelt down beside Helen. He shut out the sight against the fold of her dress. Helen smiled with quick happiness and wound her fingers in his hair.

There was no need for her to know any more. Tom would leave her with that memory of their friend.

It was the last thing he could do for him.

'I love you, Tom,' she said.

He nodded, quickly, and the jealousy that he had felt for his dead friend broke up and drifted away like mist under the sun.

He was still learning about Helen, and it was his daily pleasure to know her better and to love her more. But he was certain, as certain as he was of his own love, that Helen's dazzled devotion to Oliver was long ago over. Their memories of him were a bond between them now, liking and love that had different faces but were still shared, and precious to them both.

The Mortimores were no threat, any more. If he had almost lost her to Darcy, with his title and all his acres and priceless possessions, then he had fought back for her in time.

Helen had chosen him, and she had turned her back on all that English magnificence to come here, to come back home, with him.

'Are you happy?' he whispered against her.

Her face when she looked at him told him more than anything she could have put into words.

'You know I am.'

Tom reached up and pulled her down so that their mouths met.

When he spoke again his voice was light, and teasing. They knew that Follies, and everything that had happened there, would drift away at last into their shared history.

He smiled at her. 'So, clever. What will you do now?'

'Now? At once? What do you think?'

'I meant after that.'

Slowly, as if the thought was just coming to her, she said, 'I'd like to study some more. Does that sound very dull?'

'No. It sounds just what you should be doing. And where better? American universities are the best in the world.'

'You don't have to tell me that. I'm already more New York than the New Yorkers, remember?'

He looked at her, a slender gipsy-like girl in the careful white space of his apartment. How empty it would be without her. He thought of the mid-town theatres, the dusty stages and cramped rehearsal rooms and the opulence of Greg Hart's suite. His world, and where he wanted to be. But never without Helen.

He remembered how unquestioningly she had left the cool green and gold of Oxford to come here with him. She had embraced his home town open-heartedly.

'Thank you,' he said softly, 'for coming here with me.'

'It doesn't matter where I am,' she answered, 'so long as it's with you. But if I could choose . . .' she hesitated, and saw the flash of determination in Tom's face that they would go wherever it was she wanted, '. . . it would be right here.'

He pulled her close to him. 'In that case, will you marry me? Now at once, without a ruby?'

'Yes,' she answered him. 'Yes, I will.'

They turned away together, and above them, where the little sea picture hung the air still seemed full of the scent of flowers and the tough, salt, free tang of the sea.